THE GOOD SISTER

For over a decade Morgan Jones worked for the ~rld's largest investigations company, where he specialized ▪ Russian matters and international disputes. Under the ▪e Chris Morgan Jones, he wrote three novels about that ▪d: *An Agent of Deceit*, *The Jackal's Share* and *The Searcher*. ▪e *Good Sister* is his first novel writing as Morgan Jones. He lives in London with his wife and two children.

MORGAN JONES

THE GOOD SISTER

PAN BOOKS

First published 2018 by Mantle

This paperback edition published 2019 by Pan Books
an imprint of Pan Macmillan
20 New Wharf Road, London N1 9RR
Associated companies throughout the world
www.panmacmillan.com

ISBN 978-1-4472-3363-3

1 3 5 7 9 8 6 4 2

A CIP catalogue record for this book is available from the British Library.

Typeset by Palimpsest Book Production Limited, Falkirk, Stirlingshire
Printed and bound by CPI Group (UK) Ltd, Croydon, CR0 4YY

Visit **www.panmacmillan.com** to read more about all our books
and to buy them. You will also find features, author interviews and
news of any author events, and you can sign up for e-newsletters
so that you're always first to hear about our new releases.

'For every soul there is a guardian'

(The Koran, 86:4)

September 2014

PART ONE

1

Abraham looked up at the great painted bear and in its raised paws and flaking black eyes saw a warning: the animals here may be caged, but the men are not. They're running free with their guns and to them you look like prey.

Of course this was no place for him. The family in front, the woman at the counter – they could see it in his frown, the stoop of his shoulders, the tight smile he gave as he handed her his money. On his own, with no child, lonely or lost or far from home. The cashier smiled back, as you might at a patient who wasn't going to make it, and he shuffled through the turnstile, glancing behind him one last time.

But this was a good rendezvous, even he could see that – right in one corner of the city, bounded on two sides by the main road, only one way in. Not crowded, not empty, plenty of shade from the afternoon sun. His thoughts ran along senseless lines. Did these people hold all their meetings here? Was the management friendly to their cause? He looked down at the texted instructions: turn left at the monkey house, then keep left until you get to the gazelles and the deer, where you'll see three picnic tables in a row on a patch of grass. Sit down and wait.

The last table was under an oak whose leaves were dry and ready to fall. Legs crossed, foot tapping, Abraham chewed the nail on his little finger, watched his few fellow visitors pass and did his best to slow down, cool down, breathe. This was the first time in, what, two whole fevered days that he'd come to a stop, and it was a surprise to find the world still in order; mothers pushed pushchairs, children darted ahead to the next animal, a father hung back to talk into his phone, ignoring his daughter's pleas to look at the tiny muntjac fawn, the size of a rabbit, nibbling at the grass.

His nerves peaked. He became conscious of the dark patches under his arms and the smell of sweat that rose up from them. The man was late, almost certainly not coming, and Abraham would have to do this himself, because no one else had any reason to care.

Two old women strolled and talked confidentially, arms linked, while the monkeys chattered and whooped. He felt in his pocket, found the two pills in amongst the change and the keys to the flat he would never go back to, and left them where they were.

Then there he was. Plainly him, with a heavy walk that took its time, his black eyes fixed steadily on Abraham as he approached, one shoulder drooping a little and a frown on his face that suggested he might be in pain, from an injury perhaps, a legacy of the war. If he was a soldier who could no longer fight, that might explain his new trade – a rebel who had found another way to engage the enemy. Abraham wanted to trust him. He watched the man's face and told himself to concentrate, pay attention, read it well.

Abraham held out his hand, and after looking at it for a moment, the man shook it and sat down.

'You are good man, I can see. Good father.'

'Not so good. Or I wouldn't be here.'

'Children. They are bad for fathers.'

Good and bad. Abraham nodded.

'Much money, crazy ideas.'

The man across the table tapped his temple with a thick finger, so hard that it made Abraham blink. The money and the ideas seemed to be linked, but it didn't seem right, or useful, to ask him to explain.

'Yes,' was all he said in the end, and wished again that he had some experience of worlds beyond his own.

6

'When she come?'

'Two days ago. Monday.'

The man gave a slow bobbing nod from side to side.

'Possible. Possible still here.'

'You think?'

Don't look too keen. He's reading you while you're trying to read him, and he's better at it than you are.

'Possible. Some time they cross like this –' the man clicked his fingers with a snap – 'some time they wait, go four, five at one time, some time they just wait. When time is not good – you know, trouble with Kurds, police, Free Syrians.'

'Can you find them here? Do you know where they are?'

Abraham studied his new contact. A contact. He wasn't sure he'd ever had a contact before. It could be a good face, under the hard shell, behind those hard eyes; imagine what they had seen in the last five years. Even in London a stranger's eyes might let you in and tell you something, but here everyone needed a dark lens between them and the world, didn't they, or how could they bear the horror?

The man ran his nails slowly along the iron-filing stubble on his cheek; they made a scratching noise like sandpaper on wood. He seemed to like it, and for a moment sat with his face held up to the light that filtered through the leaves, eyes closed, scraping his skin.

'How old she is?' he asked at last, without opening his eyes.

'Seventeen. Just seventeen.'

'She come with girls, boys?'

'Alone, I think. The papers say alone.'

'Name is Sofia.'

'Sofia Mounir.'

A decisive nod now, the answer found.

'I try. I know people, they know people, you know? In Gaziantep are places Daesh go, places they hide, I think maybe

I can find. Not for sure, understand. No guarantees, my friend, no guarantees.'

With the stress on the second syllable, guaRANtees, sing-song in his gruff bass.

'Maybe we lucky. Maybe. Some time there is luck, okay. I can make luck, but for this I need money, lira, understand? I give money to people, they give money to people, understand?'

'I understand.'

'You have money?'

'How much?'

Negotiate. Don't take his first price. Who knows what else you'll need your money for, or how long you'll be here.

'Thousand dollars.'

'I don't have a thousand dollars.'

'You say you have money.'

'I'm not a rich man.'

'Thousand dollars cheap price. Difficult work, my friend, difficult.'

'I'm a pharmacist, a chemist. I'm not a rich man.'

'Much danger, to me. To my friends.'

'I can pay five hundred.'

The man whistled, turned the corners of his mouth down in an exaggerated frown.

'Five hundred not my costs. Costs more than five hundred.'

'I don't have any more.'

'Okay, too bad, okay. Five hundred not good for me, not good for you. Okay, we can leave.'

Giving Abraham a final shrug, no hard feelings, he swung one leg up and over the bench.

'Wait. Seven hundred. I can pay seven.'

'Thousand dollars, my friend. One price.'

'Eight hundred.'

Abraham felt it slipping away from him, as he had known it would. Now he asked the question.

'What's your name?'

'Aziz.'

'Aziz. I'm Abraham.'

They shook hands, like people who wanted it to mean something.

'English?'

'Egyptian. I live in London. I lived in London.'

'You look not English.'

No. Certainly he rarely felt it. Instinct told him to broaden the conversation, to appeal to the humanity he was sure he could sense in this man.

'Do you have children?'

Aziz made him wait for the answer.

'I have children.'

'Where are they?'

'One in Aleppo. One here. One, she is dead.'

The shell softened and Abraham felt he was looking into the man's eyes for the first time.

'I'm sorry.'

'Bad war.'

'I know.'

'I must eat, Abraham. My wife, my son.'

Racing here, jettisoning his old life, Abraham had felt as if all the pain in the world had been channelled at him, but now he knew he was surrounded by stories far worse than his own. He felt it, as you might damp in the air. A nation of suffering that cut across borders, and now he was just one of its citizens, waiting in line for some unlikely relief.

'If I pay you the money, please, do your best. She's all I have.'

Aziz nodded, and a look passed between them, of understanding and regret. Under other circumstances we might have been friends, it seemed to say. That was how Abraham read it, at least.

'She's been tricked. She's been poisoned.'

'Nine hundred,' said Aziz.

'Please. Find her for me. I don't have long.'

'Deposit.'

Abraham counted out the three hundred dollars he had brought with him, watched Aziz leave, and waited for five minutes, as instructed. Nine hundred dollars. He was going to have to be careful. But then, what was the money for?

No one stopped long at the deer enclosure, and that was a shame, because the gazelles were beautiful. Abraham could have spent all day looking at them. The hind legs curving into the strong back, the fur flashed with a touch of fire, and that streak of black on the flank that seemed to have no purpose but to make them look fiercer than they really were. The shyness and the sureness of them. In the eternal blackness of their eyes he searched for some encouragement.

2

Badra comes back in the early evening as the sun is going down and tells us all to get ready, there are mujahideen coming. I ask her what she means by ready and without looking at me she tells us to wash and wear our best niqabs. The twins are excited, they spend half an hour in the bathroom with the door shut, giggling, and when they're finally finished Umm Nahar and I manage to get in there to wash our faces and brush our teeth. We are not veiled.

The four of us wait in the sitting room, all squeezed together on the long sofa, silent. Badra says no phones, and I'm not even allowed the Qur'an. It's so warm in here without the air conditioning, and I'm exhausted from the endless airstrikes over Raqqa last night.

I don't mind who I marry. It will be according to His will, so why would I give it any thought? As long as my husband is devout, dedicated to jihad, and a good Muslim – and I know that he will be all those things, or he wouldn't be here. In my heart, though, I long for someone who burns with a pure fire. Someone with beauty in his soul. I tell myself that here it could hardly be otherwise.

Qadira and Jameela start to fidget. The wait feels long, though it can only be an hour. Then I hear a buzzer, and Badra leaves the room. Moments later there are men's voices in the hall greeting her. They're speaking Arabic, deep and clear, and I feel a thrill to think these men have even today been fighting the infidel. What in my old life could compare to this?

They spend a moment in the hall talking to Badra, and I catch enough to know they're talking about us. How many? Where are they from?

And then they're here. Three of them, two young, one older, maybe in his thirties, all with beautiful great black beards. I start to stand up as they come in but Badra signals with her hand that we should sit. The two younger ones have machine guns slung over their shoulders and she tells them to leave them by the door.

These two are in camouflage clothes, but clean and neatly pressed so I know they haven't come straight from the battlefield. They've made the effort, as we have. The older man is wearing a long white dishdasha and a keffiyeh on his head. He has the blackest eyes I've ever seen, they seem to swallow the light, and as he stares at each of us in turn he smiles in a way that suggests he knows things we don't.

But it isn't enough to describe these brothers by the way they look. There's an energy I can feel as they stand before us, an aliveness – and some of that life passes to us, to me. I feel it fill my whole body and pull me towards them. It's a strange feeling, like a calm excitement – not a cheap thrill, like you'd get at the cinema or from music or something, but real, and

11

lasting. Qadira and Jameela have gone quiet, but I am waking up.

The brothers greet us, and we greet them. As-salamu alaykum. They ask more questions of Badra, in Arabic, like we're not there, like I don't know what they're saying. How old are they? I expect them to talk to us, but they don't, and when I look at Badra she makes it clear that we're to let them make their inspection. They're in charge, and I'll speak when I'm spoken to.

Grinning, one of the younger brothers says maybe he'll take the Belgians, both of them, imagine. He'd thank Allah twice every night. But if he has to choose he likes the smaller of the two.

Not this girl here, she looks afraid. He means Umm Nahar. I've seen better women on the streets, says the older man – I've seen better-looking Yazidis. This makes them all laugh. My last wife, he says, she was a cunt but she looked better than this. I know the word. Kuss. It pains me to hear it, but I'm not fresh from battle. I really don't understand anything.

She looks scared, he says – I like that. She should be scared. They laugh again.

What about the English? She's okay, says one of the younger brothers. She looks intense. Passionate, maybe. He digs his friend in the ribs. No, his friend says. Too dark. Look, no breasts, and her skin is bad, across her cheeks, on her forehead. If Allah has given her spots what else has he given her?

I glance at Badra, but she looks away. She knows I'm getting all of it, and whatever her problems with me I wonder why she's letting this happen. Now I'm scared, and angry. I try not to flush. I try to remember that I really know nothing.

Trouble, that one, says the older man. A heap of trouble and nothing like worth it.

He holds his hand out to Umm Nahar, who looks to me and then takes it. She's Pakistani, she doesn't know what they're saying but you can tell she gets it, it's in her eyes. He pulls her to her feet, stands back to look her up and down, has her turn on the spot. He holds his beard, frowning, has her turn again. How old, he wants to know. Sixteen, Badra tells him. A virgin? No. Married before. Her husband was executed for cowardice.

At that he raises his eyebrows, like he finds it interesting, and while he's making his decision goes back to stroking his beard. He makes me think of a judge at a dog show. Then he sniffs, nods, says something to Badra, and Badra takes her away.

The two younger men discuss who is going to take who, and agree quickly. Qadira and Jameela sit still beside me. Badra has returned, and tells them to go and get their things together.

'You,' she says to me. 'Back to your room.'

Hers isn't a face you argue with.

3

Every girl in Gaziantep, the face was hers and not hers. It was a sort of blindness. Half of them wore headscarves, of course, as she had, so that any woman of her height was a candidate, and Abraham began to grow feverish with hope and swift disappointment. It was crazy, anyway, to think he would see her in this city of a million. He might as well bump into his mother. But that one, walking in front of him now, she had the same walk, that slight bounce on her heels and a lightness about her that he was sure he knew. He quickened his step, jogging a few paces, drew level and saw that it wasn't her. The girl's boyfriend, young and slick and innocent, gave him a look that said leave, quickly.

So he wandered on, because he had to do something while Aziz did whatever Aziz did, and what else was there? In shopping malls that might have been in London he sheltered from the heat, but they weren't her places so he sought out the back-streets, where the smell of coffee and cumin, the smoke from cigarettes and pipes, the fumes from the harsh little mopeds that zipped about, and the shouting, and the haggling, and the music of lutes and flutes broadcast from every tenth shop all seemed to find their way to him deliberately and pull him back ten years into Cairo, which had once been home. That boy in the imitation leather jacket with the thick eyebrows and the wary look could have been him, at eleven or twelve, given the run of the city and not wholly sure what to do with it. And every little girl he saw, in floral print dresses, hand in her mother's hand, reminded him of Sofia.

The language was alien but the feeling was so familiar, of a city run by its people without interference from above. He slotted into it, it seemed to accept him, and briefly he felt comfortable, even wistful. He allowed himself the fond idea that when this was done he would come here with Sofia, show her how rich the world was, how her grasp of it was as narrow as his perhaps had been. They could travel together. Learn about each other. Help her fill the hole in her spirit with good things.

Even in September, the sun was strong and relentless; he could feel it burning his neck and arms. By the castle he bought a baseball cap and suncream, stopped and drank a coffee, and for the tenth time since arriving saw a face he was sure he had seen before. Yesterday it had been the young man with the mirrored sunglasses; today it was the woman with the navy headscarf and a way of turning away, always naturally, just as he was almost certain. Or they could be ten different men and women, the light was so bright, the crowds so quick to pass, and his mind so shot. Probably he was just seeing what he thought he ought to see. But who would come for him? He was an irrelevance, a speck. Unless the police in London had notified their counterparts in Turkey – unless they thought he was on his way to join Sofia – unless they were following him in the hope of finding her.

He should stop. Leave it to the men who did this work. The fighters, the strong, the ones who knew what they wanted and took it. This was no job for a man like him.

Abraham retreated to the Ambassador Hotel, where three men were lounging on the oversized leather chairs in the lobby. One Abraham's age, the other two younger, chests and arms straining against their T-shirts, the phones they were tapping at tiny in their hands. Their faces told him they had seen and done things that no man should see or do.

He had noticed men like them all over town; they had a way of fixing you briefly with their eyes, as if making some instant calculation of your potential threat, and these three did this now – let their gaze sit on him with that lazy intentness, then looked away, satisfied that he was nobody.

The gaunt receptionist was on duty. Abraham nodded at him as he walked to the lifts, received a blank stare in response, and as the doors closed saw him pick up the phone. It meant nothing. Receptionists made all sorts of calls.

Room 312 was long and thin, with a window that overlooked the main street, lively with cars and shouting and music coming from a cafe a hundred yards away. The noise came in through thin gauze curtains that had yellowed with age. The bed, a largeish single billed as a double, was in the middle of the long wall and perpendicular to it, so that it cut the room in two and forced Abraham to turn sideways and press himself against the other wall to walk from one half to the other. From somewhere inside the hotel he heard a man's voice shouting, then another in response. They could be fighters. They could be perfectly normal people who just happened to be yelling at each other in the heat of the day.

The safety chain on the door was broken. He could jam the

wooden chair under the handle, but anyone who really wanted to get in would get in – and besides, there was no other way out, short of tying the curtains together and abseiling down from the fourth floor.

So few routes were open to him. What would be would be.

He took a fresh T-shirt and shorts to sleep in, his toothbrush and toothpaste, put the bag in the tilting flat-pack wardrobe and went to wash in the tiny bathroom. The water ran brown for thirty seconds when he turned on the tap.

The mattress was small but sagged from every corner as he lay on it, and he struggled to find a comfortable position, folding the single pillow behind his head, bringing his knees up and resting his computer on his thighs. He could sleep right there – take a pill and it would all go away – but he fought it and, willing himself to look, set off into his daughter's new world.

For hours, sickened and compelled, Abraham wandered this way and that, no longer hearing the noises from the street or the voices shouting from floor to floor. Chatrooms, videos, Facebook, Twitter. It was like a great city where everyone shouted their grievances endlessly without restraint. A free market whose currency was anger, offence and horror, and where the worst examples won. There was no looking away.

So now she was Umm Azwar. An ugly, warlike name to his ear, and probably to hers. The first search brought up her Twitter page and there she was: a photograph of a young woman taken in sharp profile, the tip of her nose just showing beyond her hijab, and below it a tagline, a sort of motto.

No rest until the khilafa is built on earth.

He scrolled down. Quotations from the Koran, in English and Arabic, posted and retweeted by her. Links to stories about the war, about bombings, about the viciousness of Assad and his soldiers and his spies. In amongst them, retweets of sickly messages of peace and brotherhood over stock photographs of flowers and mountains and horses.

Her own messages were plain and direct, and effective. It was like listening to her in the different modes he knew so well: fierce, pensive, hectoring. Sentimental. In many her anger was clear.

Assad and his evil will not survive the edge of our sword.

If we let him the kafir will wage war against the Ummah until no Muslim is left standing.

Filthy coward US dogs kill our brothers and sisters from the safety of their shores.

Attached to this was a photograph of a building crumbled into bits, its dust covering bodies in the foreground. *Drone strike, Peshawar*, said the caption, and gave the date. From the same incident she had posted a picture of a dead child, its head hanging limply from the arms of its mother. This had no caption but the one Sofia had given it, in Arabic and English: *Kafir Genocide*.

Every fourth message contained an image he broadly recognized: soldiers waving black flags, SUVs patrolling tired cities, children dressed in black being taught by women covered head to toe in it, men thrown from buildings and flailing in mid-air, balaclavaed fighters holding up knives that looked as if they'd cut a bar of steel clean through. Vast stacks of cash being counted and oil refineries ringed with guards (*We are not only rich in spirit!*). Here was a blank-faced man in an orange jumpsuit kneeling, beside him some faceless black demon pressing the knife into his throat; but here too was the desecrated body toppled onto the sand, the head held up high towards the sun. These were the photographs that no one showed. Bodies smashed on the tarmac where they fell. Bodies crucified in the midst of crowds. Backs whipped, hands severed, heads stoned.

Abraham scrolled, looked, shut his eyes in sadness and disgust, moved on. But the head had imprinted itself on his mind, and was there whenever he tried to turn away. Had she gazed at it? His daughter, whose innocence had been the most beautiful thing in the world, had gazed on this and run towards it with her arms out wide.

And here was her endorsement: *Shia scum laughs for the last time.*

Abraham imagined her writing the words and felt nausea starting in his stomach; wondering at the mystery that had brought her to this point, knowing her no better than a patient who had wandered in from the street.

What these men had done to her. They knew the receptors in the soul and had applied the right amount of poison unerringly to each.

4

The girls in my school, I'd look at them and wonder why any of them bothered. Why get up in the morning? For a good job? A good job. A teacher shovelling sand into empty minds or a doctor stretching out lives that mean nothing till they're so thin you can see right through them. And the question in my head the whole time was, for what? The gift you've been given, this gift of life, why sacrifice it to these false idols? For personal satisfaction. That's a joke. My satisfaction doesn't amount to a single atom in the whole universe. It's like saying you should pray to get what you want, it's not why we're here. A bird doesn't fly for its own pleasure.

So many souls in the world and so little to fill them, like prayers that are never said or food left out to rot.

While their souls starved, I watched those London girls – even the good ones, the ones who had been my friends – I watched them stuff every crack in their bodies full, like they were crazed with hunger and thirst. They were ill and they didn't even know it, I felt so sorry for them. Smoke in their lungs, music in their ears, gossip clogging their minds every second of the day, skin perfumed and shiny with fake tan, even the food they ate was as far from God's intentions as their blasphemies were from the holy purity of the Qur'an. Floating in pollution, they absorbed it through every pore.

It wasn't their fault, they were blind to other possibilities. Blinded by a system that doesn't want them to see. I don't even mention what else they brought inside themselves, the depraved stories they told, the pride they took in it. Life for them was seventy years of flesh and appetite and abuse of their God-given soul.

That world held nothing for me, and I'm not alone in that.

Very far from alone.

5

When I finally get signal, I set myself up online again. Before I left on my journey I deleted everything for security reasons, just like Nadia told me – she was very clear about that – but also because I wanted to leave behind every piece of what I was before.

So. New Twitter, as Umm Azwar this time. Finally under my true name. I follow a bunch of people and send a couple of tweets and it feels good to be connected with the community again. One day soon I guess I will meet Nadia. She was so wise, so supportive. So clear in all her instructions – everything she said would happen happened. There was faith in me coming here but really, she made it so easy. I haven't heard from her, I guess she's super busy with other sisters making the journey so I send her a message and leave it at that. Someone replies to one of my tweets straight away. He's a brother from Germany. I recognize his name.

Congratulations! Mahbrouk! You the English sister, my dear?

That freaks me out a bit. How did he know? There are so many false agents out there, cowards who dare not show their faces and try to trap us with their lies. Also, 'my dear'? 'My dear' is odd.

— Thank you. I am a citizen of the khilafa, my friend.

I look over his account. I don't think he can be a spy – he's been around too long. He comes back quickly.

If it's you you're an example to us all. Good luck!

I thank him, and google my name – my old name. It's everywhere. Such a weird feeling, like I've travelled back in time and can see my former self. 'English Schoolgirl in Syria.' '"Genius" Student Joins ISIS.' There must be fifty articles. There's a picture of my house, and an old picture of me from Facebook. I don't know how they got it because I deleted that account.

How terrified these people are. One seventeen-year-old girl leaves their country and I end up on every front page! Scared out of their minds, and I know why. Because I'm right. Because their decaying, stinking society cannot survive on corruption and money-lust, blind to everything that is good and true. It will rot to nothing and the dogs will eat the rest. Before I left I went into town to buy some stuff I needed and from the bus I watched Oxford Street go by with my mouth hanging open at the emptiness of it all. Literally hanging open. Shop cafe shop McDonald's shop. Shoppers with shopping bags, huge pictures of nearly naked women advertising shops. Is that it? Is that all you dream of? The West is a house with no foundation and no walls, a paper house, it will blow away or it will burn.

Why fear us? We are a hundred thousand in the khilafa, and they are billions.

Because every tree in the forest is dying except for ours. We are the power that will hasten their end. And they know.

Scrolling through these pages I see my father's name. It seems so foreign to me, like it's written in a language I no longer understand. For the first time I imagine him finding me gone, and wonder what he'll tell my mother, if he tells her anything.

When the shock is past he'll come to understand that our family died a long time ago, and that without him, and the part he played, I wouldn't be here. Out of pain will come good. That is how history is made.

6

Abraham's job, mostly, was to avoid mistakes. Sometimes he might do some good, offer useful advice, make someone better a little quicker, but he was paid to not screw up. Give the right number of the right pills to the right patient under the right label. Don't make anybody worse. Say no to the scammers and the addicts and the ones who routinely try it on. Above all, don't poison anybody, and protect the company. How did they put it, in their emails and their training videos? Control the risk. But risk wasn't something you could control. Risk was something that sat patiently waiting for the right moment to sink its teeth into you. And it wasn't interested in the company, it was interested in him.

They had come at lunchtime, after the Monday methadone rush and the deliveries and the careful stocktaking of the controlled substances, with a small crowd of shoppers gawping and his colleague Amanda looking on as if she was sorry to say she'd been expecting that moment for some time. Abraham had been trying to tell a jumpy young man with one heavily bloodshot eye that he couldn't sell him four bottles of cough medicine, no matter how ill his family was, when he caught sight of the uniform walking across the supermarket floor towards him. After a moment's fear that they had come for him, he had known without doubt what it meant. He had been on the verge of calling them himself.

At the station, the plain clothes had done most of the talking. Sofia was on her way to Syria; last seen at a bus station in Istanbul, flew through Budapest to cover her tracks, but definitely her, no question. That was yesterday, Sunday, and for all they knew she'd crossed the border by now – either that or she was holed up somewhere close to it waiting for the right time. The newest recruit, a coup, someone that young, that bright, the papers would be all over it.

The words were black stones that he couldn't get down. His throat closed.

What had they done to stop her? Abraham wanted to know. These powerful men, they must have been able to stop her.

The officer laughed. She wasn't high-risk. They weren't mind readers. His breath smelled of coffee and a diet of bread and meat.

Had Abraham known she was going? Had he heard her use the name Umm Azwar? That was her ISIS name, the one she went by online. Was he sure he had no sympathy with the cause? With all those brave brothers fighting the good fight?

'I'm a Christian, a Copt. My daughter converted and I had nothing to do with it.'

'When did she convert?'

'Three years ago.'

'Why?'

'She had good reasons, reasons of faith.'

The questions came like darts. Which mosque? Which imam? How often did she go? Who were her friends?

Where was her mother?

Her mother wasn't well. She lived with Sofia's grandmother, mostly, and didn't take calls from anyone. Hadn't done for a long time.

They were preoccupied with money. If he hadn't funded her trip who had?

He had no idea. Perhaps that was something they could investigate. Maybe it had been sent to her, he had read they did that, these people.

So he did have his fears then, of the road she might be heading down?

This didn't come out of the blue. He had been worried in the same way that a parent might worry about drugs, or pregnancy, or any of the thousand pits a daughter might fall into. Sofia wasn't one to do anything by halves but she was still a child, foolish, susceptible. Didn't policemen fear for their children?

'Yesterday she was a child, Mr Mounir. Now she's a terrorist.'

Just how far off the track had he wandered? To be tricked by his own daughter, who lived in the next room. The blindness of it, and the foolishness, not to know his own flesh and blood. How easy to slip out unseen, with a father who never looked too hard for fear of driving her further away.

He had known none of it, and all of it. Like the patients who went to their doctor too late to address the symptoms they had been ignoring for years.

Abraham had walked the three miles home from the police station, head roaring so loud that no single thought settled. She'd left forever. She'd come straight back when the reality bit. She'd be dead within weeks. He saw the crowd of journalists and cameramen who clamoured at him outside his flat but they didn't register; he might have been watching himself on the news along with everyone else.

So hard, to be a father. The thousand mistakes to be made, and that thin line through them growing thinner by the day, and the worst of it how late you woke up: stray for years, wander miles off course – and no one would tell you, you had no idea, you thought the line was still under your feet.

Any word from her, they had told him, you call us immediately. And don't go anywhere. He had almost laughed at that. Where would he go?

From the table by his bed he took the paracetamol bottle that held the oxycodone. Instant release, just two for now. A glass of water from the night before sat ready by his lamp, and for a moment he contemplated the pills nestled together in his palm and imagined the job they would quietly do, and the pain slipping away as surely as a headache.

But the pills wouldn't resolve anything; they simply froze the pain in time. Enough foolishness for today. He opened the bottle and slipped them back inside.

If the place had been searched it barely showed. The books still lay in piles, glasses lined up unwashed by his chair, on his desk his notebook displayed the latest neat scribblings towards the book he would never write. In the kitchen, dirty plates and mugs sat by the sink.

They had been in her room. The bed had been stripped and the linen bundled in a heap on the floor. Her neatly ordered books had been slotted back chaotically onto the shelves. They wouldn't have found much. A Koran, if she hadn't taken it, other devotional texts, school clothes pressed and ready, polished school shoes side by side, a desk, a chair, a computer that they would have taken if she hadn't already, all encased in white walls that would have told them as much as they had told Abraham in the last two years. Sofia might have revealed herself to her God in here, but not to anyone else.

On the other side of the bed was a table whose single drawer had been pulled out and emptied onto the mattress. Once it had been full of pens and postcards, plastic necklaces, a stopped watch with a rainbow face, a girl's precious rubbish. None of that remained – cleaned out years before, he imagined. Some tissues, a box of ibuprofen and two new batteries in a pack of four were all that was left. If her old diary still existed, the one with the floral cover and the clasp that locked with a tiny brass key, it had been taken.

Abraham sat on the bare bed, stared at the wall and felt a physical rupture, as if all this time he had been conscious of the warmth and weight of her body and someone had finally torn her away. As Ester had been torn away. He lay down, on his side, one arm across the space his daughter had left, and let the tears come. They flowed from him like blood from a fresh wound, and he feared the moment they ran out.

Sofia had left long ago, of course, and he had already mourned it. But not to say goodbye – why wouldn't she say goodbye in some way? Why deny every particle of the girl she had been? Like a man looking down from a high wire for the first time, he saw great depths appear beneath: was it him? Had she done all this just to get away?

The thought stopped his tears, shunted him from grief to a sort of horror. She must hate him. She must. She'd scrubbed herself clean of every association, as if the merest hint of him would cause her careful creation to collapse.

The tears had been warm. Now he felt cold, and wretched, and alone.

One thought remained. Since he had heard the word Syria it had been growing, first as nonsense and now as a certainty. He had to follow her.

7

When they get back in the evening, Idara invites me to eat with her and Badra. I think she asks me because we can talk to each other easily and the rest of the time in here communication is quite difficult. Last night we all spent an hour or two together in the sitting room, most of us anyway, crowded round a tablet watching videos and saying prayers and that was great, all bound together by the universal language of faith. That's the magic of those videos, I realize, I hadn't thought of it before. You don't need to know Arabic to appreciate their power.

Anyway, most of the time there's a lot of nodding and gesturing and as a result the women here haven't bonded as they might, families eat separately and tend to keep to themselves.

Idara talks more than her friend. She's telling a story about an Iraqi fighter who got scared and tried to leave when he saw how many brothers were being killed by the Peshmerga. He was found cowering in one of the tunnels we've dug round the edge of the city to hide from drones and spy planes when we need to – three brothers literally bumped into him during last night's airstrikes. At first they thought he was a terrified local woman, but when they pushed her out into the night one of them saw her combat boots. A fighter in a niqab. We know what God says about that. They cut off his head and put it on a spike, says Idara, and she makes a spitting noise – if you hurry up and get married maybe you'll be out of here in time to see it.

Sometimes I think she might be teasing me but I don't mind – I'd rather we talked. She asks me about my childhood, and my father, and my mother, and I'm happy to tell her. I never used to talk about my life but now it seems so far away it might as well belong to someone else. Idara's response is amazing. She says my mother's illness released me to come here, to travel the path I was always meant to take – that if she had still been well I might have found it hard to break away. What a blessing it is to be with others who have been guided by the Prophet and can help me illuminate my journey. I don't tell them about my father, and the type of man he is, but suddenly all that makes sense too. If he'd shown me more real love maybe I wouldn't be here. Of course it happened this way! There could be no other.

Badra is pretty quiet still. She's from Germany, and Idara told me she came here with her husband, a Turk who died during the battle for Sadad. They used to be al-Nusra, committed before the khilafa even existed. My respect for her grows.

Idara's from Sudan, but she was living in Egypt before, and when we talk about Cairo I feel so close to her. Her husband is away in Libya training our people there. She laughs when she tells me that he has just taken another wife, a fifteen-year-old local girl. When I ask her how she feels about that she shrugs and tells me it's the law, and the will of Allah, praise be upon Him, and who is she to question it? Besides, she's here and he's there and this is another fact of life. Do not trouble yourself with things that cannot be changed, she tells me. She is a wise woman, Idara. She has seen a lot, and she understands. Would it bother me? she asks. If I was worried about my emotions I wouldn't be here, I tell her. She laughs again, and nods. She looks at Badra. You see? She will do well here.

Dinner is pasta in tomato sauce, Idara makes it and it's good.

When we're washing up I ask Badra and Idara about the cigarettes I saw the brother take at the checkpoint as we entered the city. I've been thinking about it a lot, and wondering whether to keep quiet about it, and in the end decide to ask their advice. Apart from anything else I can't be sure that I'm not meant to say something, that the whole thing wasn't a test. I do my best to be subtle.

'Are any of the laws of the khilafa relaxed for the mujahideen?' I ask. 'When they return from battle.'

'The laws are laws for all,' says Badra, but Idara is looking at me, just a little sideways.

'What kind of thing?'

'Just generally.'

'A general question?'

I nod, and Idara half frowns, half smiles.

'You have an example?'

I hesitate. 'In the way they treat their wives. How they behave. Smoking, that kind of thing.'

'There's something on your mind?'

'Seeing the brothers here. Wondering what it's like for them, coming home when they've seen what they've seen.'

Maybe this is what I'm worried about. Maybe the cigarettes are a distraction. Idara breathes in deeply through her nose, nodding.

'The brothers are men like any other. And they are at war.'

'What you think of them is not important,' says Badra, looking hard at me.

I don't understand her hostility. Everything I say she twists.

'I just want to understand.'

I think I flush as I say it but I can't help that.

'You are not here to understand,' says Badra. Her face is so pale and hard. 'You are here to serve. You will never marry if you do not change.'

All the things I wanted to say go out of my head. I'm confused, and I ask Him for clarity.

'The khilafa can't be built on hypocrisy. There are laws. There is sharia.'

Badra just stares at me. I muster the strength to meet her stare, to stand my ground, but there's something else in her eyes. They look almost sad.

'You have no idea what we're building here.'

8

Abraham fell into an uneasy sleep on the sagging bed, sweating in his clothes in the heat of the evening.

He was woken from dreams of deserts by a persistent noise, separate from the cars and the mopeds and the call to prayer and the endless shouting. A knocking, not loud but insistent. With effort he swung himself from the bed and went to stand by the door, wishing there was a spyhole.

'Yes?'

'Please to open door.'

The voice was high, but a man's, with an odd rasp to it.

Abraham wished he had said nothing. What should he do? This man could be here to help him or arrest him. Or to kill him. A Turkish policeman, or a Daesh recruiter come to stop him from meddling. For the first time he felt his own vulnerability in all this, like a physical thing, a shrinking of the muscles.

'Who is it?'

'I am next room.'

What did that mean?

'What do you want?'

'Please, to power phone.'

'Reception. Reception will have one.'

'They do not.'

This was crazy. No one knocked on hotel rooms and asked for things from strangers. But in this lonely place it seemed wrong to assume that anyone's reason to be here was worse than his own. The Christian thing to do was to open the door. The human thing, regardless.

'Wait please.'

Abraham took his pills and his laptop into the bathroom, stood on the toilet seat, popped open one of the cheap tiles that made up the false ceiling and balanced both inside. Before finally opening the door he straightened his shirt, closed his eyes for a moment and took two deep breaths.

If the man who stood there had come to kill him he was going to do it with a smile. He beamed all the way across his face, which was wide and pockmarked around the cheekbones. Behind fleshy lids his big eyes smiled, too. There was oil in the smile, and sweat on the hand that he offered Abraham to shake, and the threat Abraham had felt gave way to a faint revulsion, and that in turn to guilt. So the man was unfortunate. Shouldn't two unfortunates feel a sort of kinship in a place like this?

'I am Vural.'

At least that's what it sounded like. Vyooral. He gave a deep nod as he shook, then a wet-sounding sniff. Abraham looked down on the thin hair that he had combed carefully across his bald skull, on the thick black moustache that hung over his top lip, on the cheap grey-green suit that needed a press, and had the strong instinctive sense that this man's life had fallen apart – that he was only here because he had nowhere left to go.

That was kinship.

'Sami.'

Sami was the name he had given to the receptionist. Sami Labib. A Cairo doctor who had treated his mother twenty years ago.

'I am next room.'

Vural let go of Abraham's hand and pointed to the room next door.

'Ah.'

'I have better hotels.'

He refreshed the smile, sniffed again. His eyes were sad and yellowish.

Abraham found himself smiling.

'Me too.'

'You stay long?'

'One day. Maybe two.'

'Ten. I do business –' he pronounced the 'i', busyness – 'in Antep. I sell – wait, I show.'

He was gone for a minute, during which Abraham could hear him rooting around in the cupboard that, if their rooms were laid out alike, backed on to their shared wall. When he returned, he had a book in one hand and in the other a ladle, which he held up like a baton.

'Kitchen things. Look.'

He held the book towards Abraham and flicked through it, a thick brochure full of cookers, fridges, washing machines, knives, chopping boards, colanders, orange juicers, saucepans, every single thing anyone had ever needed to use in a kitchen.

'For you. Please.'

Abraham took the ladle, inspected it with due gravity, and gave a deep nod of his own, more touched than he might have expected. To be given anything here felt extraordinary, and against the odds it seemed to have meaning: here is something for your home, if you ever return.

'Thank you.'

Vural returned the nod.

'My phone, the power, is kaput.'

He fished in his jacket pocket and pulled out a phone in amongst several used tissues, one of which fell to the floor. In the same movement he stooped to pick it up and with his other hand passed Abraham the phone, sniffing on his way down.

'Dead. You have power?'

It was a Samsung, like his own. Abraham handed it back, from long professional habit imagining the viruses clinging to it.

'Perhaps. Let me see.'

He squeezed past the bed and went to his bag, found his charger and turned to see Vural reaching for his bedside lamp.

'It doesn't work.'

Vural tried the switch anyway.

'Kaput.' He shook his head. 'I have better hotels. You want my light? I do not read.'

He picked up the book from the table. A history of Istanbul, which Abraham had bought years ago and never found the right time to read. Vural seemed pleased.

'Istanbul. Yes? You go to Istanbul?'

Maybe with her, when this was over. 'I plan to.'

'I go one time. My eyes cry with beauty.'

'I'm sure.'

Abraham handed him the charger, and Vural tried the jack for size.

'Is good!' He beamed. 'I can?'

'Of course.'

'I bring. Later.'

'Of course.'

'Thank you. Teşekkür.'

Abraham wanted to repay Vural's openness with conversation but could find nothing to say. His energy was low, most probably. Vural's was not.

'Small bag,' he said, pointing at Abraham's case. 'Not much things. You do business?'

'Not really. I'm just passing through.'

Vural frowned, not understanding.

'I come and go. I travel.'

'Aaah, traveller. I understand. Travel is best thing. For this.' He tapped his temple three times with a fat finger. 'You are writer?' Replacing the history of Istanbul, he picked up the notebook that had been underneath and began to flick through the pages.

'No. Not really. Please don't.'

'Is good, to write books. You must have big brain.'

Ridiculous though it was, Abraham was strangely flattered.

'I'm not a writer. Really. I'm a chemist. A pharmacist.'

'Aah, okay, is good, good job. Important. I have, how you say . . .' he sniffed, and waved his hand under his nose.

'A cold.'

Vural grinned.

'Yes, cold. Funny to have cold when is so hot, no?'

'Here. Wait a moment.'

Abraham went to his bag and from the small store of medicines he had brought took some aspirin and some vitamin C. Vural took them as if they were jewels of great value.

'Sami. This is kind. This is good, thank you.'

But now he was shaking his head.

'You, you are good man, I see, clear, clear. But Turkey, now, I am sorry, is bad men everywhere. And Gaziantep?' He let out a low whistle. 'Five years, beautiful city.' Beeyootiful. 'Now, everywhere bad men. You see?' He gestured to the window. 'With beards, and guns. You see?'

'Yes, I see.'

'Best thing, you go to Adana. Beautiful city. The most beautiful that is not Istanbul. Bridges, houses, old old. Beautiful. And no bad men. The Sabanci mosque, oh my goodness.'

Goodness. Abraham wondered where he had picked that up.

'After here, Adana, do not stay in Antep. Is not safe for strangers.'

Vural was shaking his head and beaming at the same time.

'Teşekkür ederim.' He raised the charger and the aspirin. 'You go today?'

A strange question to ask, at five in the afternoon.

'I stay tonight.'

He beamed at Abraham a last time from the other side of the bed.

'Tomorrow, Adana. No bad men there, yes?'

9

Two sisters came to teach us Arabic today. They stayed for the whole morning. I explained that I already spoke it, that I grew up speaking nothing else at home and spoke nothing else at my mosque – but they insisted I join their classes anyway.

I tell Badra that I don't need to be taught a language I've spoken since I was two, but all I get in response is a silent stare and then a line about me not being in charge of the khilafa. That woman has a way of winding me up so tight with just a word or a look. I hate myself for letting her.

After class I go to bed in the afternoon and listen to the planes in the sky and the bombs falling all over the city with no pattern to them. I'm not afraid, but thoughts come that I don't want. It's like the bombs open them out. I didn't tell my friends I was coming here and now I think I should have. I should have left some sort of a note or message. For Nana, too, her pain won't matter but there was no need to cause it.

I can see my bedroom in Cairo, and the warm round arch of my mother's back as I lie in bed and she sits by me reading. Why do I see that now? Why do scraps of her music come in?

I do my best to remember why I'm here: to serve Him, however He sees fit. I must think of these times as preparation, as making myself ready for the next stage, whatever it is and whenever it comes. There are tears in me, but that's where they'll stay.

We have a new arrival. Her name is Namaa, she's from Iraq, and although she's more like Badra's age she sleeps in my room, on the last mattress in the corner. She doesn't say much. I try to talk to her but she just smiles – not a real smile – and doesn't talk back. Most of the time she spends lying on her side on her bed with her back to me.

Her husband was a deserter, and his head is now on a spike.
I ask what will happen to her. Allah will provide for her, Badra
tells me. She will mourn for the decreed period and then she
will marry again.

Poor woman, to be married to such a man. I pray for her,
and for me, that God the most high might find me someone
whose faith is equal to mine.

10

Aziz phoned the next morning. At last, and just as Abraham
had more or less given up on his three-hundred-dollar deposit.
Meet me at the zoo, same bench, same time.

For the rest of the day, Abraham walked and searched, and
stayed in his room and searched, and found nothing that might
help. No news of English schoolgirls, no news of anything. No
chance-in-a-million sightings. Just normal people going about
their business, and dotted amongst them, like wolves mingling
with the flock, the fighters, the hard men with the thick shells
for faces and the eyes that followed every step you took. They
huddled on street corners, sat on car bonnets, milled about.
Gangs of them took over cafes, lolled around in the sun, smoking and talking, smoking and not talking, watching each other
pass like predators taking time out from the fight.

Abraham learned to walk past and not catch anyone's eye,
and soon became as used to them as every other resident of
Gaziantep. The men he worried about were the ones behind
him, the ones he looked for but couldn't see.

Years before, newly arrived in London, Sofia briefly loved the
zoo. She would head straight for the rainforest house, crazily
hot in a London winter, the sloths hanging by their tails and
the little bearded monkeys jumping from branch to branch.

Spotting the iguanas, which she called gwanas, in the dead leaves that lined the floor of the cages. They'd been many times with Ester and once on their own, when she was in hospital; the sight of Sofia there without her mother had been too much, and though they lived close by they never went again. It was expensive, and anyway, Sofia soon came to see the cages and not the animals they held.

If she were here now, she'd be railing against the zoo, no question. Everywhere he went, he was arguing with her, her voice in his ear an irritant and a comfort; he wanted her to be quiet, and he wanted her to keep talking. It was so like grief, this, and it occurred to him that he was waiting for news of her death – if she had crossed the border she might as well be dead, and slowly the peace cracked, replaced by the fear that had become his usual state.

'Do you have news?'

Aziz sat down on the same bench as before and nodded, in no hurry to start. He took in a deep breath, nodding slowly.

'I have news.'

Abraham couldn't bring himself to ask the next question.

'Is good and bad.'

'Go on.'

'She is in Syria.'

Abraham closed his eyes and quietly shook his head.

'She is in Dabiq. Small town. In a makkar. You know makkar?'

'No.'

Makkar. It had a horrible sound. He saw her in a kind of barracks in the dust, lined with bunks and fighters and guns.

'Where woman go. When they arrive. And families. She is there, we know the place.'

That was better, if it was just the women. But really it made no difference. It was over. She was beyond his reach.

'Is that the good news?'

36

'Good news is we can get her out.'

When Abraham opened his eyes, the gazelle that had been chewing grass by the fence had lifted its head and was staring again, as if it could sense the conflict in him.

Good news. It was good news. He had no choice but to think that.

'She won't want to come.'

'She have no choice.'

'How would you do it?'

'We do it before. Three times. Two girls, one boy, his mother took him, we took him back. My people, my friends, very good, very professional.'

'But it's like a prison.'

Aziz snorted.

'Bad prison. They kidnap from our land, we kidnap from their land. No guards at makkar. We go, we look like Daesh fighters, we tell her she has to come with us, she comes, we bring her here.'

'What about all the checkpoints?'

Aziz raised his eyebrows, intertwined his fingers and pushed them out until the bones cracked.

'For this we need money. For whole thing we need money.'

Abraham barely heard him. His hand went to his mouth and he bit at a hangnail that wasn't there. He was trying to pick out a single question from the dozens crowding him. To intercept her was one thing, to get her to see sense, even to say goodbye, but taking her back – it would never work. She wasn't ready.

'I don't know,' he said, wishing he had a single person to discuss it with.

'Ten thousand dollars.'

That was all he had, almost exactly. Even if it worked, there would be nothing left to rebuild their lives together somewhere.

Perhaps this was the universe's way of forcing him to prove his love for her.

'It's a lot.'

Aziz shrugged.

'How much your daughter is worth?'

'She won't be ready.'

Now Aziz turned to him, his belly shifting under his shirt. The hair on his chest ran up into the stubble on his neck.

'Your daughter, she is pretty?'

Abraham felt his hand stiffen.

'What do you mean?'

'She is pretty, she marry quickly. They will marry her. And when she is gone from the makkar she is gone. Like this.' He slapped his palms together twice like a man disposing of a problem.

What would Ester say? The money wasn't a consideration. It came down to an impossible calculation: take her now, and she might never see that she was wrong; delay too long and she might be too far gone to recover. Did the poison wear off? How long did it take?

'I need time to think.'

Aziz sighed and shrugged, as if he was tired of his clients but understood.

'Tomorrow. After that, too late. And nine hundred dollars now. Minus deposit is six.'

11

Sometimes the kitchen is left in a real state, plates and mugs in the sink, food out on the sides, no one bothers to empty the bin and when they do the bag sits there because to get to the bin store you have to go outside and none of us are allowed to do that. When the air con's not working and there's no breeze there's a real stink. The sitting room as well; people just leave stuff and I tidy it up and then it's a tip again within minutes. I don't even want to talk about the bathroom.

So I have an idea. A roster. I spend the afternoon drawing one up, and when Badra comes home that night I show it to her. The boxes are blank for now – I want her advice on who should do what.

She nods as she looks it over.

'Thank you.'

'You're tired now, I'll leave you. We can talk about it later.'

'We can do it now. I do not have a pen. You have a pen?'

I say of course and hand her mine.

She thanks me for it and starts writing in the blank boxes. My name in the first, in English script, just Umm Azwar. Umm Azwar in the next one, and the box after that, and in all the boxes on the top line. I think she wants me to do all the washing-up, but she keeps going, speeding up and eventually just writing the letters UA in every single box. I feel like I'm turning to stone as she's doing it, I want to speak out or walk away but I can't, it's like I can feel the blood freezing in my veins.

When she's done, she hands the paper back to me and there's a cold fire in her eyes.

'You are right. The makkar needs work. You can start tomorrow.'

It takes me all day. Idara looks in and teases me. This means Badra likes you, she says. I laugh what you'd call a hollow laugh but she says no, really, she does. Of course. Right. By the end I'm dripping under my abaya and I can smell my own sweat rising up off me. Everything looks so much better. I'd like to beat the rugs but I can only really do that outside.

I eat early because I don't want to see Badra, but when she comes back that evening she comes to find me. I'm in my room, reading hadith. She stands over my bed for a few moments, as if she's inviting me to say something, but I don't want to give her anything to work with so I put my book down and look up at her, waiting.

'I didn't say do it all today,' she says at last. 'I thought it was a roster.'

She uses the English word, and a mocking sort of tone.

'It needed it.'

'It's better.' She leaves a pause. 'Remember you are on duty again tomorrow.'

Then she goes, and I lie in my bed wondering what I have to do to be accepted by her.

12

His daughter was gone, and tonight he would drink. The Golden Lion was the last bar remaining in Gaziantep: dark, airless, tomblike, dank with the smell of old beer and last night's cigarettes. Erol, the proprietor, brought him a bad Turkish whisky, and as he set it down Abraham ordered. The place suited his mood; somewhere that had known fun but wasn't expecting to see it again. The photographs of parties that lined the far wall had an ancient feel to them, historical documents only.

By the time the second drink arrived Abraham had finished the first.

'Two more whiskies, please.'

Erol looked at him with great subtlety. I am happy for you to drink as much as you want, but understand, not everyone in this city will share my tolerance. Abraham was grateful to him; more than that, he was filled with a great love for the man and what he represented. A last bulwark against the darkness.

'And something for you. Please. At least until you get busy.'

Erol nodded, went to the bar, took bottles from the shelves and started preparing something out of sight. When he returned he had a tray, and on it a single tumbler, a two-thirds full bottle of whisky and a Martini glass full of some bright pink liquid and sporting a cocktail stick.

With different appetites, each went at their drinks. Erol sipped at his like a connoisseur.

Perhaps Gaziantep had been cosmopolitan once, the real gateway between East and West. In its own way it was cosmopolitan still, no? Abraham thought of all the fighters that had passed through on their way to sign up. English, Swedish, Russian, American, Moroccan, Belgian, Czech. A great clearing house for the scattered scum of the earth.

What has happened to your city, he wanted to ask this decent-seeming man across the bar from him. How have you allowed it? But he knew Erol wouldn't understand, and so he smiled a smile he didn't mean, drank the whisky until he felt numb, and took himself to the blankness of the hotel.

13

Abraham shifted in bed, conscious of trying to escape something in his dream, some noise or unpleasantness he didn't want to confront. He did his best to stay under but the noise came again, and as he began to wake he realized that it wasn't in his head but in the room. A banging, a hard banging on wood. On his door.

The only light was the dull orange from the street lamps outside. He sat up, tried to rub his eyes awake and as the banging started once more rolled over and out of bed.

'Wait. Please.'

His laptop and phone lay on the floor by the bed. He took them, went to the bathroom and by the light of the phone lifted the tile and placed the computer inside alongside his pills, letting the tile drop gently back into place.

'Who is it?'

The breath caught in his throat as he said it. Outside, someone grunted something he didn't catch: a man's voice, that was all, and then a fist making the door shake. One, two, three, deliberate, violent.

Oh God, I hate this place. Please deliver me from it. Deliver us, God, Sofia and me.

The voice said something else and now the whole door shook. With a silent prayer, Abraham turned the handle.

Two men stood there, one at the shoulder of the other. The moment the door opened, the first of them walked past Abraham and in one motion reached up, dragged him into the room and pinned him by the neck to the wall by the foot of the bed, so quickly that Abraham barely registered what had happened and with such force that he felt the breath go from him and his feet lift from the floor. Christ, the man's grip was strong, like his fingers were cast in metal.

Each man had the same build, short and broad with thick arms, and the same solid, heavy head. The second man switched on the overhead light, stopped for a moment to stare hard at Abraham and after a swift scan of the room crossed to the bedside table and pulled the drawer right out, turning it upside down and dropping keys, change, receipts onto the floor. His movements were quick and forceful, in an established pattern. Squatting down, he picked up Abraham's passport, leafed through it, tossed it away, did the same with his notebook. He wore a cap; Abraham thought he recognized him from the hotel lobby, he had seen him sitting there – had done his best to avoid seeing him there.

'What is?' said the man holding him to the wall.

'Notes. For my work.'

'What work?'

'I'm a pharmacist. Medicines.'

After another minute of studying Abraham's scrawled handwriting the searcher threw the book impatiently behind him. Now he kneaded the pillows, lifted the mattress and pushed it onto the floor, squatted down briefly to check underneath. With another look at Abraham he edged round the bed, took the suitcase from the wardrobe and emptied it, began to sift through the contents, scooping things behind him as he was done with them.

Abraham tried to speak. Tell me what you're looking for, he wanted to say, and I'll help you. But the moment he tried, the grip on his neck tightened and nothing came out. This man was a professional.

Finished with the bag, his friend went to the wardrobe and examined every piece of clothing, went through every pocket, until the wardrobe was empty and the floor behind him covered. When he was done, he ripped the curtains to the floor in two big heaves, flapped the fabric like someone making the bed, and seeing nothing there stood for a moment with his hands on his hips, looking round the room and shaking his head. Muttering something to his friend, he picked his way through the mess to the bathroom, flicked on the light, and Abraham heard the little he had in there – toothbrush, toothpaste, soap – being thrown on the floor.

'La shay' huna,' he said, coming back into the room and stepping right up to Abraham so that his face was only inches away. Six inches shorter, he must have been.

'Phone. Mobil, now.'

Abraham still had it in his hand; he held it up. The man took it, tried to unlock the screen and passed it back.

'Number. Now.'

The grip on Abraham's neck released and he felt himself sliding the two inches down the wall to the floor.

'Here,' he said, rubbing his neck. It felt grazed, it was so sore.

For a good minute the man's thick thumbs flicked here and there over the screen of the phone, in and out of every app.

'La shay' huna.'

Nothing here. The man with the cap threw the phone aside and reached up to Abraham's face. Abraham pulled back, expecting him to go for his neck, but with a firm open palm the man stroked one side of Abraham's face and then the other before pinching his cheek, hard, between finger and thumb.

'Taqlim hayatik.'

'He say cut your beard,' said his friend, and left the room.

The man in the cap stared hard at Abraham, and without warning slapped him round the head. Pointing with two fingers at his own eyes and then at Abraham's he walked away, leaving the door open behind him.

Bent over, Abraham rubbed his neck and with each deliberate breath swung between terror and defiance. The room was wrecked, his thoughts in chaos. He knew nothing here. Any more out of his depth and he'd go under.

He stood up and with his hands on his head surveyed the ruin, trying to find the energy and the will to start setting it straight. He could just leave. Should just leave – pack up his things and go, right now, pay the bill and a bit extra for the damage and take the first bus to Adana, as Vural had suggested.

And yet he knew he couldn't retreat now, at the first encounter with actual danger. There would be worse, and no way of avoiding it. Wasn't that why he was here, to confront all this? This was the world Sofia lived in now. If he couldn't save her from it, he should at least live it alongside her.

First, he found his passport. How stupid, that as an outlaw in this lawless place, he should still think it important. Then he put the drawer back in the bedside table, and was recovering all the odds and ends it had contained when there came another knock at the door, and a cough, and a sniff.

He looked up to see Vural in a pair of striped blue pyjamas, mouth open in apparent horror, slowly shaking his head.

'Sami, my God, what do they do?'

'Pretty much everything.'

'Who do this?'

'I don't know.'

'How they look?'

Abraham picked up the last piece of change, dropped it in the drawer and went to pull the mattress back on to the bed.

'Here. I help.'

Together they heaved it back. Abraham sat down on it, and Vural sat beside him.

'Two men. Short and strong.'

'And feet?'

'Excuse me?'

'What on feet?' Vural pulled his leg onto his knee and pointed at a leather slipper.

Abraham thought about it.

'Boots. Like workman's boots.'

Vural nodded slowly with some dark realization.

'Fighters.'

'Yes.'

'What they say?'

'Nothing.'

'Nothing?'

'They told me to cut my beard.'

Vural let his head loll back and looked up at the ceiling, as if in prayer.

'Sami, Sami, Sami.'

'What?'

'They think you are Daesh. ISIS. I wonder, your beard, all

this time. In Cairo, okay, a beard. Here a beard means bad thing. You must . . .'

He mimed lathering his face with a brush.

'Understand. Antep, there is Daesh, Free Syrian Army, Al Nusra, more, the Kurds. I think maybe this is Kurds. And then is you. In middle. Like ant with many elephant.'

With unnecessary emphasis Vural ground his slipper into the carpet.

'Sami. We must talk. You and I.'

'Vural, I just want to get my room straight and go to bed. I'm very tired.'

'Sami, no. We must talk. I know why you are in Antep.'

'I know. I told you.'

'No, the reason you do not tell me.'

Abraham tried not to frown, not to give it away, but Vural's expression told him that he had nowhere left to go.

'I know you are Abraham.'

Abraham turned from him, fitted the drawer into the bed-side table and started to pick coins and papers from the floor. His London keys were there, his driving licence, his boarding pass.

'You must work with me now. Or I cannot help you. Abraham, listen to me.'

Abraham stopped, closed his eyes, wondered where he would find the strength for this new encounter.

'How do you know?'

'I know things.'

'And you know why I'm here.'

'Of course. You are not so clever and we are not so stupid.'

'And what now? Why are you here?'

Vural sniffed, took a handkerchief from the waistband of his pyjamas and loudly blew his nose.

'To save your life.'

'I'm not here for that.'

'I know. You are hero, on special mission. I know. And now, right now, you are alive and free. You do nothing wrong, okay, for now, and this guys, they fuck up your room but they leave you. Okay. But your daughter she is gone, and you start stupid things, and best you are arrested, worse we find your head here and your body here. Yes?'

'How do you know she's gone?'

'I know things. Okay?'

Vural put his hand on Abraham's shoulder and grudgingly Abraham turned to look at him.

'You know already she is in Syria?'

Abraham didn't respond but he knew his face was giving him away.

'Okay. You know. How you know?'

'Through a man.'

'What man?'

'I don't know.'

'You give him money? How much?'

'A few hundred.'

'And now more to get your daughter, yes?'

Abraham nodded as a deep sense of foolishness started to unfold in him.

'Okay. This is job for him. Understand? Antep is full of fathers, mothers, brothers, all want information of their children, sisters. It is business, big money.'

'But he knew she crossed the border.'

Vural laughed.

'Is easy, to say this. What else he say?'

'Just that. That she was in a town called Dabiq.'

'Okay. Not Dabiq. Raqqa.'

Abraham watched Vural's slumped face and his quick eyes and somehow knew that he wasn't the one who was lying.

'How do I trust you?'

Vural smiled, almost grinned.

'Because I do not want money.'

'Then what do you want?'

'Name and everything of the man. Yes? And everything about your daughter.'

Kind she had always been, but hard with it. A powerful imagination and a preference for action over outrage: if you were hurt, she'd feel your pain and work to make it stop, perhaps because that stopped the pain for her.

At eight she had stopped eating meat, acting not on anyone's example but on principles she seemed to have discovered for herself. When friends finally came, she was the one who wanted to ease tensions, isolate bullies, redress grievances. She had bound their little group together, as far as he could tell – in those days she would tell him things – and in the process had fought anyone she needed to fight: older girls, older boys, teachers. Injustice drove her, and if he looked carefully he could begin to understand how her old compassion had transformed into this new anger. It was there online, you could see the connection. This was her response to the horror of the world.

Some of this he struggled to explain to Vural, but for his own benefit he worked at it.

'She is violent?'

Vural had moved to the room's one chair, and was leaning back with his arms crossed looking tired but unstoppable; Abraham was still sitting on the bed. The room was in one piece again, and talking was doing something similar for his thoughts.

Violent, no. Far from it. He had never seen her hurt a thing. Not so much as a mosquito. And understand, she is kind to everyone, she has respect for people, she would stop and give money she didn't really have to beggars on the street. Whatever her purpose now, it wasn't to express some deep cruelty she'd contained and hidden for years. It wasn't in her.

'She has friends in Syria?'

'I don't know. She stopped telling me things a long time ago.'

'Boyfriend?'

'I don't think so.'

'You have talked with her?'

Abraham closed his eyes and shook his head.

'She changed her number. I tried.'

'She has not called you?'

He shook his head again.

'How long, in Raqqa, before her mind changes?'

That was the question. How long?

'I don't know.'

'How long you wait here, Abraham?'

14

It feels like I've been running fast downhill and just as I was getting close to the bottom this invisible rope has yanked me back. I'm not ready. My old life isn't ready to let me go.

I remember the imam saying to me – he was so wise, I thank God in His wisdom for sending him to me – that my father was a man who had become defined by what he was not. That was how he put it. I told him how he wanted to be a doctor but had to stop studying when my mother got sick and he said exactly, there you are, he is not a husband, not a father, not a doctor. Such people are sad, and we have compassion for them, but we must see they are dangerous, they can pull us from the path of faith. I resolved not to let that happen. And in that I think I succeeded.

I may be free of him. But not of her. At night, the more I read from the Qur'an, the more I really, really concentrate, the less she's there when I close my eyes, but she's always somewhere – like moisture in the air, you can't see it but you feel it on your skin, on your face, every time you breathe.

I thought when I threw away my diary I'd be over the pain, and again when I converted, but it's still there, I can feel it now. And like a shock right through my body the revelation comes. This is the rope I've tied round myself.

They call on idols that can neither harm nor help them. That is the extreme error.

How could I not have seen before that my love for my mother has become an idol? I cling to it as my father clung to me.

I must say goodbye to her, and set us both free.

15

The interrogation over, Abraham had asked a single question of Vural, praying for the right answer, like a man receiving test results.

'How many come back?'

Vural had known at once what he meant.

'As human beings?'

'Yes.'

Vural hadn't answered straight away; this required thought. For a good ten seconds he waited, stroking his moustache between thumb and finger.

'The men, they are not human when they start. The men, the real men, from Iraq and Chechnya and hells on earth, they are devils – they know what they want, they just move their hell. And even the stupid boys, the sick ones, they want to kill, or why go?

'The women. Some are stupid, some clever. The stupid

ones, from far away they see a palace and when they are close they see it is builded of shit. They want a husband with a gun and a car and money and a big cock but it is someone like me –' he had patted his belly – 'fat and ugly and disease down here and when they see this they cry and they want to go home. These, they are children. Babies. Is she one like this?'

'No.'

'Other ones, they come here because they think.' Tapping his temple. 'They have reasons. Crazy reasons. They come to Syria they are already crazy, yes? So they see the palace of shit and to them it shines, it is like diamonds. They cannot see the shit. They cannot smell the shit. The shit it smells like a flower. You understand?'

Here Vural had paused, shrugged, shaken his head.

'Some, some they wake, yes. Like from black dream. But to what life? They cannot go home. They are in prison also. You see, just now they execute a fighter, a Daesh fighter, for wearing burka and trying to leave, to escape. It is black hole, my friend, nothing leaves.'

A black hole. The words stayed with him long after Vural left. Abraham looked for hope, some implausible scheme, at least a berth of some kind that his faith might make for him, but found nothing, and when he could stand it no longer he got up, showered under the lukewarm water, dressed as smartly as he could manage, and opened his computer.

It was dawn in Raqqa. The temperature today would reach thirty-five degrees. Pictures showed an anonymous city, apartment blocks and office buildings, wide streets, and everywhere ISIS fighters and the black ISIS flag. Books burning in a great bonfire in the road. Crucifixions, beheadings, lashings. It was under occupation and you had to look carefully to see signs of life persisting in the few cracks that had been allowed to remain open. There were markets. During the day you could move around, if you were a man or had one with you (a relative, of course). That was about it. When she saw all this – the girl who had railed against injustice since she was young enough to think – surely she would wake from the trance they had induced? She would feel for these people as she had for the faceless millions she believed to be oppressed, and come home.

He longed to ask her. What are you doing? What do you think you're doing? Have these people made you crazy or is there some cold purpose in this sacrilege?

And it occurred to him that he could. Not those questions, not straight away, but he could talk to her. Here, he could be anybody.

New to Twitter? Sign up.

His name and his email, it wanted. Irene Massud. imassud574@gmail.com, which took two minutes to create. Country, France. In half an hour he had followed sixty accounts that he hoped would make Irene appear plausible: some French imams, Al Jazeera, and several handfuls of the sort of monsters, chancers and hotheads that Sofia herself followed, taking care to range more broadly but to leave some overlap. Then a photograph. Rather than a face he found an image of five hands, each clasping a wrist in a circle, that seemed to represent the Ummah, the universal brotherhood of Islam.

Finally, he needed to say something about himself, a slogan. From a French Koran website he copied a likely phrase and pasted it in. *Bienheureux sont certes les croyants, ceux qui sont humbles dans leur Salat.* Blessed are the believers, who are humble in their prayers.

Then he sat back and inspected his work, checked it for errors, wondered what to do next. Go straight at her, was his instinct. Irene had read the news of Sofia's journey and been inspired by it to finally act on her own plan, secret until now, of one day making pilgrimage to the khilafa. Sofia would be her mentor, her guide.

Irene's English was okay, but not perfect, her tone gushing, rapt, a little naive. Her first tweet took perhaps half an hour to write, it made him sick to write it, and when it was done the morning sun was showing above the rooftops opposite.

> — My sister! Ma soeur! You have made it! Truly you are an example for me. If you will, please pray for me I can follow in future.

Abraham clicked send and saw the message register on the screen. Tweets, one. A nervous excitement ran through him. He sent another, to everyone and no one, about the glory of Allah, the most glorified, and a third, telling Sofia that her courage was an inspiration. For perhaps half an hour he watched for a reply. When it didn't come, he showered, dressed, and went to walk through the city, his future now hanging in front of him by the thread that he had spun.

16

I'm resting in the sitting room after dinner trying to read the Qur'an and doing my best not to be distracted by two of the children, brother and sister, who are playing and squabbling and refusing to settle down. I'm not annoyed with them. I'm annoyed with their mother, who should be putting them to bed, but she's on her phone – and maybe she's doing something important on it, I don't know, my mood is all over the place. I think my mother's still on my mind.

Badra comes in, and the woman finally snaps at her children to be quiet. Even at the best of times Badra's stern, and right now you wouldn't want to argue with her. She looks at me, tells me to follow her and leaves again. At the end of the corridor she waits by her room for me to go inside. She and Idara share, but there's space in here for two proper beds and two wardrobes, and they have a view over the city from two big windows, one on each wall. They have a bedside light. Badra sits on her bed, which is neat like you'd expect, and tells me to sit on Idara's, which isn't.

How am I getting on? I'm wary of her, after the whole cleaning thing, and she's not doing anything to make me feel more comfortable. I tell her fine, thank you, that it's amazing to be here and I'm looking forward to being useful to the khilafa. I try to make it sound as positive as I can.

She takes it in. How did I feel when the other girls got married so quickly?

Envious, to be honest, and I will be honest with her. Envious because they were getting out into the khilafa and could start to do good work. I ask her to forgive me the impatience of youth, I just want to be useful straight away, and to my amazement she smiles, just the smallest shortest smile like a twitch of her mouth, but still.

'You are learned. You know your Qur'an, and your hadith.'

'I'm not perfect.'

'But you try. Not everyone knows as much as you know. And your Arabic is good.'

'I need to work on it. It's too Egyptian.'

She takes a deep breath and tilts her head from one side to the other, watching me closely like she's looking at a painting or something. It's a strange feeling, because whatever she wants to know I'm sure I could just tell her.

'Your family. You are close? It was difficult coming here?'

'My father is a lost man. A sinner. My mother is ill.'

'Brothers or sisters?'

'No.'

'What is wrong with your mother?'

She's so direct, it throws me. I've never really had to explain it to anyone before, except my imam, but he asked from a place of kindness and I still don't know what Badra wants. But she represents the khilafa and I have to remember that, I have to trust her. I want to trust her.

'She . . . I don't know the word in Arabic. In English it's schizophrenic.'

'In German also.'

'She got ill when I was young.'

'That was difficult.'

'Yes.'

This isn't natural for her. I think she wants to be nicer than she knows how to be.

'Where is she now?'

'Sometimes she lives with my grandmother. Sometimes she's in hospital. It depends how she is.'

'Did you see her?'

'When she wanted to see me.'

Badra waits for me to explain.

'She imagines things. The headscarf was frightening to her. Some days she didn't really know I was me.'

Badra just nods, and that's okay, because there isn't much to say to that.

'Were you frightened? Ever?'

'She's never tried to hurt me.'

'I mean for yourself. For your own mind.'

Now I lurch. Right down. Is this a test? An evaluation? Is she trying to work out if I'm going to go crazy too? If I'm a liability?

Of course, I want to say. My father didn't have the guts to tell me but I read it for myself. My risk is greater than yours. So what?

'Not since I found the true path and the love of God, the most glorified, the most high. I will be content with what He wills for me. "There is not a creature on the earth whose destiny He does not govern."'

I feel His spirit animate me and with great clarity I see no reason to hide anything from this woman. She is a member of the Ummah. She should be my friend and if she is not that's her failing, not mine.

'I took care of her. My father couldn't, or wouldn't, at the end. He is not strong, and his strength left him. I was her mother.'

My voice is strong and if Badra's purpose was to rile me or find my weakness she'll be disappointed.

'I used to take myself to school, come home every day for lunch, make my lunch. This was when I was ten, eleven. One day she was waiting for me and she had a bag packed for each of us, and she put us on a train and told me it was a special trip, the school knew, it was something really special. We ended up by the sea, and there was a house in the woods, in the middle of nowhere – it was beautiful – and I remember thinking this is it, we're leaving London and we're going to live here, and she's going to be better. I hated London, and now it all made sense. The city was the problem. But we didn't go to the house. She took me to this old hut with no roof and got out sleeping bags and started taping up the windows. She took my phone off me so there'd be no radio waves.'

Now Badra's really listening. That's so important to me. This is my safe space. I've never told anyone this story before, even my father, not all of it, not the details.

'I told her I was going to watch the sunset and I went to get help. I got her home, I made her take her medication, I put her to bed. If He in His wisdom has the same thing in store for me I will embrace it. I will know the journey He planned for her. But until then I know I'm stronger for it.'

I am filled with His fire. The words stream from my mouth. Badra looks like she's watching something she's seen before but wasn't expecting to see today.

17

Sister hello. Tell me, how do you know about me if you only opened your account today?

God. There she was. Abraham watched the words flash into being on the screen and stared numbly at them for a while, imagining her fingers typing them out, her eyes following the letters as they appeared. Alive at least. Half alive.

His mouth had dried to dust but it didn't occur to him to drink.

This isn't your sister. This isn't Irene. It's me. Your father, who loves you more than the brothers and sisters who are not your brothers and sisters will ever love anybody. Are you with them because they're not me? Because they're everything I'm not? Active, decisive, energetic, certain, bold. Foolish. Couldn't you have done what daughters have done throughout history and found yourself an unsuitable boyfriend to do the same job?

This is what he wanted to say. Understand, they have seduced you. You are young and where there ought to be knowledge and resilience there's a pool of hope and innocence that these people know exactly how to fill. They fill it with their hatred and you take it for certainty. They don't want you. They want the victory your being there represents. They want people like me to be terrified that the safety we work so hard to create means nothing, has no weight, is mere convenience.

As Irene, he replied.

— You were in the newspapers. Even in France. You are famous.

Sister I have to be careful.

— Of course. If we cannot talk I understand.

You are a good Muslim?

— I try to be. But I will not be happy – God the most high
will not be happy – until I am in Sham.

Sham. An ancient word for Syria that he had seen her and
others use.

You must come.

— Always I dream. But I am alone, no friends will come
with me. And it will hurt my parents, they are good
Muslims but old, they do not see.

If easy to come, where is the glory to Him? swt.

Swt. Subhanahu Was Ta'ala. Glory to Him, the Exalted.
Before Abraham could reply, she sent another.

Good Muslims will understand, even tho it hurts. They
know glory to Him more important than their pain, swt.

— Did your parents understand? Do you speak?

As he sent it Abraham felt a stab of fear: that was too much,
and too soon, she would suspect. But a moment later the reply
came, and he had new reasons for regretting being direct.

My mother is ill. My father is dead to me. A kafir and
weak man led into darkness by false gods.

That was the story, in twenty words that cut him as surely as
twenty knives. Every one had weight. He had thought, fondly,
that he had failed her as a lifeguard might fail a drowning girl;
that he had stretched out his hand and found her beyond reach.
But in her eyes he had pushed her in and held her down.

Enough. This way lay only more pain. It had been a stupid
idea in the first place, to pull the scab off the wound – the

sensible thing to do was to let the conversation die over the next few days and then walk away.

— Sorry for yr mother, sister. What is wrong with her?

For two minutes, no answer.

— Did you tell yr father when u left?

Almost immediately her reply came.

Nothing to tell. In my mind had already left. My true family is here, sister, so is yours.

Abraham sat back in his chair. God, she was so hard. An absolutist from the moment she was born, sure about everything and so often right about it, too. To think that he was going to persuade her back was nonsense, stupidity.

And yet what else was there? Through the screen they were joined, as somehow he knew they remained joined in life. Neither of them had the power to cut the bond clean through.

18

Aripiprazole was the first drug they tried. Sold as Abilify, which sounded friendly, and purposeful, and seemed to promise the only thing Abraham wanted: Ester made able again. Able to laugh when it was the right time to laugh, to talk, to greet him with the old life in her eyes. To sleep through the night and stay awake during the day. Able to tell the difference between a police car that happened to be driving down the street and a government operation to steal her thoughts. Little blue pills, lozenge-shaped, full of power and possibility, imprinted with an identification code that ten years on he still remembered, two boxes of twenty-eight to start with because they might take as long as eight weeks to work. The side effects would come sooner.

Abraham understood all this. A year short of becoming a doctor himself, he had brought Ester back to London and listened to a careful, frowning psychiatrist tell him what he already knew. Drugs were essential. She wouldn't get better without them. She had too much dopamine racing round her brain and the only thing that would begin to help was to close down some of her receptors, block them off, stop the overload that caused the behaviour. The new drugs were much better than the old drugs, more precise in their action, and while they came at a price they would almost certainly help – unless they didn't. Abilify might suit one person and not another, and the only way of knowing was to plump for it and see. Wait and see.

How he willed them to work. Prayed as he handed her each blue pill and watched her take it. In Cairo, life had been in balance; Ester worked, he studied, Sofia went to school and was happy. A steady breeze and the sun at their backs. But even on their best days in London, Ester trailed behind, low in the water, her bearings gone, and in a moment the winds that drove her might rise from nowhere and send her tumbling wildly across the waves like a kite cut loose from its string.

She had always read to Sofia, in English, every night; and when she stopped, Abraham thought she must have a flu of some kind, a virus. He told her to rest, not to go to work, and was pleased when she seemed to listen and stayed in bed. But then for three days she didn't wash, didn't even clean her teeth – this, the most precise and careful of women. When he came into the room she would raise a hand to dismiss him and shake her head, saying nothing. Viruses can do this, he told himself, they can bring you down, and he squeezed oranges for her and made chicken broth. But she stayed away, far away. For weeks and then months, until it became clear that his prayers had no power. The woman who had pulled him along with her purpose and her stubborn joy about life had simply left – had been taken from him – and on his worst nights Abraham wondered at the God who could dream up such cruelty. If you're going to take her from me, take her from me. Don't take her and leave her here to force me to remember.

And all this in London, over a long winter, where the damp settled in his light Egyptian clothes and he was never, ever warm, and Sofia would ask him how long it would be until the sun came out again, and he had no answer for her. They were close then, he and Sofia, weren't they, constructing their new lives? Ester walked when she was feeling expansive and watched television when she wasn't, and no matter how much he might want to care for her she simply didn't need him. This was terrifying in a new way, but it left him time with Sofia, who was terrified too and needed him more.

Christ, she was courageous though, his daughter. He told her what was happening, used the word for it, wished there was a better one, something less scary. Schizophrenia. They couldn't have made it sound more jagged and alien if they'd tried.

And Sofia listened, asked questions, helped him tidy their new flat – always unbidden – prayed alongside him in church and went to school with the apparent faith of someone who still trusts that adults have solutions for everything. Her mother was ill, and illnesses were things people recovered from. Only at night when she asked him to read her the old books, the picture books, the ones she knew by heart, did she show any sign that her world had crumbled alongside his. Her courage made him feel weak, because he knew she was determined not to add to his burdens. If she could do it, why couldn't he?

19

This morning at breakfast Badra is no different. As if our conversation never happened. Stern. Dark. It's like living with your worst teacher.

'Tonight, be ready to go out. At five. Make yourself clean. I will come for you.'

That's all she says. What on earth does that mean? I nod and mutter something and spend the whole day switching between hope and a terror I've never known.

Badra's late, in the end, and when we leave it's almost six – the sun has lost some of its heat and the buildings are beginning to glow orange. There's a breeze, and it feels so good on my face, like a blessing. I realize this is the longest time I've ever spent indoors, and an old memory comes to me, of my father coming to my bedroom to tell me to go outside and spend more time in the fresh air. I blink it away.

Badra takes me to a car that's waiting for us and the driver sets off. I want to ask her how it's okay for us to be out without a mahram but she doesn't seem to want to talk any more than usual.

Raqqa is beautiful. Now that I finally see it, up close where the life is, with people everywhere on the streets and the roads full of cars. It's dusty, a desert town, and even though it's big, and modern, there's something simple about it. The car windows are open and I can smell the heat from the road and petrol from the cars, the smoke from a grill as we pass a market that's busy with men in dishdashas and women in their niqabs, going about their business and buying simple things that He has provided, and above everything I can see that they're all living a simple life, a holy life that doesn't need fancy clothes and excess. In accordance with His will.

How stunning it is. In England I read all the time that the people of Raqqa were oppressed and unhappy. The lies they told us! It's like the memories I have of Cairo when I was very young, the memories that until now I wasn't sure I could trust. Of course Cairo was like this. This is the Ummah! This is how Muslims should live. And will live, soon. There is damage, from the bombs I guess, but we didn't ask for that. We're not destroying the city, we're protecting it, nurturing it.

Most amazing is the black. Fighters in black, black flags, cars and trucks painted with the flag. The flag is everywhere. So black, and so simple. Why don't other flags have words? I've never thought about it before but the answer comes to me straight away, as if Allah the most glorified had sent it directly to me. No other flag means anything. No other flag has anything to say. And here you can't escape it. What would get you arrested in Britain is a symbol of pride in Raqqa. This whole city is black, and it is ours.

Badra is watching me. I turn to her, our petty difficulties forgotten, and wish that she could see the effect this place is having on me. If she has any sensitivity at all she will feel it. She looks away and tells the driver to take us through Clocktower Square.

I thank her. I know about Clocktower Square. It is the heart of the khilafa.

We have to slow down now and squeeze our way through the people. I guess this is rush hour. Everyone is out.

Badra tells the driver to stop and motions to me to get out. I find walking in the veil and niqab hard to begin with because I'm not aware of my feet as I walk. It's a strange sensation, I feel a little unbalanced in the crush of people on every side, and I can't really use my arms to steady myself. But how liberating it is not to be seen. In London, if I walked down Oxford Street, or even where we lived, men would look me up and down every five steps. A sixteen-year-old, in a headscarf, and they'd be checking me out. Diseased, all of them, but it's not until this moment, finally walking in Clocktower Square, that I realize I played my part in it. Here, any brother who might go astray cannot be tempted from the path by any sister. How simple is that, and how safe?

The infidels run up sins to their hearts' content and then ask their god to forgive them. In His compassion, the one true God makes sure that we cannot stray.

Badra leads me through the crowd until we reach a clearing, and I become aware that people have stopped to look at something. She puts her hand on my shoulder and nods ahead of her, and I follow her gaze. Against a wooden hoarding is a man on a cross. I shut my eyes for a moment, but force myself to open them again. I am meant to see this.

The cross is wooden and not all that big. The man's feet are close to the ground. They've been tied to the wood with thick rope, and two black nails have been driven through them. The surrounding skin is red and black with blood. He's wearing normal clothes, grey trousers and a white shirt that's stained with dirt and blood and pulled open over a grubby white vest. His body hangs down from his arms, which are held up by rope and nails in his hands. That's not true. One of the nails has ripped through the skin and the hand flops down from the wrist. The blood is fresh there.

When I saw pictures of Jesus on the cross, a great prophet himself, there was always a peace about him. His head rested on his chest. Here the man's head is twisted upwards in pain, and his face is swollen and purple around the red and white gag in his mouth. There are dark holes where his eyes were.

People walk by on their evening business, hardly noticing. Some of the women turn their heads away as they pass.

I don't find it revolting. When I first saw it I expected to but I don't. I'm sure Badra expected it too. I can look at it. And that tells me something. If this was wrong, if this man didn't deserve to die like this, as an example to others and as a sign of his shame, would I be able to look on it? I couldn't watch an innocent brother being crucified, because that would be against the true order of things, which we call His will. The kafir will never understand this. He sees justice and mistakes it for horror.

So many revelations in the khilafa. I can feel wisdom growing in me by the minute.

'What did he do?'

Even when I can see her eyes Badra is so hard to read. Right now it's impossible.

'A drinker. They told him but he wouldn't stop.'

It could be my father. I look at him again and wonder how much of that purple colour in his face is from the drink. It's no wonder he doesn't inspire pity.

'I am commanded to exercise justice amongst you,' I say. 'Sura forty-two. Counsel.'

Badra looks at me a moment longer and turns into the crowds of people flowing round us.

The driver stops in front of a house on a wide street. My sense of direction isn't the best but I think we've crossed the whole city. There are houses here, not flats, modern ones, and more space, but a lot of the buildings have corners that have crumbled away and further down the street two next to each other have completely collapsed. I guess there were airstrikes here, but when, I can't tell. Badra and the driver are carrying on as normal and I do the same.

Outside the house there are two fighters, in combat clothes, camouflage, with guns across their chests, talking as we walk up the path – joking, relaxed. If I knew why I was here that might make me feel safer. In the street there's a lot of debris and dust but someone has swept the path clean. Two cars sit in the driveway, both clean and shining in what's left of the sun.

The fear I'm feeling isn't for my safety, it's for my future here. It's like I heard someone say once, I'm not afraid of dying, I just don't want to stop living. I haven't started my life here yet.

One of the fighters takes us inside to a sitting room where the air conditioning is turned up so high even the evening sun coming in through a big window to my left has no effect. On one of the sofas are a man and a woman, unveiled. I recognize her as an Arab woman who was in the makkar on my first day. The man has grey hair and the ends of his beard have turned almost white. In all I've seen and read about the khilafa there haven't been many old people, and there's a feeling he gives off instantly of holiness and wisdom. The whole room has a calmness to it that I think must come from him.

Both are quite short, their feet only just touch the floor. I look away, embarrassed to have noticed.

There is a third person in the room, a young man who has stood to greet us. I am so hit by his beauty I feel myself blushing under my veil. This is what Adam looked like. Not the hairless white man of the paintings they showed us at school but a real, dark, black-haired man, bearded and handsome but at the same time so . . . delicate, so human. His pale blue eyes are all I can see. His smile is shy and hardly there. He looks right at me and then down at the floor.

Badra introduces Imam Talib and his wife, Karam. We bow, and he invites us to sit down on the sofa next to his, so that we're opposite the young brother. I can't help but snatch glances at him, even though I'm sure Karam is watching me to see if I do, and I curse myself for not being in control at this most critical moment. His beard runs along his chin but his top lip is clean. He seems so contained, like a warrior who has proven himself so utterly on the battlefield that he has no need to impress anyone any more.

Imam Talib says some words about welcoming us to his home, and me to the new centre of the Ummah, but he speaks in a slow, high voice and I'm finding it hard to concentrate on what he says, though I'm sure it's beautiful. Then he says something I don't catch and there's a silence I know I'm expected to fill. Badra looks at me expectantly and then tells me in a loud whisper that I can undo my veil. I hesitate, and she nods at me, and I unhook the veil so just my headscarf remains. She does the same, and turns to the imam.

'Thank you, Imam Talib, for welcoming us into your home. Your hospitality is equal only to your wisdom. This is the young sister I was telling you about.'

What has she been telling him? Imam Talib looks at me for a good twenty seconds, not smiling, then nods. He is a serious man, I can tell.

As if he caught the word from my thoughts he says, 'Is she a serious person?'

'I have seen many young girls come to the khilafa, and she is one of the most devout. She knows the Qur'an, and she knows many hadith. Her intentions are correct. She is not here to take but to give. And she speaks Arabic, Egyptian.'

I am stunned. This is like hearing your greatest enemy was all along your greatest friend. I don't know what's going on, but my heart lifts. Partly because I'm not afraid any more, but mostly, and this is so confusing, because Badra is saying these words. I thought I was beginning to hate her and I'm so happy to be saved from that new sin.

Imam Talib is looking at me calmly, and his face is different. He gives another one of his little nods but this time it's not so stern.

'And she wants to be married?'

'Of course,' says Badra.

'This is true?' He says it to me. Karam is smiling, I think at me, but she has one eye just off and it's hard to tell where she's looking. She has a kind face.

I am so nervous. It strikes me that here I must be near the centre of everything, the heart of jihad, and I'm ashamed for being so impatient and ungrateful. I hope they can't see my thoughts or the mood would change so quickly. I cast my eyes down and see his feet not quite touching the floor and I'm sure I go red, this is so stupid, I'm ashamed of my weakness and do my best to meet his eyes.

'I will serve Him however He sees fit, the most high, the most glorified.'

He's watching me intently. I can feel his eyes on my thoughts and instantly I'm aware of all the bad ones, all the fears and doubts and the lingering pieces of my old self that aren't worthy. The indecision, the vanity, the selfishness – they're all so clear to me and must be so clear to him. Even at this stage I could fail.

'And what do you want in a husband?'

Honestly, it isn't until this moment that I realize why I'm here. It's instantly so obvious, but I'd made no connection at all between this wise, searching imam and the beautiful young man sitting opposite me. That's how I come to be so unprepared for the question.

I hesitate, no words in my head, and when they come they stumble out.

'I want a man who embodies all the strength and grace God has given us as a species, so together we can help our great civilization to triumph.'

I'm not sure what I've said makes any sense. With this man of deep faith and real learning listening to me I suddenly appreciate how little I really know, and I watch his face closely for signs of a reaction. If he has one I don't see it. His skin is grainy like pumice stone.

'This is Abu Khalil al-Hazmi,' he says, opening his hand towards the young brother. 'He is a mujahid who has distinguished himself in battle and in service of Allah, may He be praised. A serious Muslim. It pains me to say that not every young fighter is as serious, but it takes many types of craftsman to build a house. Yes?'

I nod, nervous still, excited. I don't mind how slowly He is talking because I cannot believe what he's saying. Never before in my life has a dream like this come true. When people say their heart flutters? Mine feels like it wants to break loose and fly round the room. While Imam Talib talks I give thanks to Allah, and wonder at His generosity.

'His father was Abu Fayiz al-Hazmi, who was a fighter for Islamic State in Iraq. A great man, and a great friend. His son is precious to me, and so is the question of his bride.' He turns to Abu Khalil. 'What do you look for in your wife, my son?'

He pauses, glances at me, and thinks about it – not because he's nervous too but because he's confident enough to take his time – and when he speaks his voice is like the evening outside, warm, and light, and full.

'Someone who in devotion and eloquence will match the strength of my faith,' he says, and his eyes stay on mine. They are so pure, so deep. I see the smile in them, and know I am that woman.

20

Aziz called; called and called again. How Abraham wanted to pick up. Maybe Vural was wrong about him. Maybe Vural was deliberately wrong, and had his own reasons for wanting Sofia to stay where she was.

One of them was lying, but what Vural had said, that it was impossible to get anyone out unless she really wanted to leave – that was plainly true. It was one thing rescuing prisoners, another to rescue the guards. Every argument ended in the same place. But the universe didn't care about argument. God wanted faith, not thought. What if the only way to recover his daughter was to sacrifice everything else – pay the money, be left with nothing, take the same crazy step into nothingness that she had taken?

At least it would be doing something.

Abraham watched the phone and let it ring out.

21

— I think I have found the one

What do you mean, sister?

— a husband. This evening. The head of the makkar took me, specially, like we were a prince and princess or something

You are married?

— tomorrow

So quick. Who is he sister?

— the most beautiful man I think I ever saw

Are you sure he is the one? Beauty is not everything.

— He has ordained it swt. It feels like it was always meant to be, like the sun coming up in the morning. He's a warrior and the son of a warrior. I feel like I'm in a story!

Make sure he is good to you.

— he has the most noble spirit I can see it in his eyes, they burn with fire and faith.

You are so young sister.

— in my heart I am ready. u must not fear these things.

when u come here u will feel it urself, all doubts will
disappear

I have to go.

— okay sister you take care and wish me luck!

22

Khalil and I are husband and wife.

My husband! I can't believe I get to say those words. I will
never tire of saying them.

Imam Talib married us, in his house. I wore my best abaya,
which is the same as the others but had never been used. Khalil
wore a thawb that belonged to his father, in memory of him and
his brave death. Part of me wishes that I had a father who was
worth remembering, but at least now I have someone to talk to
about things like that. I've never had anyone before, not directly,
anyway, face to face. I can't wait to get to know him!

Badra was there, and the Imam's wife, and Umm Karam,
and Idara. We didn't need anyone else. Two minutes, two
simple, profound vows, and it was done.

At the end of the ceremony my husband and I kiss, and his
lips are strong and tender and so, so sweet. My first kiss. The
whole world is there.

I hope it's as good for him. I'm sure it means as much.

We have tea, and cakes dripping with honey, and afterwards
Khalil drives me away across the city. It's the middle of the day
and I can feel the heat pressing down on his car, a Toyota that
feels nearly new, it has that smell. I ask him where he got it but
he won't tell me – says it will spoil the surprise. There's an ISIS
flag strapped across the bonnet, and as we left he tied a black
headscarf round his head and picked up his gun. I realize as we
drive that Raqqa is now open to me. I'm not just married – I'm

married to an ISIS fighter, and no one will ever stand in our way.

Yesterday, out with Badra in the city for the first time, I felt excited, but now it's like I'm a new being altogether. As I look around at the sandy buildings and the dusty roads and the black fighters I have this sense that I understand it all, how it fits together, how it was made, what it's for. It's like I suddenly speak a new language. The language of His will.

We see a patrol, two trucks that have pulled over a civilian car on one of the main roads, and as we pass Khalil winds down the window and gets me to pass him his gun and fires three bursts into the beautiful blue sky. The noise goes right through me, it thrills me like the sound of thunder or the crash of waves.

'Allahu Akbar!' he shouts, and I shout with him, and I know that we are joined by one energy, one light, one faith.

This is a nice building. You can tell it's well built. He presses the button but the light doesn't come on and after listening for a moment he smiles and says, 'Electricity,' and taking my hand we walk up the stairs.

We stop two flights up, on a landing with a door at either end. He takes the keys, selects one, and hands it to me. With a nod, he gestures to the door on the left.

Oh my God. This is ours.

I turn the key in the lock and the door opens into a hallway with so many doors leading off it I can't take them all in. I look at Khalil, and he shuts the door before turning to me.

'Our home,' he says. 'You can take off your veil now.'

Even that is like the most beautiful shock to me. Of course I can. This man is now my mahram. I unhook the veil and stand before him as his wife. He bends down to kiss me – he's so tall, I come up to his shoulders – and for the second time that day his lips are on mine. This is a longer kiss, and still it feels so right. Skin above and beard below, the best of both worlds.

'Come. Look.'

He takes my hand and almost pulls me round the flat – he's as excited as I am. It's all perfect, like a show flat. The sofa in the sitting room still has plastic on it. Whose was this, I ask, and Khalil tells me it was some Shia family, he doesn't know anything else.

Two bedrooms, both white and clean. Khalil leads me into the bigger one, bright from the sun pouring in through the net curtains. He stands me by the bed and looks into my eyes and in his I see sparks of fire burning in the blue. I don't know if I'm equal to it, that intensity. It's like half of me is being pulled up to him and the other half is heavy on the ground. Can he possibly be seeing in me what I'm seeing in him? Yes. Yes, we were meant to be. This is ordained. I'm in the way, and I close my eyes, breathe, and tell myself to have faith. That's better. His breath is sweet and there's heat coming off him and even before I touch him I can sense his strength, the fullness of his chest that doesn't give when I lay my hand on it. The softness of his lips and the scratch of his beard.

That slow fire begins to burn in me. I realize I've never really known it until now, just a hint of it. Up and through, until it's in my fingers and my cheeks and every part of me seems to be vibrating like life itself. It's in him as well, I see it. Feel it in him as he holds me.

His grin disappears for a moment as he pulls his thawb over his head, and soon he is as God made him. Energy seems to run round him like blood. A thin trail of hair leads down from his belly button. Everything about him is as it should be. Fear rolls through me, I can't help it – of not knowing what lies ahead, of not being ready for him, of not being worthy. I think there's fear on my breath. I'm sure there is, my mouth has gone dry and sour. His body is perfect, a warrior's body, and like there are little lights in them I'm conscious of every flaw on mine. My ankles.

My wide hips. My skin. I'm not a physical person, my path has been different.

He starts to pull up my abaya but I stop him and tell him to close the curtains. I take off my abaya as smoothly as I can and fold it and lay it on the ground. I trip on my jeans and everything seems to be taking so long, it's like every graceful thing he does I'm matching with clumsiness. But soon I'm naked, and in the half-light Khalil smiles, and the smile gives me faith. I am as God made me, too. I am standing in my home, wife to my husband, servant to my God. To doubt Khalil is to doubt God's plan. My anxieties are just echoes, nothing more.

Khalil watches, smiles, comes to me, runs his hands up and down my back. Somehow I know I am with a great fighter, his righteousness and his beauty proclaim it.

He lays me down on my back, kisses my breasts and my stomach, lays his weight on me and before my faithless brain finds anything more to say, we are one. One being, one flame. There is pain, but like the fear it starts to go, swirled away into the wholeness of us, and I find myself thinking that this is like my crossing the border – without some struggle, it would mean less, or nothing. I hold Khalil tight, this man I hardly know and yet know better than anyone I have ever known, feel his sweat mix with mine, and wonder if it's the same for him.

We move together, and then it's done. An instant, and an eternity. The flame dies, but I continue to burn as he lies heavy inside me.

Now we are truly husband and wife.

I tell him I love him, and he tells me he loves me, and we lie in our bed – the marital bed! – and hold each other, eyes locked. He seems satisfied. I know he isn't a shallow man, a restless kafir, but still I want to perform my duties as a wife to the standard he deserves. Between my fingers his beard is soft as I twirl and twist it. I can feel him relaxing into sleep. It's warm in here and the only light is two bright shafts coming through the cracks in the curtains. Part of me would like to talk to him, because we haven't talked, not yet, but he's been on the battlefield for three weeks and right now he needs to rest. I watch him for a while, breathing so slow, and the rhythm of it finally makes me calm like a lioness in the shade in the middle of the day.

23

Sister!!! It has happened! I am married! He swt has provided!

So happy so happy so happy. So blessed. #iswearthekhilafaisthejannah

Now I am truly here sister. Now I am truly free!

Sister come! Come. Every moment you waste on the kafirs is an insult to Him swt.

Sister where are you?! I wish you were here to share my joy!

24

Even whisky on top of two pills barely touched him. The Turkish stuff tasted okay but there was no fire in it – it dulled but it didn't warm and God he needed warmth, against the cold that sat at the heart of him and in every eye he caught. They knew. They all knew, and if they didn't hate him for his complicity they scorned him for his weakness. He had lost his wife to disease and his daughter to the devil and at least one of them was his fault.

Tonight he was sitting at the bar, and for an hour or two or God knows how long Erol kept him topped up, and then there came a moment when he wouldn't pour any more. Effendi, he said – home. Effendi, please. Abraham could see the pity and concern in the man's face and knew they were genuine. Good for us we can't communicate. If he knew what I'd done – what I'd let happen – he wouldn't have me in here at all. He's as much a fool as I am. All fools. All the drinkers, trying to drown our responsibilities in this muck and all we dissolve is our wits.

Why did she hate him? Being here forced the question that had been waiting beneath his thoughts. For taking away her friends and her life and dropping her on the edge of a vast, cold city, that was why, and it was enough, surely – even if it had been unavoidable, because the decision could have been made no other way; the help Ester had needed couldn't be found in Cairo. But that wasn't the reason. The reason wasn't too much reality but not enough of it. He'd never mourned. His wife was gone as surely as if she were dead and he'd let the pain sit in a corner of his soul, screened off, unfaced, deadened to an ache that never left him.

There was poison. It had made them both sick, and when those men came to groom her they found traces in her system already.

They hadn't started it. He had. All this was on him.

'Erol. My friend. Tell me. You have children?'

It took a moment, but Erol understood.

'Evet. Children. Yes. Two children, a boy and a boy.'

'They are good children? Good boys?'

'Very good boys.'

Erol said it gravely, as if no question could be more serious.

Abraham nodded, thinking and not thinking.

'It is a tightrope. Understand? A rope you walk on like this and nothing either side. I thought I was on it. But I was so far away. So far.'

With an arm across his shoulder Erol helped him down from the stool and walked with him to the door.

'Effendi. Taxi. Please.'

'Erol, I can walk on my own. Thank you. Sorry. I have to walk on my own.'

He was asleep in his clothes when the door burst open and the light came on and the voices started shouting, and he felt it all before he registered any of it. There were men there, more than he could count, men in black clothes, and one of them, maybe two, pulled him off the bed and dragged him into the corridor and before they handcuffed him behind his back and marched him away he saw others emptying his case onto the floor.

'Hey,' he managed to say, and that one word brought him into himself and released a great pain in his head and a greater sickness in his stomach and it was all he could do not to vomit. The hands on him were strong, they gripped hard, and they took him past the lift and half hauled, half threw him down the stairs, just supporting him. The sickness mingled with fear. These weren't Kurds. They had polished boots, proper uniforms, they looked like police, they had the same disciplined rage as that English pair who had come to see him in his old life that no longer existed. So they'd found him. Now there'd be an interrogation and in a place like this maybe they'd beat him and then what? A Turkish prison and deportation and a legal fight and his reputation shot? His reputation. He'd never had a reputation. He was about to get one.

And the worst of it was that he didn't care. This crusade was always doomed. He'd failed as a doctor, he'd failed as a father and now he had failed in this. Even as he was being thrown about there was a sort of peace in knowing it. He had found his level.

At the first floor they didn't shove him down the next flight of stairs but along the dark corridor that ran under his own. Some of the doors were open and guests, all men, had been drawn in their pyjamas and vests by the noise. At the far end three police officers stood by the last room, arms crossed, guarding whatever was inside, watching Abraham as their two colleagues drove him towards them, and now they stood aside so that he could see, or be seen.

Abraham didn't hear the shouting back and forth that followed; even if he'd been able to understand it he wouldn't have heard it. His eyes, which had been slipping around, were set on one thing, the body that lay hunched awkwardly in the corner of the wall and the wardrobe, its head dropped onto its chest, its blood soaked into a white T-shirt that was now barely white at all.

An officer was crouching by it. Now he stood and came to Abraham, stopped with his face only six inches away, chin up, eyes hard.

'This man, you know?'

'No. No, I don't.'

The officer shouted back into the room and another policeman went to the corpse and pulled the head back by its hair. Abraham saw the dead face and the strange echo of fear in its blank eyes and turned away.

'You know?'

Oh Christ. This was bad. Oh Christ. Why had they come for him? They knew something but in this fucking state he couldn't work out what they could possibly know, this whole world was beyond him, he wasn't made for it.

'He came to my room.'

'Who is?'

'I don't know. He came to my room with another man. They were looking for something.'

The officer jutted his chin, said something in Turkish, and the two men holding Abraham began to drag him away.

'I didn't do this.'

But the officer just turned and went back into the room.

*

His cell had damp walls that had once been white, a filthy mattress on a metal frame, and a single bulb in a cracked yellow plastic casing that gave out a sickly light. Bars ran across the foot of the bed; at its head the end wall had been stained brown where a thousand prisoners' heads had rested, and above it, like a taunt, hung a photograph of forested mountains in a white plastic frame. Abraham sat with his knees drawn up and his head in his hands and did his best to breathe in the airless stench that filled the place, a heated stink of damp and disinfectant and piss.

Time passed, he had no idea how long. Once, someone came for him, and despite the bleakness of his situation he felt the most intense surge of hope; but the policeman who stood there just said four or five words in Turkish through the bars and then left before Abraham could ask the questions he desperately wanted to ask. The waiting for heaven-knew-what resumed.

The next time, two policemen came and took Abraham up through the police station and along corridors to a bright office where dawn was beginning to show through the blind that covered the one high window.

Vural was there. Dressed in his creased suit, and as lively as Abraham had seen him. His eyes were sharper, whiter, less hooded. He nodded at Abraham, and said something in Turkish to the two policemen, who hesitated for a moment, unsure. Then he nodded, and waited, and thanked the pair of them as they left, shutting the door behind them. He had a white mug in his hand and now he set it down on the desk in front of him and pushed it towards Abraham, gesturing to him to sit. Black coffee. If anything, the smell made things worse.

'Abraham, I know this will happen. Something like this.'

'Vural. Is that really your name?'

Abraham's tongue stuck in his mouth as he said the words. Vural nodded.

'Vural, can I have some water? I need water.'

Vural frowned.

'I can see you need. Is thirsty, your work last night. One moment. But please, no tricks, yes?'

'I don't want any trouble.'

'I know this.'

Vural stood and left the room. Abraham looked at the open door and wondered what was going on. Was it an invitation? Did they want him to run so that they could shoot him in the back?

Before any answer came, Vural was back, a small bottle of water in each chubby hand.

'Here. Drink.'

The water was ice cold and brought him back to himself, a degree. Vural waited for him to finish with his forearms resting on the desk, hands clasped together. Somehow, he was transformed. No sniffing, no oiliness. His voice was hard and his eyes shone.

'Vural, I didn't kill that man.'

'You are here to go to Syria, to be ISIS, to be with your daughter.'

'I . . . I don't want to be with her.'

'The dead man, he knew this, and last night he exposed you. So you killed him.'

'I didn't kill him.'

'Where were you last night?'

'At the hotel. I went to that bar, the Golden Lion, and then I went back to the hotel. To my room.'

'When were you there?'

'I don't know. I . . . I drank a lot. I was drunk. I had some bad news.'

'What news?'

'My daughter. She's married.'

'You see? So you must join her in Raqqa.'

'No, I don't—'

'What time you were in your room?'

'I don't know. Nine. Ten. The bar owner, Erol, he would know when I left.'

'Someone saw you at the hotel?'

Each question came quick and crisp.

'No. I don't know. I didn't notice.'

'How much you drink, Abraham?'

Abraham closed his eyes tight. Enough.

'I don't know. A lot.'

'You go right to bed?'

'I passed out.'

'What time?'

'I told you. I don't know.'

Vural paused, nodding, then set off again.

'Abraham, do you keep a knife?'

'A knife? No. Of course not.'

'There is no knife in your room?'

'No.'

'If my friends in the polis look in your room they will not find a knife?'

He smiled as he said it. It wasn't a question, it was a hypothetical. A new avenue of fear opened up. They could do that. Of course they might do that.

'No. No knife of mine.'

Another pause.

'What if someone saw you come from your room at two a.m.?'

'No one saw me. I didn't leave my room until those men arrived.'

'Which men?'

'The police. Your colleagues.'

'I am not their colleague.'

Vural reached across the table for the mug of coffee.

'You don't want?'

Abraham shook his head. He was beginning to think that his mind had really unravelled. Vural thanked him and took a sip.

'Perhaps I saw you.'

'I didn't leave my room.'

'Perhaps I saw you and went after you to the first floor and saw you and the dead man in a fight.'

Abraham was still shaking his head, and when he spoke again his voice sounded loud and twisted in his ears.

'You didn't. I never left my room.'

'I heard noise, the door of your room. I had concern, because you had trouble last night. I came in the corridor, and I saw you, and I went after you.'

'What do you want?'

Vural slurped coffee once, twice, then drained the cup and set it on the desk.

'I know you do not kill this man. But they, they think it. They want it. Someone has seen you, they say. The Egyptian, last night, on that floor.'

'I haven't . . .'

'I am sure. They are not. The polis do not like ISIS. Kurds they hate more but you are second.'

'I'm not ISIS. You know that. Help me.'

Nodding, Vural sniffed, like a man steeling himself to do his best.

'Abraham, I am not polis. They are different kind of man, not like you or me. But I will try.'

'Please.'

'I try.'

25

Time in the cell was measured in meals. For breakfast, rice and kidney beans and a small loaf of bread that turned out to be lunch. For dinner, rice and chickpeas. Rice and tired green beans for breakfast the next day. Abraham ate the food because it was there and because he had nothing else to do – no book to read, no plan to make, no thoughts that he wanted to have. He craved water more than freedom. Two glasses a day in this heat; he felt like he was slowly turning to powder.

No one came for him; his story wasn't required. By the first evening he was sweating and an ache ran through him and he began to think about telling his guards that he needed his medication. They might not bring him water but maybe they had to bring him medicine if he was sick, maybe there was some convention in place, some international agreement. Failing that he could bribe them. But by now they had his things and anything valuable would have gone, including the pills themselves, and it was hopeless even to try.

So this was how it felt to stop taking those things: like someone was pulling out your bones through the top of your head. Like being cored. He didn't read the warning leaflet that he pulled from every packet, of course, no one did, but he knew what they said, and they didn't begin to cover it. Muscle ache, fatigue, depression, sweating, shaking. Coughing and occasional bouts of diarrhoea. Listlessness. Disgust at one's self. A strong sense of detachment and presence at once, of wanting to be anywhere else, anyone else, but knowing that you were stuck for all time with the soul and body you had been given. Shivering, yes, but not from real or imagined cold so much as the frozen vastness of the universe.

Praying didn't seem to help. His God was nowhere to be found, but Sofia sat with him all day, ever present. Happy to watch him sunk to this, but resisting the temptation to wag a finger because her piety wouldn't allow her to score cheap tricks. You have suffered, she told him, but we all suffer, and in the face of that suffering we can choose to stretch up to Paradise, as I have done, or slip down into hell. I take no pleasure in seeing you there, nor any pride in my own choice. In his weakness, he just lay there and took it. Maybe she was right – maybe it was better to aspire to something wrong-headed than to aspire to nothing at all.

But she was in her own cell, of course, the one of her making, somewhere across the border. They were both captives. Did she see that yet?

26

I am a woman now. Yesterday I was just a girl, with nothing, and now I have a husband, a house and a job. I begin to understand how a caterpillar can turn into a butterfly, but the miracle is to think all this was in me always, waiting to find wings.

My first day on the brigade is training. The Al-Khansaa Brigade – the most fearsome women on the planet. I've seen the pictures and now I'm one of them. My breath is actually short with excitement, I have to control it.

Umm Karam is there, Idara, others I'm getting to know. It's a real team. Umm Karam gives us a short speech about how women are the foundation of the khilafa, and how if they're allowed to ignore sharia the whole building will come down. I get it. It fills me with pride, and nerves.

For the rest of the day she trains us. What to look for. Who to look for. The appropriate punishments for transgressions. How to record punishments, and how to verify people's papers.

Tomorrow, she explains, you will be apprentices. Watch. Listen. Smell. You are His senses in the City.

The next night Khalil comes to pick me up and we go for dinner at his favourite place. I'm still pinching myself. I'm tired, more tired than I think I've ever been, but I don't feel it like tiredness, it's just like every part of me has done what it was supposed to do and now I can take a moment to reflect, and relax. I don't think I've ever known what work was before. Such fulfilment. Such release!

The restaurant is full of our people, hanging out, chatting, taking it easy. We all work hard. We all deserve a bit of time before rejoining the front. Brothers are here with their wives, with their kids, it's all so . . . natural. So right. No alcohol, no pressure, no one who isn't on the same path.

One of the things I love about the khilafa is that everyone is here for a different reason *and the same one*. Everyone has their own story to explain why they don't fit in the world of lies and killing and greed, and no matter what that story is, somehow they slot into the khilafa like they were always made to be here. And that's because we share the same faith, in every way. It's like a universal language we all speak. A safe harbour for true souls.

Khalil orders and he's patient with the waiter, who seems nervous for some reason and doesn't hear right the first time. Other fighters might shout at him but not Khalil, he patiently repeats what he said and leaves it at that. He's so handsome tonight, I swear a light shines from his eyes, it's like the sun sometimes. He has this way of just looking at me so that his eyes smile but the rest of his face is still serious – it's hard to explain but it's like he's sending his love straight from his soul to mine.

Tonight I have so much to tell him. What a day! My first catch, there's no way I can keep it from him, but I wait till our food comes.

'How was your day?'

'Good. Just chilled. Prayed, watched videos. Building up my strength.'

He grins as he pulls another wing apart with those strong soft hands.

'You need your strength.'

'If I'm not careful you'll use it all up.'

He grins again and I hope he can see that behind my veil I'm doing the same.

'I made my first catch today.'

'What do you mean?'

'I went out on patrol. I'm the new girl.'

'That's cool.'

'There are four of us and they use me like a scout, I don't have a gun so no one knows I'm in the brigade.'

Khalil nods and picks meat off a bone with his teeth. So white!

'We went to a market and they just told me to get on with it. And at first it was like my eye wasn't in, you know, it's difficult to see things when you're not used to the background yet.'

'Yeah,' he nods. 'I know.'

'So for a while I just couldn't see anything, like a good half hour, and I was beginning to think Oh no, what if I don't find anything? They'll throw me straight out and how would I explain that to you? Stupid, I know, but I just wanted to impress them.'

'Yeah.'

'Umm Sharik – she's the leader, she's great, so focused – she has targets for our team each day. She told us that's what the kafir police do but there's no reason we shouldn't learn from them.'

Dear lamb, he's deep in his food, and I realize I'm not being very interesting. I need to get to the point.

'Anyway, I couldn't see anything and every woman looked completely fine and every veil was correct and everyone had a mahram and I was thinking, Oh great, my first day and the whole of Raqqa is suddenly under perfect sharia, and then I smelled it.'

I wait for him to respond, and he looks up at me frowning. 'What?'

I know he's going to be proud of me.

'I smelled her. Perfume. Kind of faint at first and I thought I'd lost it but then I got a real hold on it and I followed my instincts and then it was just me and her walking away from the market with me calling Umm Sharik to come to us. She really stank, some horrible smell, like a kafir smell, you know? Like a London smell.'

'Some of these women are so fucking stupid.'

'I know.'

We eat for a bit, letting each other's words sink in.

'So I caught up with her and questioned her and then Umm Sharik came with the others and gave her forty lashes.'

'You didn't do that yourself?'

'She said maybe when I've settled in.'

Khalil nods sympathetically and smiles. He tells me to eat, he wants to get home quickly to be alone with me. I love that about him, he's so direct, and there's more than one kind of hunger in his eyes right now. I want to talk to him about all sorts of things like his family and his poor mother who died at the hands of Assad and when he came to the khilafa and if he has brothers and sisters and on and on and on, but there's time for that when he wants it. It will come.

27

Deep in the night, sunk in some shallow and disordered dream, Abraham felt himself being dragged by the feet like a carcass, and woke to find a hand around his ankle pulling him down his bed towards the bars. The grip was insanely strong, and for an instant his only thought was that he was being called to hell.

Pain stabbed at his knee, which was being crushed between the metal; and as he pushed back with his other foot he found himself looking into the wild face of a young man, teeth bared, the veins in his temple pulsing. A guard had him round the neck but the man seemed possessed, there was no way he was letting go.

'Murdering scum. He was ten times the man you are, Daesh cunt.'

Wresting his free arm from the guard he grabbed Abraham's T-shirt, pulled him up to the bars and spat in his face.

'You're going to fucking die in here.'

He spat again, and Abraham pulled himself back up the bed, wiped his face on his T-shirt, and watched the man draw his finger across his throat with a final leer as another guard came and helped to pull him away.

From down the corridor came a new noise, half shout, half wail, a terrible noise that made his senses vibrate at the pitch of fear.

'Free. Syrian. Army. Free. Syrian. Army.'

One voice at first, then a second, then five or six together, chanting without any urgency, knowing their time would come.

28

Sometime long after dinner on the second day, when Abraham had given up hope of seeing him or anyone else ever again, Vural appeared.

'Abraham,' he said, silhouetted against the light in the corridor. 'I hope you have rest. Come.' And he simply walked away, leaving the door to the cell open and the policeman who had unlocked it waiting with crossed arms for Abraham to leave.

'Where are we going?'

Abraham had to trot to keep up with him.

'You will decide.'

They left the building, past sleeping prisoners, past the few policemen on duty, Vural going with such confidence that no one seemed to think to challenge them, and out into the car park, where he unlocked an old Toyota and ushered Abraham inside.

'Quick. Before policeman changes mind.'

Vural drove just as he walked – quickly and surely, darting from one empty street to the next – and the abrupt motion after two days in one place made Abraham so disorientated he could hardly watch the streets as they slipped by. Gaziantep slept; dawn was just beginning to show, and they saw barely a soul. He felt it like limbo: he was here, and he wasn't here. Just him and this unknowable man who might be his enemy and might be his friend.

Neither said anything. After five minutes, Vural pulled over swiftly to the kerb, braking with a jerk. They had arrived at the bus station. Eight white buses neatly lined up and the first passengers setting down their bags on the kerb.

'You look very bad, Abraham.'

Vural frowned, as if somehow this was unexpected, and in response Abraham nodded.

'Very bad. Here.'

From a baggy jacket pocket Vural pulled Abraham's phone, and his wallet. From another he produced his passport.

'What about the rest?'

'What I could get.'

'I need my things.'

'You have papers? You have money?'

'Yes.'

'You have everything. Come.'

'I have medication.'

'Abraham. You are not sick. Are you sick?'

Vural raised his eyebrows and looked hard at Abraham, who dropped his head in response.

'You are man, not patient. Okay. Now you have choice to make.'

'Okay.'

'One. You go home. London, Cairo, what you like.'

'I don't want to go home.'

Impatiently, Vural held up a hand.

'Please. Hear. Two. You cross border and you work for me.'

Abraham frowned his question back.

'Inside Daesh.'

The sky was light in the east now, and a breeze was blowing through the open window of the car. On Abraham's skin it felt like balm. Another clear blue day, beautiful, free, full of promise: somewhere, for someone, life was good.

'You mean it?'

'Of course.'

'I'm a Christian. They'll kill me.'

'You look like Muslim.'

'It's a crazy idea. I never heard a crazier idea.'

Vural rubbed his chin, apparently unconcerned, as if the choice was simple and balanced. An apple, or an orange. You pick.

'This way, you can find your daughter from inside. How you will do this if not? Raqqa is big. And they, they are like fortress.'

'I have some ideas.'

'So you will go there? This is your plan?'

'Until half an hour ago I didn't need a plan.'

Vural shifted in his seat and waited for Abraham to look at him.

'You killed a Free Syrian. A kafir. You are already Daesh.'

'My God. You mean it.'

'Of course. Is easy. Fits like this.' He laced his fingers together. 'You go now, we report you escape, you go to Akçakale, cross border. Someone there take you, easy. I give you phone, we talk. Safe, no problem. Then maybe I help you back to Turkey when you or your daughter you have enough.'

God, it made sense. Did it make sense? How was someone like him meant to judge something like this?

'Give me a day. It's too much.'

Vural reached across and put his hand on Abraham's shoulder.

'Abraham. You go on bus this way or this way. You are problem or asset. Or, you want, I give you to polis. I do not mind.'

'Till this evening.'

Vural chose not to reply.

Raqqa he had imagined. Getting there somehow, finding a room somehow, sneaking around, talking to Sofia through Irene, ready for the moment when it came. But not this. Not becoming one of them.

Vural gripped his shoulder.

'Is okay, Abraham. Now you know what you will do. Time for home.'

29

— Sorry I am slow to respond, sister. You must be very happy.

— tell me. What man is he? Is he young, old, handsome?

He is young and so handsome and we are so happy!

— Where is he from sister? A foreign fighter or local?

Syria! His father was a great man, a hero before the khilafa

— I am sure he will treat you well sister, you deserve it.

he is a good Muslim and a fearless fighter. Better to marry him than to fight him!

— What is his name?

Khalil. I looked it up. It means friend! We will be great friends.

he understands me, my background, my family problems

— be sure you look after yourself my sister

he will do that for me now

are you coming? when?

— I am less sure sister. My faith is tested.

30

The haze that Abraham had taken for some welcome cloud burned away and heat began to build and press in the metal shell of the bus. A relief, no, to be back in London soon, with its low skies and the leaves turning and the mornings growing cool? Where nothing could be changed and nothing could be done? There was peace in that. He had mistaken himself for a man with passions, when they were only fears that he would never outrun. They were his lot, and to think he could finally be rid of them through what, some heroic rescue, that was vanity, a sin, a fond rejection of the role God had given him to play. You couldn't buck that, any more than Sofia could avoid her destiny.

She had her line, he had his, and they had diverged, that was all. No one could will them together again.

The bus powered along through a rough cutting in the rising hills. Abraham let his eyes slip on the chalky rock and his mind empty of thought; the decision was made, and the tiredness that had been building over days began to catch up with him. But she was there as he closed his eyes. Newborn, scalp thick with fine, wayward hair, asleep on his chest or straddling Ester's arm like a cat in a tree, the distinct weight of her. Dancing, with her hands in his hands and her feet on his. That erect, bobbing walk, on the brink of becoming a skip. The seriousness in her eyes as she drew.

Strange, that as she had grown the physical memory of her should remain somehow the same. Her skin, her warmth a constant.

About fifty miles outside Gaziantep, Abraham told the driver he wanted to get off, stepped down into the heat, and crossed the road to wait for the bus coming the other way. Vural was wrong. This wasn't a test of his limits. It was a choice between two deaths: of one cut, or a thousand; with honour and love, or an eternal shame.

And all this; all of it was on him. He was her father.

For an hour he sat cross-legged on the verge, a handkerchief on his head in place of a hat, visions of sand and mirages and death from thirst playing across the sun-beaten yellow scrub that only ended at the sky. Unchecked miles of plain, and somewhere in them this fabled evil city that held his daughter, like a dark castle that only appeared to those who had the faith to seek it.

Vural's plan was insane. You could never leave ISIS – you could as easily tear up a contract with the devil. No. He would do it his way. Find someone to take him to Raqqa, God knows how; pose as a merchant, as Vural had, and live there in some quiet hole; keep talking to Sofia through Irene until an opportunity presented itself. He was insignificant. The city held hundreds of thousands and wouldn't notice him. He would keep his head down and wait. If he had to, he would wait for a year.

The bus came and took him east again. No one was waiting for him in the city; no police, no Vural. He passed through as invisibly as a single tiny fish crossing a great burning sea. In this vast land he was alone, making his way as she had, south to the border.

PART TWO

1

Akçakale: gateway to the khilafa. Two hours south-east of Gaziantep, and popular, for a town no one wanted to go to. The final bus turned out to be a battered minibus, old and straining and so full that for the first twenty minutes Abraham stood in between the rows of seats, stooping and hot and feeling increasingly sick. His clothes smelled terrible on him. But for all that he felt a little more human, in amongst other humans again. The sweats were beginning to be just sweating, the headache just an ache.

In time, the bus stopped to let a woman off at the side of the road. Abraham had to step down himself to allow her and her two swollen shopping bags to pass, and as he stood in the dust and the heat he scanned the landscape for some sign of where she might be heading; but he could see nothing, just gently rising and falling sandy scrub for mile after mile. Back on the bus he went to take the empty seat and remembered as he began to sit, prompted by a momentary stiffening of the people around, that he couldn't be next to a woman he didn't know. Without saying anything the woman opposite shifted across the aisle and sat in the empty spot, and Abraham, thanking her, conscious all the while of the smell coming off him, sat next to her husband, or her brother, or whoever he was, and as the bus drove off he watched the woman they had let off walking resolutely, a plastic bag in each hand, on a barely visible track towards the edge of the world.

These were normal people. Poor people. Their clothes were well used, their shoes dusty and battered, the bags on their knees full and heavy. Each of them, Abraham thought, was there because they had to be; the mood was purposeful, but there was tension in it, and even his neighbours who had let him sit were wary of him. This was a new kind of conspicuousness, and it forced him to wonder how many strangers they had seen pass through their town on their way south, how many deluded people, how many fighters. How many killers. My mission is different, he wanted to say. I'm not like that. If I could explain to you, you would understand. As it was, he sat and watched the land roll by, trying to calm his nausea and the nerves building in him.

Akçakale felt like the last town in Turkey, which Abraham supposed it was; low, built for purpose and without much evidence of love. Outskirts of simple white houses and dry walled-in yards, and in the centre boxy breeze-block shops and office buildings lining wide streets set out in a grid: a petrol station, a police station, a supermarket, an empty park dotted with trees beginning to yellow. Water towers and a pair of slender minarets rose up against the sky. But there was no doubting its purpose now: even from two miles outside, Abraham could see the wire fence that stretched across the whole landscape from east to west, barely separating the country from Syria, and as they drove into town he kept glimpsing it down side streets, in the gaps between buildings. A border town once, now a frontier town, which no one visited by accident any more, still less passed casually through. Seventy miles due north of Raqqa, the only reasons for being here to flee death or to run towards it.

After Gaziantep, the streets were quiet, faded. A hot wind blew hard from the south and passed right through; with the sun, it seemed to bleach the place of colour and life. Groups of men sat outside cafes watching the world. Abraham sensed that the atmosphere outside was as it was in the bus: everyone had their heads down, in the hope that they might get through the day without being noticed or challenged. Fear had got into the place.

Abraham waited for all the women to leave, thanked his neighbour and the driver, and stepped down into a central square by the mosque, bright and functional in the full morning light. He needed somewhere to buy a phone, and clothes. Feeling like a tramp, he approached two of his fellow passengers as they got their things together at the kerb, but each shook his head and slipped away.

The driver of the bus got down from his cab and with a glance at Abraham walked slowly across the tarmac to a cafe in a row of shops. Outside were plastic tables and chairs, unoccupied, and in the doorway stood a man smoking. He asked the driver something as he approached. The driver glanced back over his shoulder at Abraham, met his eye, and turning back with a jerk of his head said something in reply. His friend looked hard at Abraham for a moment, flicked his cigarette away towards the gutter, and together they went inside.

2

Abraham started to walk. At a supermarket on what seemed to be the main street he bought water, and in bad Turkish asked the woman at the checkout where he might find a hotel. That was where to start. A base. And in a hotel, even a bad hotel, you paid money and could start a conversation on the basis of it. It was the only place a stranger could establish a claim on someone's time. The woman pointed down the street and turned to the next customer.

He kept walking, past an empty barber's, nondescript offices, a mobile phone shop with six old phones in the window, and more functional cafes, white tables in white rooms. From a shop whose shelves were nearly bare he bought shirts, underwear, a pair of trousers that fit him well enough. Life was going on here, but only barely; what had to be done was getting done, and no more. Shopkeepers stood outside their shops, talking, smoking, accustomed to the new reality. On the other side of the road three bearded men were smoking silently, two of them leaning against the bonnet of a car, all in black: black jeans and T-shirts and zipped jackets. One of them pointed at Abraham with his cigarette and the other two turned to look, their faces young but hard, forever set in menace and cold calculation. Abraham felt himself being swiftly and efficiently assessed – friend, foe, civilian – and realized that he fit none of those categories. He walked on, eyes firmly on the ground.

He saw no hotel anywhere, but his nerve had gone and he failed to ask new directions from each person he passed. Where the shops ran out and the pavement became a track he stopped, peered down the street at the more scattered buildings ahead of him and seeing nothing remotely promising turned and looked back the way he had come. The three men were still there, still watching him, and opposite them – of course, it would be – on the side of a building was the painted word 'hotel'.

Walking back, into the wind and the dust and the men's stares, he passed a man whose face he knew he recognized from somewhere, Antep or the bus or maybe just now, he was so preoccupied he couldn't remember. Without even a glance across the street he turned into the door of the hotel and went up a narrow flight of stairs into a dark room at the back of the building. Two of its walls were lined with low, battered, vinyl-covered chairs, and on them sat two young men in T-shirts and trainers, staring intently at their phones. One looked local, the other was white, with black hair closely cropped at the sides and razored with straight, stepped lines. At a desk opposite sat a squat, heavy-shouldered man in a white shirt that was too tight and showed between each pair of buttons a glimpse of string vest. All three looked up at Abraham as he entered, and their eyes stayed on him as he approached the desk and asked, in his guidebook Turkish, if there was a free room.

The squat man sniffed, took a deep breath and let it slowly out, looked Abraham up and down.

'No room. You go.'

Abraham glanced round at the two men and found them staring up at him. Unblinking, like lizards.

'Nice beard,' said the one with the shaved head, in English. English English. He was young, maybe twenty, and clean-shaven. His accent sounded northern.

Abraham had no response to that.

'Why are you here?'

'I want a room.'

'No mate. In this shithole. Akçakale.'

'I have family in Syria. I need to see them.'

'Family?'

'My wife's family.'

The man nodded, emphatically, like he didn't believe a word.

'That be in Raqqa, by any chance?'

He meant something by this but Abraham had no idea what. There was so much he didn't know.

'Not just Raqqa.'

The young man looked at his friend, stood up and walked towards Abraham until he was only six inches from him, fresh garlic harsh on his breath. Abraham was the taller.

'You don't look like a fighter, mate.'

'I'm not a fighter.'

'Why else go to Raqqa?'

'I don't want to go. I have to go.'

'That's what they all say.'

That was a joke, it seemed. He turned round to grin at his friend. He was wearing a white T-shirt that showed every detail of his pumped-up chest, and combat trousers with bulging pockets.

'Really. I'm not here for trouble.'

'Only trouble here, mate. That's all there is.'

What should he say? I'm searching for someone. I'm here by mistake, more or less. I'm not even a Muslim.

'How'd you feel about Assad, my friend?'

Bad. He felt bad about Assad. Without him there would be none of this. Everyone hated Assad, didn't they? Unless they were trying to trick you.

'The sooner he goes, the better.'

'That's good, that's good. You're doing well. So that's why you're here, is it, to fight the good fight?'

'I'm not here to fight.'

The man pushed himself up on his toes until his face was an inch from Abraham's.

'If you're not with us, my lanky fucking friend, you're against us.'

'I'm not here to fight anyone.'

With another grin the young man grabbed Abraham's upper arm and squeezed.

'I believe you. I believe you. Fuck me, pal. You'd take a lot of training up.'

He turned to his friend again and for the first time in a very long time Abraham wished he were stronger, and fitter, and capable of beating this character into being quiet. Shrugging his arm free he started to walk away.

'Hey.'

He kept walking.

'I'll catch up with you later.' Then to his friend: 'Fuck me. Scraping the fucking barrel now.'

Back on the street, Abraham stood by the entrance to the hotel, his head empty of ideas. The three men had gone, and for now he was alone.

3

That afternoon we take a school and Umm Sharik has me administer forty lashes to a teacher for smoking. We don't find any cigarettes on her but one of her colleagues tells Umm Sharik that she came in early three days ago and found her round the back in a storeroom, puffing away. I'm amazed that after over a year anybody can still be so stupid.

Without evidence, I want to refer the matter to the court, and have a judge decide the punishment, but Umm Sharik insists that in cases like this we must act quickly, stop the rot before it spreads, and I can see that. I'm prepared to bow to her experience, but as I take the lash from her I'm unsure whether this is truly the honour she says it is. At best it feels like a test.

I don't mind tests. I'm getting used to them. The lash is heavier in my hand than I thought it would be, and the weight is in the rubber, which is stiff and floppy at once. People don't understand the lash. They imagine long whips, slicing through fabric and drawing lines of blood, but this is really quite a gentle punishment. I've seen it often enough to know how to do it – lift the lash up to shoulder height and bring it firmly down across the back, not that hard, letting the flex in the rubber do the work. One thing I'm not expecting is how solid the connection is. If you're just watching, the clothes seem to take some of the impact, but as I deliver the first one I can feel the lash cracking into her bone. It will leave a bruise, for sure, but that's the idea – for a week she'll be thinking about what she did and chances are she won't offend again. Most don't.

Forty is a lot. You have to find a quick rhythm and stick to it, not slow down when you see it taking effect, but I have the discipline. I am doing this for her. She starts to sob, but after half way it gets easier. When I'm done I feel the urge to help her to her feet and that surprises me. I resist it. Instead she pushes herself up and limps back into the classroom, an example to the girls and herself.

The flat feels pretty empty that evening. It's been a full day and I long to talk to somebody about it. I've sent a load of texts to Khalil, too many, but I guess the reception's bad because he's only sent me one back. Right now he's with a platoon, at least that's what he calls it, in a house outside Kobani. There's a stand-off between our fighters and the Kurds, who we've pushed back to a group of buildings on the edge of the town. No one's moved for three days, and he says he's bored, but I can tell he's frustrated really. A spirit like that won't be contained for long, but in war as in everything we have to be clever. Take your time, I tell him. Trust your commanders, they are guided from above.

More than anything I fear his fearlessness, and when I lie awake at night I picture my lion tearing a dozen of his prey to pieces before some coward from the shadows takes him from me with a single bullet. But it will be okay. I know we have something up our sleeve. We just need the weather to change. Then they'll see who are the true fighters of Allah, the most glorified.

Patience in progress. That is what this place is teaching me.

I don't feel great when I get back, and put it down to being out in the heat all day and not drinking enough, but even after two glasses of water I'm not myself. Still, I know it's important to eat, and I'm making myself a salad when the intercom goes, and as I go to the door I can see on the screen it's Badra downstairs waiting, and I'm pleased to see her. I could do with the company, and she's proved herself my friend.

I buzz her in, but she rings the bell again and over the intercom tells me to come down straight away, there's no time, we have to go out. I sort out my abaya and my veils and leave the flat as quickly as I can.

Even by Badra's standards she's in a strange mood. She's cold to start with and says nothing much in the car, except to tell me that this is work, whatever we're doing, and we're heading a little way out of town. It's a sweaty hot evening and for once the clouds are covering the whole sky, and the city seems quiet, heavy somehow. I want to tell her I'm not feeling good but really there's no point with her. She'll only see it as weakness.

On the edges of the city we drive through industrial buildings, and past them I can see the desert, a dead gold in the dull light. Just as we're leaving Raqqa behind, Badra turns off the main road and towards a group of cars and 4x4s that have stopped between an old warehouse and what looks like an old factory, most of its windows smashed. The cars are in a semi-circle pointing inwards and the light of their headlights is shining on a crowd of maybe a hundred people who are all gathered round to watch something.

'We're late,' says Badra, pulling up.

As we walk towards the crowd I can hear a voice I think I recognize, a man's voice, high-pitched and cutting. Everyone is listening hard and I listen too. I find great beauty in it, so sharp and clear.

Of all the sins, there is none greater than this, it is saying. When a woman fornicates with a man who is not her husband she is an apostate, she has forsaken her faith, in that moment and from that moment she is an unbeliever, only she is worse than the kafir because she was given the gift of faith and she chose to cast it aside to satisfy her lust. The khilafa cannot tolerate this insult to Allah, the most glorified, the most high, this insult to the Prophet, and the punishment is set and unchanging.

The voice stops, and everyone stands silent, expectant. Badra pushes through the people in front of us so that we can reach the front, and we arrive to see Imam Talib throwing the first stone, not so hard because he's not a strong man, but hard enough. He must be six feet from the woman's head, which is bare and all that's showing above the ground, just her neck and head. She's so well buried that it's hard to imagine there's a body beneath. The stone – the rock, it's the size of a fist – connects with a heavy crack and drops back onto the sand. Her black face twists in pain but it can't recoil, it can't move, and only when I bring myself to look fully at her do I realize who it is.

Badra crouches by me, stands with a rock in each hand and passes one to me. I don't say anything but I don't need to. We both know exactly what she's doing. The ache in my head is clamping hard.

The circle around Idara tightens and the rocks beat down. I hear some miss and fall dead in the sand, and I hear some hit, and I hear her crying, wailing, an animal noise I haven't heard before, high and strangled, like foxes fighting. The crowd shouts in a virtuous rage but her wailing is above it all. I keep my eyes on Badra, because I don't want to look, and if I could shut my ears right now, shame on me, I would.

I imagine that I'm her encased in earth and I can't move my arms or my legs, not an inch, not a finger, and the rocks are coming for me and I can only twist my head from side to side, there's no escape from them.

The rock is still in Badra's hand. I wish I could see her eyes. Are they full of His light, are they righteous? Would I see in them that mix of regret and certainty that ought to guide the punisher? Or is there victory in them, over me or the woman in the sand?

All she is right now is a black form and a choice. My choice. No choice.

I take the rock and turn towards Idara. My eyes slip off her, no matter how hard I try to keep them there. The sand around her neck is spreading black.

This is the just punishment. I know that. It is written. If I cheated on Khalil this is what I would expect, and I would want it. I would want to be cleansed. If she's guilty this is the only outcome, and who am I to doubt her guilt? What, I know better than Imam Talib, the man who found me my lion, the man who married me? I think about his words. We, the community.

I raise my hand, ask Him to forgive my weakness, and throw.

4

My head is full of knives as we drive away, the sickness from earlier is churning through me, and each time the car jolts I seriously think I'm going to throw up. I watch the road as hard as I can, because my weakness is lingering and I don't want to see the images that are there when I close my eyes. If I wasn't feeling ill I'd be stronger, and I curse myself for it.

The elation I ought to be feeling at passing the test won't come. Maybe in time.

As if she's picking up on my anxiety Badra turns to me.

'You did well.'

I nod and thank her.

'Some people find it easy. But they have violence in their hearts and they do it because they want to. To do it because He wants you to, the most glorified, this is something else.'

I nod again. Part of me – most of me – wishes she'd be quiet. With what just happened, and still nothing from Khalil, and feeling ill myself, I don't need to be wondering for the fiftieth time what this woman wants from me.

'What did she do?'

Badra takes a moment. 'Her neighbours heard her. Through the walls.'

'Who was he?'

'Some fighter. A young guy. She was stupid.'

'Does her husband know?'

'I have no idea.'

'Now he has two wives again.'

She doesn't reply, and for a while we're silent, driving through the city. It's dark now, and the place is still quiet. A question's been eating away at me and in the end I have to let it out.

'Were there witnesses?'

'To what?'

'To Idara. To her crime.'

'I don't know.'

'Was she pregnant?'

Badra takes a moment, and I can feel the heat growing behind her veil.

'You are doubting the decision of the judge?'

'Not at all. I was just wondering how we know.'

For a full minute she doesn't speak, but when she does the heat is in her voice.

'We account to you now, is that right? You are the caliph? If you are in charge, maybe you can tell me why you hesitated to throw your first stone? You think a caliph would have doubts?'

I stutter no, of course not. That wasn't what I meant.

Without warning she pulls over to the side of the road, brakes sharply to a stop. She is speaking English to me for the first time since the makkar.

'Fuck Idara. Fuck Idara. Fuck what she did. She knew, and I tell you, this was not the first time. Not the first, not the second. Don't trouble yourself with whether she deserved to die.'

As she pauses, her head drops, as if it's been heavy with some burden for years. She sits like this for a moment, then reaches up and unhooks her veil and pulls it aside. It's dark now, but even by the street light I can see her eyes are red.

'You. You are one of the good ones, and they are the worst. Fuck your idea of good. It is a Western thing, corrupt. There is no "fair" in sharia. Only justice. It has contempt for you and your fairness, and if you do not change it will cut you in two. Do you hear me? This is not some fucking utopia. It is a fortress and sharia is our sword. We are building a fortress because we are at war. The West, it would destroy us. Not just the khilafa, all Muslims, every last one. The whole Ummah, because we are the only true threat to their creed of money and endless pleasure. Every other enemy has gone. You are too young, too fucking young, but think, just think if you can. Stand back and use your big brain. The Americans, they wage war for a century against communism, they suck it dry until the whole thing crumbles into dust. Because there is no money in a better world. So they sweep the body aside, ask themselves what is next, and what do they do? Invade Iraq. Start the whole thing over again, because they are not stupid. They know where they can be hurt. In here, and in here.' She holds a finger to her temple, then beats her fist against her heart. 'We fail, and they have won forever. This is the last great war, and if we do not win we will be finished. So fuck Idara, and the witnesses, and the truth. Forget them. Burn them in the fire of faith. Harden yourself, or you will not survive.'

Her words cut right to the heart of me, and at the same time seem to rush past. I can barely take them in. My head is splintering and I can feel sickness in my throat. I want to take my veil off, to breathe, but I don't trust myself to hold it together, not after what she's said. I long to see Khalil, and the days until he will return stretch out in front of me like the desert around us. I just want to go home, and shower, and sleep, and concentrate on my work. But I cannot say nothing.

'When the war is over, what then? There must be beauty, and love for Allah, the most glorified. Or we'll lose the things that make them fight us in the first place.'

Badra looks at me and her eyes seem old and so tired. They were full of rage but now their light has gone out. She takes my hand and brings it up to her breast, places it there, and holds it. Her chest is flat, like a man's.

'My husband was a good man. When he died I did not want to marry again. But I understood I should build a home, to serve the khilafa. Have the children I couldn't have with him. And then I began to see. Fighters would come, and they would inspect me, and when they saw I was old, and only had one breast, they would leave, with disgust in their eyes.'

She releases my hand and lets the words do their work. Ashamed, not knowing why, I clasp my hands in my lap.

'The khilafa is for men. It is not for us. Women mean nothing here. It is for men to fight and fuck, and they will never do anything else, because they are men. They will kill the men and rape the women and marry the fucking children because they can. And we need them to. Nothing else will defeat the kafir.'

With effort, I look into her eyes, and see something else there, some old trace of softness. I think I understand now. And I do not want to become like her.

'There are brothers and brothers.'

She laughs, if you can call it a laugh.

'Love is impossible here. Your man will not save you.'

5

we cannot understand Justice. Only Allah the most high, the most glorified understands

pretending we know anything is arrogant and an insult to Him who knows everything swt

how many times must I realize that the khilafa is so much bigger than any one person?

so many lessons here – every day every minute

— is everything okay sister?

all fine i just have a lot to learn

important lesson not to get ahead of yourself

— what do you mean sister? sorry I don't understand

you have to know how far you still have to go

no matter how close you feel to Him swt He is always so far ahead

6

In figures of eight, Abraham walked around Akçakale, not wanting to stop in any one place for long, hope warmed a degree by Irene's last exchange with Sofia. He wandered to the beginning of the plains where the sparse traffic thinned and the workshops and factories looked like they'd been abandoned years earlier. He stood on the edge of the empty no man's land straddling the border fence that divided the town from its Syrian double, just a few hundred yards to the south. Saw the neat, low, new town of tents, like an army encampment, where thousands of refugees were failing to find a home.

Something had unsettled her, and that could be a good thing.

There had to be a way into this world that didn't want him. When he came across a bench he sat for a while, until he sensed someone looking at him, or felt the hostile energy of one of the bands of men casually patrolling. He recognized the types from Gaziantep, but here they were so concentrated they seemed to outnumber the locals, who kept their eyes straight ahead and zigzagged from one side of the street to the other to avoid them.

Abraham had his eye in now; he was beginning to be able to distinguish. The beards were the giveaway. North of the border ISIS trimmed theirs; all the other fighters simply didn't shave in battle.

The Kurds, the Peshmerga, in their military boots and their fatigues and their flashes of camouflage, appeared predictable, disciplined, almost reassuring. They might kill you but they'd have a reason for it. No beard and no set uniform were the Syrian rebels, the Free Army and heaven knew how many breakaway groups. Western clothes, jeans, sunglasses. Those two from the hotel, they fit in there somewhere. But ISIS – ISIS were less organized, scrappier, wilder, more like a gang than an army, bound together not by authority but by some unseen, unstable animating force. They wore black T-shirts, sweatpants, trainers, and in any one group it was impossible to tell who had command. But more than that, as he made his lonely way past them Abraham could see in their eyes that their first and constant thought was whether he would be better dead. Every man and woman they idly tracked was an invitation, a taunt. Life was an insult to their power.

Abraham kept his head bowed as he walked and tried to look as weak and unthreatening as he could – not difficult today, his third in these clothes, with his shopping bags and the sweat stains under his arms, more tramp than fighter. But he had to work hard to stop his hand going to his chin. This fucking beard. He had to keep it. Here it marked him, but in Raqqa it would let him disappear.

Twice he passed police patrols and fought the urge to duck his head and run, but they paid him no attention and let him on his uneasy way. He longed for coffee and something to eat but the cafes had all been commandeered by one group or another, little impromptu headquarters in the field. The only one that hadn't was in the main square, where the bus had dropped him off. That seemed to be a local place, and he needed a local.

There was trade between Turkey and Raqqa, he had read about it, and what there was would pass through here. Someone was profiting in this hell.

The Tarcin Cafe, it was called. A handful of Turkish men sat outside in the shade of a jutting concrete canopy, smoking and drinking tea while the proprietor stood in the doorway and followed Abraham with his eyes each time he passed, like a man warning off a stray dog that was circling for scraps.

As the heat was beginning to go from the day, Abraham drew near again and saw that the cafe was busy now. Behind him a car turned over its engine; the noise startled him, and he turned to see where it was coming from. A hundred yards back two men were trying to start an old van, paying him no attention, and walking in his direction was the man that he had passed outside the hotel earlier. It was him, no question; the same fringe of hair and the same gait. God, this was exhausting. Who was he? Police? Fighter? Spy? Impossible to answer and better not to try. In Akçakale no face was friendly, and every look seemed to carry some dark purpose. Abraham walked a little faster, slowed for a moment as he neared the square to let a police car ahead of him idly cross his path, then half jogged the remaining distance to the cafe.

Still no one out on the street, but the tables inside were almost full, a row down either wall of the narrow room. Old men, young men, paunchy middle-aged men, some with moustaches, some of the younger ones with a few days' stubble, all in dark clothing and engaged in what appeared to be one large conversation. Locals, here to talk and smoke, a different energy altogether. As Abraham entered, some of the men looked up at him, nudged the arm of a neighbour, until all talk stopped and every man in the room had turned to look at him. Not hostile, not yet, but wary. One of the younger ones said something in Turkish and two of his young friends laughed.

Trying to project confidence he didn't feel, Abraham walked

to one of two empty tables, sat down, and told the cafe owner that he wanted tea. This was the man who had flicked his cigarette butt at him earlier, and now he just stood and stared Abraham down: you're not getting served here.

Someone shouted something in Turkish, and a moment later in Arabic.

'For twenty bucks I teach you to shave.'

The joker of the group. Twenty years old, perhaps, no more, wearing a natty tan leather jacket and a white T-shirt, full of himself and enjoying the attention. Some of the older men stared at him with weary disapproval.

'And wash,' someone shouted. That got a laugh.

'I have a scar,' said Abraham, meeting the kid's eye. He brought his hand up to his cheek.

'You sure you haven't been fighting, my friend?'

The kid laughed at his own joke, looking around for reinforcement.

'I fell when I was a boy.'

'Where are you from?'

This was one of the older men, his voice deeper, carrying more authority. At the sound of it the kid sat back in his chair, no longer quite so sure of himself, conceding the arena. The man's eyes were deep-set and tired, the lines in his face all cast downwards.

'Cairo.'

'And what do you want in my town?'

Abraham realized that he had made a mistake: he had walked past these men to his table, and now they were between him and the door. Not that it makes much difference, he thought. If they want to get me, they will get me.

'I have family in Raqqa.'

The man continued to stare at him, not satisfied.

'I need someone to take me there.'

The kid couldn't hold it in. 'He needs a taxi!'

Ignoring him, the man kept his eyes right on Abraham.

'Why did you come here?'

'A friend sent me.'

'Who?'

'A man called Erol. He runs a bar in Antep.'

The man thought for a moment more. He was greying, balding, a little out of shape, his authority settled in him like his paunch.

'Have you been here before?'

'I've never been to Turkey before.'

'Can you prove that?'

What was there to lose? From the back pocket of his trousers he produced his passport, and hands passed it to the head man, who started to flick through it.

'You haven't been anywhere.'

'Not really.'

The man thumbed through the pages once more from start to finish, as if it were a flick book, then threw it spinning back to Abraham, who trapped it awkwardly on the table.

'If someone here wants to help you that's their business,' said the man and, holding up a finger, signalled to the owner for more coffee.

Now Abraham was of no interest, and slowly the conversation started up again. First the talk was about him, and then it seemed to move on, and he was left to drink his tea at the corner table in peace.

Peace, of course, he didn't want. The sun had gone down, the call to maghrib, the fourth prayer of the day, had been sung – two men had left the cafe, the rest appeared not to register it at all – and before long the minarets would sound for the last time. What he was going to do when night fell he had no idea.

But no one seemed to want his business. The men were still talking, more confidentially now, conspiratorially, leaning in over the tables. The cafe began to empty as they left in ones and twos, and at last the final prayer began to be called. The owner was clearing up, emptying ashtrays and noisily stacking plates and cups. Abraham got up and went to stand by the nearest table. The kid was still there, with two of his friends and two older men. The head man had gone home, or wherever it was such people went.

'Hey, it's the beard.' The kid was still grinning. 'I thought you'd left.'

'I can pay five thousand lira.' About a thousand pounds – a lot, here.

'You have papers?'

This was one of the friends, but he had a different quality to the others. Calmer, less excited by the moment, his voice deeper, slower. He was sitting with his back to the wall and his legs crossed, one elbow on the table and in his hand a cigarette with no filter that he seemed in no hurry to smoke. The others were all in nondescript clothes but he wore a suit, a sharp grey suit with thin lapels, and under it a cherry-red shirt. He might have been in the wrong place: a film set, or the bar of some Buenos Aires hotel. In this little group, he had authority.

'I don't,' said Abraham. 'I need papers.'

The man took a drag on his cigarette, letting the smoke out in a slow stream. Next to his friends he was handsome, too: black eyes, a narrow face, brown hair that was neither messy nor neat, and about him the air of being more experienced, wiser, though he couldn't have been older than twenty-five.

'You want everything, don't you?'

'I just want to get to Raqqa.'

Another drag. Abraham felt everything slipping from him.

'Why don't you tell me why you really want to go?'

'I have family there. My wife's family.'

'What are their names?'

Christ.

'Labib. Sami Labib. That's her father.'

'And his wife?'

'Ester.'

'Where do they live?'

'I don't know.'

Next to him the kid laughed and shook his head. His friend went on.

'You don't know? What you going to do, knock on every door?'

'I have the address, just not here.'

'With all your other things?'

'That's right.'

They didn't believe a word.

'You're going to have to tell me why you're really going or this conversation is going to end real soon.'

Abraham looked from him to the others and back again. If he was going to come clean he didn't want an audience.

'Just you.'

The man jutted his chin at his friends.

'Go on.'

'Seriously?' said the joker.

'I'll be out in a minute.'

'Fuck sake.'

It took a minute for them to collect their cigarettes and their matches, drink the last of their coffee, demonstrate that they were only going on sufferance.

'Here. Sit.'

Abraham glanced at the owner, who was wiping the table next to them. They were the last ones left now.

'Don't worry. Sit.'

Abraham sat opposite the self-possessed young man and wondered where on earth to start.

'I'm Abraham.'

He held out his hand. It was hard not to shake a hand.

'Murat.'

'Thanks for talking to me, Murat.'

'I'm just talking.'

'I understand.'

Murat crossed his arms. Go on. Convince me.

So Abraham gave him everything. The truth. Who he was, why he was going, how little he knew about what he was doing. How his daughter had been tricked, duped at least, and how he feared that she'd be dead within weeks.

'The women can last a long time,' said Murat.

'I think that might be worse.'

With a flick of a finger Murat spun his packet of cigarettes round on the table, twice, three times, then picked it up, opened the lid with his thumb and held it up to Abraham, who told him no, thank you. Murat took one for himself, lit it, blew out the match and let the smoke out in a thin stream. Everything he did was self-conscious but at the same time relaxed, controlled.

'I go. But I don't take people.'

'I need to get there.'

'People are unpredictable. They do stupid things. Or they lie to you.'

'I'm not lying.'

'You lied to begin with.'

'I'm sorry. I'm not lying now.'

Murat raised his eyebrows and drew on the cigarette.

'Also, the price. Five thousand is nothing.'

'I have more.'

'Hundred thousand.'

'I . . . I don't have that.'

Twenty thousand pounds. Impossible.

Murat shrugged, sighed, tapped the ash off his cigarette.

'My friend, you're asking too much.' He pushed his chair back. 'I can't do it.'

Unconsciously, Abraham reached out and rested his hand on Murat's forearm.

'Please. I have to get there.'

'I can't do it.'

'Do you know anyone?'

'Come back tomorrow. Maybe some bastard's crazier than me.'

'I have to go as soon as possible.'

Murat frowned mid-drag, squinting against the smoke rising into his eyes.

'What's the hurry? Don't you like it here?'

Maybe if he mentioned the police it would be a good thing. Establish his credentials as a serious person.

'It doesn't seem safe.'

'Not safe for any of us, my friend.'

Murat stood, pulled a wallet from his back pocket and from it a note.

'I'll pay for this,' said Abraham.

Murat thanked him, said goodnight to the owner, and left. Abraham caught up with him outside.

'Here. My phone number.'

He had written it down in preparation.

'I'm not going to change my mind.'

'Please. If you think of anyone.'

Murat took the piece of paper as if it was a bill or a summons or something else he didn't want, and with a nod stuffed it into a pocket and began to walk away to his friends, who were waiting for him in an old white Nissan.

'Can you tell me – I'm sorry.'

Murat turned slowly, eyebrows raised again. The square was almost dark now and almost empty; the last worshippers had left the mosque and were hurrying in twos and threes down the side streets that led into the square. Four or five cars had gathered in the far corner, their doors open and the young men inside shouting from one to another, lolling like cats in the heat.

'I have nowhere to stay.'

'You're serious.'

What a sight he must be. No one would have him. But it was a warm night, and maybe there was an empty house, or one of those abandoned-looking warehouses he had seen on the edge of town.

'Is there a park, or a . . .'

'You tried the hotel?'

Abraham nodded.

'Son of a bitch. You're serious.'

'I'll be all right, I just need . . .'

'You can't sleep on the street.' Murat shook his head, looked across the square, and for an instant held the eye of a man who was standing there against one of the cars, arms crossed. 'You won't last till morning. Son of a bitch. Here.'

He beckoned Abraham to him, put his hand on his shoulder and pointed beyond the mosque.

'That street there? Take the third left off it and five or six houses down you'll see a white house on the right, very neat, there are two olive trees growing outside. A crazy old woman lives there. Sometimes she takes people in. That's all I can think of. I'd take you myself but I've got to go.'

Abraham tried to fix the directions in his mind.

'Get fucking going, Cairo. You don't want to be out when it gets dark.'

Murat slapped him on the back and left him standing alone in the square.

7

As Murat drove away, Abraham dropped his eyes to the floor and set off across the square, quickly but not so quickly that he might become more interesting than he already was, the only moving thing in the last of the dusk. Somewhere towards the border, a little way off, came four flat cracks that were almost certainly shots being fired. Christ, what a place this was.

The street he turned into was empty. All the worshippers had vanished into the low houses either side, every window dark. It was as if some silent siren had sounded and shut down the town.

Abraham kept his head down and walked faster. A left here would bring him up past the mosque to the street Murat had pointed out. Then right and second left. Easy. Just keep your wits about you and go as quickly as you can.

He broke into a jog, almost unconsciously, feeling a prickle of fear start across his back and up the nape of his neck.

As he approached the crossroads he slowed and pulled in to the wall of a building so he could peer round the corner back towards the square. If it came to a chase, he was done for. His lungs were burning and he could feel sweat damp on his chest.

Fifty yards away, ten men were walking towards him. Ten, a dozen. The loping, casual walk told him they were the same men from the square, not locals, not the good Muslims who had come out in the dark in this hellhole to pray to their God, but the fighters, as they called themselves, full of that aimless purpose, as if they needed something to do and the first person they met would be the best prospect they had. In their hands, silhouetted against the light from the square, he was sure he saw guns.

He pulled back against the wall. If he was quick and fast he could go back the way he had come and make a loop around them, maybe. But the street he was on was too long – he'd never clear the bottom before they appeared at the top.

As quietly as he could, he retraced his steps, staying close to the wall, until he felt it give way behind him. Set back from the street was a chain-link gate about three feet high and beyond that what looked like a patch of garden, thick with plants; he fumbled for the catch, cursing it as it clinked in the silence, and when it wouldn't open he straddled the gate awkwardly, dropped his shopping bags on the other side, and half fell onto the dry ground, shrinking into the darkness.

The breeze and his breath, that was all there was. He kept his eyes shut because he thought that would be better, but it wasn't; the fear built inside him until it was only with great effort that he managed to stop himself bolting over the gate and running, feet slipping on the loose surface, running across town and out onto those endless dark fields to some place where he might forever lose these bastards and himself. He opened his eyes. Nothing. No one there, no sound. They had kept straight on. They weren't coming this way.

In his corner, Abraham crouched right down. Now he could hear the individual crunch of boot on dirt. Keep still, barely breathe. They don't know you're here.

Through the leaves he saw feet, three pairs. His breathing stopped. The men were quiet, too, walking slowly and not talking now, until they were a few yards past him and someone hissed something in Arabic that Abraham didn't catch. Two men stopped, the rest kept walking. Abraham looked up and saw a figure coming back towards him, taking its time, scanning the ground. It came to the fence, perhaps twelve feet away, looked over it, left and right, saw enough and turned to join the group; thought better of it, and turned again to make sure. Abraham squeezed himself still closer to the wall.

'Here!' the figure shouted. 'Fucker's doing some gardening. You. Up.'

Abraham pulled himself awkwardly up by the fence and unconsciously raised his hands in the air. The man in front of him had a machine gun that he held down low, pointing at Abraham's belly.

'What the fuck are you doing? You a fucking spy?'

'No. No. I'm not a spy.'

'Well who the fuck are you, brother?'

The others were grouping round now, some laughing, some shouting, all enjoying themselves, all terrifying. Maybe ten of them, younger than him, stronger. Four had guns. By the light coming from the house Abraham thought he recognized two of them from outside the hotel earlier, and coming up behind them the Englishman from the lobby.

'Get the fuck out of there, Daesh cunt.'

The one who had found him grabbed hold of his shirt at the shoulder and hauled him hard over the fence. Abraham landed awkwardly on an outstretched hand before feeling himself pulled up again.

'Get the fuck up. What you doing in there, motherfucker? Weeding?'

Money. Could he offer them money, or would it make things worse? How could they be any worse?

Abraham raised his hands in a futile conciliatory gesture.

'I . . .'

'Hey, it's the lanky fuck. Why you hiding, motherfucker?'

The Englishman came forward and stood all of a foot away from Abraham, tobacco and beer on his breath and in his right hand a pistol, which he brought calmly up to Abraham's face, touching the barrel to his cheek. So young he looked grotesque. He was no man. He was a boy with a gun, twenty at most. Even his voice was trying hard to be older than it was.

He waited for Abraham to answer the question.

'I . . . I thought you might be Daesh.'

The gun drove harder in, pushing the flesh towards his eye.

'Fuck does that mean? I look like fucking Daesh?'

'It's dark, I couldn't see.'

Now the man twisted the gun's barrel hard into the skin, into the upper jawbone. Abraham felt the cold of the metal through his beard and found himself praying, please God, not here, I'm not finished yet.

'What sort of Arabic is that, cunt?'

'Egyptian. Cairo.'

Still pressing the gun into Abraham's face, he turned, grinning.

'Fucking Egyptian.'

Some laughter, not from everyone. He turned back to Abraham.

'Why you here?'

Probably there was no correct answer. The truth would get you killed. A lie would get you killed.

'I've come to deliver a letter.'

'The fuck are you talking about?'

'My wife died. She was from Raqqa. I have a letter for her family.'

'A letter. Really? Important letter, for you to come here.'

'It is important.'

'There money in it?'

'No money.'

'Where is this letter?'

'I don't have it.'

'What do you have, brother? Apart from this lovely beard.'

He laughed, others laughed. Abraham felt them pressing closer, impatient now for this to move on, for the fun to start.

'You going to Raqqa with the letter, is that it? You planning on putting down roots?'

'Please. I'm not part of any of this.'

'Any of what? What are you part of?'

'Nothing. I'm on my own.'

'You want to tell me why I should believe you? Empty your pockets. Empty your fucking pockets.'

Before Abraham could do anything, another man stepped forward from the pack and pulled the Englishman out of the way. He was older, squat, with a thick neck and the blackest eyes, and now he shoved Abraham hard in the shoulder with the heel of his hand, so hard that the bone seemed to crack.

'Get on your knees.'

'I . . .'

'Get on your fucking knees.'

With his foot he buckled Abraham's legs and drove him down towards the ground.

'I don't give a fuck if you're Daesh or not. If you are, they're one down. If you're not, so the fuck what. But first I'm going to shave off this fucking beard and then who fucking knows.'

From his belt he drew a hunting knife and with his free hand pulled taut the skin on Abraham's cheek. The others crowded in, shouting and laughing with release.

Then Abraham heard a single shout above the rest, and the grip on his face relaxed. Space opened around him, and through the men's legs he saw the headlights of a car and black against them a figure walking towards him.

'What is this?'

The voice was like iron.

'You. What the fuck do you think you're doing?'

The man with the knife let go and stood. No one was interested in Abraham any more; he might have not been there. Kneeling on the ground, he felt his shoulder.

All he could see was this new man's outline against the light: huge, stocky, thick arms, thighs so big his legs splayed out. He walked up to one of the fighters and with the flat of his hand pushed him hard in the chest like a punch, sent him staggering back.

'Didn't you hear me?'

He pushed him again. Everything else was quiet now; it was impossible to imagine anything outside this tiny circle of light.

'I'm guessing you didn't hear me earlier, either. Huh? Were any of you cunts listening?'

Pulling the fighter out of his way he moved closer in. No one was about to answer, let alone challenge him. In his right hand by his side hung a pistol.

'Who the fuck is this?'

Silence.

'One of you cunts is going to answer me. You.'

He pointed at the Englishman, who looked down at the ground and started muttering a reply.

'Daesh maybe. We were finding out.'

'This guy?'

The Englishman kept his head down.

'This sack of shit? I should shoot the fucking lot of you. This is how you win a war? This is the respect you show your commanders?'

No one so much as looked up at him. He took a step towards the Englishman. 'Have you been drinking?'

'No sir,' he said, shaking his head violently. Abraham could feel the fear in him now.

'Any one of you cunts has been drinking I will shoot them here and now.'

He looked around at them, taking his time, staring hard at each face.

'Babies. You call yourselves soldiers but you need to play like fucking babies. Now fuck off to bed. Tomorrow we have more than one cunt to send to hell. Fail and I will come for your heads. Better you die in battle. Understand? Go. Go!'

As one the men scattered, ran together up the street the way they had come. Abraham watched them go but without relief. It wasn't over.

'Get up.'

The voice was still hard. Abraham didn't so much hear it as feel it in his chest. Pushing himself up he stood, and against the pain and the natural recoiling of his body did his best to face the man.

'Who are you?'

Abraham brought his hand up to shield his eyes from the light.

'An Egyptian. A good Muslim, trying to get a message to family in Raqqa.'

For a good ten seconds the man stared at him. His face was like his body, round and blockish.

'Lucky for you you're not important today. Now fuck off.'

8

Abraham went. Recovered his bags and ran with them swinging out of sync at his side. A car started and its lights swept across him but he just ran, all the way to the crossroads and round the corner and finally into the street Murat had given him, until he was outside the house with the two olive trees, just discernible in the thin moonlight. Now it was really night. No one, surely, would open their door, and if they did they would close it the moment they saw him.

Panting, he put his bags down, smoothed his hair without effect, did his best to straighten his stinking shirt, and knocked.

A wind was getting up, and as he waited, straining to hear, two cars raced past at the bottom of the street. A good minute he gave it, knocked again, and when he could no longer fool himself he bent down to pick up his bags and turned to leave. Where to? He couldn't go on and he couldn't go back. No one would have him inside and he couldn't be out on the street. He was nowhere. Nowhere was all he had.

If he had some oxycodone he could take four and curl up under a bush and nothing would matter.

Behind him he heard a voice, a woman's voice.

'Who are you?'

When he turned he saw the door was open an inch, on a chain, but the woman herself wasn't there.

'I . . . Murat sent me.'

'Murat who?'

'I don't know. Murat. From the Tarcin Cafe. He said you sometimes take lodgers.'

'Not after dark.'

'I was . . . some people attacked me.'

'That's what happens after dark. You'll have to leave.'

'Do you know where I might go?'

Behind the door there was a cough, and a pause.

'Your Arabic is strange.'

'I'm from Egypt.'

'Then why are you here?'

'I have to go to Raqqa.'

'My advice, go back to Egypt. Go now. Don't go to Raqqa.'

'My daughter is there.'

Another pause, and when it spoke again the voice was harder.

'Is she one of them?'

'I want to bring her back.'

The door shut, with great finality, and then after a pause it opened again, and standing in the light was an old woman, holding a walking stick but completely upright, her eyes burning into his.

'My husband, he would take anyone, but he is a fool. He would rather have money now than a house later. But you are not a devil. Devils do not come with plastic bags looking like they have been dragged across the desert. Devils are vain creatures, all of them.'

She had a long, straight nose, and tilting her head back she looked down it now from hard, frank eyes. Her forehead and cheeks were crossed with deep wrinkles, her mouth a fixed line across her face, and she wore a headscarf, tightly tied and covered in bright yellow and orange flowers.

'Come in. But I have more questions.'

Abraham picked up his bags and stepped into the hall. Outside, the house had looked nondescript, featureless. Inside, it was decorated like the houses of the grander families Abraham remembered visiting in Cairo with his mother as a child: fading yellow walls, oil paintings of scenes from country life, dark wood furniture, lace curtains across the windows, the air cool and smelling richly of wood polish. Abraham keenly felt the filth on him, and with a measure of shame. He shouldn't be polluting this poor woman's home.

'What is your name?'

'Abraham. Abraham Mounir.'

She nodded to herself, as if he had passed the first, minor test.

'I am Mrs Demirsoy. What is in those bags?'

'Clothes. I had to buy new clothes.'

'Hm. Are you a holy man?'

Abraham hesitated. That wasn't the question he'd been expecting, and probably it wasn't for him to say.

'I go to church.'

Mrs Demirsoy's head clicked a degree, like a bird's, and she frowned.

'I'm a Christian,' said Abraham. 'A Copt.'

'I know about Copts.'

It wasn't clear if that was a good or a bad thing.

'I'm not a good Christian. I try to be holy and mainly fail.'

'We all fail. How could we succeed?'

This question didn't require an answer, and she asked the next immediately.

'Your wife. Tell me about her.'

'She is ill. Lost. In her head.'

'She has devils too. I am sorry. You have sons?'

'No. Just my daughter.'

'Probably she thinks she is special. Does she think she is special?'

It was like being back with Vural, only with better questions.

Yes, she probably did think she was special. It had never occurred to him before.

'Perhaps.'

'Of course she does. She is young and has no family to keep her hands in the soil. And you? You think you can change her now?'

'I'm hoping she'll wake up.'

'All is dark there. Waking, sleeping, it's the same thing.'

The eyes that looked up at him were full of a hard sympathy: I have no consolation for you, but then there's no consolation for anyone.

'So you are alone? In the world?'

Abraham nodded. Part of him felt like he might cry; not from self-pity but simply from relief in having it acknowledged.

'And you seek death.'

'I don't . . . I just want to save her.'

'But not yourself. You would give yourself for her and it would be a relief. Some parents are like you. I am more selfish. How can we expect our children's lives to be better than our own? There is no right way.'

Maybe she was crazy. Maybe all the death and horror had found their way into her. But her eyes were clear, as they stayed on his, and sharp, there was a lifetime of sharpness in them. She gave him one last look and nodded.

'Some things are easy. Washing is easy. Sleeping is easy. You, you need both before you know who you are. But I am satisfied. You are a man and not a devil. Definitely a man. Come.'

Mrs Demirsoy opened a drawer in the desk, picked out a key, took her stick and led Abraham briskly up the stairs to the first floor and a room at the back of the house. A neat, clean, single room furnished with a bed, a bedside table, a chest of drawers and nothing else besides a small rug on the floor and a sink in the corner. A thick velvet curtain had done little to keep the heat of the day out, but it was wonderful, perfect, like falling into paradise.

'You smell like old meat. Bath is next door. Clean it afterwards.'

'Thank you. Really. I don't think I deserve this.'

'Are you hungry?'

'I'm fine.'

'Nonsense. You are hungry. Wash, put on your new clothes, come downstairs, I will find something for you. Full board is a hundred lira each night. How many nights?'

'I have no idea.'

'Really, it is a miracle you have come this far. God must smile on you.'

9

My dreams are a mess of animals, sand and blood. I wake ten times in the night soaked through and each time I fall straight back into sleep, but I don't want to be there. Nothing's right, I have no control, all I can do is watch.

When I come out of it the sun is burning against the curtains and my hair is cold and wet on my face. My first thought is for Khalil, and just for a second I feel so low that he isn't here to look after me, bringing me water, changing my sheets. Talking through whatever the hell it was Badra was trying to tell me last night.

Then I see the time.

I have three missed calls, all from an hour ago. Two from Umm Sharik, who usually picks me up. I call her straight away. No answer. I want to call again but there's no point, they'll be out on patrol already.

My head splits right open as I get out of bed but I force myself into the shower and turn it to cold and wish I had longer because it seems to be doing some good. By now my team will be out on the streets, and I have no idea how to find them or what to say when I do. I don't want to tell them I'm ill. Only weak people get ill, and I curse myself for my weakness. Every bit of me aches and I get exhausted just drying myself.

It's a sign of how bad I'm feeling that I don't realize until I'm leaving that this isn't just random, it's a test of my strength, of course it is, like everything else. I can do this. I will not fail Him.

But I'm sweating before I even leave the building, and in the heat of the day each step needs will. The clouds have gone and my niqab feels like it's pulling in all the heat from the sun, as if every ray was channelled right at me. The sound, too. It's so noisy today, and there's nothing I can do to escape it, the horns and the engines and the shouting. My gun's as heavy as a body on my shoulder. Even the smells are getting to me, and each breath makes me feel like the world doesn't want me here.

I will tell them I'm ill. The truth is all I have.

It's a mile and a half to the brigade office. The harder I work the more I think I'm not going to make it at all. I need a bench, to rest, just for a minute, but I can't find one. When we aren't at war and Badra's been proved wrong and peace flourishes here then there will be benches, and green parks, and the sound of birdsong everywhere and we will assume our true role, the women, the foundation. I picture the parks, the people in them, the ancient balance of the world in place again, but Badra's words are still in my head, all broken up and shuffled, more images than words, Khalil polishing his gun and tanks in the sand and the fortress we are building here, the war we are fighting because we have no choice, she's so right about that, we didn't start this war, and the brave brothers, the brothers killing the kafirs, brothers killing brothers, the commanders commanding and the stones rain down from a clear sky so that when I crouch down He will protect me—

*

132

I wake in darkness and it must be the end. I have died failing Him. My body is dissolving back into heat and water and I await His judgement without thought. Love and fear pulse through me, the sounds of the world die away.

Then voices nudge me. Voices I don't recognize, women's and men's, ghostly, questioning. In time I understand them, but I can't reply, it's like they're out of range. Leave her where she is. Take her up. We cannot leave her. I am being judged.

I feel a touch on my arm. It lifts me, supports me across my back, which is cold and hot at once. It pulls my veil down for a second and light comes in, and as I focus I see another veil in front of me and behind it people standing and cars passing. The world's noise returns. My head feels like it's going to crack.

The veil is asking me if I'm all right. I have no idea. I look up at the faces above me, the men stern, the women veiled, all dark against the sky-blue sky, and I think I say something.

Leave her, someone says, a man's voice. Would she do the same for you?

I long for water, and air. I try to stand, hold on to the figure by me, feel my legs buckle like straws. Something weighs on my shoulder. I reach for it and take a moment to recognize my gun. It brings me to myself, and I clutch it close. For the first time I realize the danger I'm in, and I shrink away from the figure's touch.

'Are you all right?'

If I could just get on my feet. I use the gun to push myself up but it slips from under me and I fall back down. New voices come, louder, and the people around me move away.

A brother is there. He has a gun round his neck and it swings forward as he bends over me. I can see the brown skin through his beard and the dark bags under his eyes. I have the strange sense of wanting to reach out to him and at the same time to pull back.

He tells everyone to leave, and then it's just him and me.

'Who are you?'

I tell him my name. Umm Azwar, Al-Khansaa Brigade.

'What's wrong with you? Why are you here? Your ankles are showing.'

I apologize, and try to sit up.

'You're not safe with that. Fucking joke.' He wrenches the gun from me and my eyes follow it as he hands it to someone behind him. 'Are you drunk?'

It's even an effort to shake my head. I manage two words.

'I'm sick.'

'Where are you going? Who knows you?'

I reach out a hand for him to help me up but he doesn't take it, and then the heat and the pain in my head are too much and I feel a surge of sickness and try to unfasten my veil in time, but I vomit against the cloth, a stream of it, and the wet and the stink of it panic me.

'Fuck. Fuck.'

The brother steps back in disgust.

I tear at the veil, and finally pull it away, and use it to wipe my face and mouth. Only now I see myself as the others must, and a deep shame washes through me, and a deep fear follows it, more powerful than this illness. My time here is over. I have insulted our faith, and if I do not die now they will be right to kill me.

10

How I got from there to here I don't remember. I wake up in my old bed in the makkar, on my own, under clean sheets. It's dark outside but the door is open an inch or two and some light gets in. There's a glass of water on the floor beside me, and as I prop myself up on an elbow and reach for it the pain in my head returns. I give up and lie back. Planes fly overhead but no bombs fall, none that I hear.

At some point Badra comes. She's her usual self, impossible to know what she's thinking, but she brings me more water and asks me if I want medicine. Something for my head, perhaps, Nurofen. Paracetamol would be better, she says, and gives me three pills to swallow. The water tastes like metal and feels like it doesn't belong in my throat.

She lays her hand on my forehead and tells me I'm still burning up. I want to know who's doing my work, what will happen to me, but she doesn't answer. Just rest, she says.

I'm not well enough to read, but I pray. I pray for the strength to get through this, and to take whatever punishment is due to me. I expected to wake up in a cell but with Badra you can never tell. Is she curing me or holding me? I can feel the sense of disgrace waiting for me, just there, waiting until I'm well enough to realize how bad it truly is.

When I get reception I manage to text Khalil that I'm ill, I don't mention anything else, and then the signal goes and I wait hours for his reply. Not knowing if he knows what I've done is worse than everything else.

I know I should sleep but my dreams are still crazy and I'm not enjoying them. Nothing makes sense in there. Sometimes I'm inside this huge machine, and that's all there is, wheels and cogs and steam and noise, banging and crashing and clanking. It's like a metal hell. I want to find a way out but I can't.

I get a text back from Khalil, telling me to hang in there. I have so much to say to him but don't want to burden him with my weakness when he's fighting. I let him know I'll be okay. Not long now, he says. And that thought, which should be the happiest one, is the one that eats me up. When I disgraced the khilafa I disgraced him. I should tell him now but I can't bring myself to because what if he leaves me?

Badra comes to me and says I have a visitor. Just like that, you have a visitor, no explanation, no suggestion of who it is or what they want. This is it, I think. Of course, they wouldn't punish a sick person because the punishment wouldn't register. If you're out of your mind, how are you meant to understand? Where's the pain or the improvement?

It's Umm Karam, and when I see her I actually feel relief, like someone who's been condemned to death who finally sees the electric chair. I sit up in bed, try to make the covers neat. My heart is still going at a thousand beats a minute, and in my pyjamas I am so exposed. Ready for judgement, I guess. She's unveiled, and I look for signs in her face, but she's like Badra, a sphinx, there's nothing there. Badra follows her with a chair from the kitchen, sets it down for her and she sits. I say nothing. I don't even have the confidence any more to greet her.

After a minute she nods and says she's pleased to see me looking better. She came yesterday but I was sleeping.

'Thank you,' I manage to say.

'You have been through a great deal.'

'And I disgraced my position. I failed the khilafa.'

Umm Karam looks at me and her eyes are the most piercing I've ever seen. I feel like there's nothing she doesn't know about me.

'You were weak, but your spirit was doing what it could.'

I barely understand her. I don't know where this is leading.

'That was your first stoning.'

'It was.'

'Did your first stone hit?'

Badra might have told her. And anyway, I cannot lie.

'No.'

'Your second?'

'My third. I'm not good . . . it's not so easy to hit.'

'If your arm is guided by Allah, the most glorified, the most high, it is easy. If you mean the stone to hit, it is easy.'

Her eyes are so clear. She can see right inside me.

She's silent again, leaving me to consider the truth she has just shown me. Badra was right to test me that night. I wasn't ready. Where there was justice I saw horror.

'If I had the chance again I would not miss.'

'You would not want to. But you would. You are not a punisher. Your intelligence is your strength and the source of your weakness. To destroy a person with stone after stone until the life leaks from them you must be fully righteous or part of your brain must be dead.'

Now I feel like I'm in Badra territory. She's right, but it leaves me nowhere. I long to know what she wants, where she's going. Then she tells me.

'You will no longer work for the brigade.'

I close my eyes. How will I explain the disgrace to Khalil?

'I understand.'

'There is new work for you. A chance to redeem yourself.'

I can't believe it. Of all the blessings He could have given me, this is the greatest. An energy starts spreading through me that I thought had gone forever.

'Thank you, Umm Karam.'

'Think on your weakness. Try to understand it.'

11

'Murat Felek, this is him?'

Mrs Demirsoy said the name like a schoolteacher remembering some errant child.

'I don't know his name.'

'Murat Felek. It will be Murat. Tall boy, hair like this, thinks he is a little better than everyone else.'

'That could be him.'

'I know his grandmother. I know his mother. He should have gone away but I see him in his suits, he thinks he can make money in hell. Maybe he can. Maybe he is the clever one. But he will not take you?'

'I can't pay him enough.'

'How much does he ask for?'

'Hundred thousand lira.'

Mrs Demirsoy had been topping and tailing long yellow beans but now she stopped with the blade of the small knife held at her thumb.

'For this I would want Raqqa to come to me.'

Shaking her head, she went back to her work.

'I will talk to Beren.'

After breakfast Mrs Demirsoy went out, and when she returned she found Abraham still in the kitchen where she had left him.

'What are you doing?'

'Nothing. Thinking.'

'Good. You should think. We should all think more.'

She had bags of shopping, and Abraham got up to help her with them.

'Thank you. He will do it. You must see him at one o'clock, at the cafe. He will charge you twenty thousand, which is expensive but fair. There is risk for him. Your papers will take time but he will arrange everything. In the meantime you will stay here.'

She passed him a bag of coffee and pointed to a cupboard above the table.

'There. Empty it into the tin.'

How long will it take, Abraham wanted to ask.

'Thank you,' he said, nodding to himself, tearing the top off the packet, trying to imagine this real future that was now upon him.

'Your poor daughter,' said Mrs Demirsoy, who was watching him tentatively begin to sift the coffee, 'without a woman in her life. Here. Like this.'

She took the packet from him and upended it in one swift action into the tin, shaking out the last of the grounds.

'There. Useless. Don't worry. Only a madman would want to go. My family is in Raqqa, my cousins, but I do not visit, and the devils are scared of me. They are scared of all women, but most of all they are scared of old women, and the older we are the less they like it. We have a power they do not understand. They do not kill old women, it is the last thing they will do, but still I will not go there.'

'Do you think I should?'

'You? You have to. Not for her but for yourself. What, you would go home and for all your life you wonder? Of course not.'

12

Mrs Demirsoy had Abraham under house arrest, and he didn't mind in the least. What's the point of going outside, she asked him; it's hot and dry and there's nothing to do except watch the devils strutting.

'I loved my town. But now it is a waiting room for death. And I thank God I will not be in it for long.'

So Abraham stayed at home. He helped prepare food, he washed up, he sat on his bed and looked for news of Sofia – and he talked to her, as Irene.

Mrs Demirsoy continued to comfort and scold him. She wanted to know about Ester, what kind of a woman she'd been before, who had cared for her, who had been there to help. That was the problem with families now, they had shrunk. Mrs Demirsoy was one of seven, her mother had been the youngest of eight. When someone died or fell ill others would take their place. But here was this man and this girl, expected to make a family on their own? It was like a piano with two strings. No music could come from it.

A great tragedy, all round. Not improved by you and your self-pity and your fear, though I understand both. The girl sounds as if she craves life, and yet she was shut in as surely as you are shut in here. When I was a girl we didn't know life existed, and maybe that was better. A cage is not a cage if you cannot see beyond the bars.

I had no idea I had gone so wrong, he told her, and with a look she let him know that she'd tolerate none of that – the self-pity – and besides, if God let us see our own mistakes we would have nothing to learn on the Day of Resurrection.

Throughout these conversations, as Abraham sliced tomatoes or picked parsley leaves from their stems or spooned soup into his mouth, the more or less silent Mr Demirsoy would occasionally catch his eye and give him a rich look that said, My wife is an extraordinary woman, and I greatly respect what she says, but I am thankful that for once she isn't saying it to me.

After lunch on the second day, as Mrs Demirsoy was bringing coffee to the table, the doorbell rang, and so timeless was life in the house that to Abraham the noise was instantly jarring, wrong. Mr Demirsoy made to get up but his wife held up her hand to stop him.

'I will go. It might be important.'

As she turned, Mr Demirsoy smiled at Abraham fully for the first time.

'If not important she also go.'

Looking pleased with himself for making a joke in Arabic,

he poured the coffee and they sat in silence, Mr Demirsoy contented, Abraham unsettled, for reasons he couldn't grasp. From the hall he heard a man's voice speaking Turkish, and Mrs Demirsoy replying, curtly at first and increasingly firmly as he seemed to persist.

Mr Demirsoy reached across the table and put his hand on Abraham's.

'Polis,' he whispered, and put a finger to his mouth.

Carefully he half stood, lifted his chair back from the table so that it made no sound, and with a glance at the door Abraham followed him, dazed, like a man who'd just been abruptly woken. Beyond the kitchen, screened off by a curtain, was a storeroom, and set in the far wall a small wooden door, a good size for a child. Mr Demirsoy opened it and impatiently ushered Abraham inside. Wooden steps led down into darkness. Abraham did his best to take them quietly and surely, crouching lower as he went; behind him came Mr Demirsoy, who closed the door and for a moment left them with no light at all. Then a click, and by the thin beam of a torch Abraham saw he was in a narrow cellar, the height of his shoulders and maybe three feet wide. Buckets and paint pots were piled on the floor, lengths of pipe and timber. There was nowhere to go. If anyone bothered to shine a light in here they were found.

'Here,' said Mr Demirsoy, and steered him by the elbow to the far end of the cellar. To their left was an external wall, bricked and finished; to the right, boxes and bottles and what looked like old phone directories were piled up on a ledge. Mr Demirsoy took one of the boxes and placed it on the floor, then another, and shining the torch through the gap that he'd made revealed a shallow space, at most a foot deep, between wooden floorboards and compacted earth. It ran under the whole house, and the torch barely reached its furthest limit.

'In here.'

Abraham looked at him and realized he had no choice.

Above their heads a door closed and footsteps sounded on wood. He crawled head first into the darkness, floorboards brushing against his back as he went further and further in, lips shut tight against the dust. Behind him Mr Demirsoy replaced the boxes and crept softly up the stairs; the door opened and closed and in the pure black Abraham kept going, as far in as he could, squeezing through the narrow points where the rough floor rose up. Now he was under the kitchen, most probably, now the sitting room, and as his eyes grew used to the darkness he saw pale shafts of light showing through the boards above. Finally he stopped, let his head drop down onto his forearms, and waited. The earth was cool on his skin, its heavy musty smell somehow comforting, and Abraham listened to his breath panting and his pulse racing and imagined them slowing, slowing, slowing to a stop. Not a bad place to be forgotten. Not a bad place to be buried. Somewhere nearby he thought he heard a scratching in the dust.

Two men, at least two, their solid clumping sometimes obscuring Mrs Demirsoy's tread altogether. They all seemed to go upstairs, and in two minutes they were back and in the room directly above, inches from Abraham's ear. He heard Mrs Demirsoy say something and then they all left and he followed the footsteps as they made their way round the edge of the house, into the kitchen, into the storeroom. The cellar door opened, as he knew it would, and now there was quite a lot of talking, so much that he began to think that they'd decided to move on; but they hadn't, they'd been waiting for a torch, and now one of them came down the steps, cursed in the near darkness as he hit his head on the low ceiling, and shone his torch round the cellar. Barely breathing, Abraham kept his head turned and watched the dim reflected light play on the earth below and the wood above. Something scratched in the dust again and he saw a grey mouse scuttle past, not a foot away from him. Don't give me away, he thought, but the searcher had seen all he wanted to see and was on his way back up.

'So you killed a devil?'

Mrs Demirsoy had left Abraham in the cellar for half an hour after the men had left, and from his hole underground he had listened to her talking quietly and urgently to her husband. He knew he must go. When night came he'd leave. Murat had said his papers should be ready by tomorrow, and then he'd be gone anyway – or detained at the border, one or the other. Even a night on the streets of Akçakale was better than the thought of bringing more trouble into this house.

'I'm so sorry. I never meant this. What did they say?'

'The idea of you a murderer. Dogs, they are, they make me rage. Look at our town. A thousand killers on our streets and they treat them like they are pashas. Who are they here to protect? A thousand killers and they pick a man who can't even control his own daughter.'

Abraham felt like he'd been lanced by those crystal blue eyes. What had she told these people?

'I wanted to say this but I did not. Before I give up a guest in my home I will decide if he is guilty.'

So Abraham was on trial. The three of them were in the storeroom, where the windows were too small and high for anyone to see in. Mrs Demirsoy stood in the doorway with her arms crossed; Mr Demirsoy was beside her, looking down at the floor and not taking sides.

'Thank you,' said Abraham, covered in dust and standing stiffly so that he didn't dirty the place any more than he already had.

'You may not thank me yet. Now. What is all this?'

'A man died in my hotel. In Antep. They pulled me from my bed and accused me.' Despite his innocence he was finding it hard to hold her eye. 'They need someone for the murder. I didn't do it.'

'How did he die?'

Abraham hesitated.

'I have seen more horror in my life than you, Abraham. I can look on horror.'

'His throat was cut.'

'You saw it?'

He nodded. 'I can see it now.'

'And they have met you, these police?'

'They questioned me, and put me in a cell.'

'They said you attacked a guard.'

Abraham shook his head and laughed at the banal horror of it.

'Yes. That was me, too.'

Mrs Demirsoy breathed deeply and nodded once, with emphasis, as if congratulating herself on her initial judgement.

'If you have ever so much as slaughtered a chicken I would be very surprised.'

He had no answer to that.

Until nightfall Abraham stayed in the storeroom. Mr Demirsoy brought him a cushion, and his phone, and the two Arabic books they had: a Koran and a guidebook to Damascus. When the curtains were drawn throughout the house he was allowed out, but not upstairs, since there was a window on the landing that couldn't be covered, and Mrs Demirsoy wasn't the type to take chances. That there were any policemen left in Akçakale after dark was as likely as Murat Felek doing anything for free, but the impossible was only impossible until it happened. The three of them ate, and as they ate she told Abraham how everything was going to work.

13

I count them when I come in. Nine women and five children, all girls. I asked Umm Karam how many there would be but she didn't know, and neither did the brother who drove me here.

They look dirty, like they haven't washed since they arrived, and tired. Every one of them has bags under her eyes, and none of them are veiled, though some of the women wear head-scarves. Their clothes are garish and need a wash, you can smell the old sweat on them as soon as you come through the door, and worse, and they make me realize how ordered the khilafa is and how used to it I've become. The colours they wear look so cheap and unnecessary. Arrogant, even, as if the way they look is more important than what God wants.

Most of the women must be in their fifties or sixties but through the dirt it's hard to say. The girls are young, tiny, inno-cent, confused – they've been through so much. The oldest is maybe eight, and she's the only one who's with her mother, a big woman, younger, with fat arms that hold her child foolishly, like they can protect her from anything. The rest are grand-mothers, I think. Probably their daughters and sons died in battle.

We're all lucky to be here. We all have a chance to save our-selves. But from how they're looking at me they don't see it that way – the children are sullen, the women full of a silent rage that they're doing their best to drill right into me. I feel like every new teacher must have done when she came into our class for the first time and all the idiots who'd never amount to anything would stare her out. What did they think she was there for if not for them? It used to drive me crazy, but it taught me how not to respond at least, and not for the first time I'm full of a sort of wonder at how He has quietly prepared me for my life in this place.

Yazidis. Pagans. Pagans! I almost shake my head. How can pagans still exist anywhere? Soon they will not, as we clear them from their lands.

I asked Umm Karam why they hadn't been killed. She has a look when she's thinking about the best response, it's not like she thinks I'm stupid, it's just that she's so far ahead of me, so full of knowledge and grace.

When we kill a sheep, she said, we do so knowing that it is one of God's creatures and should not die in vain. So we take the meat and we eat it or salt it. We eat the kidneys and the liver and the heart and the sweetbreads, the eyes, anything that will not injure us. We use the wool for clothes and we tan the skin for leather. The bones we boil for stock. At the end, God can look at us and say you have not wasted My creation.

It is the same with the Yazidis. We kill the men because that is war. The boys we teach the one true faith and train to fight. And the women, the strong and healthy ones, they meet our fighters' needs when they return from battle, or they are taken into our homes to do honest work, and the rest we must make use of as we can. The ones you will be teaching are the guts and the bones. They will require preparation and patience to yield anything of value, but we would rather not throw them away. The girls especially, they can grow up to be good Muslims and the khilafa needs all the future mothers it can get.

But they must be good Muslims. When we force them to convert at the edge of a sword their hearts remain unchanged and in a week they are wailing and disobeying and betraying us. So we are trying this new way.

Very good. You have two weeks to decide the fate of these people. You are a convert yourself, and know what it is to be born into the wrong faith. Succeed, and the khilafa will be stronger. Fail, and you will have hurt only yourself.

They're all sitting against the far wall on a mess of grubby blankets and some of them look close to sleep, it's so hot in here. The wind is up today and it's blowing heat and sand in through the broken glass of the two small windows. I unhook my veil, and very deliberately inspect each of the women and children in turn, not saying anything.

To me they look like Iraqis, but some have wild hair with blonde in it and eyes between blue and green. The youngest girl is maybe four, she's tiny, and you can tell just by looking at her that she hasn't been corrupted by the nonsense of her family's religion. Then there are two who are older who are on the verge of being sucked in. There's resentment in their faces but they've learned it from somewhere. The oldest girl is very beautiful, peering shyly at me from her mother's arms – or she would be beautiful after a wash, with clean hair, with the wildness combed out. I can see wisdom in her eyes, which seem to run deep into her, and I wonder whether she can see it in me. Here's something I can work with.

I try not to blink as I move from face to face, even though I am nervous, I realize. My future is on the line as well.

The first step is to see who speaks Arabic. According to Umm Karam some of them do, but not many, and no one in this group has admitted to it. It suits them to pretend even greater ignorance than they have.

'I am Umm Azwar,' I say. 'I am your teacher. You have a choice. A simple choice. You can convert to our faith. Or your children will be taken from you, and you will die.'

They all just stare. I try to work out who's in charge. In every group someone's in charge. One woman, the oldest, stares at me with her eyelids half shut so that I can't tell if she's close to sleep or just can't stand to look at me. Her face is yellow, wrinkled, unbelieving, a godless face, and her lazy eyes are like a snake's, watching and waiting. If these people really do worship Satan she might be the high priestess.

'Who speaks Arabic?'

I look from face to face, getting nothing. They're like kids in detention, sulking, refusing to engage.

'I know one of you does. Which one of you is it?'

One of them says something, not to me but to the floor, and the others mutter and make a sort of twittering noise. They're so primitive, like a troop of monkeys. I half expect them to start picking bugs out of their hair.

I tell them to be quiet and take my time.

'I know you understand me. Work with us, and this will be easy. You think this is as bad as it gets? It can always get worse. We can learn here together, or I will separate you and you will never see your children again. Talk it through. Don't dwell on what you've lost. Think about what you still have left.'

As I say it I keep my eyes on the old woman and the two others whose heads are still up, and all I see there is defiance. I almost admire their spirit, but it would be better for everyone if they had less of it.

I veil myself and walk slowly from the room, closing the door behind me. It's a steel door, this was some kind of storeroom, but the whole place is badly built and there's a gap between the wall and the corrugated iron roof and I wait in the corridor outside to listen. The two brothers are squatting down against the wall and take no notice of me. It must be hard for them, not being at the front. Having no noble purpose.

This place is disgusting, a mess. I don't know what it was, an old factory or workshop or something. There's one big long room that takes up almost the whole building, full of workbenches and machines that look like they've been stripped for parts or scrap, then a corridor with three smaller rooms off it, and a bathroom, which even with the wind blowing through the place stinks like you wouldn't believe. Some of the roof has been taken and there are weeds growing through the dirt floor. These women were captured five days ago but others have been held here – the stench is so bad and in the other rooms there are piles of clothes and suitcases and shoes, some women's, some men's. In town we have proper prisons for criminals awaiting trial but I guess that out here this is where we keep prisoners of war, the few we let live. They don't know how lucky they are in there.

I lean against the wall and listen. It takes them a while to start talking and when they do they're quiet at first, before the volume rises and they start really arguing. I don't need to know Yazidi, or whatever they speak, to know what they're saying. There's disagreement, and that's enough. If they hadn't understood a word I said they wouldn't have anything to disagree about. I let the talk peak and calm down before going back in.

The old woman is the only one looking at me now, and she just stares, without any urgency, from under those heavy eyelids.

I shout for one of the brothers, and just his presence changes the whole situation, there in his fatigues with his gun over his shoulder and that deadly lazy look in his eyes that so many brothers have. The old woman doesn't move a muscle but there's a general shrinking back amongst the rest, and the mother pulls her daughter close.

'You have made your choice. Today I will take one of your children, and they will be raised in a good Muslim family in the khilafa.' I watch them all so carefully as I talk. 'Tomorrow I will take another, and the next day one more.'

One woman can't help it. She's sitting by a girl with wild unbrushed hair and black eyes, and as I talk the fear grows on her face and she reaches out a hand and places it on the girl's shoulder. I've got her.

'You. What did I just say?'

Her eyes are full of fear but all she does is tighten her lips into a line and clutch her granddaughter harder.

'Why don't you explain it to your friends?'

She's paralysed. Even her skin looks tight across her bones.

'I'll take yours last. In five days' time.' I turn to the brother. 'Take the youngest girl.'

As he takes a step forward the women start to shout, at her and at me, and she hasn't got the strength for it. It's such a good feeling to have won.

'Don't!'

I hold my hand up and tell the brother to wait.

'Is that the only word you have?' I ask her, my hand still raised.

It takes her a moment to find the strength.

'No.'

'You have others?'

'I can speak it.'

Her voice is quiet, nervous. She's looking at the floor by my feet, maybe to avoid the stares of her friends. Without turning to them she says something in their tongue, and I let them settle again.

'You've explained?'

She nods, and as she glances up at me I get a glimpse of the hatred and resentment in her eyes. If she only knew the wonders I will open up to her!

14

— believe I will come soon sister, no more delay.

— I have been trying sister but the journey is more difficult than it appears

if it was easy what would be point in making it? thru struggle we know Him swt.

— when I am there can I see you?

if you make it of course

Khalil is away fighting but I'm busy with work

i have new job, getting some pagan women ready for conversion

— seriously?

yazidis sister, they're crazy it's a real challenge

— that sounds good for you

it's going to be hard but an honour, so important for the khilafa

— you will be good to them I'm sure

also remember you'll be in makkar to start with but maybe I can come one evening or just get married quickly! sure you will

— probably I am there next week I will tell you when I arrive

inshallah you have a smooth journey sister

— any last advice?

bring good moisturiser! I bought mine here it's really greasy lol

15

His first night at the Demirsoys, Abraham had slept like a stone, a rock, a boulder. Now he skittered about on the surface of his unconscious, thoughts bouncing between the police and Sofia, the path to her clear and terrifying. He would soon be on his way, to the city that sat in his thoughts like the black shadow of a recurring dream.

When the banging woke him he was sitting up and listening in an instant, as if he had been waiting for it. Four hard, certain knocks, almost immediately another four, then footsteps going down the stairs. In the dark, Abraham got up and heard Mrs Demirsoy muttering to herself before she shot the two bolts back and opened the front door on its chain. She snapped something in Turkish, but the reply came in Arabic.

'Open the door.'

'Of course. Of course I will open the door. You must all come in.'

The door closed with a bang, and Mrs Demirsoy let them knock for half a minute before she opened it again, still on the chain.

'Stop your noise. And don't tell me to do stupid things. Then you can explain what you are doing, waking an old woman and the whole street in the middle of the night.'

Across the landing, Mr Demirsoy had appeared in his pyjamas, and now he gave Abraham a look that was half fearful, half abashed. He should go and help, but his help would make things worse.

'Open the door, or I'll break it down.'

'For devils you are very stupid. We can talk like this, and then you can go away. Now tell me what you want.'

There was a pause, and in it Abraham imagined what was about to happen. The time had come. The end had come. He reached for the light and began to dress.

Mrs Demirsoy's voice came from downstairs, shrill with impatience.

'There is no one here. You people see phantoms everywhere.'

'He killed one of our men.'

'And you killed one of his no doubt. Everyone kills everyone now.'

'Why would you protect a murderer?'

Abraham slipped on his shoes and started to tie them.

'Murderer my foot. The only man in the house is my husband, and though he'll die soon he doesn't need to now.'

'Old woman, please. I don't want to hurt you. I don't even want to hurt your door. If you're telling the truth just open up and let us look around.'

Mrs Demirsoy clucked with irritation.

'I'm going back to bed now.'

'He slit his throat. From here to here. You want a man like that in your house?'

Abraham stepped out onto the landing and walked to the top of the stairs. It took a moment for Mr Demirsoy to notice the movement, and now he stepped forward to stop him, holding an arm out and shaking his head. His eyes were insistent: not yet, wait, give her a chance. Abraham looked down at the tiny figure by the door, and back at her husband, and nodded. Another minute, that was all. These poor people had given enough.

Mrs Demirsoy was standing so her face couldn't be seen through the crack, leaning forward, head up and alert as ever.

'Who did he kill?'

'A comrade, a fighter, in Antep. Slit his throat.'

'What does he look like?'

'He's an Egyptian. That's all I know. I haven't seen him.'

Mrs Demirsoy paused, glancing up at Abraham as if she had known he was there all along.

'That was him.'

'What do you mean?'

'What do you think I mean? He was here.'

'When?'

'An Egyptian. Yesterday night. It was dark so I didn't let him in.'

'What time?'

'Eight. I don't let anyone in after dark. I asked him where he was from because his Arabic was strange, and he said Egypt. Cairo. And he was a rough creature, dirty, with a look in his eye I didn't like. I knew I was right. My instincts are always right.'

'What did he say?'

'Some lies, I don't know. I told him to try the hotel or to pray to God that the mosque might have him. My instincts are always right. The police came for him today and I said to my husband, you see, that's the kind of person you want to bring into our house. He always wants the money but I tell him what use is money when our throats are slit? A hundred lira and the two of us dead in our beds. That's what I said, when our throats are slit. And I had no idea. Allah the most glorified must have put the thought in my head. It makes me shiver to think of it.'

'If you're lying . . .'

'You are a fool. I'm too old to lie. When you're young you think God doesn't see your lies but when you're as old as I am you might as well lie straight to Him. Now let me sleep. Not that I'll sleep now, not for hours, and I have you to thank for that.'

'If you see him again—'

'If I see him I'll take him in and when you come again you can break down the door because I won't be alive to stop you. You people are idiots. Your poor country will need better to set it free.'

Without waiting for a reply, she slammed the door shut, slid the bolts into place and stood for a moment with her head up and her eyes closed. Then with a sort of shudder she came to, muttered something to herself in Turkish and marched up the stairs, looking Abraham up and down as she passed him.

'Where are you going? Don't be ridiculous. Goodnight. Omer will wake you at dawn.'

16

At daybreak, a sleepy and silent Mr Demirsoy drove Abraham through the town and out onto the plains towards the rising sun. He had checked the surrounding streets and if anyone was about they were too well hidden for him to see.

Akçakale looked peaceful to Abraham for the first time; they were the only people about and it was easy enough to imagine life here before the trouble, as Mrs Demirsoy called it. The light was soft, the air still and fresh, the place full of promise. The trees held their slowly browning leaves. On their way out of town they drove past the camp, the endless tents like bubble wrap, and after ten minutes turned north onto a stony track that slowly rose to what in this level landscape constituted a hill. By a thick line of cedar trees Mr Demirsoy stopped the car.

'Land,' he said, with a possessive sweep of his arm.

Abraham took his bags from the back seat and looked across at the town. From this point it was all so clear. North of the border, Akçakale, south of it, Tell Abyad, the two separated by a tall chain fence and a few hundred yards of no man's land on either side. Clustered on the Syrian side were cars, trucks, cattle and people, waiting for the gate to open.

Mr Demirsoy tapped Abraham on the shoulder and led him past the wall of trees, which leaned and rustled in the steady wind. On the other side and bounded to the north and west by the cedars was a huge kitchen garden, laid out in well-tended rows. An immense area for one old man to tend. Most of it had been harvested but Abraham saw cabbages, potatoes, leeks, beans growing up cane frames. Some of the rows had been freshly ploughed for sowing, their soil darker and softer than the rest.

Mr Demirsoy had taken a key from his pocket and was standing by the door of a shed that somehow Abraham knew he had built himself. The walls were made of planks of dark wood laid not end to end but on their side, so that the whole building felt solid; to call it a shed didn't seem quite right. The door was five lengths of greying pine that had split and warped over the decades it must have stood here, and above it sat a gabled roof that sagged a little at the sides but was otherwise intact. A single window, unglazed, was covered with iron bars that looked as if they too had been bent into place by this one man.

Inside, the air was cool and smelled of earth and compost and the musty boxes of chemicals that sat on one of the countless shelves. Such organization; Abraham marvelled at it. Tools hanging in their place from nails set into the walls, brooms to the left, then spades and shovels, hoes, forks, trowels, secateurs, saws, all aged and shaped by long use. Seeds in their packets lined up and labelled. Neatly rolled lengths of plastic and netting against the far wall. Thick paper bags full of potatoes and onions on the floor.

'Wait,' said Mr Demirsoy, and left. When he came back he had bags in each hand and a bedroll under one arm.

'Here,' he said, and handed it all to Abraham. 'Home.'

Sheets and blankets in one bag, neatly folded, and in the other parcels of food and paper bags full of fruit.

'Teşekkür ederim.'

Abraham nodded gravely as he said it. He wasn't sure he'd ever been as grateful to anyone for anything, certainly not a stranger, and tears rose at the unimaginable kindness of it – but he checked them, more for Mr Demirsoy's sake than his own.

Mr Demirsoy took a knife from the wall, cut off a length of plastic sheeting, laid it out carefully on the floor and waited for

Abraham to lay his mattress on it. Then together they made the bed, tucking in the sheets and the blankets down each side.

'Is no . . .' Mr Demirsoy pressed his palms together and tilted his head onto his hands.

'Pillow.' Abraham smiled. 'I'll be fine.'

Mr Demirsoy looked around the shed, nodded with satisfaction and beamed at Abraham.

'Good here. Come.'

Between the shed and the cedars was a water trough and a tap on a standpipe. He turned it on and after a second or two a trickle of water came out.

'Good for this.' He splashed it on his face. 'But no drink.'

'What can I do for you? While I am here. What work needs to be done?'

When Mr Demirsoy understood, he held a finger up and led him round the edge of the field to its far corner, where a barn stood, thin planks attached to a wooden frame, a less finished construction than the shed. Behind its double doors was a wheelbarrow, a cart, some sort of seed-sowing machine and a rusted metal contraption that he began to pull outside. It looked like one half of a scrapped bicycle: two long bars in a V, a spoked wheel where they met, and behind that a crude curving blade like the prow of some ancient ship. A hand plough, so well worn it might have been medieval. Mr Demirsoy left it on the ground outside the barn, took Abraham up one side of the field and with great care explained that those rows had been ploughed, and those harvested, but these in the middle all needed to be turned over.

Of course, said Abraham, already too indebted to ask how the thing worked.

By ten, left alone with the land and the sun, Abraham had found a sort of rhythm. The soil was heavy and full of stones and the blade too blunt and rough to glide right through it; with a horse or a motor he might have left the bit in the ground and watched the thing go but he hadn't the strength for that, so he devised a dipping action, driving in, pulling back a little, driving in again. Sixteen rows, and the first took him a full hour. The sun pressed down on his back and tried to find its way through the sun hat he'd fashioned from a pair of boxer shorts and the cap he'd found in the shed. Sweat dripped from him. Push in, pull back, go on. Sofia should do this. We should all do this. Maybe this was what she had gone to find. Honest work uncorrupted by the world.

Thought left him, and soon there was only the heat, and the flat rows ahead, and the dark earth newly crumbled at his feet.

17

I texted Khalil last night to tell him I was thinking of becoming a Yazidi, but he got quite worried and I had to tell him it was only a joke. He sounds tired. Only three days until he's back, and every moment seems like a week. Three Kurds, he has killed! Three he knows about, it could be more. Yesterday he was part of a troop that used the wind and the sandstorm to ambush this house on the Peshmergas' front line where their snipers had been based. That's the weather they were waiting for. So clever! He's going to tell me exactly what happened when we see each other and how I long to hear every second, every detail. I'm so proud, imagining him there, hidden by the dust, gun across his chest, not an atom of fear in him. And I so want him to be proud of me.

I must remember not to crowd him when I see him. I'll want to cover him in kisses and smother him with attention but after what he's been through he'll need time.

I send something about the Yazidis to Irene but she doesn't reply.

My phone rings. I don't know the number, and I have this strange feeling, for no reason, that it's going to be some kind of intrusion from my old life. I look at the phone as if it's some kind of impostor before I answer.

It's Umm Karam. She's never phoned me before, and hearing her voice comes as a relief, first of all, but then she says she wants to come and see me and that rocks me a little. Has she heard something about my first day with the Yazidis? Who could have told her?

I tell her that I wasn't planning to leave for another hour at least and of course, she is always welcome in my home. Then I make sure everything is super tidy and wait, my thoughts going this way and that and preventing me from reading, even. Finally, I write out my lesson plan in case she wants to discuss it, and as I'm finishing it she arrives.

Badra is with her. They come in and unveil, and Umm Karam smiles. Badra nods, like she does. I lead them into the sitting room. Umm Karam has a way of seeming to glide under her niqab, and her face is the same, somehow, always calm and unmoved. It's impossible to imagine her getting worked up.

I ask if they'd like tea and she says no. We sit, and for a moment she just looks at me with the same kind, wise, almost blank expression.

'I have news for you, my sister.'

The way she says it I think it must be good, and I almost feel nervous at the luck being heaped on me. I'm sitting on the edge of the armchair, expectant, and I don't say anything.

But something changes in her eyes, something most people wouldn't notice, something I wouldn't notice if I wasn't trying desperately to read every sign. I'm sure I see sympathy there, and straight away it makes me panic, my heart goes up into my throat. I manage to say his name. It's not even a question.

'Khalil.'

She nods. 'Khalil.'

I close my eyes and all I can see is his sweet innocent face the day he went back to battle, so strong and young. There was no mark on that face. Allah had not marked him out, I knew it! I felt sure I couldn't see it on him, that I had some special power to read his future, that he would be back. That he would be different. That we would.

'When?'

'Last night. A rocket to the house he was in. He died with one other brother.'

'Peshmerga?'

'American.'

I know how it looked. The explosion, the burst of flame, the crumbling of brick and tiles, the dust and the shouting and Khalil inside it all, blind to his brothers screaming and searching for him, finally at peace. The finger of some kafir pig pressing the launch button and the rocket firing through the air to do no more real damage than send my lion to his rightful place in Paradise, to sit by the side of Allah, the most glorified, the most high. The Americans do not realize that we are stronger in death. I see him there, happy, free of the pains and torment of this world, his work done, blessed by the love of the one true God.

I see all this in an instant, and my heart feels like it has truly been split in two. One half mourns, the other rejoices. My lion, my lamb.

Umm Karam has leaned forward and taken my hands in hers. I barely notice.

'The greatest death of all is to die for jihad,' she says, her eyes piercing mine.

'And to be the widow of a jihadi the greatest honour.'

Badra is looking at me with proper sympathy, I can see it in her eyes.

'If I was not married to an imam, I should wish it for myself.'

It is not a worthy thought but right now I wish Khalil had

been an imam, that his battleground had been the spirit and not the body that is weak and fails. I am more proud of him than I have ever been, but I don't think I'm ready to let him go. Twelve days! Twelve sweet sweet days are all I have spent with him. And one of those was really only half a day. I do not question His wisdom but how I wish it could have been doubled. To have spent even a few hours more together would have been the greatest blessing.

He is a martyr, but he was my husband. I am tossed up and down between Paradise and hell.

'You will survive this, my child. We will support you.'

Her warmth and her practicality bring me to myself. I think I'm crying, but these few tears are so few and so controlled that they're the same as the driest eyes. They do no good, nor any bad. I breathe, deep and slow, the air catches in my throat but I just keep breathing, in and out, and soon I manage a nod and a smile that is not a smile.

Umm Karam smiles back. For a moment I think she is going to hug me but she doesn't, and thank goodness because I'm not sure I could take it.

'I will take you to your work, and when you return tonight Badra will help you with your things.'

I don't know which part to try to take in first. Of course I should work, what else would I do, just sit here and mourn? I cannot let myself descend into that prison of self-pity. That makes sense.

I thank her and ask her what she means about my things. Badra answers.

'You cannot stay here now. A widowed woman cannot live on her own.'

I try to be strong, but I realize that almost without thinking it I have imagined being here, with him, letting his spirit go slowly from me. I need it. A little more time with him.

'Just tonight.'

Umm Karam shakes her head. The line is clear.

'We must move you tonight. You will like the place. There are other widows there. And then in time, when you have grieved, you can marry again.'

18

The words come out of me that day but I don't hear them. I like to think they're guided by Him, the most glorified, but maybe they're just nonsense, nothing, the dust of my grief. And maybe the women don't notice or care.

Two things happen that day, neither good. The old woman, Emina, she challenges me. That wakes me up. When I finally get Besma to translate what she's said I find out that what I thought were little pieces of encouragement were terrible blasphemies, some of them I couldn't bring myself to say. She's been calling me a liar, and a she-devil, and a hypocrite, which in their basic stupid language is she whose heart fights her tongue.

I don't argue with her. I'm sending her out of the room when I hear shouting outside and three brothers come in. It takes me a while to place them but they're Russians, they speak Arabic with a weird accent and Russian with themselves, I recognize the niets and das.

I'm wary of them, straight away, the moment they come in the room. They treat me like I'm nothing, and most brothers don't do that – they may not show respect but they know we're in this together. Not these ones. There's something wild and alien about them, like someone's kept them in a dark room their whole lives and the rules they play by aren't our rules, aren't anybody's rules. They have pale skin like animal fat and bad teeth. I know I shouldn't react to them like this. Honestly, they scare me.

The leader – God has blessed most brothers, you can see the

blessing on them, but not this one. His black beard is patchy, I can see the whitest pockmarked skin underneath. He leers at me like a dog, showing his shining teeth, and from instinct I step back. I almost pity the enemies that have to face him.

They've come for women, but when they see there are only girls and grandmothers they lay into me like it's my fault, then one of them starts on Niran, touching her face, running his fingers down her arm. She takes it. She's terrified, watches him like he's a scorpion, but knows she has to sit still and do nothing to provoke him. Her mother keeps her hand on her shoulder and she's looking at me like I should do something. I want to pull him off her but that would be the worst thing.

How old is she, he wants to know. I tell him eight. You sure she's not nine? She must be lying, she's clearly old enough. Either she's lying to you or you're lying to me. How do you know she's eight anyway? None of these kafirs have papers. It's bullshit.

I tell him to watch his language and for a moment there's a stand-off, and then the leader loses interest. Leave the girl, he says, and the fighter stares at me, squeezes Niran's chin in his great fist, stands up and yanks her mother up by the hand.

Old but okay for now, he says, and marches from the room, dragging her screaming behind him. As the leader leaves he holds his gun up and silently sprays it across us all, back and forth, laughing.

That night Badra comes to help me move. She doesn't smile, or offer me any sympathy, but there's a softness about her I haven't seen before. I wonder if she's remembering the day her husband died, or knows I'm suffering like she did. Both, I guess. We don't say much, but there's an understanding between us and it feels like the only silver lining on this dark dark cloud of a day.

I pack my things, and she sorts out the kitchen, empties the fridge, makes sure everything's in good order. Then I find some black sacks and take everything from Khalil's drawers and stuff it all in. I can hardly bear to look at it, let alone touch it, I just want it to be gone. One T-shirt I take. The black one, his favourite, with Islamic State written across the front in bold white letters. He looked so handsome in that.

In the wardrobe there's one smart jacket and his father's thawb, the one he was married in. The jacket goes, but I take the thawb from its hanger and fold it carefully until it's a neat square. As I'm opening my suitcase Badra comes in, sees me, and stands for a moment watching me repack and then zip the case.

'You should leave that.'

This isn't stern Badra. She's not telling me off, she's giving me advice.

I don't reply, I just look at her.

'It is easier to forget. Really.'

'I don't think I can forget.'

'Your pain now is healthy pain. But in dark times it can be bad to look back at the light.'

19

How quickly a man could forge a routine. Rise early, and walk in search of a signal to check his phone. Find nothing, breakfast on crackers and water, work until the heat grew unbearable, then lunch and a doze in the shade of the shed, because by noon it was too hot to be inside it. A phone run, then work and food and finally the phone again, carefully switching it off after each attempt to preserve its precious charge.

The day was hard, and he came to relish it. The pain in his arms and legs, the headaches, the drops into that habitual fear he couldn't remember being without – while he was gripping the plough and the sweat was running from him and his heart was going hard in his chest, all that might never have existed. He began to feel strong, like he could accomplish things. The future was no longer something that needed to be dodged. What might the last ten years have been if he had learned this sooner?

He saw no one; he was alone on his plot. The noises from the road a mile away reminded him that the world was still there, and on the third evening it came for him. A text from Murat, telling him to be ready to make the crossing the next day.

20

sister he's gone my precious boy my beautiful man

— what do you mean sister? gone where?

to Paradise, to sit alongside our God swt

— sister I am sorry

i wish i could join him

— don't say that sister, you don't mean it

never meant anything more but i won't, not what He swt wants for me

— who's with you sister?

no one i'm in the widows' house

— stay safe sister

you always say that, why? why do you say that?

— I don't know

you need to stop. safe isn't important, He swt doesn't care about safe

Khalil wasn't safe but now he sits in glory in Paradise

— just worried there's no one to look after you

i don't need looking after i have Him swt that's all i need

— everyone needs someone

worried about you sister. i have someone, i have a whole family, the khilafa is a family and i have Allah the most glorified the most high

— Okay good sister as long as someone is there for your grief. I am sorry.

don't be sorry it's His will swt

— of course. Still I will think of you.

21

Abraham was woken by a dull sense of noise outside the shed, tyres crunching slowly on stones, and as he opened his eyes he saw the trees briefly lightening through the window. A car door slammed shut, and footsteps started in the dust. He didn't need to consider his options to know he didn't have any.

Arms feeling in front of him, he went to the wall by the door and reached for a tool of some kind from the dozens hanging there, setting them knocking against each other in the near silence. He came away with something, a hoe by the length and weight of it, and stood in the crook of the door with his mouth as dry as the field he'd been ploughing all day. The muscles in his arms ached as they tensed.

But whoever this was, they were in no hurry, and the

footsteps took their time before stopping just outside. In the silence Abraham closed his eyes and forced his breath to come slow. Then a polite knock, one two three, like a neighbour worried about intruding.

'Abraham.'

That voice. He knew the voice.

'Abraham. Sorry to disturb. Please. Open door.'

Please God. Why couldn't anything be simple?

Resting the hoe against the wall, he opened the door and stood back a pace. Vural was there, the dim silhouette of his form against the little light outside.

'Hello, Abraham. Is good to see you.'

Abraham nodded in the darkness.

'You have light here?'

'No.'

'Come. To car, there is light. Sit.'

'I'm not coming with you.'

The familiar sound of Vural sniffing.

'I can force. But okay.'

Checking each of his pockets, he finally found his phone, switched on its torch, and swept it across the shed.

'Nice. Nice room this is. You are farmer now?'

'How did you know I was here?'

'Please, Abraham, I can sit? We must talk.'

Abraham knelt down, straightened out his bed and gestured for Vural to join him on his bedroll. With a groan Vural sat, holding his knees and ending up awkwardly cross-legged with the phone's light shining on the patch of sheet between them. He smelled of garlic and his breath was sour in the clean cold air, but Abraham was strangely comforted by him being there. After a pause and a sniff, he spoke.

'Abraham, what you do? Why not go home?'

'I don't have anything else.'

'Is stupid move. Stupid move. Here police want you, Syrians want you. Now London police want you too. You know this?'

Abraham didn't answer. He didn't. He hadn't thought about London for days.

'You go home when I say, you okay – but no, you come back, you are like cat in the night and now even London police want your head.'

Abraham shrugged. He had given his explanation.

'Okay, my friend, here is facts. Before, there was choice. You go on, you go back. Now choice is you go on or police find you here.'

'Why are you threatening me?'

'Not threat, facts.'

'Okay. I go on.'

'To Raqqa?'

'Of course.'

'And in Raqqa you talk to me. Yes?'

So we were back here.

'I'm not joining them.'

'You want your daughter, no other way.'

Lit dimly from below, Vural's face looked severe, stony. His rheumy eyes were now black, and Abraham could see no way round him.

'How did you find me?'

'In Akçakale, good market for secrets. Only market now.'

Murat. Or one of Murat's friends. Or one of their friends, God knew, but it wasn't good.

'Talk to you how?'

'You SMS. I will tell you what I want to know.'

'They'll check my phone.'

'Delete as you send. But they all use their phones, all the time. Abraham, they are clever. But they are stupid also.'

Vural was smiling now. It was meant to be a charming smile.

'Will be good work, Abraham. Useful work.'

Abraham looked down at his hands, clean now but for the neat lines of black soil under the nails. The hands of a chemist turned fugitive now spy.

22

Two o'clock, was the rendezvous. Abraham let the Demirsoys know, and by noon he was waiting with his bag packed and the last row finally dug, looking across the field with a certain pride in the order he had left; if he achieved nothing else he had at least achieved this.

Keep your arrangements, Vural had told him. They seem fine. And true, real, they will believe, this is good. Before leaving with as little fuss as he had appeared, he had given Abraham a telephone number and a clutch of advice – beard long, trousers short, pray all the time – and that was it. No support, no escape route, no tricks of the trade. What should I do if something goes wrong, Abraham had asked. If I had power there I wouldn't need you, was the answer; but if I can help get you out I will do whatever I can.

As he watched the old white car shaking up the track, throwing out dust behind it, he saw that Mrs Demirsoy had come too, no doubt with food and advice; and as they drew near, that a second car had just turned off the road a quarter of a mile behind them. A tan 4x4, of the kind that sat on the street corners of Akçakale and Gaziantep with fighters inside.

He stared at it stupidly for a second, then came to; ran to the shed, threw his bag inside, and took an old spade from the rack by the door, the heaviest thing he could see. Out of sight of the track he waited for the Demirsoys to reach him. They weren't quick. Mr Demirsoy parked the car carefully, and Mrs Demirsoy needed to retrieve a bag from the boot, and as they walked towards the shed Mrs Demirsoy began to shout Abraham's name in a puzzled tone, wondering why he had been there one minute and the next had disappeared. Abraham closed his eyes and prayed that they would hurry. By the time they rounded the corner the second car was pulling in behind theirs, and Mr Demirsoy was turning to notice it for the first time. As he stood and frowned, his wife and Abraham exchanged a single look of understanding, and Abraham darted behind the shed.

Two car doors opened and closed, but he only heard one voice, raised against the wind.

'Where's your friend, old man?'

'She is my wife.'

'You're very funny. Now tell me.'

'I don't understand.'

'Sure.' Then, in a different tone: 'Find him.'

'You people are crazy.'

Mrs Demirsoy had walked round to confront them. Abraham could picture her, arms crossed, staring fiercely. Her voice was imperious.

'You. Are you the one who came to my house? Didn't you hear me then?'

'I heard your lies, mother. Get out of my way.'

There was nowhere to hide out here. In the barn, in the shed, or behind the shed in the angle of the trees, where he was now. Immersed in the trough of muddy water next to him. Abraham looked out at the bare horizon through the line of cedars that bordered the plot and wondered how far he would get. Yards, at most. There was no cover, and he felt his shoulders tighten at the thought of the bullet in his back.

Christ, where were they? He couldn't look without being seen and the wind was blowing too hard in the trees for him to hear footsteps. Even Mrs Demirsoy had gone quiet. Standing with his back to the wooden wall, spade raised, he watched the corner and prayed that neither had thought to come up behind him.

The shed door opened. He heard it, and he felt it through the wood. Here was a chance; for once, just take the fucking chance. With a deep breath he made his decision, stepped to the end of the wall, and saw away on the other side of the field a man in fatigues with his gun held up walking towards the barn. Abraham moved silently to the doorway, saw a figure inside with his back to him; raised the spade behind his head and brought it down with all the strength he could find. In that moment by some instinct the man turned and the spade caught him on the neck and jaw. Abraham saw his face crease and distort, felt the power of the blow in the crack it made, hit him again as his knees buckled from the shock so that he sprawled forward heavily, his arms still by his side, his face in the dirt. God, such a weight to him, he seemed to rattle the floor as he went down. Appalled, electrified, past regret, Abraham readied himself again but it wasn't necessary. The man was out. Blood began to pool in the corner of his open mouth. Dropping the spade, Abraham squatted down to pick up the gun that his fingers still loosely held.

Across the field the barn door was open and there was no sign of anyone; at the top of the track Mr Demirsoy was reversing his car into a turn. Only when Abraham saw Mrs Demirsoy next to him – her little mouth open and silent, watching the scene as she might some collision she was too old and too slow to avoid – only then did he become aware of himself, of his dry mouth and the pain in his throat where the sides seemed to be clamped together, of the insanity of the life he had fallen into. A chemist, a man of inaction, standing in no man's land with a price on his head and a meaningless gun out in front of him. He had never shot a gun. Never held one. Strange, how it could feel so alien and yet sit so comfortably in his grip.

He raised a hand to her as he ran. It meant goodbye, and sorry, I never meant any of this to happen, and go, get out of here as quickly as you can. But she didn't seem to register it.

Her eyes were on something behind him, and now she turned to shout at Mr Demirsoy, who was trying to find first gear, grinding the gearbox. Please hurry. Please go. Abraham ran behind them to the 4x4, opened the door, and in the moment that he saw there was no key heard a shot sound and the window by him crack and splinter. By instinct he ducked away and turned to see the other fighter running clumsily over the ploughed earth, maybe fifty yards away, gun for the moment by his side again. He could be the second man from his hotel room that night, the one who had done the searching while his friend had pinned Abraham to the wall. He had the same cap, the same build.

Feet skating on the dust, Abraham swung himself behind the 4x4, and as he did so the car lurched forward with a rattle. A second shot hit the metalwork of the jeep with the same flat finality. He willed the Demirsoys on their way. Fate would run its course, and they weren't part of it. Besides, fate had evened things up. He had a gun, and he had the advantage. He had something to hide behind.

'Get in.'

From behind the bumper he saw Mrs Demirsoy's face looking at him, as exasperated and as sure as it had ever been.

'Go. God, would you go?'

'I will not. Language.'

Next to her Mr Demirsoy was watching the field and the man charging across it, seconds from them now.

Her eyes decided it. She wasn't going to move.

Abraham stood, aimed the gun past the car at the fighter, and pulled the trigger. The blast forced his arms into their sockets and knocked him back, but he was ready for it and in an instant he was running to the car and pulling at the handle and firing again at the figure crouching all of thirty yards away in the earth.

'His tyres!' shouted Mrs Demirsoy. 'Shoot his tyres, you idiot.'

Half hanging out of the car, with the door flapping as Mr Demirsoy drove off, Abraham took aim at the nearest wheel and fired; missed, and fired again, and the tyre collapsed. He steadied himself to try a second wheel but they were too far away and the car was bouncing and then he was recoiling from a third shot, not his, that shattered the driver's window and sprayed glass all over Mr Demirsoy and sent the car jumping across the track onto the rougher ground at the verge. Mrs Demirsoy screamed, and Mr Demirsoy's head slumped onto his chest, and sliding across the back seat Abraham felt beside the terror a sort of stabbing helplessness, even in the chaos and the noise and the speed of it all, the strongest urge to pick these two innocents up and set them down a long way away, beyond the reach of this vicious world that now seemed to be his. The car carried on, jolting over rocks and ruts and beginning to slow, one door still hanging open like a broken limb, and while Mrs Demirsoy reached for the steering wheel with one hand and held the other to her husband's face, Abraham managed to twist round and look back at the fighter who was standing at the top of the track, feet set, both hands holding his gun motionless before him.

The back windscreen shattered. Tiny pieces of glass showered him, scoured his face and arms. More to put up a fight than to accomplish anything he tried to steady himself and take aim, return some fire at least, but the car gathered speed and changed direction and sent him sprawling over the seat towards the open door. He grabbed at a seat belt, managed to steady himself, and when he looked up saw that Mr Demirsoy was in charge again, head down between his shoulders and his eyes just over the steering wheel, but driving, and muttering Turkish under his breath, taking the car back onto the track. Blood was staining his collar.

'Silly goat,' said Mrs Demirsoy, leaving her hand on his shoulder.

Another two shots; the first hit the metal of the boot, and the second either sailed clean through or missed altogether. Abraham rested his hands on the back seat and tried to aim, but he didn't shoot; he wouldn't hit anything, not at this distance, and in any case the fighter had given up, and was running to his car.

Now they were halfway to the road. Abraham had time to register the heat, and the glare from the sun, and the emptiness all around. No one was going to help them as these people had helped him. Who would help them?

He looked along the road to Akçakale, looked back up the track, and tried to gauge how long they had before they were caught. Mr Demirsoy was still muttering, and his hands were tight on the wheel. He was leaning forward with a concentration Abraham hadn't seen in him before; but the car was old, and disintegrating, and behind them the 4x4 had turned in a wide circle, ignoring the verge, and was racing down at them, clouds of dust rising in its wake, back end squirming on its one good tyre.

Mr Demirsoy slowed at the junction with the road, and looked carefully left, then right, then left again, so slowly that he had to wait to let a truck laden with watermelons amble past on its way to the town. Abraham saw the fear in his eyes and would have done anything to ease it. Imagine how many times they had made this same journey at their own pace, the boot laden with lettuces and courgettes, Mrs Demirsoy talking, Mr Demirsoy half listening and half not. Now they were silent, and the 4x4 was so close that Abraham could hear its engine screaming; it wasn't slowing, it was going to shunt them across the road, nose first into the ditch, and while they struggled to get out the fighter would come and calmly shoot them, if they weren't dead already. With the same care, Mr Demirsoy made sure nothing was coming and finally turned, so late that Abraham braced himself for the 4x4 clipping their bumper and sending them spinning forward. But sedately the car settled onto the tarmac, and through the back window Abraham watched as the 4x4 braked too late on the dust and stones, started to veer and spun across the road; it seemed to stop there, caught in time for an instant, and then with a great crunching, tearing sound it crumpled, and splintered, caught like a steer on a cowcatcher by the cab of the eighteen-wheeler that was shunting it down the road, helpless and ruined, away from Akçakale.

Like a thunderclap it was everything and then it was gone. In shock, Abraham watched the scene recede, scarcely believing it; then he faced the front, and closed his eyes, and let out a breath that seemed to come deep from the earth beneath.

'By the heavens what was that noise?' said Mrs Demirsoy, twisting a little in her seat and catching Abraham's eye. She hadn't seen it. Possibly she had had no idea they were being chased.

'An accident.'

'Nothing happens for years and then everything happens.'

'Are you all right?'

'I'm fine. I'm quite all right. He, he is a mess, but this is normal.'

She dusted his shoulder, and with a look she let Abraham know that if he asked her again he would regret it.

23

With the Yazidis I feel like a lion roaring at a herd of goats and hoping that if I roar loud enough they'll become lions too. All I have is the roar, and the threat of my bite, and although I try my hardest that's not enough. Faith, faith will make the bridge, and when I'm at my lowest, and all I can hear is their bleating, on and on, with no sign that I'm getting through, I just keep going, knowing that He would not have sent me here unless it was to accomplish something with meaning.

I breathe slowly and will myself to concentrate. Niran is the key to this. Since her mother went away she's been pale and lifeless, like she's suffering from some illness, the light has gone from her eyes, and I know that the only chance she has of salvation is me.

Today is day seven. We're on Zakat – charity – and I can feel my enthusiasm building. I'm in the flow, He's guiding me, but then this is one of my favourite things, perhaps the best one of all. How amazing is it, I ask them, that every Muslim has to give – and is happy to give – a percentage of everything she earns to those who have nothing? What other religion does the same? Not Christianity. Not Judaism. Does your religion say anything so simple, so powerful, so pure? I have them here. Usually old Emina has something to say but this shuts even her up. What did you do for your poor and your sick, I ask her. The sick we tended, she said, and the poor, we were all poor.

As I begin to tell her that there's a reason for that, that they've been forsaken by the one true God, the door opens. I'm expecting a guard but it's someone I don't recognize, which means that I've been so deep in my teaching that I didn't hear anyone arrive, as I usually would.

He's a brother but brother is the wrong word for him. He looks different. Even the way he stands is like no other brother, like he's never been afraid of anything.

He's also paler, the palest man I've ever seen. His skin is white white, except under his eyes where there are dark bags, and his beard is the same colour as wood that's just been cut. He's wearing a long white dishdasha that stops just below his knees and white puttees above his black combat boots, the only dark thing on him. He has no gun. One or two brothers have frightened me, I'll admit it, but it's because there's a craziness about them that they need for the battlefield and can't always contain. This man isn't crazy, he's containing a great power and the moment I see him my breath goes tight. I do my best not to look away from his burning green eyes.

I start to veil myself but he shakes his head and somehow I know he doesn't want me to stop what I'm doing, that he's come to watch, standing a yard inside the door with his arms crossed against his solid chest. Two brothers have appeared behind him, the Russians from yesterday. He nods, once, as if to tell me to carry on, but my head's empty. The women seem to have shrunk back towards the wall and are just watching him, not making any noise now, and that thought helps me. I have nothing to fear. He is one of us. I am one of us. The kafirs have every reason to be scared, but I don't.

So I start again. Not quite where I left off. No one of the five pillars is greater than any other, I say, but Zakat is indispensable, and no Muslim would ever think to . . . all Muslims are happy in their hearts to know that their faith is supported . . .

My flow has gone. Besma translates even more hesitantly than usual, as if she's caught it from me, and her unease distracts me further, and I find myself concentrating on her Yazidi words and not on the ones that won't form properly in my head. All the time I can feel the brother behind me, or whatever he is, those eyes burning into my back.

I try again. This man will find me out, I know it. Discover how thin my learning is. How weak my faith.

We build hospitals with this money, I tell the women, trying to concentrate on their faces, which are now familiar, even comforting. Poor children are sent away to study at schools paid for entirely by Zakat. In London, where I once lived, there was a child who was born with great problems, problems in its bones, and the parents could not afford the operation abroad, and so my mosque raised extra money, outside the two and a half per cent, to pay for the child to be healed. I realize as I'm saying it that these people may have no idea what an operation is, but it doesn't matter. I'm reconnecting again and the eyes are burning less fiercely into my back.

He says nothing, and I don't hear him move. Occasionally I see Besma glance nervously at him, as if she knows she mustn't but is drawn to him anyway. I will her to keep her eyes on the floor in case she gets us both into trouble, but at the same time I understand. I long to look round.

Five minutes this lasts, or ten, or twenty, I have no idea, I'm just talking and my sense of time is gone. Somehow the women know not to interrupt, and they don't, until Emina kicks off. She's been staring over my shoulder at the man for the whole time, she hasn't taken her snake eyes off him, and when I pause for a second she jumps in and asks him a question. I have no idea what she says but it's a question, and it's short, and Besma doesn't translate it, she just looks at me and back to Emina. I have to give it to her, for all her crudeness she has some sort of authority, and I feel like a child stuck between the two elders in the room. I start talking again, just try to ignore her, but the brother tells me to stop, in Arabic, in a voice that's harsh and cuts right through me.

I stand aside. The room is silent. His expression hasn't changed – he's watching her without curiosity or anger or amusement. He has as much interest in her as a man has in the rubbish he throws out. The old woman, though, she takes his look as an invitation to keep ranting. I tell Besma to tell her to be quiet, but before she can translate my words the brother asks his own question, quite calmly, his voice not raised at all. His Arabic is good enough but his accent is strange.

'Ask her if she wants to die now.'

Besma looks from him to me and I nod. Unable to raise her eyes she translates the words, and when she's finished Emina takes a deep breath, shakes her head, and makes a gesture with her hand, flicking it at him off her chin. Still looking right at him she says maybe ten words.

'Tell me what she said.'

The calmness in his voice is like ice and the cold settles on all of us. Besma hesitates again and he repeats himself, word for word.

'She said . . . she said you hate your God so much you kill your people. She said when you die you fall into hell.'

Silence again. He gives off such a sense of dominance, force, untouched by whatever his feelings might be. His feelings don't come into it.

Now he nods to the two brothers and says something in Russian.

Emina stays where she is, but the other women shout, and the children pick up on their fear and start to cry. The brothers say nothing, they just grab her by the arms and pick her up off her chair. I haven't noticed before how light she is, how skinny – between them they carry her easily, like an empty sack, and haul her out of the room, her feet just dragging on the floor. She's too proud to say anything, but her eyes burn at this fearsome brother, and at me, and even though I'm full of conviction from the lesson, and fuller still of His love, I find it hard to look at them. Maybe it's because with her I've failed, and as I watch her go I feel a great guilt that if I'd done my job better this wouldn't have needed to happen.

But she was never going to see the light. An old creature from a dark and ancient world.

The commander follows her out.

I'm concentrating so hard on her that I barely notice all the noise from the women left behind. When I come to, I shout at them to stop. I've had enough, I can't take that any more. They quieten down a bit but then the wailing starts, that low and sort of fluttering noise they make and although it's doing my head in I do my best to ignore it.

I have a whiteboard now, like in a proper classroom, and I've been writing basic concepts down, showing them the beauty of the words. Now I wipe it off and start writing so that they'll have something else to concentrate on.

'Pay attention. Okay. Pay attention. It's time for our Article of Faith.'

From outside there comes a single dead crack, a noise we all know well in this city, and for the shortest time the wailing stops.

24

'My God, what happened to you?'

Today Murat's suit was sober, his shirt white. He was on time, in the appointed place. Everything was toned down, professional even, but he looked at Abraham and Mrs Demirsoy now as though they were the first truly surprising thing he'd ever seen. While the two of them went at each other in the quiet, dusty street, Abraham looked up and down it, certain that in the next moment a jeep full of fighters was going to swing round the corner and it would all start again.

'Never mind what things have happened. What has happened is not your concern. Concentrate on what happens now.'

Murat tried to control it but his face was pure puzzlement.

'I have a right to . . .'

Mrs Demirsoy stepped towards him with her finger raised. After everything she was still immaculate; a pale blue cardigan despite the heat, her flowered headscarf tightly tied. Murat's eyes went to the finger as if there was some special power in it.

She spoke in Turkish, quickly and quietly, and Abraham never knew what she said, but whatever it was it made Murat lean back from her and raise his hands, and by the time she was done he was shaking his head and saying okay okay, in the tone of a teenager who knows he might rebel but in the end has no choice. Abraham glanced at her husband, who was still sitting in the car, looking straight ahead with unseeing eyes.

'Okay,' said Murat a final time, and then to Abraham, 'Cairo, open your case.'

Abraham hesitated, not because he was reluctant but because he was still dazed and didn't understand.

'Are you awake? I need to look at your case, and your phone, and any other fucking thing you've got with you.'

Abraham watched him closely. There was strain in his face, a thread of fear, but it was open still, it had that same naivety.

'I need to know who you told about today.'

Murat frowned deeply and quizzically, baffled.

'Told who about what?'

'Did you tell anyone you were taking me?'

'Why the fuck would I do that?'

Mrs Demirsoy tutted, but her eyes stayed sharply on Abraham and his on Murat.

'You promise me you didn't?'

'My paranoid friend, think about it. If I'd betrayed you I wouldn't be here now. And you're paying me way more than I could make selling you out. So yes. I promise.'

'If he promises . . .'

Abraham looked at Mrs Demirsoy and she gave a little nod. That would have to be good enough. What choice was there?

'We okay?'

There was a smile in the corner of Murat's mouth.

'Sorry. We're okay.'

'So who knows?'

'Everyone, apparently.'

'Then we should go. Open your case.'

Abraham kept his hand tightly on it.

'Look, brother. They'll go through them. They find anything

– cigarettes, booze, the wrong fucking aftershave, you're dead. I'm dead. If there's anything you want to lose now, lose it.'

'None of that language,' said Mrs Demirsoy, who was watching the two of them with her hands behind her back, keenly, like a crow. Murat glanced at Abraham with his eyebrows raised, and Abraham wondered at his bravery.

'Of course,' said Abraham. 'Sorry.'

He opened it and Murat crouched down to sift the paltry contents. Abraham went into his phone, deleted his Twitter app and handed the thing over. In there was Vural's number, saved under the name of his friend Albert. What if someone knew it?

'Okay. All right. What's in your pockets?'

Abraham emptied one, then the other, and Murat inspected the keys and coins in his hands.

'What's that?'

'What?'

'There.'

His hand went to Abraham's belt.

'What the fuck is this? Are you serious?'

Abraham had forgotten he had it. Murat pulled the gun from his waistband and held it up.

'This is nice.' And to Mrs Demirsoy, 'What did you say, innocent as a child?'

'It isn't his.'

'It isn't mine.'

Murat looked from one to the other and shook his head.

'I must be fucking crazy. Here. Take it.'

He passed it to Mrs Demirsoy, who looked at it for a moment as if it was a dead mouse, or some other mild unpleasantness, and then took it.

'Get rid of it.'

'Young man, I'm not going to keep it.'

Murat sighed, shook his head again, and ran his hand through his hair.

'A Koran. Where's your Koran? You need a Koran. And some hadith. Luckily I keep spares.'

He looked at Abraham and shook his head for a final time.

'Okay. You are clean. Now that we've got rid of the fucking murder weapon, you're clean. I must be crazy. Okay.'

He went to the car and took an envelope from the glove box.

'Your papers. You aren't whatever the fuck you're called. You're Aref Jandali. Born in Aleppo. A businessman, and not a murderer.' He grinned, not meaning it. 'You can pretend not to be a murderer for five minutes, yes?'

Mrs Demirsoy clucked.

Abraham inspected the document. It looked fine, but then he wasn't the audience for it. A strange sensation, meeting your new self, confusing even, as if he'd stolen this identity from the real Jandali, who happened to have his face and his height and, he noticed, his birthday.

'Anybody asks why you speak like a fucking retard, tell them you grew up in Cairo or some shit. They're not that clever. Now, give me your old passport.'

'Why?'

'You serious? Anyone finds it, you think they might figure it out?'

'I don't like that.'

'You don't like that. Are you for real? I don't like any of this.'

Abraham took the passport from his jacket and handed it to Murat, who squatted by the car's open door, pulled a corner of the plastic panelling away, popped the passport inside and snapped the panel back again.

'There. Okay. We can go. Before some other shit happens. Say goodbye.'

Abraham looked at Mrs Demirsoy, and she looked up at him. What can I give you, he wanted to ask. How can I improve your lives as you have forever changed mine? But he knew he had nothing, so he nodded when she nodded, and managed to say the one thing that came close to expressing what he felt.

'Teşekkür ederim.'

Thank you. Two of his five words of Turkish.

'It's nothing at all. The bad people will always hurt the good. But without them how would we have good to do? Your daughter. I hope she sees what you are.'

Abraham nodded again, to himself as much as to her, and while his emotions were still in check got into the car.

'What do you think you're doing?' said Murat.

Abraham looked up at him.

'Are you serious? You're a murderer. Murderers go in the trunk.'

25

At the border crossing Abraham felt the car slow to a stop, and heard Murat talking, relaxed and easy. He was a pro, and that was good. In the boot, wedged up against his case, nose full of exhaust and hot rubber, Abraham felt his heart going and marvelled at the man's calmness. Where did they come from, these people? How could the world hold two men so different from each other?

After a full five minutes the car moved forward again and picked up pace. Straight ahead for maybe two minutes, cautiously enough, then swinging round corners with an abandon that suggested some punishment was being dished out.

Then with a jolt the car stopped, and the trunk opened, and there was Murat, grinning down against a brilliant blue sky.

'Welcome to the Islamic State, motherfucker.'

He gave Abraham his hand and pulled him out.

'What do you think?'

He held his arms out and gestured up and down the

street. Low breeze-block buildings, beaten-up cars, graffiti on the weathered walls. It looked just like Akçakale. Exactly like Akçakale.

'Have we gone anywhere?'

'To the other side of the world, brother.'

Murat laughed and handed him something. A case, and inside it a pair of sunglasses, gold-rimmed, either expensive or diligently faked.

'Put these on. Look at me.' Murat shook his head. 'May the Lord protect us.'

In the car, Abraham pulled the sun shade down and looked in the narrow band of mirror. Without the tired, hunted eyes he wouldn't have known himself.

'Remember, you do not talk. I talk. If someone asks you a question, I answer it. If they ask you again, you give the answer I gave. Understand?'

Three times Murat made him say he understood.

Tell Abyad was simply the mirror of its sister to the north, in all but one respect: here the fighters had control. This was like the pictures he had seen. Black flags flew from houses, lamp posts, cars. Soldiers with machine guns patrolled the streets, the only officialdom. Here they wore camouflage, desert-coloured kit, big black boots. Murat pulled over to speak to one group, who he seemed to know by name, and this time Abraham understood them, and marvelled at how little was said. Hey. What's up? Raqqa, you know. This is my cousin's friend. He has family there, he's been away. No, he's good.

From behind the dark lenses Abraham watched the street. It was hot, tired, functioning. It worked. Life was going on, less tense than it was just across the border. Here the war had been won.

They drove on. When they were clear of the town Murat lit a cigarette.

'Is that wise?'

'They all fucking smoke. Away from the street. You want one?'

Murat offered him the pack, and Abraham shook his head. What he would have done for a drink. Just one swift Scotch to stop these skittering nerves.

North of Akçakale there had been fields, irrigation, life; here there was dirty red sand and patches of stubborn grass and the husks of forgotten buildings that seemed to have risen from the desert of their own accord. They saw few cars, and no people. A tank passed them, heading north, the colour of mustard, black flags flying from it front and back and a goggled, bala-clavaed head above its gun turret. Half an hour in, Abraham saw in the haze above the ground something that might once have been a house, now a crooked pile of rubble and concrete blocks – the first signs that the fighters really fought. This was no man's land. The whole landscape had been abandoned, and Abraham felt as if he was crossing from one realm into another, from the world into hell, with this unconcerned young man, this boy as his ferryman.

'So who came for you?'

'Sorry?'

'You thought I shopped you. You must have had a reason.'

Abraham breathed deeply and thought about the conse-quences and decided he had had enough of them. Why not tell him? Why not simply trust someone?

'A man called Vural. I think he's a spy.'

'For who?'

'For you. For the Turks.'

'He's not spying for me, Cairo.'

'He wants me to report to him.'

'Report what?'

'I join up, I tell him what I see.'

'What d'you mean, you join up?'

'I join ISIS.'

'Serious?'

'He was.'

Murat threw his head back and laughed hard at the roof of the car.

'Seriously? Cairo, you'd last five fucking minutes.'

'I know.'

'So don't do it.'

'If I don't he's going to hand me over to the police.'

Murat took both hands off the wheel and gestured at the miles of scrub to the east and west.

'You see any fucking police, Cairo?'

It really was hell. The afterlife. Nothing mattered here. Nothing that had pursued him in the world could reach him – the police, the Syrians, Vural – and in that moment Abraham felt a shock of strange freedom. All his daily fears consolidated into one pure source of terror, which with God's will he might overcome. Few people got this chance, this strange privilege.

'Seriously, my friend. Get to Raqqa, find a place to stay, look around, keep low. It's the only way. I can help you.'

'Thank you. This isn't my world.'

'Isn't anyone's world now, brother.'

Clouds covered the sky, and the heat grew sticky, and in his languid way Murat asked Abraham questions about Cairo, and being a pharmacist, and his wife.

'You love your daughter?'

'Of course.'

'My mother says that without children life would be a dance.'

Abraham nodded. The thought upset him. He imagined a life in which Sofia had never existed, and found himself wondering whether in sum it would have been better – whether the

187

pain she had caused had yet cancelled out all the joy. But he had limited the joy himself. He felt as he had when his father had died, that their time together had been too inhibited and too short. But with Sofia that was his fault. He could have relaxed. He could have given her the freedom that now she had come to this prison to seek.

In return he wasn't much of a travelling companion. His questions to Murat were practical. What happens in the city? Can you just move around? Where can you buy food?

Life went on, he said, slowly. It was like the city was in a coma. The schools were shut, the university was shut, half the cafes were shut, most people had no jobs.

'My friend, his job was to mend the roads. I mean he organized it, he had an office, a good job. Daesh told him, we are the government, you work for us now, or you don't work at all. So now he stays at home, he doesn't go out, his wife and his kid in the apartment all day. He'll leave. He says he won't, that Daesh should be the ones to leave, it's his home, but he'll go. He'll have to. Otherwise, what are they going to do? They stay there, they want any future for the kid, she'll have to go to Daesh school, and then she's one of them. You know?'

Abraham didn't really know. He had read about these things but could hardly imagine them.

'How many are there?'

'Who?'

'Daesh. In Raqqa.'

Murat shrugged.

'I don't know. Ten thousand. Not so many in a big city. But it doesn't matter. They have fear on their side. No one wants to end up with their head on a stick, you know?'

He looked across at Abraham and grinned.

Food was okay. Expensive if you weren't a fighter, but it was there. Trade hadn't died just because these fuckers had control. They all liked to eat. Coke, candy, Red Bull. Chicken. They all fucking loved chicken. You look on Twitter – you do Twitter? Go on Twitter and look at all the pictures of food these idiots post. Unbelievable. But hey, they were good customers. In Turkish, there was a saying. The silver door closes, a golden door opens. It was good for business.

'What business?' Abraham asked, but Murat just grinned and shook another cigarette loose from its pack.

'Look. All you need to know is, keep your head down, don't do anything stupid. Don't take any photographs. They hate that. Don't look the fighters in the eye. Then they'll leave you alone. It's simple. You've got a good beard, you're a good Muslim, that's all they want.'

After an hour, they reached a checkpoint, two 4x4s parked off the road and four fighters with guns across their chests. Murat slowed a long way off, stopped by the men and passed them his papers, folded round three or four banknotes. This time he wasn't subtle about it.

'Hey, cousin, you still here? You need a new gig, man, there's no action here.'

The fighter took the notes, handed back the papers without looking at them and smiled.

'If they keep me here any longer I'm going to have to put the price up.'

'You're in charge, man.'

'Who's this?'

'This? He's my actual cousin. He's good.'

The fighter stepped back. Murat grinned, raised a hand in goodbye, and drove away.

'You got to keep these people sweet. Business is always business, anywhere you like. When these fuckers are gone, there'll still be business. I'm going to do this for a while, build up some capital, wait to see which way the wind blows and then when all this shit is over, boom, this part of the world is going to go crazy, like a river that's been dammed for years, you know? Opportunities everywhere. You come back in ten years' time, cousin, I'm going to own this road. Own this country.'

26

Two hours was all it took. The sand turned to dry fields where nothing seemed to be growing and in the haze of the horizon Abraham could begin to see minarets and a pinkish line of buildings.

'Raqqa,' said Murat, and grinned again. 'City of the Damned.'

Two hundred yards short of the city walls was another checkpoint, more permanent: a concrete shelter on one side, draped in black flags, and on the other an armoured jeep, its mounted gun trained on the road. A fighter in a khaki flak jacket with a chain of bullets across his chest and carrying a machine gun leaned against it. Two fighters stood by the shelter, and a fourth was checking the papers of the car in front. With a nod he signalled to the others to check its boot.

Abraham stiffened, wiped his sweating palms on his trousers. None of these men were wearing sunglasses. He wasn't sure about the sunglasses – he should get rid of them.

'It's okay, my friend,' said Murat, quietly and calmly. 'This is all normal.'

He took off his own and Abraham did the same, hoping that his eyes wouldn't betray the fear in them. Wasn't that what these people looked for? Couldn't they smell it, like dogs?

'New guys,' said Murat.

Ahead of them the fighters had put a suitcase on the floor and were roughly going through it; Abraham could see shirts, pants, T-shirts. One of the fighters lifted up a can of something, showed it to the other, then took off its cap and sprayed it in the air.

'Perfume,' said Murat. 'Stupid.'

Abraham kept watching, though part of him felt he should look away. Don't catch anyone's eye. The man checking the papers took the can from his colleague, held it up to the driver's face and asked him something. Abraham saw the driver shrug; in response the fighter half turned, threw the can hard off into the wasteland by the side of the road, and stood for a moment with one hand on his hip, one hand on his gun, staring at the driver in the car. Abraham didn't breathe, and even Murat stiffened a little. But all the fighter did was shout at the man, loud enough for Abraham to hear some words – banned, unIslamic, an insult to Allah, the most high, the most glorified – and then with a parting command not to be caught with rubbish like that again he waved the car through.

'You see? Not so bad.'

Murat eased the car forward and wound his window right down. Abraham kept his eyes straight ahead but sensed the man well enough, the usual: black beard, the top lip shaved, the air of violence imminent.

'As-salamu alaykum,' said Murat, relaxed but respectful.

The fighter said nothing. Abraham could feel him looking at him.

'Here,' said Murat, and handed him his papers and Abraham's new passport.

The fighter took his time leafing through them.

'You live Raqqa?'

'Sometimes,' said Murat. 'I do business. Trade. Food, clothing. I'm known here.'

'Who is this?'

'My partner. He has a clothing mill in Egypt. They make niqabs, veils.'

As stories went it wasn't bad. Until now Abraham had been

nervous of Murat's confidence, his casualness, but maybe he'd picked a good one. He was alert now, on his mettle.

The fighter took two steps back.

'Open back of car.'

'Abu Waheed knows me. I source things for him. He can vouch for me.'

'Open car.'

Murat said nothing, and his silence told Abraham that the mood had changed. Murat was a talker, and if he wasn't talking that was bad.

He nodded, as if deciding something for himself, opened the car door and got out onto the road.

'I come this way the whole time. Where's Abu Nazir?'

He had put the smile back in his voice.

'At Kobani, fighting. Open car.'

'Okay, no problem. It's open.'

Murat walked to the back of the car and in the mirror Abraham saw the boot lid pop open. His own case was in there, and two of Murat's, regular-looking suitcases.

For a minute all Abraham heard was the wind and the car that had driven up behind them idling. In his side mirror he could see Murat, one hand on his hip, the other in his hair, watching the fighter go through the bags.

'You see? Just some samples, some clothes, that's it.'

Now Abraham felt the car rock a little, and listened to the sounds of rummaging coming from the boot, and then of something heavy dropping on the ground.

'Brother, I don't know what you're doing, but there's nothing there.'

Maybe another ten seconds passed. Murat ran his hand through his hair, shifted on his feet. Abraham closed his eyes and prayed he was wrong about what was happening.

'What is this?'

At first Abraham hardly heard the fighter's voice, but then

he repeated himself, coming up to Murat and shouting, pressing something into his face.

'You. Get the other one.'

Abraham's door opened and a gun appeared, pointing at his chest. Raising his hands, conscious of the sweat now pouring from him, he swung his legs slowly out of the car and pulled himself upright. Another fighter, another dark, blank face. With the gun he motioned to Abraham to move to the back of the car.

Murat was standing there, a different man, hands up, jacket hanging off him, his face red, flushed with fear and impotence. The fighter was rummaging in the boot again, and now he came up with three clear plastic bags, each the size of a grapefruit, full of small brown pills.

'They're not mine. They're for Abu Waheed. He knows me.'

'On ground. You. Knees. Both of you.'

As he knelt by Murat, Abraham instinctively put his hands on his head, and realized that he had seen this scene before, online, in the videos he had stopped watching before the inevitable end. Now he looked up into the fighter's face: it was animated, on fire with righteousness, strength, almost lust.

Murat was still playing his one card.

'I do this for Abu Waheed. Understand? He places an order, I fill it. You know him, yes?'

'I know him.'

'He's a big fucking deal, brother. Really. You don't want to be messing with this arrangement.'

The fighter had opened one of the bags and was smelling the contents. His face was narrow, angular, the nose fine, and his eyes seemed to swim with a strange poison. The Arabic he spoke was bad.

'These illegal. How much you sell for?'

Abraham hated him with a hatred he had never felt for anyone. Here was the lie that had fooled Sofia: where she had seen virtue and energy there was only this angry little man lusting after money and death.

'They're not mine to sell, brother. They belong to Abu Waheed.'

The fighter sealed the bag, put it with the others on the ground. His eyes went from Murat to Abraham and back to Murat, where they stayed.

'They're not yours either, brother.' One last try.

'Abu Waheed dead. Two days.'

Abraham kept his hands on his head and began to say a new prayer.

Forgive me, Lord. This has not been the best use of a life.

Murat sniffed, loudly, took his hands from his head, and when he spoke his voice was quicker, shriller.

'Brother, I'm sorry to hear that. He was a brave man.'

'Dead man now.'

'I hear you. The pills are yours, destroy them, sell them, do what you want. It's not my business but he asked me, you know, he wasn't a man you could refuse. Take them, I have some cash, take anything, whatever you want . . .'

With no warning the fighter swivelled on his heel and brought his boot up hard into Murat's face. Abraham heard the bone crack and Murat sprawl against him, sending them both over onto the hot tarmac.

Murat groaned, brought his hand up to his jaw, with slow eyes saw the blood on his hand as it came away, and for a mere instant he and Abraham shared a look of terror and understanding.

'Dead man now.'

Four flat cracks. No echo, no fanfare. No glory. Abraham felt Murat's body twitch and shock against his, put his hands to his shoulders to support him, saw two dark holes in the back of his jacket. Felt his body go slack as the last signals left the brain and the blood from his exploded heart slowed to a stop.

'Wait!' He looked up at the fighter, who without hurry had turned the gun on him. 'Wait!'

The body's full weight was on him now and he tried to scrabble out from under it, adrenaline pulsing through him, making his own heart race, lighting every cell with energy. Standing over him the fighter turned to his friends and laughed.

'He wants me wait.'

He lifted the gun up an inch until it was pointing at Abraham's head.

'Listen. Please. I'm not with him.'

He laid Murat's head down on the road and pushed himself away. So quickly gone.

'Stop. I'm a doctor.'

The fighter cocked his head, turned again to his friends, a big grin fixed on his face.

'You are doctor? Heal friend.'

'I'm a doctor. My name is Abu Ibrahim. I have come to join Islamic State.'

PART THREE

1

'You are Egyptian?'

'Yes.'

'Why are you here?'

'I have come to make jihad.'

'What made you come?'

'Islam in Egypt is not Islam. My country had its chance. Now they kill the Muslim Brothers in return for money from America. I must live where there is sharia. Then I can return and build the khilafa there.'

The words that streamed from him had the right sound but no substance; like bricks he piled one on top of another and hoped they wouldn't fall. The shots still rang in his head, and even with his eyes open he saw Murat's empty face nestling on the ground. Yet the more scared he was the more easily the words seemed to tumble out.

'There is no mention of you on the internet.'

This he hadn't prepared for. Of course they would look for him.

'I don't go online.'

'One Ibrahim Mounir in England. One in Texas. No doctors in Egypt.'

'I don't like computers. I read books.'

'Spies have no background.'

Christ. Think of an answer to that.

'Yes, they do. Someone makes a background for them. I'm just an ordinary man.'

His questioner looked at him for a long time, as if that might force him to confess that everything he was saying was nonsense.

'Can you fight?'

'If you require me. But I know you need doctors.'

That was a mistake. He knew it was true, but he shouldn't have said it. How did he know, apart from reading the infidel press? The man across the desk stopped and drilled a look into him.

'Our health facilities are excellent.'

Such pride in the rat pit. And such thin skin.

This man looked like all the rest, in his sand-coloured shirt and thick beard with the bare top lip, and he had the eye of a fighter – calm, deliberate, vicious. But his job was in this office, in this hot little room with its tiny barred window and its peeling lemon walls – an administrator for this new state, or some part of it, and proud of his work. Two fighters in fatigues stood to each side of him cradling machine guns.

'Everyone says so. But I read that kafir doctors have left. They have betrayed you.'

The man leaned back in his chair and eyed Abraham for a moment, mollified, turning over the blue Egyptian passport with the fingers of one hand. He was older than the others Abraham had seen, and his eyes held a wariness that suggested experience: the violence there was of a practical kind, the bloodlust dulled to a calculation.

He opened the passport.

'Ibrahim Mounir.'

Abraham nodded.

'You are Sunni?'

He said it with a faint jerk of his chin, and his look seemed to harden.

'Yes.'

'You don't sound sure about that, brother.'

'Of course. All Egyptians are Sunni.'

'So, Egyptian. How many times a day do you pray?'

Abraham tried to find his balance. He had reached a state of pure fear, and his mind had emptied of everything else. How many times? How many times had he heard the call to prayer over how many years? His whole childhood. It was five. Or four. One at dawn, one at noon, one in the afternoon, and two at night. Definitely two at night.

'Five times. Five.'

'And what is the name of your mosque, in Cairo?'

Muhammad Ali was the famous one, but if this man knew Cairo he would know it was the most obvious. There was one, near where he had trained, it was where his friends had gone to pray.

'Khekia Mosque. In Shubra.'

'Khekia. I don't know Khekia.'

Now he locked his eyes on Abraham's and held them there.

'Your favourite hadith. The one that means the most to you. Recite it.'

Hadith. The only ones he had ever read had been sent by Sofia to her followers, in amongst all that chaff. Desperately he cast back for one.

'You shouldn't have to think.'

'I . . . I am ashamed by this.'

'You'll be worse than ashamed. Are you serious? One hadith.'

Without turning he held up a finger and the fighters brought their guns up to point at Abraham, who looked at the black barrels and raised his hands.

'I have a memory disorder. Lacunar amnesia. Please. There's a hole in my memory. I can remember everything except words. For years, I have suffered the deepest shame from this. Every day I have to learn my prayers and by the next they are gone.'

The administrator's expression did not change.

'My Koran, it has all gone. I . . . I didn't say this before, but one of the reasons I am here is to reaffirm my faith. To make amends for this shameful deformity.'

'One hadith.'

'Please. If I was blind, if I was lame, you would see it. This is the same thing but inside my head. I cannot control it.'

The administrator sat back, crossed his arms and for ten seconds didn't speak.

'Doctors are useful. Traitors and spies are deadly. If I kill a doctor, it's not good. But if I fail to kill a spy the whole khilafa may fall.'

'I am no risk.'

Again he was silent, and then he stood.

'Kill him. But not here. Outside.'

Abraham rose from his chair and instantly one of the fighters was by him, pushing him back.

'I killed a man in Antep. In our name.'

The administrator stopped with his hand on the door.

'I was held in jail for it. You can check.'

'What man?'

'Free Syrian Army. He knew I was coming here.'

'How did you kill him?'

'I slit his throat. In his hotel.'

'But you are not a fighter.'

'It was a great test of my faith.'

His decision was tipping back. Abraham could see it.

'Please. Check. You must have ways of checking.'

'How did it feel?'

'Like I was closer to God, the most high, the most glorified. And to the khilafa. Please. I have come so far.'

That was a good answer; he knew it as it came out from wherever it had been waiting. The administrator scratched at his cheek and nodded at the guards.

'Lock him up. I will make two calls. Your life hangs on them.'

Once an office block, the building was now part government department, part police station. The khilafa's Ministry of Fear, or one of them. Outside it, motionless, stood a dozen armed men in camouflage, black masks across their faces and machine guns held at their chests. Machine guns mounted on two 4x4s watched the street. A pair of vast black flags hung from the second storey either side of the door they guarded, and a black banner ran between them to create a sort of arch, like an open mouth.

Now, marched down stairs and along anonymous corridors, Abraham had time to wonder how many people had been brought here in terror, never to leave. That man just now; the easy choice was execution. He would lose nothing by it. There was no risk to getting it wrong. Alive Abraham might be useful to them, dead he would certainly be, and that was the genius and special savagery of the whole place. There was no obvious benefit to letting any one man or woman live. Death became the safe state.

His cell was a storeroom, two floors below ground, lined with shelves that still held pots of paint and bottles of detergent. A thick alien smell in the hot air, and a single fluorescent bulb giving out a tired blue light. Abraham sat against the wall in a gap between the shelves and took inventory. Buckets, rags, a broom. Various chemicals, none useful, though they'd kill him quickly enough if he was minded.

He wasn't minded. They could do it. Let it be on their souls, or whatever passed for them. Mingling with his fear was a simple repugnance, as if with every breath he was still able to make he was taking in a gallon of the stink and poison they exhaled. Heavy with the smell of the dead, there was only so long you could breathe it in. What was that line? From Revelations. That Death and Hell would be given dominion over men, to kill with swords and famine and the beasts of the earth. Well here they were, the beasts of the earth, pinning him down and waiting to tear him into pieces. Evil didn't cover it. Evil was too good a word, too noble. In the eyes of his interrogator and the guards and the checkpoint patrols he saw nothing but an indiscriminate hunger, and no thought beyond the need to satisfy it. He had sensed this in his reading, and seeing them close up, he knew it: there was nothing captivating about ISIS. No dark charm that drew you in, no glimmer from the black flame. The blackness was simply the absence of light, and somehow that quietened his fear. In the end they had nothing, and would return to nothing, and as he had seen it so Sofia would see it, in time.

It could have been worse for me. I tried – at the end, I tried. Better this than a lifetime of slow regret. Better this death than that one.

Somehow, he slept, and when he woke his head was numb and his clothes were wet and standing over him was a soldier with a gun.

'You. Now. Up.'

Abraham blinked, rubbed his eyes, and before he could stand the soldier kicked him hard in the thigh.

'Up.'

Now they would give him his orange overalls. His death suit. Why were they orange? Was there some special significance or did they just like the way it looked against the sand and the sky? Or perhaps he was too lowly to merit publicity and could be dispatched in the clothes he stood in, without cameras, without ceremony.

Up to the second floor, and back to the same interrogation room. One by one thoughts dropped from his head – half-baked plans, regrets, new sources of fury – until, by the time they arrived, only blankness and white noise remained. The soldier opened the door and pushed him through; there was the administrator, at his desk, and with their backs to Abraham a man he hadn't seen before – small, white-robed, ratty – and beside him a woman, fully veiled. The little man looked up at Abraham as he entered and fixed him with an eye like a dagger. The woman glanced his way and then looked straight ahead. Even by that movement he knew her.

2

My thoughts aren't thoughts. They're noise, like ten songs playing at once. I see him, and I know it's him, and even though I look away it doesn't change the fact that he's here, or that it's impossible he's here. If Khalil had walked in it would make more sense. It's like seeing a dead man in this world. A kafir in Paradise. If I look out of the window will I see red buses everywhere and all the mosques turned to churches?

He says my name and they tell him to shut up.

The commander is talking, but I don't hear him. If I was braver, stronger, I'd look up again, confront the reality, but I'm not, I'm weak, and I keep my eyes on the desk. I can't. I can't take it. I feel crazy, properly insane. The man I love is taken from me and this excuse for one is returned?

The commander repeats what he said.

'Umm Azwar. Do you know this man?'

What is he doing here? What can he be doing here?

I force myself to look. My heart is not closed to him, however hard I want it to be. One of his eyes is black and his clothes are dusty and his jacket is torn. He has suffered, and my first reaction is pity, it shouldn't be, but then I'm off balance, staggering. In his eyes I see some of what I'm feeling and I'm so glad of my veil, I don't want him to be able to look inside me. But no, his reaction is different. There's that sentimental longing there, that attachment to the idea of me that blinds him to who I am.

That's why he's come. For that version of me. He isn't complete without it.

'I know him.'

'Who is he?'

'He's my father.'

'Do you know why he is here?'

'I don't.'

Imam Talib is looking at me with that way he has of searching right inside, but he doesn't say anything, the commander does all the talking.

'Did you know he was in the khilafa?'

I shake my head. To say no but also in disbelief. He's going to ruin this for me. The one thing I had that was finally mine and he's found a way to destroy it. It's like in order for him to exist, I can't.

The commander takes a piece of paper from his desk and holds it in front of him, taking his time to read it. They'll think we're here together. Of course they will, and when they find out he isn't a Muslim they'll kill us both, as they should.

'What does your father do? What job does he have?'

I can feel my father's eyes on me.

'He's a pharmacist.'

The commander takes his time, keeps his eyes on the paper, puts it back carefully on the pile on his desk, looks at my father and then at me.

'He has told us he's a doctor. That he wants to work for Islamic State. That your journey opened his eyes.'

That can't be true. Crazier than everything else. Can it be true? Have I led him here for the right reasons?

The commander is staring at me. Everyone is concentrating on me alone.

'But we don't need pharmacists,' he says. 'We need doctors.'

If I don't lie for him – as he has lied to them – they'll kill him. And if they find me out in my lie they'll kill me.

How can it be that we are still joined? I thought I was free.

'He was a doctor. In Egypt. Then we moved to London and he worked as a pharmacist. Because my mother was ill and then he looked after me.'

This barely makes sense. And I can't believe I'm saying it, even though it's close to the truth. I shouldn't be saying it, but what if it's true, that he's here for the khilafa? Who am I to deny him what has been given to me?

'You said you came from Egypt.'

The commander says this to my father.

'I do come from Egypt. It's my home.'

'But you travelled from London.'

'I'm not proud of my time in that place.'

His eyes are wide and terrified. The commander and Imam Talib exchange a look, and then the imam speaks to me.

'You understand the khilafa, my child. You have shown yourself to be part of it, and you know that it must be pure to function. Are you close to this man?'

'Once. We had grown apart.'

'Can you vouch for him?'

'He is a good doctor.'

'He says he killed a man in Turkey. One of our enemies.'

Now the world is upside down and inside out. I look at him again. My father. Dressed like a local, beaten, defeated. My father the convert, the jihadi, the killer in His name.

I close my eyes and pray to Him to help me. This is the gravest test yet, it makes stoning Idara look easy. Then, I knew what to do but could not do it. Now I have no idea, and everything rests on what I say. My father's life, and my soul.

Holy words appear to me in the darkness. I don't select them, they just make themselves known to me.

God's curse is on the wrongdoers who debar others from the path of God.

Who am I to block my father's path?

Who is more wicked than he who invents a falsehood about God?

Adjacent verses, and everything I need to know is in them. If my father wants to be saved, I would be the last person to stand in his way. And if he is lying, God will punish him. I do not need to protect either of them.

'He has been a weak man, but it is within us all to change.'

Imam Talib nods to me, and then he nods to the commander, and the man who was my father is taken from the room and out into my city.

3

It was easy to see what Raqqa had once been. Wide streets split down the middle by lines of plane trees, solid apartment blocks, the odd fine stuccoed building looking down on the quiet from its arcaded balconies. Grand municipal buildings in grand squares draped with black flag after black flag. Rows of jumbled shops painted green and pink and blue faded in the strong sun, their business hidden now behind grilles and shutters. Maybe one in three was open; shopkeepers stood in their doorways and watched the world like men who expected nothing good to happen. Once, there would have been shouting and car horns and the buzz of mopeds flashing through traffic, but now Raqqa was hushed, doing its best to do what it needed to do without being noticed.

Black flags everywhere, on cars and lamp posts and draped across dead shopfronts. Abraham's jeep drove past one building set back from the road that had been painted black all over, the finish so fresh it glinted in the sun like oil. Fighters in khakis and black kufiya, and women like black ghosts going silently about their day, each with a man to escort her – except the troop of black-clad vultures darting between them with machine guns slung awkwardly across their backs. Sofia had been one of those. Had she moved like they did, swooping from victim to victim with that erratic energy? Was that her under there, transformed into something less than human? From the back of the jeep Abraham watched them make their progress up the street as they checked every woman, looked them up and down, challenged them, leaned in to their necks like vampires sniffing for blood. This was what the world looked like when everyone in it was consumed by power or fear.

Why had she vouched for him? The safe thing would have been to expose him. It had taken courage, and she gained nothing by it.

Children sat on the pavement in the shade begging and selling matches, shoelaces, string. Around one shop a crowd of men and children jostled for the attention of a man who stood above them, and it took a moment for Abraham to realize why he was so popular. He had bread, a pile of flatbreads balanced on one arm, and was passing them out to the hands outstretched in front of him. Everyone carried plastic buckets and when they took the bread they stayed in place, as if expecting more. A soup kitchen. He studied the faces and saw not fear but resignation, and tiredness, and repulsion. Raqqa had been occupied for nine months, and already its people had endured a lifetime of it.

Along with his passport and a sheaf of Islamic State documents, they had given him his phone back, and as they drove he restored his Twitter app and sent Sofia a message. Simple and direct.

— When can we meet? It would be good to talk.

Nothing for Vural. Vural could assume he was dead. After all, it wasn't so far from the truth.

The jeep found a space in the traffic and lurched forward, sped round corners and down narrower streets, the jihadi at the wheel driving like the teenager he was, in unchecked spurts of speed, until he was forced to slow for a queue of cars. The driver leaned on the horn, but as Abraham looked ahead he could see they were going nowhere: half a building had come down in an airstrike, sheering into the street in a pile of grey rubble and leaving room for one car at a time to inch round. Fresh dust still blew in the wind. Panels of corrugated iron hung off what was left of a wall, and a length of carpet spilled from one of the first-floor rooms that had been destroyed, its floral pattern stained with blood that had not yet dried to brown. Men stood and talked and surveyed the damage; women threw their hands up and cried behind their veils. Here, in death, there was finally life.

'Government scum always miss,' said the fighter beside the driver, half turning to Abraham. His accent was odd, flat, European perhaps. 'Hit everything but us.'

What a shame that was. Why had God forsaken this place? As the jeep bullied and pushed its way through the gap, Abraham saw in the eyes that turned to him the strongest possible hatred, and felt for the first time a deep unease about his mission. He had rushed here without stopping to think, oblivious to all this suffering, and with no intention of helping these people, of doing anything but saving someone only he wanted to see saved. It was like heading into the sheepfold to rescue the wolf.

Raqqa's main hospital was half a hospital, maybe less than that, and what was left had been divided into two again. It had been bombed three weeks earlier, and the main entrance was now a precarious heap of concrete and rusted metal rods. One side had collapsed onto itself like a drift of grey snow, and inside the blasted facade gurneys and bedding and cabinets and bits of shattered equipment lay piled and smashed. The 4x4 drove round to the side of the building and Abraham was told to get out by the driver's sidekick, who jumped down from the cab and with that lazy swagger that seemed to be common to them all headed down a long, shallow ramp that fell away into the basement. Abraham spent a moment in the sun before he followed, looking around him and wondering whether a better man would take this opportunity to run.

Around the ramp, pressed into the patches of shade against the bruised buildings on either side, stood some local men, perhaps fifteen of them, waiting. Anywhere else they would have been smoking, and they watched Abraham with that same look of quiet resentment he had seen from the car. One day, they said, when this is all past, you or your soul will pay for your part in this.

The fighter seemed to know where he was going. He led Abraham down dark, humid corridors whose blue-green paint was peeling, past makeshift wards in what appeared once to have been storerooms. Small windows set high in the wall and surrounded by sandbags gave the only light, enough for Abraham to see injured men lying on the beds inside, legs elevated, faces bandaged. Others that he assumed were fighters walked the halls in flip-flops and sweat pants, some on crutches. To his right he glimpsed an operating theatre, or what looked like one, with dead surgical lights ranged round an empty operating table. One was working, and he thought he could hear the generator responsible humming in the background. A doctor in scrubs looked up at him as he walked past.

Then he was in another office, at the core of the building, almost dark but for a circle of light thrown on the desk by the single working lamp. At the desk sat two men, one senior and clearly in charge, the other as clearly in thrall. Beards, black tunics, taqiyah caps. The older had big, heavy eyes that he was working hard to make stern. Together they looked like a priggish father and the son he quietly despaired of.

'General practice?' said the older, reading the papers he had been handed. Without great confidence, the younger did his best to stare Abraham out.

'Yes.'

'No surgery?'

'No.'

'But you can assist?'

Probably, yes. In fact, almost certainly. Three years of medical school and you could tell one end of a curette from another. And the drugs he knew, the anaesthetics, the antibiotics, the analgesics. Provided no one asked him to cut anyone open he could play his part. It was even possible, against all the odds, that he might do some good.

'You chose not to fight?'

'I thought I could be of more use here.'

'Allah alone, the most glorified, the most high, will know if you are right. But even here you are at war. Disobey an order and it is treason. Fail, and it is treason. The punishment for treason is death.'

Abraham managed to nod. How they loved to say that word.

'You are under watch. Huq will work with you. Any signs that your behaviour or your performance are below par and you will answer for it.'

Probably he had been a manager, this one; he had the delivery and the tics, the facile approach to complexity.

'Huq will tell you what you need to know. And he will report to me every night.'

With that, and a hard look at Abraham, he left. No shake of the hand, no welcome aboard, no looking forward to working together, but in other respects this wasn't so different from the old job, Abraham thought. Maybe all organizations resemble each other.

Huq was no fighter. He was even an unlikely doctor. Young, no older than twenty-five, chinless under the feeble beard, narrow-shouldered, pot-bellied, the head too small for his body, the eyes mean and uncertain. Abraham's mother would have called him unfortunate. Through the adolescent whiskers peeped a tight red little mouth that was cruel and vicious and petty at once, and the voice that came from it sounded strangled, odd, as uncomfortable with itself as the rest of him was. Doing his best to establish some authority, he sat for a moment looking his new recruit up and down.

'You've never worked in a hospital?'

'As I said.'

'You'll never have worked in a hospital like this.'

That didn't make sense, but Abraham let it go, and turning his face away from the man's meaty breath listened to the rules he was counting off on his fingers.

One: men could not be treated by women. There were no female doctors left in the hospital, however, which was a solution sent by Allah himself. Nevertheless, men could not be washed or directly treated by any female nurse, who even then must of course be properly covered and accompanied by a male doctor at all times. Men could treat women but not for anything that involved the breasts, abdomen or reproductive areas. Most of the conditions the local women presented were false, hysterical, and the rest gynaecological. Allah, the most glorified, the most high, would in any case decide whether a child should live or die, and any that did not survive were not strong enough to serve the Islamic State. This was efficient.

Two. Women must not be given the opportunity to provoke the men. Doctors were responsible for ensuring that their female colleagues obeyed the rules on appearance. Gloves and the veil must be worn at all times. Breaches would result in the offender being punished together with any colleague who had failed to report the offence.

Female patients must be accompanied to the hospital by their mahram, who must then wait outside the hospital. If any mahram was found inside the hospital he and his woman would be thrown out and punished. If the mahram was not a blood relative, the patient would be thrown out and both punished.

The hospital was split into two. This floor, the basement, was for members of Islamic State: leaders, fighters, and their wives. Priority was of course given to them, and this was where those central to jihad were safest from government attacks. The American dogs did not bomb here but during the day Assad's kafir army had tried, so inaccurately that the safest place to be was exactly where the bombs were meant to fall, but after the last successful attack it had made sense to come down here.

Nevertheless, the dawla provided healthcare to all its people, and so the rest of the hospital was given over to their needs. A quarter of a million people in Raqqa and bar two surgeries this was the only place they could come. Their claim on drugs, equipment, procedures and beds was secondary. The civilian staff was liable to forget this, and any indication of false favouritism should be reported.

Hours were not fixed. Abraham would work until there was no more work to do, within reason. Pay was four hundred dollars a month, payable at the end of the month. Once every four weeks he was entitled to one day off, unless the hospital was overwhelmed, which it usually was.

All work except critical operations already underway stopped for salat five times a day. A room had been set aside for the purpose.

'I say again. This is a field hospital in a Holy War. It is not a cosmetic surgery clinic. We have many good doctors here but there are never enough. Truly you have found an opportunity to be valuable in God's eyes, the most high, the most glorified.'

Abraham's head ached. He needed aspirin, and water. Food, too, he realized, he hadn't eaten anything all day. This man wasn't a doctor. He was an idiot and probably a psychopath, a pinched, bullying spirit that had come here not to cure suffering but to cause it.

Forcing a look of respect, he nodded. Probably he should bring himself to say something, something zealous and committed, but he didn't have it in him.

'I will do my best,' was all he managed to say.

'I will find you scrubs.'

Abraham thanked him, but he wasn't done.

'The doctors with black armbands are ours. The others are civilians. We have them under control but do not trust them.'

Abraham nodded again, now an impostor twice over.

4

That night I don't feel like eating, I feel a bit sick, and so I go straight to my room and try to read but the words won't stay in one place. Khalil and my father, my father and Khalil. My brain flits from one to the other, seeing nothing, learning nothing. I hate being like this. So weak.

Do not fail this test. None will be more important.

If Khalil was a lion – and if the Yazidis are sheep and I am their shepherd – then my father is a crippled dog dragging himself round the world in search of food and water and some pitiful love. He sent me a DM today. I can hardly believe I am saying those words. What is there for us to talk about? I don't even want to hear him explain himself. In the end, I deleted the reply I had started to write.

I miss Khalil. I realize I shouldn't but I do. The good part is I can feel his spirit by me, always there, but when I'm down like this it doesn't pull me up, it just reminds me of what might have been. I guess I'm taking longer to adjust than I imagined. Even my body isn't coming round. I'm late. Everything seems to have stopped.

In the night, the woman who runs the widows' house comes and wakes me from a deep sleep full of frenzied dreams. She's never touched me before and it's strange that she's even in my room, and through the haze I can hear fear in her voice like something's urgent.

'Brothers are here for you. You must get dressed.'

They drive me in silence through the dead streets to a big house with a heavy guard on it, four more brothers in a circle of light by the front door. They greet us with 'allahu akbar' as we get out of the car and let us straight in. Inside it's like Imam Talib's house, clean and marble everywhere, with the air conditioning turned right up. The brothers take me into a room that looks like a dining room, with a table and eight chairs, and tell me to wait, and that's when my mind starts racing again, turning over the possibilities – that I'm here because of something to do with Khalil, or my father, but the one I keep coming back to is I failed to control that old woman and now I'm going to lose that job too. Why is life suddenly so difficult? Why am I not equal to it? Thank God my husband isn't here to see my disgrace.

I wait for ten minutes, twenty minutes, and although the brothers closed the door on me I can hear noises from inside the house, voices, shouting, and what sounds like a baby crying but through the walls it's hard to tell. Dim fears build in me. I don't know whether I should sit down so I stay standing. It's icy in here and I'm starting to get cold when the door opens and the brother from yesterday comes in, from the classroom, the huge pale fighter with the straw beard and the green eyes that own you.

This is his home, I know it. Somehow he has even more command here. For a moment he stands and looks at me with that same look of calm and control and underneath my veil I'm probably blushing, not from embarrassment but a sort of shame for my faults as a Muslim. I get that same sense that he can see each one.

'Take off your veil,' he says, pulling a chair out with one hand and sitting down a yard back from the table, his legs wide apart and the skirt of his dishdasha hanging down. His voice is higher and clearer than the look of him. 'Sit.'

I unhook my veil, hoping the blushing doesn't show, and sit

close at the table, straight as I can, clasping my hands together in my lap. I want to wipe them on my niqab they're so cold and sweaty but something tells me I should keep as still as possible.

First he just looks at me, as he looked at the old woman, as he looked at Besma, as I'm certain he looks at everyone. Any question could be going through his head. Whether to sack me, or kill me. He doesn't project any emotion but I'm not sure there is any. The control is on the inside.

It's like he's inspecting every last cell. I can almost see the blood rushing in panic round my veins.

'How old you are.' His Arabic is fine but the words are in the wrong order. Also it doesn't sound like a question, there's no rise in it.

'Seventeen.'

He doesn't answer straight away.

'English?'

'Egyptian. My family . . . my father moved me to London when I was seven.'

Again there's a long pause, and this time I try my best to hold his eye.

'Why you come?'

At first I don't understand what he means and then I realize he means to Raqqa, to Sham.

'To build the khilafa. To honour Allah, the most glorified, the most high.'

'You are good person?'

'No. Not yet. I am weak and I make mistakes.'

'You know the Qur'an?'

'Yes.'

He sniffs, and jerks his head like a nod. I can't tell if it means anything or if it's just a physical thing.

'You are widow.'

'I am.'

'Also virgin.'

This is so abrupt I don't know what to say. And I don't know why he's asking. What choice do I have but the truth with him?

'I am not a virgin. My husband, we . . .'

I expect him to help me but he doesn't, he leaves me hanging, and now I feel myself blushing bright red. Why does he want to know? Are they considering me for some new position, some special mission that can only be performed by the pure? I expect disappointment to register in him somewhere but he keeps asking questions.

'Your husband, when he die?'

I don't have to count the days, I know.

'Eight days ago.'

He sniffs again, takes in a roomful of air until his chest is pushed right out, then he bites down on his lower lip, keeps his teeth there, lets the lip slowly spring back. Like he's deciding something.

'You live in widows' house?'

I tell him yes.

'Now you live here.'

I don't understand. I want to say so but daren't.

'Someone bring your clothes.'

My face must show my confusion because he answers my question.

'You live here. You are good Muslim. I make you my wife.'

I think my mouth drops. I can't help it. My confusion has turned to horror.

'I have been a widow only eight days.'

'Virgin. Special case.'

This man sets his own truth. Something in his eyes has changed, from a lion at rest to a lion near the end of its hunt, and I realize Khalil was no lion at all.

He stands up, sniffs again, as if we're all done, and leaves, leaves me sitting there wondering what my life has just become.

5

I'm sharing a room with one of the Russian's other wives. She is called Maysan. She is his second, I am the third.

At a guess she's younger than me, a local. She reminds me of girls I knew at school, the ones who had the strictest parents and you hardly knew they were there, they spent their whole time trying to disappear into the corners. Pretty, but skinny, and timid. She comes in while I'm unpacking and nods a greeting before busying herself in a chest of drawers, looking for something that I'm not sure exists. I leave her to it.

The first wife shows me round. A big woman, under her abaya, she must be nearly six foot, a proper wife for him. I can't tell where she's from. She has an odd accent, not Russian, her voice is hard and harsh, and she barks out short sentences like she doesn't want any conversation. I don't think she's thrilled to find me here. I get the impression she's been told to take charge of me but would much rather the house was hers alone.

There are rules. So many rules. Which bathroom I'm allowed to use and when, the places I'm not allowed to go (his office, the dining room and sitting room unless invited, the garages for his cars, the basement, the main bedroom, the main bathroom), when I will be eating my meals, what to do if I need the toilet in the night. Mealtimes are complicated. If he is away fighting, the three wives eat in the kitchen at seven, but when he's home the four of us sit down at eight, unless he has fellow commanders in the house, in which case he may choose to be with none or all of us, with the rest making do in the kitchen. The children eat separately, except on feast days. Under no circumstances can he see any of his wives before he has had his breakfast, unless he has spent the night with them, in which case he may ask that wife to join him, or he may not. To be safe – the way she says it it's more like an order than advice – it is best to wait until he has eaten before going to wash. The same goes for the children.

We aren't meant to cook, but together we are responsible for overseeing the Yazidi girl who prepares all our food. If it isn't good enough, he will punish us and we will punish her, and she's Yazidi, a teenager, so you have to be on top of her the whole time. Basically we do quite a lot of it. He likes chicken, and fattoush, and the bread has to be very fresh, as does the baklava, so she checks it at the baker's each day and if he tries to palm her off with yesterday's muck – well, he tried that once and he probably won't try it again. Still, it's important to look over his shoulder, make sure he's concentrating. Sometimes if she can't do this, when she has other things to do, maybe I could go there in her place, with one of the guards (we do not speak to the guards). When I tell her that I work all day with the Yazidis she throws her hands up and asks no one in particular what she did to deserve two such useless wives.

There are three children. She doesn't say who their mothers are, or whether they're girls or boys, but I know from the crying I've heard that one of them is a baby. They all share a room. I'm not to go in it.

Her name is Hafa. His is Borz. He is from Dagestan, a great warrior in his homeland who established a caliphate there before joining this greater battle. She corrects herself. This greater war. That is all I need to know, except that some of our most glorious victories have been his, and that it is a great privilege to be his wife. As she says it she tries to give me the kind of stare her husband does but it has nothing like the same effect.

Borz and I are married in the house the next day, Saturday. When I lay my best niqab out on the bed that morning it's like the old me is still inside it, being joined to Khalil, first by God and then on earth. The only time I ever put it on was my wedding day. I swear I can feel him in the room with me, and it's all I can do not to break down. I'm honoured, of course, to be the wife of a truly great warrior. When I left London how could I ever have imagined such a thing? It's a fairy tale, and I should be glad. First I married a prince, and now I am marrying a king.

As I come downstairs I see Imam Talib in the sitting room. It's fitting, that it should be him again, and it must mean that I am a special case after all, that the waiting period can be short-ened. That puts my mind at rest. To maintain the dignity of the occasion he doesn't look at me as I come in. Umm Karam is there as well. It feels like they are there to bless me into my new family.

Borz is in white, as he always seems to be. He nods to me as I stand by him. His eyes are at rest again.

The words are said, and we are husband and wife. After-wards Borz leaves the house and says nothing to me before he goes.

6

sister it's me. how are you? are you coming?

— Nearly there, sister. Crossing tomorrow, inshallah

may God swt give you safe crossing sister.

— Merci ma soeur. I'm ready I think. How are you?

pretty good. my life here gets more and more amazing

— Why sister, what's happened?

i'm married again. yesterday, to a great warrior.

i know it's soon but it's fine, the first one was so short. the imam married us.

221

— Who is he sister?

one of our greatest fighters. such an honour. Khalil was a boy but he is a man.

— Does he have a name?

of course he has a name. Borz. Khasan Bórz.

— He seems a famous man sister. I can see pictures of him. A serious man.

not as famous as he will become.

— Why do you think He swt has chosen this honour for you, sister?

i don't know sister. must go now. i don't know.

7

I eat with the other wives in the kitchen. Borz will not be home tonight. I ask whether he has gone to the front and Hafa gives me a look that says I'm not to concern myself with such things. The Yazidi girl puts the food on the table and then disappears, and I don't ask her her name because I know Hafa won't think it's important. She is young, I think maybe just thirteen. A little younger and she could be in my class. It's strange having her around us, clean and dressed in a niqab, so unlike the ones I teach during the day. I don't suppose she's had any education, before or after she was brought here.

No one says a word. Hafa sits at the head of the table and Maysan opposite me. I watch them eat but they don't see me because their eyes are just on their food. There are currents flowing about between us that I can't begin to pick up. I think

Hafa might hate me but anyway, I don't much feel like speaking either.

I find it hard to sleep. I have work in the morning and no idea how I'm going to get there – I mentioned it to Hafa but she didn't seem to register what I said, just waved me away with a hand and went to sit in the sitting room where I couldn't follow, she doesn't invite me in. I don't want to be late tomorrow. I text Badra and tell her where I am and what I'm doing and ask for her advice. Funny, how I didn't used to trust her. She doesn't reply, at least not before I eventually drift off.

Khalil is in all my thoughts. I wish he wasn't because now I'm married to someone else, it's time to move on, but every time I close my eyes there he is, so young, so innocent. I can even feel him, the warm push of his skin on mine, his breath on the back of my neck, the curl of the hair on his chest. My legs round his. I feel close to him and so far away, warmed by him and yet so lonely, so cold, like a moon that's lost its planet and is spinning out into space.

I'm woken by a hand on my wrist jerking me out of bed so hard I'm still asleep as my feet hit the floor. The hand is strong and rough and dry, and it holds me tighter than it needs to. I want to pull against it but I daren't. If I'm his wife, I'll come when he asks. He doesn't need to drag me.

Borz is naked. Pale skin gathers at the base of his back, which is thick with pale hairs. The landing is lit by the light from his bedroom, where Hafa is wrapping a dressing gown around her, her face full of sleep and irritation, her cheeks and eyes puffy, and this unwanted image enters my head of me in her place some years from now, thrown out of my own bed by the new arrival – and it's strange how the mind works, because in that instant I think two things that seem to mean very little, that I will never be the first wife, and that I have no idea where Hafa is going to sleep. Perhaps in my bed.

This is my husband. It's natural, what's about to happen. I concentrate on my breath, letting it out slowly. To be married to him is an honour, and I must honour him. I keep my eyes on the bed, because I don't want to look and because it seems decent not to, but I'm conscious of his big white form in the room, all that skin and flesh, and I can feel a shaking in my legs that I can't control, a quivering I don't want to show through my pyjamas. He says something to Hafa in Russian, the first time I've heard him speak it, and whether it always sounds like that I don't know but there's something fearsome about it that fits with the rest of him. He has power, and power is everything.

Hafa says something back and Borz shouts at her, tells her to get out, I guess, and she goes, shutting the door.

How I want to follow her.

'Your clothes.'

I hesitate, and he says it again, his eyes now hungry, lazy. The sight of him, he's so big, his chest inflated, the full strong belly, his penis – even like this – looks small against it all. I cannot see us together. I try to tell my body to accept it but it won't. My legs won't stop shaking. We are like two different species, and somewhere between my mind and my senses I feel the fit Khalil and I had, the belonging, and with the same certainty I know that there will never be belonging with this man.

But that is the test. If it was easy, there would be no progress. And has not each test brought me closer to Him?

I unbutton my pyjama top, slip it off, step clumsily out of my bottoms, feel the cold blowing on my skin from the air conditioning. I try to stand straight, natural, but I'm aware of all my body's weakness like I never have been before, and it makes me want to wrap my arms around myself. My want of power is complete. Maybe that is the balance. He could do anything with me, and all I could do with my feeble hands is flail and scratch.

His eyes go from my face to my breasts to my loins, until every familiar flaw on my body – every blemish, everything I have ever obsessed over – is like a new and shameful discovery. In front of him I am a child and an old woman at once, not ripe enough and yet beginning to rot. I don't know what he wants, there is no communication between us. Just him deciding and directing.

He does that sniff he does and tells me to get on the bed. I am the other side of it from him, and I slide in on my back, pulling the duvet up over me as I lie back and try to look him full in the face, to encourage him to think of me as his wife. There must be a reason he took me. Perhaps it is my duty to discover it.

He yanks the covers off, and now it's worse than when I was standing. An image comes into my head of me in the desert, at night, naked and curled up on the sand in the cold under the stars and waiting not for His love but for nameless jinns and demons, creatures of the devil who I know are there in the darkness, drawing closer, ready to tear my flesh apart. The demons are Borz, I think, but then I realize my mistake, and why this image has been given to me. I have this the wrong way round. The temptation is to refuse my husband. That is what the devils want. The path to God is to do my duty.

'Over.'

Until now my husband has been standing by the bed but when I don't understand him he kneels on it and turns me over by my shoulders onto my front, brings one leg over me and pushes my legs apart. He rests against me, leans against me on his hands, I hear his hoarse breath and feel it in my hair, smell the strong scent of sweat and force on him, and something else, something bitter, stale, and then he moves into me and we are joined. Joined, but not one. The Russian words he breathes into my ear are like insects finding their way into my brain, I close my eyes into the pillow and feel his weight push into me, his hand grips my neck and tightens, grows tighter with and against his weight until my breath thins and the red behind my eyes starts to go black and there's nowhere left for me to go.

Only my faith remains. Strong, silent. Of everything unafraid.

Then he slows, and the weight lightens, and his grasp goes loose, and I wonder now what is in his eyes, whether now the hunt is over they show satisfaction or something more.

I understand his need. I understand my place. But I am glad he can't see mine.

With one last word of Russian he rolls off me, and when I bring myself to look he is on his back, staring upwards, completely separate. The dark energy in him has not been spent. The muscles in his jaw are working, and when he closes his eyes for a moment it isn't to rest but to gather strength, or to curse my image, I can feel it. I want to turn my head away from him but I don't dare, because if I move he may remember I'm here, and right now he might be a thousand miles away. I want to turn on my side, wipe myself clean, be dressed again, search for sleep, but instead I lie as still as I can like a mouse pretending to be dead in the hope that the cat will move on. In the space I've made, ashamed by my tears, I try to remember the lesson. He is my husband now. A man of strength, a man who has killed a thousand times as many enemies as a boy like Khalil. And what, I want him to be gentle? I expected my innocence to end when I crossed the border but maybe this is the real border, right here, from being a girl to becoming a woman.

I lie in the dark for a long time and somehow I sleep. I wake to the sound of a child crying.

It's definitely a child, not the baby. It sounds like a girl, yelping in pain. I still haven't seen any of the children – their room is next to this, at the other end of the house from mine, and they seem to stay in there. For a while I lie in the dark and listen to it. A word comes to me, I don't know where from. Keening. I think she must be ill, the crying has a weird inhuman quality to it, like she has a fever or something.

No one seems to be doing anything about it. As I get used to the darkness and being awake I realize that Borz has gone, there's no one else in here. I have no way of telling the time but perhaps he's already gone to work, or even to the front.

After some fumbling I switch on the bedside light and find my pyjamas. I have a headache, and my stomach churns a little when I stand, and it occurs to me that when the house is awake I might have a shower. I would like a shower. Maybe here it will be hot.

I stand in the doorway for a minute to listen as the crying stops briefly and then starts up again. Down the landing my bedroom door is shut. There are no lights on and no sounds of anyone moving about. I wonder if the brothers on guard outside can hear it and if they find it distracting. Poor child. It sounds horrible, whatever it is. She needs a doctor, or even to go to hospital. Suddenly I feel hugely protective towards her, and I wonder if that has to do with my own worries about being late, and I force that thought from my mind before it can take root.

If Borz isn't here I'll have to wake Hafa and hope that she knows what to do. Perhaps one of the brothers could drive us somewhere.

The children's door is only a few feet from me, and I tiptoe to it. But as soon as I move that way I know that the noise is coming from somewhere else, and with my ear to the door I hear only silence inside.

It's downstairs. It has to be. The stairs turn halfway down, and I stop there to listen. The crying is weaker now, but still distinct, and I'm caught about what to do. Maybe one of the children is sleeping downstairs. Maybe she left her room and is looking for help.

So I go down, slowly, listening on every step. I guess part of me thinks Borz may not be gone and while I have his children's best interests at heart I don't want him to get the wrong idea about what I'm doing. Like I'm trying to leave or something. The crying is definitely less intense, more tired, and it seems to be coming from the far end of the house, by the garage, underneath my room, and by the time I'm at the bottom of the stairs I'm sure of it. For a few seconds I stand there, and as I step off the last step I hear a whispered hiss from up above me that makes me stop. It comes again, and I can just make out a shape on the landing.

'Up here,' it says, in the same hiss. 'Now.'

'One of the children—' I start to say, but it cuts me off.

'Up. Quiet.'

As she says it I hear a door open downstairs and without really knowing why I zip back up the stairs as quickly as I can, two at a time. On the top step Hafa takes my arm and marches me in front of her into my bedroom and silently closes the door. There's barely any light and I can't see her face but the fear in her voice is as plain as day.

'Do not move around this house at night. Ever. Now. Go to the bathroom. Quickly. Flush it and return to your bed. And pray he does not suspect. Go.'

She opens the door and pushes me out. The bathroom is in between my room and Borz's, I find the toilet in the half-light, feel for the flush and leave, trying to look as if I'm not rushing.

I meet Borz as he climbs the last steps, and even in the near darkness there's something so intimidating about his presence, the great mass of him, that no matter how hard I focus I shrink back. His breathing is thick and he's sniffing, clearing his throat, so he doesn't hear me and when he finally realizes I'm there he stops and swears in Russian, and then just stands over me, working out what to do, and even without really seeing him I have a sense of his hand closing into a fist. My heart is going so fast.

'What you do.'

'I needed the bathroom.'

There's a tiredness about him now, a heaviness. I wonder what the options are that he's considering. Part of me wants to run past him, down the stairs, past the guards and out to God knows where.

But in the end he turns, walks slowly away, and falls lifeless into bed. And I have no choice but to follow him.

The bed is full of snakes. My skin crawls with them and they wrap themselves round my brain.

I try to think about it, and I try not to think about it, and neither works because all there is in my head is the smell of him and the crying of that girl like a song that repeats and repeats no matter how much you want it to stop.

I don't know her name. I don't know if anybody does. Perhaps she's forgotten herself. I think I would.

In my mind I am her, underneath that dark form, seeing and feeling that dark shape rolling and shifting, his smell working its way inside. I feel her pain, and it confuses me, because her pain should be different from mine.

Then a new thought comes to me, the worst I've had. What if this is a punishment, for all of us? What if this is what happens to unbelievers? All of a sudden my mind clears and a hundred memories rush in of mistakes and shortcomings and failures.

One begins to stand out from all the rest. I begin to realize with such great clarity what is happening to me.

8

They made doctors young in the Islamic State. The hard demeanour and brutal manner that Doctor Huq had learned from his brothers didn't sit well on him. It was like watching a child play at soldiers. Why couldn't Sofia have married an idiot like this and not one of the murderers-in-chief?

Huq may have been a fool but it didn't make him any less dangerous. His new commission seemed to torture him: an opportunity for advancement, yes, but the slightest slip might send him to the bottom of the ladder, or somewhere worse than that. It puffed him up into a quivering bubble of importance and fear. As my friend, you can expect great things, but if you do not do precisely as I say I shall have no choice but to count you as my enemy. He reminded Abraham of managers he had had throughout his career.

But he seemed straightforwardly pleased to have someone to order around. Later, Abraham might have to run some errands, everyone else was too important to leave the hospital, but for now he could accompany Huq on his rounds. For the next two hours, the two men went from room to room inspecting two dozen bearded young men who had been shot, maimed, burned, knifed and filled with shrapnel from exploding bombs. Not all had been injured in battle. Two had been crushed when the tunnel they had been crawling through had collapsed during an airstrike. And the knifing was a personal matter, according to Huq, who at first refused to elaborate and then in a low voice told Abraham that two fighters had fought over a Yazidi girl. Here in hell this sounded almost noble, until Huq revealed that the victim had been stabbed for selling a virgin who was not a virgin. He told the story confidentially, as if it might confer more importance on him, suggest some intimacy with the fighters' affairs, but at the same time Abraham thought he detected a hesitation there, something short of total commitment to the cause. Again, he could have been playing a role. His commitment to this new life seemed to be built on an idea that wasn't quite playing out as he had expected.

He was no doctor. As they moved from one bed to another Abraham watched him ask questions that betrayed his lack of knowledge at every point. Someone else must have been doing all the work. One young Bangladeshi, face screwed up in constant pain, had had a leg amputated below the knee after an airstrike on a barracks just north of Madan three nights earlier. The Americans, well-targeted. His other leg had been shredded by fragments from the blast, and yesterday he had undergone an operation first to remove these fragments, and then to graft some skin from his thigh onto an open wound on his ankle that otherwise stood no chance of healing.

Huq removed the dressing and spent a good minute carefully inspecting the leg, from the knee down a mess of blood and exposed flesh. In an instant Abraham knew that it was infected; there seemed to be swelling, although the skin was so damaged it was difficult to tell, and around the central wound on the ankle there was a raised section of skin that had turned a yellowish green. He had known it, in fact, as soon as he saw the patient's face.

'It's infected,' he told Huq.

'I can see that.'

'Is he being given antibiotics?'

Huq consulted the chart, which had been hanging on the end of the bed where it was supposed to be. It was odd, this, being in a place that felt just like a hospital and like no hospital at all.

'Of course. By mouth.'

'It's not enough. He needs intravenous. Who did the work?'

Huq brought his chin in, a defensive reflex.

'A civilian doctor. A surgeon.'

'Where is he?'

'Working.'

'Find a drip. Now, or he'll lose this leg. If you need to speak to this doctor, interrupt him. Otherwise we should take responsibility. I will.'

Huq looked at Abraham with a look that was rich with defeat and pride and some relief.

'I don't need to interrupt him.'

Abraham nodded. Huq was terrified, of his bosses, his patients, his colleagues. Any rational person would be, but then no rational person ought to be here. Perhaps the delusion that had brought him had simply worn off. The thought gave him hope.

'Then let's go.'

Huq breathed deeply and ushered Abraham away from the bed.

'I can't administer it.'

'Why not?'

'He is not a priority.'

'What do you mean?'

'His case is not a priority case.'

'Then whose is?' Abraham raised his voice and Huq raised a hand to quiet him. 'Look at him.'

'His wounds are serious.'

'Exactly.'

'He won't fight again.'

The understanding passed into Abraham like a knife into flesh. Of course. This whole place functioned on icy practicality. He told himself never again to assume that any goodness existed in the dawla.

'You're serious?'

Huq said nothing.

'Then why try to save his leg? Why not just amputate?'

'Dr Saad thought it could be saved.'

232

Abraham looked from the patient to Huq, who was once again looking down at his shoes. The fighter was no doubt as repellent as the rest, but Christ, this was a hospital.

'Double his dose at least. For fuck sake.'

And he left, disgusted, to continue Huq's rounds.

Huq was from Canada. Toronto, or a town just outside. His parents were from Pakistan, originally, Lucknow, both doctors, well, medics – his mother was a dentist – and he had followed their example and studied medicine at school, but in his second year he had become disillusioned. Why work to cure people who were diseased in the soul? Years of studying and practising to prolong lives that had no value. It seemed almost to run counter to the teachings of Allah, the most high, the most glorified – to perpetuate the spread of consumerism and individualism and greed and mindless lust. And in Canada, half the patients he would end up treating would have made themselves ill in the first place. That was the curse of the kafir, and one day it would take them all down, it was a fatal condition. Sickness in the soul spread to the body, through gorging on sugar and godless rich food and alcohol and drugs. And sex, of course. What, he should give years of life he might devote to Him, the most high, the most glorified, to rid some homosexual of the illness he had brought upon himself? Was that what his life was for?

Huq harangued Abraham while they drank water from plastic bottles at the top of the ramp, rounds over. In Arabic, because Abraham didn't want to let on that he spoke English. Huq was hopeless, and deluded, but there was a sort of twisted integrity in what he said, a diseased logic. His case reminded Abraham strongly of Sofia's, and in another place he might have brought him into his confidence. Not here. Not with anyone, and least of all someone as changeable as Huq.

But he could still be useful.

'My daughter, she's here somewhere. In Raqqa.'

'I know,' said Huq, with a certain self-importance.

'She was married yesterday. To a great fighter. A Russian called Borz.'

'She's married to Borz?'

As he said the words, Huq seemed to regret them. He should know everything about his charge.

'You know him?'

'Everyone knows him. They say he's killed more kafirs than any other fighter.'

And now he's married to my daughter. Abraham controlled the scream growing inside him.

'A great honour.'

'Yes,' said Huq, unsurely. Behind his bulging eyes he seemed to be trying to work out how this changed things. Was Abraham more important now that he was connected to the very top rung? Could he be more useful? Certainly, if the two of them fucked up it would be more visible. Despite everything, Abraham took some grim pleasure from watching the fear ebb and flow in the man's face.

'Do you know where he lives?'

Immediately Huq filled with suspicion.

'Why do you want to know where he lives?'

'Because I saw my daughter yesterday, and she told me she was getting married, and I wanted to pay my respects. Meet my new son-in-law.'

'Why didn't she invite you to the ceremony?'

'Before I . . . before we came here we had a fight. A father–daughter thing. She's a teenager, you know how it is.'

Huq nodded and frowned. He did know, but that didn't mean Abraham was off the hook.

'Why don't you just call her?'

'She hasn't given me her new number. She's as stubborn as her mother.'

Abraham smiled, as one man of experience might smile to another.

'I don't know where he lives. Of course not. What am I, your guide? And your mind should not be on personal matters. In the dawla there are no personal matters.'

Abraham felt his phone buzz twice in his pocket and telling Huq that, of course, he understood, he excused himself, desperate to read what she had sent.

But it wasn't her. It was Vural.

— Are you there? Speak to me.

9

— Sister. Je suis arrivée. Dans le khilafa. I can hardly believe it. So amazing here. When can we meet?

that's great sister. amazing you made it. i was beginning to doubt!!!

— It was scary but your example is so strong. I could not have done it without your help and direction.

— I would like to thank you face to face sister. I have something for you.

gifts not important sister. also i'm super busy right now, not a great time

— Not for long, sister. Just to see you and embrace you one sister and another.

you need a mahram sister until you are married you can't go out. i had that problem

    — I have a mahram sister, the husband of my cousin he is
      here since a year now

weird you didn't mention that sister

    — I did mention, I am sure that I did. His name is Yusef
      he is from Lyon.

oh okay sorry sister not myself. tbh so soon to be married
again.

    — what is he like your new husband? can I meet him too?

unlikely sister. unlikely

    — why is that sister?

    — okay sister goodnight I try you again soon

10

Abraham slept, when he was allowed to sleep, in a dormitory
for unmarried fighters, administrators and other minor compo-
nents of the Islamic State machine.

They were boys, each one of them. The way they jostled and
brayed and bragged. The obsession with things: the biggest
gun, the coolest car, the sexiest knife. Look at this motherfucker, that's going to slice right through anything it wants, cut
metal in two like a fucking melon. Like butter, brother. Like
fucking water.

Imagine the fucking damage this is going to do.

Which was the sweetest kafir girl to take? It's all in the teeth,
brother, sweet white teeth. Bullshit. She'll fucking bite down on
you brother, you don't want any fucking teeth. I knew a brother
he nearly lost it, brother, she bit clean through. Smash them out
first, maybe, take no chances. Some of these Yazidi girls, they're

blonde, the kafir cunts, imagine that, blonde here and down there, fucking beautiful. I'd pay for that, brother. I'd pay well for that, fucking four weeks' wages, as long as she was clean. She won't be so fucking clean after I've fucking finished with her, brother, and no way you're getting in first, no way. I'm quick as fuck. I've heard that about you, brother. You come here and say that. Come right here. I fucking mean it.

All night. Abraham felt as if he'd been dropped into a nest of rats. It smelled that way in here. A particular kind of sweat: acrid, fear-ridden, funky. These were the men his daughter idolized. This was what she'd married. This was where the family line was headed.

Going to smash those kafirs tomorrow, brother. This baby's going to do the job for me, aren't you, my beauty? Going to clean you up good so the bullets fly straight and sweet right into some kafir cunt's head, boom. You know it, brother. You, Cairo, you ever seen a head explode? At Dabiq I took this rebel fuck out, such a good shot, man, that was beautiful, I got him right here, yeah, right in the cheekbone, and his head burst all over the kafir standing next to him. Allahu Akbar, He gave me a great shot, the most glorified, the most high, and I took it. Those fuckers can't fight. All over the guy's face, he's going fucking mental, jumping around and wiping it off while his friend just kind of crumples. Hysterical. Like he was just clothes. Ain't no way you were putting that one back together, Cairo, he was well fucked, and that other cunt too, once I gave him a minute to get the taste of his friend out of his mouth.

You're full of shit. It fucking happened. Abu Kaba saw it. That would be the dead Abu Kaba? Fuck you. Don't call me a fucking liar. How many kills, brother, if you're so fucking clever?

They bickered about that for a while. Six of them there were in this room, not counting Abraham himself, sitting on their bedrolls polishing their guns and talking shit like kids on a camping trip. Dinner had been pitta and houmous and some sort of cold meat slices that could have been beef. The water was not quite clear and tasted of soil; everyone else had drunk Coke. Abraham had eaten with his head down, acknowledging the odd taunting question with a nod or shake of his head. It was a new feeling, to hate anyone so much, but he realized there was a sort of fear in them as well, and as he ate and listened he began to realize that they were as unthinking as Sofia had been credulous. Fools manipulated by knaves.

Tomorrow they were going out to the front, up to Kobani. You should come with us, Cairo, see some actual fighting. Are you kidding? Shit his pants. He's too old. No fucking walking sticks at the front, brother Ibrahim.

'I'll be waiting here to stitch you back together again.'

That got a laugh, and made him feel complicit. He didn't want these men laughing with him, even if it might be useful to establish some trust.

Don't want stitching, Cairo.

This was the youngest of them all; at least he looked the youngest, his beard so thin the straggly hairs barely covered his cheeks, which were chubby and soft like the rest of him. The unlikely jihadi, grown up too soon, a lumbering boy whose eyes were pinched and too close together. When he spoke he spoke slowly, every syllable deliberate, so that Abraham assumed his first language must be something other than Arabic, but from things the other fighters had said it seemed he came from Iraq. The others teased him about his age but not his appearance, as if obeying some unspoken code.

Inshallah I will be shaheed tomorrow, I can feel it, He has willed it for me.

That brought a solemnity on the group. Now there was no teasing.

Inshallah, brother. Inshallah.

Much murmuring, and then silence for a few seconds.

Tomorrow I shall be in Paradise by the running brook. God willing, brother, in Paradise, with the virgins with the dark eyes.

May we all be shaheed when He ordains it, brother, may we all be worthy of that glory.

The sentimentality of it was complete. They pined for God and death, which were the same thing. But the dumb energy had only gone for a moment, and for another hour the chatter went on.

In a break in the talk Abraham finally said the thing he had been wanting to say all this time, the one thing that might be useful.

'Who here knows Borz?'

'Borz? Course we know Borz. Man's a fucking legend, brother. Took out half the Iraqi army with his fists. Killed a thousand Peshmerga. What you want with Borz, Cairo? You want to suck his dick for the fucking cause? Show your respect to a real man?'

'Someone in his family's ill. One of his children. I have to go there tomorrow but the address they gave me makes no sense, I think it's wrong.'

'You want us to give you Borz's address? Serious? Cairo, you're the fucking best.'

'You think we're directories or something, brother? What the fuck?'

'It's his kid. What if I don't get there? What if something happens to it?'

'Who told you to go, Cairo? Just get the address off them.'

'They gave me the address.'

'Then tell them it's wrong. What's wrong with you?'

'I did tell them. They say it's right. But I've looked, it doesn't exist.'

'I went there once. I had to pick him up, our detail.'

'So where was it?'

'He's got this big fucking house out beyond that Shia mosque, the one we blew up.'

'Ah fuck I know those houses, man, sweet. One day I'm having one of those.'

'You'll be dead long before that happens, brother.'

'Fuck you, Khalid.'

'What was the address?'

'I don't know, Cairo, it was months ago. Looks like you just killed Borz's kid. Good luck with that.'

'It's on Hamra Street, fuck sake. It's the one with a dozen fighters outside.'

One by one the men began to undress and go to bed. They slept in their T-shirts and Calvin Kleins, Abraham in his shirt and boxer shorts. The whole thing was like a teenage sleepover with guns.

'Cairo. Turn off the light.'

He looked across at the fighter lying on his bedroll, head propped on his hand.

'Last in.'

Back in bed, his mind danced in the darkness. A boy in the hospital, his leg blasted, writhing against the pain. Murat's face pressed into the road, his eyes as empty as the eyes of the man who had killed him. Black, dead eyes that stared at nothingness.

One of these people had killed him. One of these interchangeable killers that swarmed through his imagination like an infestation, with the same face, the same clothes, the same leer, cocksure and petty, swaggering and murderous and barely formed. Cockroaches, locusts, a blight and a pestilence brought upon mankind for going its own way, swaggering into pure selfishness, heedless, stupid. In their millions they overran him and blacked out all thought.

Sofia. Sofia, Sofia. Some part of the real her must remain, or why save him? No other explanation fit. Faith in this god or that god, that might come and go, but logic – there was nothing the rats could do against logic. Abraham lay in the darkness and cherished the light of that one idea.

11

This morning I don't feel like the teacher, or the jailer, I feel like one of the imprisoned. That's why I'm here.

The Yazidis can sense there's something wrong, but I just don't have the energy to pretend. I fall back on old habits, take my copy of the Qur'an, explain to them that in each page there is wisdom and beauty and direction, and that by opening it at random we can see what God has in mind for us. As I let the pages spray under my thumb part of me is praying that the passage I find will be relevant to me and may contain some hope, but even as I catch myself thinking it I know it's a superstition, a low instinct, selfish, base. But I do it anyway, because I've started to do it, and because my need for hope right now is greater than anything else.

Niran's mother is back. I find it hard to look at her.

I close my eyes at the open page and point.

And the unbelievers say, 'Why has no sign been sent down to him his Lord?'

I turn it on the Yazidis, tell them that their insistence on signs is a sign of their ingratitude, that Allah the most glorified has no need, no desire to let them know of his existence, and the words scour me with shame because I know each one applies to me. I have treated each moment of my time here as a sign, as something to be read, as something that was intended for me, and I am eaten up with hatred for my self-absorption.

The women are quiet. They can sense a change in me and I have no patience for them. I want them to go away.

If I was one of these women, every sign I saw would be of a world without God. They have lost their husbands. They have lost their sons. Their homes have been destroyed and their dignity taken, and I cannot make them see that this is the time above all others that they must believe. The lesson applies to me as well.

Until we get past this we won't get anywhere. We all need courage. So I do something that even last week I couldn't have imagined. I get the women to tell me about their lives. Not their religion, not their god and beliefs, but their stories. I want them to understand that God was not the cause of the suffering, and that now He can lead them from it.

I start with Besma, and when she sees that I'm serious and that this isn't a trap, slowly she opens up. She was married, for twenty years, and her husband was killed in fighting on Mount Sinjar. No, that's not true. I must report what she believes to be the full truth. He was injured in fighting, and she and two cousins took him to the hospital in the town, and there he was murdered by our fighters. They came in and shot him as he lay in his bed, but she didn't see it because she was trying to find food for her youngest son, who was unwell.

I don't interrupt her, I just let her talk. I need to understand her reality.

Then she and her son and many other women and children were taken across the border into Syria, where they were separated into groups and she was moved on. Her son was taken. He was fifteen. I ask her where her son is now and she says she has no idea, that for two weeks she had news of him because people have mobiles still and they talk to each other, but then there was silence and all she heard was that every boy was taken to be converted and trained as a fighter for IS.

What was his name, I ask. His name was Mirza but now it will be different. The first thing they take from you is your name.

As Besma talks the other women play with the cloth of their dresses, occasionally mutter something to each other. They hold the children close, and the children squirm away, restless. Not one of them has been outside for weeks.

I move on. I ask the mother of Niran to tell me about her family, how she came to be here. She is sitting cross-legged on the floor and running her hands through her daughter's thick hair, picking out heaven knows what. From this angle Niran looks thinner than she was, some of the fullness has gone from her cheeks, but it might be the light and anyway her eyes are still bright and an amazing blue. Even in this place she shines. She reminds me of girls from my school who seemed to be outside the run of things, the really beautiful ones, God's creatures, their beauty something that the rest of us could never aspire to. She has a way of narrowing her eyes when she focuses but now she's just staring into the distance. I realize I've never heard her say anything, not a word.

Besma translates my question to her mother and she doesn't seem to hear it, just keeps on separating Niran's hair and playing it out through her fingers. I ask Besma to ask again and this time the woman's hands stop, and she pushes Niran gently upright off her lap. Then she looks right at me and with a dip and shake of her head says something short in reply. Besma hesitates, but when I nod she translates.

'She say she do not speak with you.'

Now she really starts, head bobbing from side to side, finger pointing at me, and the words flowing out in a stream that's been ready to break for a long time. Even if Besma wanted to she couldn't keep up. I nod, and try to look sympathetic, but having someone rage at you even when you don't know what they're saying is hard and I find it difficult to hold her eye. Flecks of her spit catch in the shafts of light from the high windows.

There is anger in me, I can feel it, like a residue from the past, but I ignore it, push it to one side. I want to know what she's said.

'She says, what good is your God if He cannot protect this little girl?'

I think if I tried to take Niran from her she would kill me with her hands.

12

What did Badra say? Women mean nothing here. We need the men to be men. Maybe. Maybe that's right in war. But what about the peace? When there is peace, we will need the women to lead, because the men will all be dead or like Borz. I don't think many in the khilafa realize this. No one's thought it through.

The Yazidi maid is called Zarifa. This evening I help her prepare dinner and we try to talk. She has a little Arabic, not much, and at first she's so shy she doesn't want to say anything, probably because she thinks I'm going to stop smiling any minute and scold her, or even hit her. I can tell Hafa hits her, not because she's bruised or anything, but just from the way she behaves around me. She can't seem to believe I'm helping as much as I can – I guess when the others are on cooking duty the most they do is just stand and watch.

We marinate chicken wings in lemon juice and oil and we shred lettuce and chop tomatoes and I fry the pitta for the fattoush – Borz likes it fried, Hafa briefs me on this.

'You can cook,' I tell her.

She knows what she's doing. Her chopping is quick, and before peeling the garlic she crushes it lightly under the blade of the knife like my mother used to do.

Zarifa nods, eyes down on her work. Always down.

'Who taught you?'

She doesn't understand, so I rephrase it.

'This. How did you learn?'

'Mother. She die.'

She says this without looking up. In that moment her world opens up to me and I see her mother dying at our hands and it takes the strongest faith to remember that I should feel bad not for that, but because she didn't have the chance to be taken into God's kingdom. It's like Zarifa knows what I'm thinking because then she says,

'Sick.'

'I'm sorry. My mother is sick too.'

I make a vow there and then to make sure that Zarifa has the chances in life that her mother didn't have.

'How old were you?'

She shakes her head and her shoulders go up just a little in a shrug, so I ask something else.

'Have you got brothers? Or sisters?'

Now she looks at me, and I can see the answer in her face, and it's not good. The skin under her eyes is so dark she looks ill. A narrow face, with something ancient about it, like one of those African masks. She's so skinny, I wonder what she gets to eat and who gives it to her. Every time I say something she bows her head an inch and her shoulders tighten as if she knows what's coming next.

She should cry. She should be able to cry. But I can tell that she's past crying, that to cry would mean hope, and she has no hope left.

If only she could join my class. Poor creature, she has nothing to lead her from the darkness.

'I will teach you,' I tell her.

She nods.

'About God. About Allah, the most high, the most glorified.'

'Yes,' she says, and even if she doesn't completely understand I think I'm getting through to her. And then I do something that surprises me. I take her by the arms and I look into her eyes and I bring her to me and hug her. Her stiff thin body shakes but after a second she relaxes and puts her hands behind my back.

'It's going to be okay,' I tell her, and at the same time I think I'm telling myself.

That night the four of us eat together in the dining room, Borz and his three wives. I sit on his left, Hafa on his right, and no one speaks. Maysan looks like she would shrink into nothingness if she could.

Zarifa serves the food and leaves as soon as she is done. No one so much as registers her presence. Borz pulls his wings apart first, before ripping the flesh off them with his teeth. I have little appetite but I don't want to draw attention to myself by leaving food, so I eat it.

Borz's face is bent over his plate, his red-blond beard drooping. I see this out of the corner of my eye, I don't look at him, but I can hear the bones tearing and the salad crunching in his mouth. He eats with the hunger he keeps caged inside.

On his fourth or fifth wing he stops and says something in Russian. Hafa looks up at him, and he shows her the meat, splays it out for her to inspect, then throws it back on his plate and sits back in his chair, arms crossed, like a man who cannot believe he has been so gravely insulted. Even from here I can see the red on the bone.

'I must know who is responsible,' he says, in Arabic now, to all of us and none in particular.

Hafa looks from him to me, stands up and leaves for the kitchen. She comes straight back dragging Zarifa behind her. She pulls her to the table and shows her the chicken wing, takes her own fork and prods at it.

'What is this?' she asks. 'It is raw. Blood. Look.' She lifts the wing up and pushes it in her face.

'Sorry.' This is one word she does have. She looks down at

the floor but I don't need to see her eyes to know she's terrified. 'Sorry.'

Hafa is scared herself, I can see it. She needs to make the situation right.

'Eat it,' she says to the girl. 'Take it. Eat it.'

'That was me. I will eat it.'

Hafa looks at me like I've lost my mind.

'You cooked this?'

'Yes.'

I didn't. I left it for Zarifa, but he'll kill her and he may not kill me. Borz's eyes are like green ice, they feel like they could burn a hole right through my chest.

I reach across the table and take the wing from Hafa whose mouth is actually hanging open. What I'm doing is a far bigger deal than undercooking a piece of chicken.

It's not that bad. In fact, it's fine. The great warrior, killer of a thousand men, floored by a drop of bird's blood. I eat it like it's no problem and put the bones on my plate. Borz sits looking away with his arms crossed as if this whole business was way beneath his dignity. Everyone else has their eyes down.

'Apologize,' says Hafa when I'm done.

'I'm sorry.'

Borz sniffs, pushes his plate away, wipes his mouth.

'Come here and say it.'

I get up and stand by him. His frame bulges out from the chair.

'Closer.'

I take a step forward, so that my niqab touches his arm.

'Look at me,' he says. He uncrosses his arms and places a hand on each thigh. 'Look at me.'

Inwardly I brace myself for whatever's coming but even then it's so quick I don't see it. He keeps his palm open but you wouldn't call it a slap, his hand is rigid and it makes a hollow sound like a balloon bursting. I fall backwards, bring my hand up to my face, fall into Hafa, who pushes me away.

'Here.'

Impatiently wagging the fingers of the same hand Borz calls me back, points to where he wants me to stand. I keep my body turned from him but he shouts at me to face him and as I bring myself slowly round he hits me again. He repeats this process four times, varying the delay each time so that I never know when the blow is coming. By the end my cheek is ringing and I can feel my eye beginning to swell. I draw my hand across my mouth and blood comes away with it.

With as much dignity as I still have I walk steadily from the room.

13

On his third day, Abraham returned to the hospital to find Huq darting about the corridors in a high state of panic.

'Where have you been?'

'Taking those drugs to Dar al-Shifa. You sent me.'

'What took you so long?'

'Al Mogmaa is blocked. You heard the bombs last night?'

'Find Saad. We need to find Saad.'

'Why?'

'There's a fighter in that room with half his fucking leg missing. And not just any fighter. Find him, or we are both fucked.'

'Who is it?'

'Just fucking go! Try upstairs.'

Upstairs the hospital wasn't a hospital. It was a place for the sick and the injured to wait and to die.

And to moan, wail, scream. A low hum of pain washed in and out of the halls, hung over the patients lying hopeless on the broken floor, settled on an old man with twin cotton pads taped over his eyes. Settled on bodies that hadn't been cleared. Clung to the airstrike victims and the thick layer of fine dust that covered them. As he wandered, Abraham felt that he occupied a different realm, that he could only look on as a ghost might, unable to act. Someone was helping these people. There were slings and bandages, limbs were set in plaster, but for every patient who had had treatment there were five waiting for it, and an image took root in Abraham's mind of waters swelling impossibly at the entrance to a narrow channel.

A ghost he might be, but he could be seen, and as he passed people looked up with a mixture of loathing and hope. His armband. How he longed to take it off. If he was in rebel country to the west he could do proper work, treat people, show the courage he was beginning to discover in himself. Here he was a lickspittle, a toady, a traitor to the oath he had never actually taken, and he hated himself about as much as everyone around him did.

But even in this chaos there must be a system, some way of deciding who was treated, some sort of triage – insert himself into it and he could at least begin to make himself useful. He saw no staff up here, except maybe a nurse or two, and he hesitated to ask them because there was no way of knowing their allegiance. So he walked, and looked for a man in scrubs without an armband, feeling more useless and ashamed with every step.

Turning a corner, he found himself in a wide hall where the hospital's main entrance must once have been, now half collapsed into glass and masonry and sheered lengths of window frame. Armed guards stood by the opening that remained, and through them now against the white street outside came a black figure carrying a child, head turned to its mother's shoulder, arms loosely wrapped around her neck. One of the guards stepped in front of her, hand on the trigger of his gun: who was she, where did she live, what did she want. The woman just shook her head, unable to speak, and behind her her husband began to answer. This was their son, five years old, he was hurt, they don't know how, they found him with a great wound, they are good people, supporters of the cause, please, we need help.

The guard stood, tilted his head, took his time.

'You tell me how this happened or you turn around and fuck off.'

Abraham walked to them and as his eyes adjusted to the light saw a wound in the boy's side, deep and dark beyond the shirt someone had ripped apart to give it air. The boy made no sound; his skin was pale and the hair on his forehead pasted with sweat. Abraham stood between the fighter and the family and crossed his arms.

'Are you a doctor?' he said. 'Can you treat this boy?'

The fighter looked uncertain. The script for this exchange hadn't been written.

'How old is he?' Abraham asked the father.

Like a man used to being trapped by such questions, the father looked at Abraham and tried to divine the answer.

'Five. Just five.'

Abraham turned back to the fighter.

'Do you think you should decide his future value to the khilafa?'

Reaching to the mother he took the child and carefully held him, one arm across the shoulders, one under the knees. There was no weight to him.

'The husband stays.'

The fighter reached out and placed his hand on the man's chest.

'I might need him,' said Abraham. 'The mother's hysterical.'

He glared into the dumb eyes of the guard and realized what it was about these people. This man was no more a wolf than he was; he was a sheep, herded and processed like the people under him. Disrupt their programming and they couldn't function.

'I'm the doctor here.'

There were no beds. Half the rooms had no furniture at all and the rest were full. Abraham went from doorway to doorway, desperation growing. Really, they had minutes to save the boy. He could feel the small store of life left in him as surely as he might see the dimming light from a bulb about to blow.

'Are you a nurse?'

He stopped a woman in the corridor and she nodded, said nothing.

'Find me Dr Saad.'

'I don't know where he is.'

'Are you ISIS?'

He didn't need to see her eyes to see that the question terrified her; she stiffened and shrunk back.

'No.'

'The boy will die. We don't want to be the ones who killed him.'

'I don't know.'

'Tell him it's a fighter's son. Anything. Bring antiseptic, antibiotics.'

'I . . .'

'Try.'

She went. Two more full rooms and then a closed door that with a nod Abraham had the father open. An office, small, hot, not used, to judge by the papers piled on the desk and the floor and the stacks of chairs against the far wall.

'Clear the desk. Push it all on the floor.'

When they were done, Abraham laid the boy gently on the desk, wiped the hair from his brow, and told him everything was going to be okay. When he opened his eyes, as he did from time to time, the pupils were shaking, delirious. The colour was leaving him, his breaths were short and the skin around his eyes was turning a dark, lifeless grey. A handsome boy, like his father, with thin limbs and a graze on his elbow, the kind of injury a boy of five should sustain, playing somewhere perhaps, in the hanging ruins of someone's former home.

'Water,' he said to the mother. 'Get water and a cloth, whatever you can find.'

She looked to her husband, and Abraham reassured her.

'You're veiled. It's easier for you to move around. Please. It'll be all right.'

The wound was smaller than he'd thought at first; what he had taken to be flesh was only bloody skin. Gently turning the boy on his side, Abraham ripped the shirt right up to the armpit and looked around for something to cut the fabric. In the drawer of the desk he found a tiny pair of paper scissors, cut round the sleeve and up through the collar, and as he knelt to inspect him noticed a second wound on his back, an inch or two to the left of the spine. Oh God. Make me equal to this.

The father knew. Half the fear on his face was for his son, and the rest for how much worse their lives might become if he told the truth.

'What happened?'

The father shook his head.

'I'm not going to hurt you. I'm not going to hurt him.'

Such sadness in the man's eyes. Such contortions.

'It will help him. If you tell me.'

'He was playing.'

'Playing.'

'He was playing football, in our street, and someone shot him. A friend dragged him away, another came to get me.'

'Why did they shoot him?'

'I don't know. For playing.'

Abraham breathed as deeply as he could and closed his eyes.

One day God would punish these people. Whose God he didn't know, and he didn't care.

The mother came with cloudy water in a metal jug and a strip of cloth that looked pristine, more or less, and Abraham cleaned the skin around both wounds. They were too low for the bullet to have damaged the liver, or the kidneys, but his appendix might have ruptured, and his bowel was almost certainly damaged. The bleeding had slowed, but then the poor boy's blood pressure must have dropped to nothing, and there was no telling what was happening to him inside. Where was the nurse? He wouldn't blame her for not delivering the message, or the doctor for not hearing it. Trapped in this tiny little hutch with the parents' eyes on his sweating hands and all their hopes pushing down on him, Abraham might feel that there was nothing more important in the world – but this was nothing, this was just a tiny part of it, one small beat in an insane, endless drum roll of suffering and pain.

'What's his name?' he asked. It was all he could think to say.

'Ali.'

'Ali.' Abraham nodded and said the name. He did what he could, what he knew to do. Raised Ali's hip on a thick pile of papers to try to slow the flow of blood, such as it was. Cleaned the wound. Checked his pulse, which was weak but steady. Really, that was it. What else was there? He needed drugs, and sterile dressings, and expertise. The weight of the responsibility, the sharpness of it – Abraham hadn't felt anything like it since Ester's diagnosis, when Sofia had been made of glass and at every step he had expected to drop her.

Without real help the boy would die. With a look, he let the father know what he was doing and left the room.

Now he ran, picking his way through the bodies and the soon-to-be bodies, round to the broad staircase and down again onto the fighters' floor, cool and ordered in comparison. Passed

Huq and held a hand up to his punchable questioning face. Worked hard not to catch the eye of a single fighter.

In the theatre, a nurse was washing blood from the operating table onto the floor.

'Where is he?'

She looked at him, or at least she turned to him, and said nothing.

'Saad. Where is he?'

But she didn't or wouldn't understand him.

Abraham found him three rooms away, inspecting the dressing on a wound to a fighter's neck, so intently that he appeared not to notice Abraham come in. The fighter's face was pained and irritable; seeing Abraham, he pushed the doctor away.

'Enough. You. What are you fucking staring at?'

The doctor turned, still concentrating, and frowned at Abraham. His scrubs were splashed with old and fresh blood.

'One of your patients. The operation you just finished. His blood pressure is dropping. I was told to get you.'

Behind his metal glasses the doctor's eyes were grave, bloodshot, searching. His gown was too big for him and the sleeves were pulled up by rubber bands at his elbows. He wore no black band.

'Who are you?'

'I . . . I'm new. Please hurry.'

The soldier closed his eyes in pain and impatience.

'Fuck off, the both of you. Would you? Fuck.'

Still frowning, the doctor looked up at Abraham as if he was simply too tired to work out the puzzle he represented, and passing him left the room, walking at such a pace that Abraham had to jog to catch up.

'There's a boy, upstairs, he's been shot through the flank, just inside the hip. I think he's going to die.'

The doctor stopped. Fighters passed and Abraham willed

him to keep his voice down. At the far end of the corridor he could see Huq, peering.

'What are you talking about?'

'I lied. It's a boy. I need your help or he's going to die.'

'Sometimes that's better.' He studied Abraham's eyes as he might a fresh case for diagnosis. 'Why are you helping?'

'I'm still new.'

'If you're fucking with me you'll regret it. Show me.'

Huq watched them impotently as they approached.

'Where are you going?'

'I need him upstairs,' said the doctor, with a finality that caused Huq to take a step backwards to let them pass, glaring at Abraham for undermining his authority.

In twenty minutes they had found supplies and the doctor was directing Abraham to fix a drip in the boy's arm while he bandaged the two wounds. There was little else to be done; for now they had to wait for any bleeding to stop and guard against infection. Later he would operate, if that could be done and would actually help.

'Do you know him?'

Abraham took a moment to realize what he meant.

'No. I never saw him before.'

'Then why come to me?'

'I knew he would die.'

The doctor wasn't satisfied, and Abraham understood.

'I'm new. I guess the discipline is hard at first.'

'That was a risk.'

'I didn't want this on my conscience.'

'You have a conscience?'

The door opened and the director of the hospital came into the tiny hot room, Huq behind him.

'We're busy,' said the doctor.

'With what? Who is that?'

'A boy that you shot.'

'Stop that now and get downstairs. A fighter is losing his life.'

'When I'm ready.'

'Stop it now.'

The doctor looked up from his work.

'How many times? Do you have another surgeon? No? So shoot me when you do.'

'What's he doing?'

The director nodded his head at Abraham.

'I needed help,' said the doctor.

'He told you to come up here.'

'One of the nurses told me.'

'Which nurse?'

'Are you serious? How would I know which nurse it was?'

'He came for you. He brought you here.'

'Fuck you people. I told you, a nurse came to tell me a boy was dying. I don't like boys to die. Not boys who are playing in the street. Not even the boys you send to the front. This one may live. He may not. Maybe if he lives he'll be strong enough to blow himself up for you one day and then you'll be a fucking hero.'

Abraham watched the director, whose eyes went from him to the doctor and back again.

'You, we need. You, we do not. Downstairs, now. Not one more mistake. And you.' He turned to Huq. 'Keep better control of your people.'

14

can I see you my sister? would be good to see you

after my work tomorrow? i can come to your makkar maybe

— bien sûr ma soeur, any time. I am here for you always. Basha street, 143

near the hospital?

— a few blocks away

take care sister, from the airstrikes, I'm surprised they put a makkar there

— it's fine, we hear them but we're okay

tomorrow probably

— can't wait, my sister, can't wait

15

I don't know what's happening to me. My head is full of snakes and doubts. A crisis of faith. My first. I feel like I'm being split down the middle.

There are some who profess to serve God and yet stand on the very fringe of faith. When blessed with good fortune they are content, but when an ordeal befalls them they turn upon their heels, forfeiting this life and the Hereafter.

That way true perdition lies.

Bed is no sanctuary. Maysan and I exchange looks when we say goodnight. I should hug her but everything is too tightly wound here, it's too soon. It's just good to know I'm not in this completely alone – although it's not like we're really together, we don't talk or anything. Another human being who understands. It's enough.

Irene helps as well. She will be a good friend to me, I think. After class tomorrow I'll go and see her, if I go straight there it shouldn't be a problem – I can tell the driver it's official business.

So: sleep, work, then back to the makkar. Things aren't so bad. The lights are out and I'm messaging her again when the door opens and there's Borz, silhouetted, huge. I must have been nodding off because it gives me such a shock my heart starts racing.

'You.'

He doesn't point, he just looks at me, and he doesn't wait, he turns back to his room and there's Hafa, a plaster on her cheek and her eye a livid black. As I pass I give her a sympathetic look, which she doesn't return. Maybe it isn't so sympathetic. Her position is the same as mine, but the difference is that after dinner I heard her shouting at Zarifa and I'm pretty sure I heard her hurting her too. The girl doesn't need that. She's had enough. She may be a kafir, but Hafa taking out her own pain on her won't make her any less ignorant.

I'm scared of Borz tonight. Last night I was nervous, now I'm scared. I know what he can do. I know what he does. And the anger in him, like his other energies, takes a long time to go. I can feel it in him as I follow him to his room.

Once we're in there he nods at me – which means undress – and starts taking off his dishdasha. As he pulls off his under-shirt the smell of him spreads through the room, sweat and something sharper, it makes me think of death and deepens my fear. My legs aren't shaking tonight but I feel a sort of ache inside, in my groin, like you get when you see someone in pain and your body imagines it happening to you.

Now he's naked, in all his whiteness. It's not like the men's bodies you see in the west on television, all smooth and taut, it's almost pudgy, like wet clay, but it's stronger, or it looks stronger, somehow, because there's no vanity in it. He's never spent a moment worrying about what he looks like. Down his left side runs a scar I didn't notice last night, all the way from his ribs to his hip, and it reminds me that whatever else this man might be he is a warrior who has done great things for the khilafa, and for all Muslims. I try to remember this.

Tonight he shows no excitement at seeing me, and for the first time it occurs to me that maybe we will just lie together, husband and wife.

As before, he tells me to get into bed and I lie on my side, facing in. I try to smile, and feel some small relief when he switches off the light, but somehow in the near dark it's as if there's more of him, he seems to fill the space.

Maybe he doesn't want me to see what state he's in. I can tell he's bothered by it and pray that he doesn't decide it's my fault. I keep my arms up to my chest but as he gets into bed beside me he pulls the upper one away and grabs my breast with his hand, which is cold and rough with calluses and damp with sweat. He leaves it there for a moment, squeezing the flesh, his eyes on mine daring me to look away, squeezing harder until it begins to pinch and the pain starts spreading through me. Something like a smile shows through his beard and in his eyes and I have to turn from him. Every instinct is telling me to push him off me and run, but I can't. It will be so much worse.

I can feel the bruises starting, and the pain is like I'm being electrocuted, like he's sticking knives into me. Eventually he relaxes his grip and I let out a gasp, but I won't cry, there's no way he's making me cry.

Now he pulls my arm to him so that I'm forced to lie on my front, and he gets up on me like before. I guess this is what he likes. His hand goes to my neck again, and the weight is there, and that's okay because at least I know what to expect and I've got through it once. And as I think that I get an image, or a sense, I feel it like a new blow, like a kick in my stomach, of a lifetime of nights exactly like this in front of me.

He's pressing himself against me, writhing, and his grip on my neck is tightening, and he rolls right on top of me, his whole weight, as the hand that was supporting him starts smacking my thigh and the side of my buttock, hard, like it hit me earlier. I can't get enough air. The pain and the pressure are nothing, I just want air. What he likes doesn't seem to be working and I have a new fear, that unless I can give him what he wants he's going to kill me trying.

I didn't see it going this way.

His grip gets stronger and stronger and I can't even cough, my breath has stopped completely, there's black behind my eyes and fire in my lungs and my body starts to panic and tries to thrash against him even while I'm thinking, okay, this is it, this is what he does, he kills. He's going to kill me.

Then he's off, and he's gone. Like a bear that's finished toying with its prey. With my face in the pillow, I see him pad heavily to the top of the stairs and then down, and I think of Zarifa and wonder how long it will take for the wailing to start.

16

My neck is bruised front and back, but the niqab hides it. The brother who's driving me to class this morning was on duty last night. Does he hear? Does he listen to her screams night after night? Does he know? Under my veil I must be flushing red from anger, and from shame. I feel so alone in here today. It hurts when I swallow, when I breathe.

I got no sleep. When Borz came back to bed he told me to leave, and that was a relief, but I had nowhere to go. Hafa was in my bed, and I couldn't sleep with the children, or with Zarifa, and I'm not allowed in the sitting room without permission. So I sat in the kitchen, in the dark because somehow the dark was better, I didn't want to see anything – not my body, my feet, my hands, no part of me. In the dark, I can find moments where I don't exist.

It was so cold in there I began to shake. Even wrapping my

arms round myself reminded me of him. Thank heaven I'd put my pyjamas back on, but when Borz threw me out I couldn't find my dressing gown as I scrabbled about in the dark, and the air conditioning in the kitchen just blew all night.

No bed, no shelter from His judgement.

In the cold my father appeared to me like some messenger from the darkness. He was young again, and handsome, and music played as he reached out his hand to me. Come back. You are not worthy to remain in the light. Come back with me where you belong.

I saw him, literally saw him standing there beckoning to me, and in an instant I imagined my life like his, empty of feeling, numbed by his drugs, meaningless. And then some last divine spark lit a corner of the darkness, and by His grace I began to see. To see at last.

My father is a jinn. He is the demon come to tempt me. And the temptation is a test, of course it is, the biggest test of all, and I failed it. When I vouched for him, when I let his black heart into the khilafa, I betrayed everything I had been reaching for, and now I am being punished. Punished, and shown what hell lies waiting for those who doubt.

How did I not see this? The day after I betrayed the khilafa, Borz came for me. Maybe he's been chosen as the instrument of my punishment. Maybe that's why he married me. One thing I do know – I am being shown a way back. For me and all I'm responsible for. I need to repair my mistake.

17

sister I can't see you

— Sister, no. why not?

too hard to get away

— Tomorrow?

maybe never

— Don't say that sister. He swt will provide. What's wrong?

He is testing me sister. The test is hard.

— Tell me.

— Sister please, tell me. I can help you. We can talk.

— Sister

18

Huq doubled his watch on Abraham. When they could be together, they were together; on rounds, in consultations, at prayer. Like a bad dancer learning new steps, Abraham did his best to copy his neighbour and prayed hard that he wouldn't be found out. If circumstance forced them apart – because Huq was needed in another part of the hospital, or when the weight of new cases simply overwhelmed them – he had Abraham report back to him at the shortest possible intervals, like a husband jealous of his new wife's minor freedoms.

Not that they felt like that. Abraham had never worked so hard, nor so intensely. Dying fighters, wounded fighters, fighters with dysentery from the filthy water, one who'd taken too many of those pills they all took; Abraham treated them as he would anyone else, doing what he was told and tamping down his revulsion by telling himself that each of these human disasters had once been a child and was probably still a son. That helped – it all helped. It was hard to think a man a monster when he was struggling for life.

At some point Vural sent him a second message that, despite the tumult, sat in his head, scratching at his conscience for no reason.

> A, your phone is on. Tell me something.

Sometimes the flow stopped, and with permission he was allowed upstairs to do what he could for the people who didn't matter. Dr Saad would often seek him out – why, he didn't really understand – and in the snatched hours he spent at his side, cleaning instruments, sewing wounds, bandaging wounds, Abraham finally felt useful, properly useful, at the centre of something, not his usual, marginal self.

After each of these trips, Huq would give him a look that said, you're pushing your luck. But Abraham thought he detected something else there, something rather like envy – perhaps because Saad had smiled on him, or because he had the courage to step outside the suffocating walls of the basement from time to time. Who could tell? Who even had time to care?

His day seemed to finish at ten, unless there was night fighting, or airstrikes, in which case it was endless, and it started again at seven every morning. Why had Sofia cancelled? Every sign could be good or bad, it was exhausting. If he was going to go to her house it had to be during the day, and even if he managed that, the chances were she wouldn't be there – she worked, she had her filthy job, whatever it was now, she'd be out all day just as he was. Friday. Friday was his only hope.

That morning his luck switched. The medicine he had delivered two days earlier should never have left the hospital. Huq dressed him down, told him they'd both be tried for insubordination or treason or some fucking thing if he didn't correct his stupid fucking mistake, and sent him on his way. Back immediately. Don't screw it up.

The Dar al-Shifa surgery was across town, maybe a mile away, but half the roads were shut and the traffic clogged. When he finally arrived, he had to argue with three people to get the drugs returned at all, and then there was a problem with the paperwork – and this was bad, because it meant that no record existed of how much had been used and therefore how much should be returned. Abraham had seen enough by now to know that when he got back to the hospital there would be accusations and shouting, but it was also an opportunity, because these were good drugs, powerful painkillers. As he drove back he took two blister packs, one from each of the fuller boxes, and slid them into his trouser pocket.

He was late now, and Huq would be fretting. Let him fret. Abraham made his way towards Borz's house and by stopping often to ask his way finally closed in on Hamra Street, which by the look of it was where the traders and the businessmen and the corrupt politicians had lived before the Islamic State had turfed everybody out. Proper houses, maybe fifteen on each side, detached, white, whole, and so utterly out of place here that it was a shock to see them lined up against the scrub and the desert and not some perfectly tended golf course.

Several had guards, a couple here, a couple there, standing in the pose that Abraham knew so well, feet spread, machine gun clutched high on the chest, chin out, beard foremost. God, the vanity of them. There wasn't one who hadn't admired himself in the mirror with his gun or felt a thrill of power in his loins every time he slung it across himself. And yet here they were, protecting the lifestyles of their leaders for the sake of the revolution. Who was going to tell them? Was there any way of making them see? As he drove, Abraham felt each pair of eyes on him and a dozen fingers tighten on the trigger. Oh, to kill something. Oh, to justify their existence with a kill.

The street ran out into wasteland, and three plots from the end was Borz's house. Plainly Borz's house, because there were six fighters on duty and two of those sand-coloured 4x4s parked on the road outside. And it was the biggest of them all, a grand villa with a portico for cars to sit under and clean windows and a roof of terracotta tiles. There were no flowers in the window boxes but it was neat, well kept. Borz was house-proud.

Abraham saw the six guards tense as he drove slowly towards them and parked by one of the 4x4s. Was this insane? Did he share their death wish? There was no reason for them to shoot him. He was their commander's father-in-law, come to see his daughter. What could be more proper? Borz might not see it that way but then with luck Borz would be at the front, killing people, or in a room elsewhere planning how to kill them.

Engine off, door gently open, lightly down from the van, hands at his side and just a little to the front in case anyone worried that he had something under his dishdasha, papers at the ready. No smile, just an easy countenance, don't look away but don't hold their eye either or they'll take it for a threat.

'Stop there, brother.' One of them moved forward from the rest and motioned at Abraham with his gun. 'Not another step. I don't know you. Tell me very carefully who you are and what you're doing here.'

Abraham stopped and by instinct held his hands up. 'It's all right, brother. Borz was married three days ago to my daughter. I'm her father. I've come to pay my respects and give the couple their gift.'

'You for real?'

'I'm for real. I have these.'

The fighter walked towards him and took the papers. This was one of the unlikely ones – plump, squat, with eyes that bulged and took in everything. He came up to Abraham's chest.

How did one of these people get ahead and not another? Did he have more brains? Less conscience?

'You're a doctor.'

'Yes.'

'And your daughter's here.'

'Yes.'

'How do I know she's your daughter?'

'You could look at her papers.'

'I don't have her papers, brother.'

'Is she here?'

'I don't know who's here and who isn't.'

'Can you find out?'

The fighter stroked the beard on his chin. Maybe it made him feel wise.

'I don't do things for you.'

To show his submission Abraham held his hands up again and looked at the floor.

'Where's the gift?'

Abraham signalled that he was going to put his hand in his pocket and received a nod of approval.

'Here.'

'What is it?'

'A gift.'

'You taking the piss, brother? You told me it's a fucking gift. Tell me what's inside.'

'It's nothing, just a gift.'

'Open it.'

Abraham ran his thumbs over the brown paper of his clumsy wrapping, held in place with string. Only Sofia could have it. He wouldn't part with it otherwise.

'Brother, you've got five seconds to fucking open it or I'll destroy the fucking thing.'

'It's personal. It's not a bomb.'

'Okay. Enough. On your knees. Put your hands on your head.'

'What? Why?'

'Do it or you're a dead man, brother, doctor or no doctor.'

He meant it. Never doubt that they meant it. Abraham knelt down and closed his fingers over his head. The guard reached into Abraham's pockets and pulled out money, leftover string, toilet paper folded to be used as a tissue, and two bubble packs of Roxanol.

'What's this, brother?'

Abraham concentrated on his breath and kept his voice as level as he could.

'Drugs. Medication.'

'What kind of drugs?'

'Painkillers.'

'You in pain, brother? Or are you planning to be?'

He was pleased with that. He grinned over his shoulder at the other guards, who stood motionless in the sun, sunglasses and guns glinting.

'They're for my patients.'

'That's a personal service you provide. Do you test the drugs yourself, brother, make sure they're okay?'

This one wasn't stupid. Why couldn't he be stupid like the rest?

'They're for one patient. A fighter, he lost a leg. He's in a lot of pain.'

'So what are they doing out here, brother?'

Over the fighter's shoulder, the door of the house opened and a veiled figure appeared at the top of the four steps that led up to it. Again, Abraham knew her instantly, just by the way she stood. Oblivious, the fighter had his hand on the package and now Abraham pulled it away.

'You serious, brother? Fuck me.'

Sofia spoke, and the fighter turned.

'Tell him to leave.'

'He says he's your father.'

'He was my father. Tell him to leave.'

'Please. Sofia. I just have a gift for you.'

The fighter brought the gun back above his shoulder so the butt was pointing at Abraham.

'Brother, shut the fuck up or I will break your fucking face.'

'Why are you here? Are you crazy? Why do you think this is okay?'

Abraham stood up and made to step around the fighter, who held a hand to his chest to stop him going anywhere. But the veil was the greater divide; if he could only see her eyes, see what was hidden in them.

'I wanted to congratulate you, and give you this. A wedding present.'

'No you didn't.'

'Please. Just take it. And I'll go.'

For a moment everyone held their positions – Abraham appealing, the fighter with his gun up, Sofia standing in judgement over it all – and no one spoke. Abraham kept his eyes on his daughter and offered the parcel to her.

'Give it to me.'

The fighter turned to confirm and received a nod. He took the parcel, and handed Abraham back his money, tissue and string. Of course. He'll keep the drugs, thought Abraham, and cursed his own stupidity. Why hadn't he just left them in the car, or hidden them in the hospital?

He kept his eyes on Sofia for as long as he dared and turned to walk back to the jeep, half dejected, half satisfied. At least she would see what he wanted her to see, and that would be more persuasive than any conversation.

The fighter was following him.

'Hold up, brother. I'm coming with you. See what the hospital has to say about these babies.'

He waved the white packs in Abraham's face and grinned a set of perfect, pure white teeth.

19

Together they waited, the director at his desk, Abraham standing across from him, Huq and the fighter against the wall. On the desk were the pills, and nothing else. After five minutes the director became restless and sent Huq to look, and he returned in a moment preceded by Dr Saad. Sweat shone on Huq's upper lip; he seemed more nervous than Abraham, who had reached a state of serene resignation. Let them do their worst. He had done what he could.

The director looked from face to face with eyes that bulged and seemed never to blink. For a long moment he said nothing, anxious to display his authority, and with something just short of a sigh Saad let him know that he was used to this sort of performance but had better things to do elsewhere.

'Do you know what these are?'

The words were meant to sound stern but they slipped dully from his mouth. Saad stepped forward to inspect the pills and then stepped back.

'Roxanol. Pain relief.'

'Do you know what they're doing here?'

Saad looked from the director to Abraham and from him to Huq.

'I imagine Mounir got them for me.'

Impassive, the director waited for him to explain. Any disappointment didn't show.

'I need morphine for two patients. I told him if he ever saw any spare he should bring it to me.'

'When was this?'

'I don't know. Two days ago.'

'Civilian patients?'

'Patients.'

The director looked at Abraham, who had come round like a man slapped awake.

'You took Islamic State medicine to give it to pigs?'

'It was extra. I saw no harm.'

'You would have fighters suffer?'

The director looked at him long and hard, a great sage weighing up the appropriate punishment.

'Then you will suffer. Eighty lashes.'

Abraham hung his head and felt the flesh on his back go tight.

'I need him,' said Saad.

'After the lashes. You –' the director nodded at the fighter – 'take him.'

'I need him now, and I need him able to work.'

'After he is punished.'

Saad sighed. The pained sigh of a tired man.

'It will take time to have him lashed. After he is lashed he will try to work but he will tire and make mistakes. And men may die as a result.'

'God's retribution is stern.'

'God would find another way. Would He want His own fighters to suffer?'

The director's eyes looked ready to pop; Saad had pushed him too hard. It was a mistake to have brought God into it.

'How dare you predict what God the most high would do? That is blasphemy, Saad.'

But Saad smiled and shook his head.

'Please. Not that track again. I'm simply wondering what happens when you lose a man because you lashed a good nurse. What his commander might say.'

The director sniffed, eyeing Saad with less confidence, and ran his tongue round the inside of his lips as if checking for undigested food. Finally he turned down the corners of his mouth in grim resolution.

'You need him?'

'We need him.'

'Two weeks' pay. No more errands.'

'Fair,' said Saad, and went to take the drugs from the desk. 'For the fighters,' he said, with a thin smile, and left the room.

Out in the corridor Abraham caught up with Saad.

'Thank you. My God. How did you know what to say?'

'What were you doing with these?'

'How did you know?'

'I knew the moment I came in the room. They think they're clever but most of them have the brains of flies. Why I bothered is another question. Here. These are yours.'

Abraham shook his head. He wanted Saad to see his eyes but he was walking fast, as he always did.

'They're for upstairs.'

'I don't want them. Sell them or take them or whatever you want to do with them but keep me the fuck out of it next time.'

Abraham reached out and pulled him back. Everyone else might misjudge him but it was important that Saad knew. Saad of all people.

'Once, I'd have taken them. In this place, my God, I'd have swallowed them all. But they were for you. They were for everyone upstairs. I'm sorry. I shouldn't have involved you.'

The irritation on Saad's face cleared, and he shook his head.

'You're a strange man.'

'I don't know what I am.'

'Find out soon or you'll get somebody killed. Understand?'

20

This is the surest sign yet. The strongest temptation.

The wrapping is terrible. His wrapping was always terrible. I look at the thing for a while and wonder if I should just throw it away. And probably I should have, because even as I pull at the string I know what it is and I know what he's doing.

It's a photograph of my mother. She's twenty-five, and she's looking down at me in my cot, in profile. You can't really see me through the white bars, but I know I'm there and so does she because you can tell nothing else exists for her in that moment. I can imagine that. I've never felt closer to her. The light is coming through an orange curtain, a thin piece of fabric that I remember so vividly even while I can't remember anything else about the room, and her skin glows quietly. She's not smiling, because you couldn't smile with that much love in you. The smiling would take away from it. I haven't seen the picture before. He must have kept it with him.

My breath actually catches, like I'm about to sob, but I don't sob. There's nothing there. It's a physical thing, that's all.

There's a piece of paper with five words written on it. In Arabic, which is cunning.

Your mother still honours you.

I screw up the paper, hold the photograph, ask myself what he's trying to achieve, why he's doing this. Did he bring this with him all the way just to give to me, or is this his final sacrifice, his last desperate act?

It doesn't matter. What matters is my response, and I see now what I have to do. To resist the greatest temptation in the darkest hour requires the purest strength.

Umm Karam will understand me. She was there when Khalil died and when my father appeared, she knows I didn't ask for any of it. The message I write to her is short but in my heart it feels like I'm crossing a chasm. I have made a mistake, I tell her. Please can I meet you later? My father should be there as well.

Because when I denounce him, it must be to his face.

21

The next day Vural texted again.

I am best hope for you. Do not forget.

Abraham deleted the message and was dressing a wound when Saad appeared and told him to get some instruments and drugs together, whatever he could find, and join him upstairs – and quickly, they had maybe half an hour. A straightforward procedure, a caesarean section for a mother whose cord had prolapsed, and no nurses anywhere because your fellow devils keep beating them for one bullshit infringement or another.

The woman was on her own, and terrified, under her veil. They shouldn't have been treating her, but there were no female doctors left, and without treatment the baby would die.

'So why do you hate women?'

Saad spoke in English, and the shock of hearing it and the abruptness of the question caused Abraham to stop and look up. Saad continued to prepare the anaesthetic with the total concentration that he seemed to bring to everything.

'I don't hate women.'

'You all do. What scares you?'

'I'm not scared. Not by that.'

'Because you are different. Of course.'

For a good minute Abraham thought carefully about his reply. It was only vanity to worry what Saad thought of him. Or anyone but God. If an airstrike killed him tomorrow and the world knew him as an evil man who joined ISIS to be with his daughter, so be it. But to be straight with one person? God, the release. Like a confession. Let Saad be his priest.

'I'm not one of them.'

Saad glanced up at him.

'You are with them, you are one of them.'

'I'm here for a reason.'

'Fuck your reason. Your reason is the problem.'

'I'm a Christian.'

Saad's hands stopped doing what they were doing and without looking at Abraham he shook his head.

'Now I have heard everything.'

'My daughter was poisoned by these animals. I came to bring her back.'

Saad was still shaking his head, eyes wide.

'I had to join them. At a checkpoint. They were going to shoot me.'

'She needs to be completely clean.'

'And I'm not a doctor. I'm a pharmacist.'

'You're a Christian pharmacist.'

'I trained as a doctor. But I never qualified.'

'Anything else?'

'That's it.'

'I'm going to go into the spine.'

'Because it's quicker?'

'And to save anaesthetic.' Then in Arabic, 'Please, turn on your side.'

Together they helped the woman and Saad ran his fingers along her vertebrae. There was another reason he liked working with Saad, Abraham realized. He felt like a student again. He was learning.

Saad said nothing until the injection was done. Then he straightened up and told the woman that everything was fine and he would operate in five minutes.

'Is she worth saving?'

At first Abraham thought he meant the woman lying between them.

Was Sofia worth saving? It was a good question. If he was to rescue one person from Raqqa how far down the list of the deserving would she come?

'She's my daughter.'

'You do know there's no way out? This is a black hole. No light escapes.'

'People get out.'

'Most don't. I didn't.'

'You should try.'

'Ibrahim – is that your name?'

'Abraham.'

'Of course. Abraham. My wife died before the occupation. Assad killed her. When the devils arrived I stayed because I figured they couldn't be worse and then I stayed because there were only four surgeons left in the whole city and now I stay because there's just me. So I will die here, like the thousands and thousands who cannot leave. If you find a way to leave, go. Take your daughter with you if you can. Save her soul if there is anything left to be saved. I am sorry for your pain but next to the pain of Raqqa it is a cut, a graze, a bite from a mosquito.'

Abraham looked at his feet and nodded. Tell the truth and it got reflected right back at you. A bad man he might not be, but how far from a good one?

Saad reached over the woman and touched Abraham on the arm.

'Nothing is right. It is all impossible. I think sometimes the only good I do is save people's lives so they can be killed some other way. We didn't create this place.'

Abraham pinched his eyes closed, and saw there a million souls in pain, without hope of peace or even rest. How could he leave? It would be like fleeing a burning building past the out-stretched hands of those about to burn.

When he opened his eyes, Saad was pricking the woman's abdomen with a pin.

'Will you teach me?'

'Teach you what?'

'If I stay, will you teach me? To be a doctor.'

'I don't need doctors. I need pharmacists.'

Okay, thought Abraham. I can live with that.

22

I feel lighter today. The sun has joy in it, it's not oppressive like it has been, and I understand why. The lie I have lived with will soon be out in the open. The khilafa can judge me and I can stop judging myself.

No word from Umm Karam, not yet, but then she isn't at my beck and call. There are processes.

When I arrive at the school there's one brother on duty out-side but the one who was guarding the room inside has gone. He's not with the women either, and the moment I appear one of them comes at me, Niran's mother, shouting and crying and shaking her head. She holds on to me and hangs there and in my exhaustion I have to push her off.

'Niran,' she says. 'Please. Niran.'

'Where is she?'

But the woman is beside herself and all she can do is hold her hands up and together, like she's praying.

'They took her,' says Besma.

From the corridor I shout to the guard at the front but he doesn't hear me or he chooses not to answer. I try the next door along, the bathroom, barely noticing the stench, but there's no one there. Beyond that there's the storeroom with all the old clothes and I don't expect to find her there either but when I open the door there she is, in the corner with her dress off, tiny and naked, powerless, and in front of her is the brother, crouching down to her level with his hand out touching her cheek.

I stop thinking. I'm too tired and too wired to think. I shout at him to get away from her but he ignores me, like I'm simply not there. I run to him and push him so he loses his balance and he falls forward, reaching out with his hand. His gun is on the floor beside him and I grab it. I point it at him and for a moment I'm just staring at the twisted filthy desire in his face and the innocent fear in hers. He holds up one hand, regains his footing, then holds up both and starts to stand.

'You get the fuck away from her.'

The surprise has gone from his face and he's cocked his head to one side and he's grinning with crooked teeth behind his scraggy beard. His eyes are wide and swimming with something like excitement. Blue eyes that don't fit the rest of him. I don't know what it is men feel when they're like this.

If I shot him now surely he would go to hell. War or no war. Fortress or not. In that moment I hate his face and his emptiness and his distance from the faith and I see no reason why he should survive, but that's not my judgement to make and somehow I stop myself.

Niran wasn't crying when I came in but she is now and it makes me come to. I start thinking about how on earth I'm going to get us both out of this.

I motion with the gun for him to move towards the door and at the same time I circle round to be by Niran, who shrinks from me as I come close. I stoop down and hand her her dress, without taking my eyes off the brother.

Brother. He is not worthy of the name.

He skulks round, hands half up.

'Above your head,' I tell him, and slowly he raises them.

'Okay, stop. Stop.' I breathe, try to keep calm. The only hope I have is that he doesn't know very much. The khilafa is so well organized, but different parts don't always talk to each other.

'You know how old she is?'

He grins harder, raises his eyebrows like the whole thing is a joke.

'Do you?'

He shrugs, says he doesn't know.

'She is eight. Eight years old.'

'Never too young,' he says.

'She is not for you.'

'Will bring me closer to God.'

His biggest grin yet. So I gamble.

'She is not yours. She is being kept for Borz.'

The grin stays on his face but his eyes lose some of their bullshit, so I carry on.

'You know Borz? Good. When she is nine he will marry her. She is intended for him and for no other. If you touch her again, you come in the same room, you even fucking look at her I will tell him you think your claim greater than his, and you can settle it with him. Understand? And I will pay your friend outside to tell me if you do.'

He's still grinning, but like a fool grins.

'Out. Go!'

He holds out his hand for his gun.

'No. Tell your commander you had your gun taken from you by Borz's wife.'

Now his face drops. I see the fear go right in, the fear this pig likes to sow in others.

'That's right. I'm his wife. Don't fuck with me and maybe I won't fuck with you. Now go.'

He's so different now, just a little man with a beard and a

hole where his soul should be. I watch him go and crouch down in front of Niran.

'It will be okay,' I say as I hold her arms and look right in her eyes, and she shrinks away. I no longer know how I can help these people.

23

i am not made for the khilafa sister

may your time be different

i do not have the strength.

24

Abraham was woken two hours before dawn as the fighters dressed in near-silence and left, taking their guns and leaving their stench behind. Sweat, fear, old breath, gun oil, farts. No air was left. It made him retch, and further sleep impossible, so he got up, splashed water on his face in the filthy bathroom – though it made him feel no cleaner – and sat alone in the kitchen watching the sun rise over the rooftops and the desert. He found tea and read Sofia's most recent messages. Still, after everything, his stomach dropped at the sight of them. The end was coming. She had started to break.

— Sister, what is wrong? I am worried for you. Tell me. Do not despair.

There had to be a way to get to her. No one else would pick her back up.

His phone lit up with a new text. This time from Huq.

— come now many casualties!

How could he come now? There was no one to drive him and he barely knew his way around. But there was reception here, and Google knew where the hospital was, so he walked, half ran, and even before he heard all the noise could sense that the atmosphere had changed.

He rounded the corner to the hospital out of breath and sweating, and found the space at the top of the ramp clogged with jeeps and 4x4s and fighters loitering and pacing and shouting in a round of anger and indignation and mutual stoking. The words kafir, American and dogs rang in the air, but so charged were the fighters that they barely paid Abraham any attention as he ran inside. 'Doctor,' he shouted at the single guard, who watched him with slack eyes.

Huq was outside the operating theatre, wheeling about without purpose and watching nurses and the few doctors rushing about in the corridor.

'Where the fuck have you been?'

'I have no car. I had to run.'

'You were meant to be here at six.'

'You said seven.'

'Never mind. Scrub up.'

'What's happened?'

'Airstrike. A barracks.'

'How many?'

'How many what?'

Jesus. 'How many injured?'

'Seventeen. Four aren't going to make it.'

Abraham ran to the changing room, threw on his scrubs and washed his hands and forearms as thoroughly as he could in the water that wasn't good enough to drink, all the while conducting a conversation with himself in the mirror. What was he supposed to do? Save these men who would never show mercy to a soul? The idea repelled him. And even if he did his best to help them, what if his work did more harm than good? Was it a sin to botch an operation on a bad man in good faith? For a moment he considered the idiot staring back at him who had contrived such a mess, then shook his head, closed his eyes and with a deep breath went to find the job that was waiting for him.

Huq was talking to Saad, standing in the doorway of a ward three doors up from the operating theatre, and past them Abraham could see a figure on a bed and blood on white sheets. Moaning came from the room, high and tight like a wounded dog.

'I'm going to have to operate in here,' said Saad. 'I can't wait for the theatre.'

'What do you need?'

'Find a nurse. All the basics. Tools, antibiotics, morphine if you can find any, whatever else is around if you can't, gloves, soap, fuck, everything. Blood. Everything. And lights. Find some lights that haven't been blown to shit.'

Saad had cut away the fighter's tunic and shirt and exposed the wound, or wounds: one deep, in his side between his hip and ribs, filled with blood, and several others shallower and smaller across that side of his belly. Judging from how tightly they were grouped he had been close to one of the strikes. His face was turned away but Abraham could see that he was biting down hard on the first knuckle of his fist, and through it the moaning continued at an even pitch.

Abraham marvelled at Saad's coolness. His eyes were bloodshot and sitting on heavy purple bags, but they shone. He was exhausted, propelled by will, inspecting each wound carefully, with concentration but no sense of urgency.

'I can't do this without blood. When I take that out . . .'

'What do you need?'

'O. Negative. We're out.'

Two fighters stood against the wall, one white, one Arab,

both in fatigues. The white man had cuts on his cheekbone and temple that bled into his beard. Now he spoke, in a voice that was too high for his heavy bearing.

'Use other blood.'

'I can't. It will probably kill him.'

The fighter was ungainly, lumbering. Abraham knew his type from his work: ill at ease, uncomfortable in the real world, here he had found his place. He wore metal-framed glasses that looked as if he'd borrowed them from someone else. For a while he and the doctor stared at each other, until Abraham began to will the doctor to look away. Then the fighter spoke.

'Much blood here.'

'There's none. Not a drop. We used the last a month ago.'

The fighter's slack grey eyes went pointedly to the ceiling and then back to Saad.

'Much blood.'

Saad shook his head.

'Uh-uh. A single transfusion won't do it. I need four or five pints.'

'They have.'

Abraham was the first to understand. It was the finality with which it was said. Anywhere else it would have been a joke but here it was simply logic. That the doctor took so long to understand simply meant he was the better man.

'No.'

'Find blood.'

'No.'

'You. You ISIS?'

The fighter nodded at Abraham, who felt his legs go weak and acid rise in his throat. No. No I am not.

'We go, find blood.'

Abraham shook his head.

'I can't do that.'

The fighter pushed himself away from the wall and came right up to Abraham, so close that their beards touched.

'You, ISIS.'

Abraham said nothing.

'Yes?'

Still nothing. The fighter looked back at his friend and said, in English, the accent London: 'Unbelievable. I'm going to gut this cunt.'

For ten seconds, he stood toe to toe with Abraham and looked up into his face.

'You. With me. We find blood. Man, woman, child. Right blood. You get blood, come back. You give blood to my friend.'

'I can't.'

'That's a fucking fighter, you prick.' In English now. 'A fucking hero. And you won't save him for the sake of some godless kafir cunt?'

Abraham closed his eyes, and shook his head once more.

The fighter looked over his shoulder, shook his head in turn, and when he looked back brought his fist up hard into Abraham's stomach, so hard that it lifted him an inch off the ground and sent him staggering backwards into the bed. He held out a hand to steady himself and in his side felt another blow that drove him down towards the floor. Saad was shouting; Abraham sensed the other fighter coming into it now, heard bone crack as a boot crunched into his chest, and then heard nothing more, because the final kick was to his ear and he only had time to see it connect.

25

Borz is out. Hafa tells me when I get back from work, and though I do my best not to show it she knows I'm relieved. It's weak but I thank Allah the most glorified, because I could not face seeing that man right now. I don't have the strength.

I was expecting to be on cooking duty again but Hafa wants to do it on her own, so instead of hiding in my room away from all the things I don't want to confront I go to check on Zarifa. I don't know why she feels like my responsibility. Because I can't protect Niran, maybe. Because each of them has been hurt, or will be hurt. The thought comes to me that maybe we're all the same in some way but we're not, I know I'm much luckier, I am on the path to the one true God and it's my duty to take them with me.

I think I'm still on the path. That man, he won't leave my thoughts. His black mouth and his blue eyes on Niran like a trick from the devil himself – corrupting the khilafa, blackening its mission, debasing us all. I tell myself that today I did a little to defend it. Not enough, nothing like enough, but then others wiser and more powerful than I will deal with his kind when the time comes. My true test lies elsewhere.

I've still heard nothing from Umm Karam, but the longer she's silent the clearer the route I must take. My father's curse will not lift on its own, and only one of us can survive here. I send her another text:

I must see you and my father. He is not what he says he is.

Zarifa is in her room, sitting on the bed, and when I knock and go in she inches back against the wall and clutches her knees. I tell her it's okay and ask if I can come in, she nods and I sit next to her.

For a moment we're just silent – I look at her and every so often she looks up at me. I notice a bruise on her wrist that seems fresh and goes almost the whole way round, like a purple and yellow bracelet, and when I bring my hand up to it an understanding passes between us. Her other arm is in the sleeve of her abaya but now she brings it out and the bruises there are almost the same. Heaven knows what else is under that black fabric.

I wish Badra could be here now to explain why it's necessary for Borz to do these things.

I have so little to give her. There's almost nothing I can do. I go back to the kitchen and when Hafa asks me what I'm doing I tell her I'm hungry after a long day and need a snack before dinner. From the fridge I take cheese and tomatoes, and pitta from the bread bin, and I put a plate together while she stares at me like I'm committing some unforgivable crime.

Back in her room, Zarifa can't quite believe I'm being straightforward but in the end she sees it in my eyes and when she starts to eat I can tell she's trying not to wolf it down. She may be a pagan but she seems to have the same ideas about decency as I do. And then I have a thought. If I'm going to help her, we're going to need to communicate better.

I point to the bread. 'Khubz,' I say, and she gets what I'm doing straight away, like there is a real connection between us. When she's finished her mouthful she repeats it, and we move on from there. Cheese. Plate. Hand. We're a long way off reading the Qur'an but it's a start. Wall, *jadar*. Bed, *alssarir*.

Dest, she says, and touches my hand. *Dest*. She nods, and I say the word back to her. Her hand rests on my arm. *Mil*. These are pagan words and it feels strange to say them. Possibly I shouldn't say them but I have to. *Mil*. Zarifa smiles and it's the first time I've seen that. Then, as if she's ashamed to have forgotten something important, she offers the rest of her bread to me. I shake my head and say it again, khubz. *Nan*, she says. We understand each other. It crosses my mind that maybe she could join my class.

The door opens and she stops chewing. Borz is there. In the doorway. I sense him before I see him, it's like he sucks all the air and light from the room. I feel my heart contract and my lungs clamp shut. Zarifa shrinks up onto her bed but to my surprise I just turn and lock eyes with him and when he tells me to get up I just keep looking. If he wants to abuse me he can do all the work.

Grabbing my abaya, he hauls me off my bed and drags me across the hall and all that's in my head is: you have no power over me. You are merely the instrument of my punishment.

With a great swing of his arm he pulls me from behind and throws me ahead of him. I land hard and slide across the polished floor. My head hits the door of the dining room. Before I can right myself he's there again, talking at me through my pain.

'Up.'

I rest my weight on my elbow and do my best to push, but his hands are on me again and he pulls me up with one hand and shoves me into the dining room, where I've never been.

'Sit.'

I fall onto a chair and try to make it look like sitting. I'm still me. I'm not a sack of bones for him to hurl about, not yet. Borz stands over me and I think he's going to hit me but he doesn't, eventually he just sits down opposite and stares into my eyes. My wrist feels sprained, I try moving it under the table, I can't tell, I think I'm still in shock. I look at him and he looks at me. His mad eyes are concentrating, the left one wide open like it's been propped. His nose is a hideous shape and covered in black-heads. I've never had a chance to really look at his face before and even though I hate it I can't turn away, it's like staring into the face of evil and it holds me. There's no beauty there, no trace of God. I have to find Him there.

'I want Yazidi girl, yes?'

When he speaks his massive teeth are like bits of broken plate. I don't know what he means. He leaves the question there for me to answer and when I don't he says it again.

'I want Yazidi girl, yes? This is what I want.'

He knows I know about his night-time visits. Why does he care? Why the pretence? He has more power than that.

'You tell my fighters what I want. A Yazidi child. You tell them. Where is gun?'

I shake my head. I don't know what he means, and then I do. Stupid. So stupid.

'What gun?'

'The fighter guards prisoners. Prisoners of war. You take his gun. A woman take his gun.'

I won't lie. And there is no good lie.

'I took the bullets and left it in the building.'

His eyes should be full of wickedness and horror but they're green like emeralds and they shine with the same cold light. An instrument of His vengeance, terrible, fearsome, final, an earthquake, a plague, a flood.

'Your school, it is over.'

'What do you mean?'

'Kafirs cannot be taught. You cannot. You all need justice.'

He grabs my arm and marches me across the hall towards Zarifa's room and I have just enough time to think that really I am Yazidi now and to be terrified by what he'll do to Zarifa before he stops by the door to the basement, draws back the two bolts, opens it, and throws me inside. The stairs lead straight down and I crash to the bottom, half turning and landing on my shoulder, hard enough that my head rebounds off the concrete floor. Above me the door shuts and I hear Borz shooting the bolts back into place.

I thought I had reached the bottom. I was wrong. I should know by now that's not for me to judge.

26

When they slapped him awake, the first thought to come through the confusion was that he hadn't expected to be alive; his second that he wouldn't be for long. One hand slapped him and another gripped his arm so he wouldn't fall to the floor. By the third slap he was back, trying to work out where he was and who was doing this to him and quickly understanding that neither mattered very much.

Thin grey light came from somewhere; a window set high in the wall and hung with a black flag. Abraham tasted blood in his mouth and with his tongue felt at a cracked tooth, upper right, a canine. His left eye was swollen shut.

'What is this?'

English. He thought he recognized the voice but in the half dark with his one less than good eye he couldn't make out the face, let alone the thing that was being thrust at him. Pulling back, trying to focus, he saw it. His phone. Open at his Twitter account.

'The fuck is this?'

It was impossible to swallow, and he had to swallow before he could talk. His mouth had dried to sand.

'And this?'

Vural had sent a final text.

Remember our contract. You report to me.

The hand slapped him again and with nothing to hold him he fell to the floor, cracking his shoulder and spreading his chest with pain.

'Know what we do with fucking spies?'

This was the fighter from the hospital. He couldn't see his face but he knew. And someone else was there; past the man standing over him he saw sandy-coloured boots and desert camouflage.

'Kafir fucking cunt.'

With his boot the fighter rolled him from his side onto his back, squatted down and spat in his face. Abraham flinched and writhed but the spittle just stayed where it was, cooling on his skin and in his beard.

The other man came forward, touched the fighter on the shoulder and took his place by Abraham. He was older, harder, and he spoke in Arabic.

'You have help, yes?'

Instinctively, Abraham shook his head, though he had no idea what this meant.

'Father. Daughter. You think we are stupid?'

Oh Jesus, no. Not this. He tried to speak but the words wouldn't come.

'She is here, you are here. She tells you things, you tell the fucking Turks.'

He held up Abraham's phone.

'Not so clever.'

'I didn't . . . I came to . . .'

The Arab shook his head.

'No explanation. What do you think we are going to do now?'

He let the question hang in the air a moment. There was no satisfaction in his face, no pleasure, just professional certainty.

As soon as he began to speak again Abraham knew what he was going to say.

'Family execution.' He nodded. 'A first.'

No, Abraham tried to shout, as they dragged him from the room, but no sound came.

Now they drove him through Raqqa for the last time. Bound, lying across the back seat, Abraham watched the sky and found more beauty in it than he ever had. The day was ending; the clear blue deepening and turning to black.

Lord, forgive me. My attempts to do good seem only to expose my vanities and fears. By trying to keep her safe, I drove her here; by trying to save her, I have condemned her to death. Is it part of Your plan, that when it's too late to redeem our failings we finally understand them? That as we finally fall, we see the line above us? The line we should have taken and now cannot reach.

The fighters talked but he didn't hear them; pain pulsed through him but he barely felt it.

He would see Sofia. That he gave thanks for. If they had to die at least they would die together, and she would see what her idols were made of. At the end, she would at least be reconciled with the truth.

If she didn't blame him. With fresh reproach that made his chest tighten he imagined the hundred arguments she might make – would make – possessed by that insane logic. That they were right to kill her, because her father was a spy. He had tainted her and threatened the foundations of the khilafa. There was no question they both must die.

That was it, of course. From the start, death was what she had come here to find. Nothing but death would satisfy her.

Abraham closed his eyes and stopped talking to his God.

PART FOUR

PART FOUR

1

'Who's that?'

My words seem to hang in the darkness and at first the only answer to them is a groan and the sound of a body in pain re-arranging itself in the dust.

'Who is it?'

'Sofia?'

'My God.'

Even though it's dark I close my eyes and ask my Lord for strength. I've been preparing myself for the end and I thought I had it all under control but now this, this has knocked me off my feet and I don't know where I am. But I'm stronger now than I was and I recover quicker. I don't let the shock of it make me forget.

Even so, his voice is soft and familiar.

'Are you all right?'

'Why are you here? What are you doing here?'

'They brought me.'

My God, please give me the strength for this. He still riles me. In this darkest hour, moments from death – unless some miracle is still in store for me, a miracle I don't deserve – he still gets right inside me and twists everything up.

'I meant why did you come? Why did you come after me?'

'I thought I could bring you back.'

I'm staggered. I'm sitting cross-legged in the pitch black but I feel myself swaying. He thought he could change my mind? Still? That's what this is about?

'You're serious?'

'Nothing else seemed important.'

'Why the fuck would I want to go back? What were you thinking? How did you get here?'

He doesn't answer straight away. I hear him pulling himself along the floor, I guess trying to sit up.

'There's broken glass.'

He thanks me, takes another moment to get comfortable. My God, this is crazy. My head can't fit it all in.

'I couldn't give you up. Not to this.'

'I'm not yours to give.'

He can't answer that. For a minute or two we sit in the blackness and marvel that two people of the same blood could misunderstand each other so completely.

'They think I'm a spy.'

'Seriously? Have they met you?'

'They've been through my phone. That's how they know I've been talking to you. I'm so sorry.'

It's like he means some other life entirely, some other daughter. It crosses my mind that this isn't my father after all, that it's a final test from Him, that it's important for me to make peace with the idea of him before I go. Like some sort of apparition.

None of it makes any sense. I may be crazy.

'Talking to me when?'

Abraham tells her his story. All of it, from the moment he knew she had left to the realization that his foolishness had condemned them both to death. That a family execution was being planned. She lets him talk, but her silence isn't just silence, it means something. It always does with her, and in the darkness he can picture her face, set and serious, some deep grievance behind it that he can never quite reach or resolve.

'You're Irene?'

'Yes.'

'My God. My God. Someone has sent you. Is that what this is? You wouldn't know how to do that.'

'I had to have some connection with you.'

'You are, you're a fucking spy.'

Though she can't see it, Abraham shakes his head.

'I'm not a spy. Try not to think like them. I love you. I came for you.'

'Don't tell me how to think.'

Her silence is different now.

'This isn't you. You wouldn't do this on your own.'

'I was always terrified of losing you. When I lost you I wasn't scared any more.'

That reaches her, he knows it, and he waits before going on.

'I knew it wouldn't work. That you'd see this place for what it is.'

'Sorry. What is it? This place.'

'It's a lie.'

'God is a lie?'

'Not God. This isn't God. The idea. The khilafa. That you're saving the world.'

'Someone has to.'

'You think that's what they're trying to do? The men in command. They want to save the world?'

'They're trying to save their people. My people. From death and torture and constant persecution. Dad, wake up. Stop taking those fucking pills and open your eyes. The world is sliding into hell.'

It strikes Abraham that in London he and she had been equally out of place. It was home to neither of them.

'And this isn't hell?'

'It's a necessary stage.'

'It's necessary to throw people off buildings?'

'The punishments are decreed.'

'What happens after the hell stage?'

'Shut up. I can't believe I travelled thousands of miles to get away from you and I'm still having to listen to your shit.'

Now we're not talking. Three feet away from each other in the last place on earth and both of us are sulking. What's more ridiculous, that I have to talk to my father here or that right now I won't? I don't know how long we just sit there in the dark but eventually I can't stand it.

He thinks he was right all along. That the fact we're sitting here now is somehow proof I made the wrong decision. I can feel it, he's just dying to tell me he told me so. But the khilafa has run out of patience with me, not the other way round. Badra was right. I'm not strong enough to make the sacrifices that need to be made. I'm in the way. I don't want to be in the way. It's as simple as that.

'That was a shitty thing you did, with Mama's picture.'

'It wasn't meant to be shitty.'

'I gave up all that. I can't have it dragging me back.'

'You gave up your mother? That's what God wants?'

'No love is more important than love for Him, the most glorified, the most high.'

'These men don't love God. They love death, and power. And money. They love what men have always loved.'

'Then why do they fight for Him?'

'They're not fighting for any God I recognize.'

'You don't know my God.'

'I've read the Koran. Your God doesn't want this.'

I wasn't expecting that. I imagine him going through it, looking for clues and objections.

'You don't know my God.'

'I know God. And I understand why you're here. You came to fight for a better world and I'm proud of that.'

He's silent for a while and I'm grateful for it. Not for long.

'This is your house?'

'I suppose.'

'It's a nice house.'

Not for me, I want to say, but I won't give him the satisfaction.

'Nice enough.'

'The fighters and I, we sleep ten to a room and every night only eight come back.'

'That's not true.'

'You should smell the stink of it.'

'I know what you're trying to do. This is a war. You show me any general who doesn't live better than his men.'

He thinks about that and when he speaks again it's in this quiet voice that he thinks will get inside me.

'How does he treat you?'

'Who?'

'Your husband. The general.'

'None of your business.'

'Does he treat you well?'

'I've been married to him for a week.'

'And in that time?'

'Leave it.'

'Tell me. Would you introduce him to Mama?'

That really gets me. How dare he exploit my mother to make whatever point he's trying to make.

'You don't have the right to talk about her.'

'She's still my wife.'

'After what you did to her.'

'What did I do to her?'

'She told me you started it. That she was ill because of you.'

He's quiet for a second and then asks me what she said.

'That you'd done something to hurt her.'

Now he doesn't say anything for a long time and in the

darkness I can sense the truth assembling itself in his head. I feel his hand reach for my leg, and rest on my knee.

'My whole life I never did a thing to hurt her, or you. Your God or mine strike me down if I did.'

A great sob moves up from the earth and through the whole of me and I work hard to control it. At least he cannot see my eyes.

It must be two years since they've talked like this, and Abraham does his best to break the old pattern of their conversations. Don't get cross. Don't be riled. Have the energy and the will to keep her engaged. This may be the last time you talk to her – may be the last time either of us speaks to anyone.

But in fact, it's easy. After a lifetime of worrying about the future, the future has been taken away, and everything seems so clear, so calm. Right here at the end, I'm being shown what love is. My poor girl, bewildered, incomplete, raging and afraid. I think I understand why you're here. And it would be better before we die if you did, too.

'Does he know you're down here?'

'Who?'

'Borz.'

'How do you know his name?'

'You told Irene.'

'Great.'

'Does he?'

'Of course.'

'So they decide I'm a spy, and you must be too? Why doesn't he stand up for you?'

Every time she's silent Abraham thinks he might be getting somewhere, but he waits, doesn't push it.

'That's not why I'm here.'

*

I've got to tell him. For one, I'm not going to lie, it's a sin, but also I don't want him thinking he's responsible for my fate. Not for this part.

So I tell him. I tell him about Niran, and the fighter, and the gun, and even as I'm saying the words I can't believe how stupid I've been and all the damage I've done.

'You did the right thing.'

He doesn't know how complicated it is.

'I put personal concerns before the khilafa.'

'Protecting an eight-year-old girl isn't a personal concern.'

'It was a test. I failed the test.'

'Sorry. Who set the test?'

'God, the most glorified, the most high.'

'Then you passed. What God would want you to abandon her?'

He just doesn't see it. He of all people ought to see it. I tell him that and he asks me what I mean.

'It was for God to spare Isaac, not Abraham. Niran wasn't mine to save. No one is. And now because of my mistake she will be lost forever. Don't you see? If I'd been true to the khilafa she would've become a Muslim, a good Muslim, raised in a good family. And instead she'll live and die in darkness. That was the test. I thought I knew best. That's why I can't be here. I'm not worthy of the khilafa.'

Tears are building in me but I hold them, keep my voice steady. His breathing is slow and deep, and I hope he's taking it in. It's so important he understands.

So twisted, her thinking. Each false thread pulls the knot tighter. She hasn't been poisoned, she's been programmed, so that everything is reversed. Dark is light, good is bad, death is life. Abraham casts around for the question to ask, the memory to invoke, the piece of logic that will magically cause it to unravel, and knows that none of them will work. But she's upset, and that's good.

'Where is she now?'

'Who?'

'Niran.'

'I don't know.'

'What will happen to her?'

'I don't know, okay? How would I know?'

'You know what the difference is?'

'What are you talking about?'

'Abraham's sacrifice was to God.'

'Yes.'

'And Niran. Who was she being sacrificed to? You think God wanted that man to get pleasure from her?'

'Of course not.'

'You think He'd use that disgusting creature as His instrument?'

'That's not the point.'

'How many are there like that, in the khilafa?'

She doesn't answer.

'You think God would work through them?'

'Can you be quiet?'

'Your husband. A man like that. Would God work through him?'

'I mean it.'

'Would He allow him to do the things he does to you?'

A raging cry moves at him through the darkness and her fists connect clumsily, striking his chest until he finds and holds her arms and wrestles her closer to him. The pounding turns to twitching and the cry to sobs that shudder through her. The stuff of her abaya is heavy and her body hot inside it; her head rests on his chest, her breath making a warm circle on his shirt; slowly the seething spirit seems to leave her.

'I'm proud of you.'

She doesn't say anything, and he wonders whether she's falling asleep.

'God chooses people like you for His work. Not people like them. Or like me.'

When I wake I'm still leaning on my father and I'm so hot and I barely know where I am. I move off him, shuffle away, blink in the blackness. I think it's daylight. I can see light coming through tiny cracks.

'Good morning,' he says.

I don't know where I am. I don't know who I am. I feel like I've been taken apart and the pieces scattered across the desert.

'Good morning.'

Saying it helps, a tiny bit. Something normal, everyday.

'Is there any way out of here?'

He's crazy. I knew he was crazy.

'There's no point.'

'Who but the lost would despair of God's mercy?'

More craziness. I thought I was already thrown but that throws me.

'Where did you get that?'

'You know where. The Qur'an.'

'That's good.'

He starts to look. Or rather he feels. I can hear him inching around the room, touching the walls, stumbling over things on the floor, rattling things about. I don't know what he's looking for, he's getting on my nerves and I want him to sit down again. What does he think, we're going to find a hidden door and a tunnel to Turkey?

'There are fighters everywhere. You don't know this place.'

'No. But you do.'

As he moves I can smell the sweat on him, hear him breathing and making little noises as he rummages about. From the way his breath catches sometimes, I think he must be hurt.

Something's missing. That sweet stale smell of drink, it's not on him, for the first time in so long, and for some reason it makes me think of him when I was little and I used to sit on the toilet in the bathroom and watch him trim his beard. I think about all the children in the world who will never know their father, and for a moment that chokes me up.

I don't know how long it takes but eventually he comes and sits down beside me, feeling his way and putting his hand on my shoulder as he lowers himself.

'Take this.'

He finds my hand, and puts something in it. His own hands are soft and dry, even in the heat down here.

'What is it?'

It's hard and cool to the touch, metal.

'I think it's a chisel. There's a box of tools. Hide it in your gown.'

'Niqab.'

'Your niqab, then. You may need it.'

'We may need more than a chisel. Have you got one?'

'No. The only other thing was a saw.'

From out of nowhere I laugh. I don't see it coming and for an instant it's like there's a third person down here, I haven't laughed in so long.

2

Sitting at the long side of the table are four men and one woman. Abraham and Sofia are made to stand opposite them against the wall and told not to look at anyone. Abraham glances up occasionally; why not, now? There are no more threats or terror in reserve. Sofia stands by him, in her niqab; he still hasn't seen her face.

The big one is Borz, he's seen the pictures. He'd know it

anyway: he has the face of a man who's taken pleasure in watching men die. White, translucent skin, damp-looking, hard and pudgy at once, like pig fat, and sticking out from it like bristles the red brown hairs of his too-big beard. Two muddy green eyes taking in everything as if all they need to know is how best to destroy it. Abraham has never met a man of this kind, the monsters who occupy the news, and he's surprised to discover that he's no longer particularly scared. Instead he feels disgust for the man, his new son-in-law, and pity for the daughter who married him.

Borz is in fatigues, desert camouflage. On his left is another large man, in black robes, a black scarf on his head. His eyes have a different strain of cruelty, born of some never acknowledged inadequacy; they watch carefully, assessing, calculating the personal risk in everything. To Borz's right is an imam, and by him a woman in full niqab, her face covered. On the other flank is a compact, hard, dry man in his fifties, maybe, who might be a bureaucrat or a general but looks used to having command. Here, the man in black seems to have the power. When he talks, the others listen and are careful not to interrupt.

A council. A jury.

They talk as if their prisoners weren't there, and Abraham wonders why he and Sofia have been called up from their confinement downstairs for this. There's discussion of timing, and place, even before the trial begins. Trial – it's their word and they pronounce it with great gravity, as if it truly means something. The trial is being conducted here because the matter is so unusually sensitive.

The man in black presides, and he starts with Abraham. The spy Ibrahim Mounir deceived the Islamic State twice, once by claiming he was an Egyptian and again by pretending to be a doctor. As they now knew he lived in London and worked as a pharmacist, he was no doctor at all. It was also clear that he had had contact with state espionage agencies in the UK before he came to Syria.

The charges go on. Mounir and his daughter were from the start engaged in a conspiracy to pass secrets back to their masters in London. What better spy than a seventeen-year-old girl? Who would come under less suspicion? They even devised a means of communicating with each other on Twitter, in plain sight, that allowed them to pass instructions one way and vital secrets the other. Before this was discovered the daughter was placed in positions of great trust, and her ascent through the administration of the State was steep. She was well trained to achieve this, evidently, and her access to sensitive information made her a valued asset of British intelligence.

This was a serious case. All spying is treason. But this is a commander's wife, a prominent person, with the ability to inflict acute damage on the State and its reputation. An example must be made.

'She is not my wife.'

'You are married to her.'

The imam speaks. 'The marriage can be cancelled.'

The man in black shakes his head. 'It is known. The British know. They will use it.'

Borz shakes his in turn. 'I will not cancel.'

At the end of the table the general or whatever he is leans forward and says he has a suggestion to make in this regard. Abraham is struck by how official the whole conversation is. This isn't anarchy, and these are not mere thugs.

'We will say that the moment we discovered the girl was a spy we brought her in close so we could investigate. We watched her, her communications, to make sure she was not operating in a ring. When we were satisfied she was acting alone we executed her and her handler, her father.'

Borz crosses his arms and sits back in his chair, shaking his head.

'This is my name.'

'This is your mistake.' The man in black looks straight ahead as he says it. 'Abu Selim's solution is correct. Tomorrow morning, at eight. Make the arrangements. Until then lock them up, but not here.'

3

I must have seen fifty of the things, at least, maybe a hundred, and before he is shoved into one of the tiny cells I see them hand one to my father – an orange jumpsuit ready for tomorrow. They keep me in my niqab because I guess the rules are the rules even in death.

The logistics I've never considered before – where the prisoners are held beforehand, when they change into their death clothes, who guards them, what they think is happening. I remember reading in the kafir press that some of the early hostages were told they weren't actually going to be killed, that the camera would cut away at the last moment and leave the rest up to the imagination of the millions who would see it, but I don't believe anyone could be in any doubt, not at this stage.

So I know the form. Beheading, for treason, unless they have something unusual in store, something creative, and I doubt that because this already has all the appeal they need. Two members of the same family would be enough, but a father and his daughter is new and fresh, and I think they'll keep it simple. I hope so. Cleaner than what happened to Idara – quicker. An instant, the soul detached from the flesh like an apple from its tree, and painless, I imagine. Like a paper cut, you only register it after it's been made. And there is no after.

This place was the local police station, I know it from the brigade – we would bring people here before trial. Before we took the town, political prisoners were kept here. Maybe we're political. I'm on the ground floor in a cell on a corridor of ten or twelve. Mine's the first cell on the left, and although I don't know who's in the others I think they must all be men – I hear them sneeze and cough and groan like men.

Before they do it I hope they let me wash, I want to be in a dignified state for when I meet Him. If I must be clean for prayer how much more important is it to be clean for death?

I wish it could be now.

When they brought us up from the cellar and stood us in the dining room of that disgusting house I looked at my father and I looked at those other men and in their strength I saw weakness and in his weakness I saw a strange sort of strength. I'd never recognized it in him before. Borz is weak because he's a hypocrite. He is not a holy man. In his eyes there is only murder and lust, nothing else. My father loved my mother so much that when she became ill life stopped for him. He lived in fear, all the time. I see it now. Borz has never known fear. He just makes others afraid.

What is in his head when he executes a woman with her hands tied behind her back or forces himself on a girl a third his size? The young brothers, the stupid brothers, the ones who came here for a gun and a wife and to think they're big, a nobody become a somebody, the ones who'll come to my class and take an eight-year-old and treat her as no one should be treated and then say it brings them closer to God – those brothers, with their eyes that turn from sparkling to dead in the instant they get what they want, when they bring the axe down or sink their weight onto some poor girl, all they want is an excuse. Badra's right. They have given as much thought to Allah, the most glorified, the most high, as they have to the life they take or the beauty they destroy.

What is in Borz's head? Does he know he is no different? Does he know he is a sinner?

My eyes are shut, and against them I see an image, I don't

know where it comes from – barely an image, it's more of a sense, maybe this is what they call a vision – of the universe in cold harmony, every part of it connected to every other and working for the whole, and of Borz naked in the desert, his white flesh writhing on the sand, eyes screwed tight and a silent cry in his throat. And flowing through everything, around and within, are His words.

THE DISASTER! What is the Disaster?

On that day people shall become like scattered moths and the mountains like tufts of carded wool.

Then he whose good deeds weigh heavy in the scales shall live in bliss; but he whose good deeds are light, the Abyss shall be his home.

Would that you knew what this is like!

It is a scorching fire.

Borz will know the Abyss. I have my answer. He will burn in the fire. The fire will scorch him to atoms. And soon I will discover how heavily my deeds weigh, and on which side of the scale I fall.

I think I sleep, a sleep with no rest in it. I will rest soon enough.

At first I don't register them, but screams have woken me, like a baby's might wake a mother. Screams I seem to know and not to know. It's dark now, the cell is black, and I both listen and try not to listen. Then there are words, rushed, strangled, and I've never heard it like that before but I know the voice, I'll always know it.

No one should hear her father like that. I can picture too easily what they're doing to him. That man I hadn't seen before at Borz's, I think I know who he was, and my guess is that they want to force all the intelligence they can get out of us before tomorrow. Maybe they really think we're spies. Maybe they just enjoy it. I don't know any more.

More screams, I press my hands to my ears. He shouldn't

have come, why did he come? Why couldn't he just live with the fact that I'd gone?

For so long I've watched him suffer and resented the suffering. But I'm beginning to understand. Wouldn't I want to keep Khalil's child close forever, that last piece of him? Don't I?

Finally it goes quiet, and I hear footsteps in the corridor and a cell door open and slam shut, and I expect them to come for me now and though that terrifies me – I can feel my body tensing – I welcome it. If he has suffered I should suffer too.

But no one comes, for a long time, I have no idea how long. They seem to know the worst punishment for me would be no punishment at all.

Then with a crack a little window in the metal door slides back and I briefly see a square of yellow light and two eyes looking at me. They stare at me for a moment and I can't see what's in them, why they're looking, but I assume my time has come. Whoever it is puts his mouth to the hole and says,

'Your father makes a lot of noise.'

The eyes return and even against the light I can see the leer in them, or perhaps I just know it's there because it's always there, in all their eyes, the brothers who took the Belgian sisters from the makkar, the guards at Borz's house, that Russian with Niran. The look wakes some fury in me and in an instant I know that Badra is wrong. We don't have to submit. There is another path to the future.

'The more the better,' I tell the voice.

The eyes move back an inch or two from the door and now I see something of his face. I don't know him, but I know him. The look is there, the same hungry greedy brazen look.

'I have no love for my father.'

'Then you are not a good Muslim, sister, and we will have to punish you.' He half laughs. This is a joke.

'He's a kafir. You want me to love a kafir?'

'I don't care what a fucking spy does.'

'I'm not the spy. My father is a kafir, and a spy, and his job was to come here and get me killed. Which you're going to help him do.'

'Won't be me, sister. No such luck.'

'That's a shame.'

He doesn't know what to say to this.

'I want to meet the man who does it.'

'Oh, you'll meet him, sister.'

I stand and move to the door. My eyes are a foot from his.

'Do I get any last requests?'

'Does this look like a fucking movie?'

I'm staring into his eyes, now, and he's staring into mine. I can see the thought starting in him.

'You could be in a movie,' I tell him.

In fact he's one of the better ones. Strong, young, I'm guessing Iraqi, the beard still on his top lip.

'Fuck you.'

I try a smile. This is taking some effort. Part of me wants to shrink back into the corner, part of me wants to break through the door and through this idiot and run.

'I don't want to go out like this. On my own.'

He cocks his head and grins.

'You'll have your dad, sister.'

'That's not what I mean.'

I give him a look. I don't know how good I am at looks but I think this one works because he grins again.

'I'm seventeen. I've been with a man three times. One man. That's not enough.'

The brother nods. He's thinking it through, I can see it.

'You ever been with a woman who's got hours to live?'

Now I smile, for the first time.

'I won't be holding back, brother.'

He takes a step away, sniffs, looks up and down the corridor.

He's really thinking – where to go? What are the chances of getting caught?

Without saying anything he shuts the slot in the door and walks away, the chance has gone, but in a minute I hear steps again and the metal of a key in the lock. I get ready.

The door opens, and he's there against the light.

'Not here,' he says.

'Wherever you want.'

I smile and move towards him, my eyes on his so that he won't look down and see what I have in my hand. He has a machine gun hanging from his shoulder. I put one hand there, still smiling, and bring the other up into his side as hard as I can manage it so that the metal of the chisel sinks right in, up towards his heart. I'm surprised by how soft it is, how easily it travels, and something about how easy it is makes it harder. His eyes go wide and his mouth opens and lets out a scream that dies in a kind of sigh and the smell of fear. He tries to pull back and get at his gun but with the chisel still inside I turn him to the wall before pulling out and stabbing him again, in the same place, in and out now while a kind of craziness takes me, a fire burns all through me and I'm not even thinking any more, there's nothing in my head but his flesh and mine and only one can survive. He's groaning, and pushing me away, but no, you can't live, you won't live, you weren't meant to live, I'm sorry my brother, I'm sorry, this was your choice, this life, this death.

I feel his weight sink against my hand and the fire calms, but something tells me this is the dangerous moment, that he's not gone yet, and I force myself not to back off, but his body slides down the wall and his eyes stop being eyes, there's no light going in or out.

I step back from him. The dead weight, so much of it, the pointlessness of all that bulk. I see the blood on my hand, on the wall, on the floor, and in the half-light it looks black, toxic, a poison that's in me now. I can feel it filling my veins until I'm a new person with sickness in my stomach and an ache in every bone.

Whoever kills a human being, it shall be as if he has killed all mankind; and whoever saves a life, it shall be as if he has saved all mankind.

Have I not done both these things?

I ask Him but there is no reply.

4

No one comes. For some time I just stand, not moving, not thinking, but then time returns and I know I have to work. I drop the chisel, and pull the brother into the cell. I take his gun, find his keys and leave him in there, locking the door behind me.

Making my way down the corridor, I quietly slide back the windows in the cell doors. No one moves or says anything, some are asleep, some assume I'm a guard and that a new bad thing is about to happen. My father is in the second to last cell on the right, awake, lying on his side, but his eyes don't even move when I call to him. When you don't have anything to tell them, they don't let up.

The key is the last I try. I step forward and put my hand on his shoulder, but he hardly seems to notice I'm there. The light has left his eyes as completely as the dead brother's in my cell.

'Dad. Dad, it's me.'

Nothing. It's like he's gone already.

'Dad.' I shake him gently, run my hand up and down his arm.

His eyes move to mine.

'We've got to go.'

Like a child woken from sleep he sits up, nods, and tries to stand, but his legs are weak and he has to rest before trying again. This time I help him up, and as I put my hand round his back I feel warmth and wet. He winces, and I know what they've done to him.

'Wait.'

I turn him so that he's facing away from the door and inspect his back. It like it's been clawed by some immense creature – deep crossed lines of red are cut through the cloth of his shirt which is meshed into the wounds and the whole thing covered with blood. The lines run diagonally both ways, as if two men have beaten him, one from each side, one left-handed, one right. I remember with a rising sickness the lashes I gave, even if they weren't like this.

The blood is beginning to clot. There's nothing I can do for him here. The cloth will have to be picked out of the wounds before they heal, but I'll need water, and something to clean them with.

'Your jacket.'

He shakes his head and tries to speak but at first the words don't come, it's like they're stuck inside.

'They took it.'

'Okay.'

He's unsteady, and for the first few steps all his weight is on me. I ask him where they took him, but he barely knows what I'm saying. I have to get something to cover his back, we can't go out into the city with him looking like that, we'd last five minutes. So I guide him into the corridor and ask him which room. He looks like he's never seen the place before and shakes his head.

'Dad.' I'm whispering now, because there's nothing except corridor between us and the lobby of the station and who knows who's around. 'It's important.'

I see him try to focus, some understanding comes back into his eyes, and he points at the second to last door on the right. I nod at him to tell him to wait here and quietly make my way towards it and inside.

I close the door as softly as I can and find the light switch. The first thing I see is the blood, spattered on the tiled walls that once were white, some fresh, some dried and brown. I can smell the blood, it makes me gag – this intense smell of metal and flesh and sweat, like no air has ever made it in here, that it's all been sucked up in people's screams. I look but I don't see. I don't want to see. But my eyes catch on handcuffs, rope, blue and red electric cable, a dial on a wooden box. In the middle of the room is a table with a wooden board that's hinged in the middle and has straps for wrists and ankles in each corner.

In a corner is a plastic bin full of clothes and filthy rags and on top of it I see the jacket my father was wearing, a grey suit jacket that I've seen him wear a hundred times before, so innocent in here, so out of place, a symbol of the line I've made him cross.

My father looks at the jacket like it doesn't make any sense to him, like he doesn't even know what it's supposed to be, and I have to feed his arms into the sleeves and hitch it ever so gently up onto his shoulders. He starts from the pain and lets out a little cry but as I hold my finger up to my lips I see that some life has returned to his eyes, he's starting to wake up. As I motion for him to follow me he holds my arm, pulls me back.

'The others.'

He turns back the way we've come, then back to me.

'We can't take them.'

'We can free them.'

'If we free them, it may finish us.'

His eyes are bloodshot and exhausted and completely serious, and I know what he's going to say before he says it.

'What's the point, if we don't?'

I breathe in deeply, close my eyes, nod. He's right.

'Stay here,' I tell him, and I take the keys and as quickly as I can I unlock all the doors, but I leave them closed. As I'm doing the last one another opens and a face appears, it's a young local, he can only be fifteen or sixteen, and he looks at me completely bewildered. His right eye is puffed up in a ball. I put my finger to my lips, finish what I'm doing and, gathering up my father, hurry silently towards the front of the building.

There's only one light on in the corridor that joins the cells and the lobby, two of the fluorescent bulbs have gone, but still I feel so conspicuous. No one's here. As we round the corner, so slowly, there's a pair of boots on a desk and a fighter asleep in a chair with his feet up, gun hanging off his shoulder. He's the only one, and I could kill him now while he sleeps. I take my father's hand and we creep past, keeping my gun on the guard the whole time, and I pray that when the door opens it doesn't make any noise, and that outside there isn't going to be a whole crew of fighters wide awake and waiting for us.

The building is set back from the street and two 4x4s are parked outside, facing it. Two trees block my view a little but in one of the cars I can see the blueish glow of a phone, and, lit up by it, someone in the driver's seat. The other car is dark. The quickest way out of their line of sight is to the right, away from the street, and then circle round behind them and away into the city.

I point the way, and looking back through the glass in the door to check on the sleeping brother see the boy we've just freed creeping slowly up to him and all I want to do is shout, no, leave him, just get out of there, but I can't, I have to watch him. He gets within maybe three feet and I know what he's going to do, he's going to make a grab for the gun.

I pull my father behind me and crouching down move away from the door, and at that moment shots sound inside, so flat and matter of fact. Immediately the car door opens and the other brother comes running past us, gun out. I move us round so the tree's always between us and him but his mind is on other things and as he arrives at the door there's more shooting, from both guns. The brother's shooting through the glass and stepping aside and shooting again. I'm willing him to go down because if he's the only brother here it'll buy us some more time. And give us a car. He steps to the side of the door and twice leans over to fire into the lobby and then carefully looks round once more and when he's certain goes into the building. The boy is dead, I know it, and my heart sinks into my gut because now we have no time at all.

'I have to finish it.'

My father looks at me and I know he doesn't understand, he just isn't made for the rules here. But I am.

I step into the doorway and the brother is there crouching down by his friend, and there's something human and innocent about the way he's leaning forward, fingers on the dead man's wrist. I register this at the same moment that I pull the trigger. He falls away from me and the force sends me backwards and him across the floor, and then his eyes are on mine, his gun still in his hand, and I see what he sees: a black crow with a gun and her eyes showing. He'll know a woman finished him. I fire again and he's gone, I know it, his blood covers the wall behind him and I can't look at it, the same sickness fills me and I turn away.

'Let's go.'

No one's coming for us. The other car must be empty, and all around I hear no noise. Shots are not unusual in this city.

I try the brother's car first, and find the keys in the ignition.

We go. My father says he can drive, but he's really slow and jerky and he has to sit bolt upright so his back doesn't touch the chair. Pain is wracking his face but he's strong, a fighter, a real one. More than I realized. I sit by him and direct him, staying on the edge of town. Coming at Borz's house from the back.

5

Abraham has never driven anything like this: powerful, certain, sneeringly superior. Even on a good day he would have felt at odds with it and now it feels always just out of his control, as if any moment it might decide to go its own way. But it gives him something to concentrate on, and he needs it. The pain seems to hammer outwards from the core of him.

Out here in the residential areas there are no shops and no lights besides those of the odd car that passes. Twice they meet bigger roads that lead into and out of the city, and twice they go straight on, hugging the rim of the place.

Sofia anticipates his question; he isn't ready yet to ask it himself.

'We can't leave yet. And I have to get something.'

God how he wants to leave. To be in Egypt, in a cool house in the heat of the day, lying with Ester in the soft light coming through the orange curtains, Sofia asleep beside him in her crib.

Hard to believe the same world can hold that heaven and this hell. He thought he was prepared, but it turns out hell is unimaginable to most human beings. They don't have the material to work with. But Sofia was beginning to see it, just as she finally became fully part of it. From time to time Abraham looks across at his daughter, this young woman – barely a woman – who has killed a man and thinks, I owe my life to her.

'Slow down,' she says, peering into the darkness, and after another few hundred yards, 'Here. I think this is it. Close enough.'

Abraham cuts the engine and the headlights. All he can see is what appear to be houses across maybe a hundred yards of field or scrub. A row of houses, lit windows in just three of them. The clock on the dashboard says two in the morning.

Sofia picks up her gun from the footwell and opens the door; the interior light comes on and instantly she reaches up to turn it off. As she leaves she tells Abraham to wait here, that she won't be long, but the thought of losing her now, after all this, is a new kind of pain to him. He'd rather die with her than be left alone.

'I'm coming.'

'This will be easy. Wait here. You have a gun.'

Abraham takes the gun – his gun – gets down from the cab and walks round to her side.

'Tell me what you're doing.'

The moon is just a crescent and he can barely see her eyes, but determination radiates from her.

'I have to pick someone up. Before we go.'

'Where is this?'

'You don't recognize it?'

Abraham shakes his head. He's sure he's never been here before, and the thought that he might be losing bits of his memory scares him.

'Stay here. If you see anyone with a gun, shoot him. But you won't.'

'I'm coming with you.'

'You can't protect me here.'

'We're here together.'

She relents, and sets off towards the houses. The terrain turns out to be much more broken than he had thought, rutted and rocky, and each time he misjudges a step the jolt sends pain to every part of his body. But he stays upright, and doesn't drop too far behind Sofia, who manages to move through the night in her niqab with the gun across her back as if this is her natural state.

At some point, as they draw near, Abraham realizes where they are.

He puts his hand on her shoulder, holds her back.

'They'll kill you. Leave him.'

'I'm not here for Borz.'

Sofia motions for him to stand by the back door and guard it. Somehow he understands her perfectly, and as he takes up his position she whispers that she'll be two minutes, no more, and goes up the three or four steps to the house and then inside.

From the moment I see the light I don't like it. No one should be up now. But I will not turn back. I will not fail anyone else.

For maybe a minute I wait in the passage between the kitchen and the garage and listen. Nothing, not a sound, not from the front where there will be two brothers standing guard, and not from the kitchen, even when I press my ear to the door.

I open the door slowly, slowly, pressing down as evenly as I can on the handle and willing it not to creak. It leads into a laundry, and the door into the kitchen is open a crack. Hafa is there, at the head of the table, facing me, deep in her phone. In her dressing gown. Apparently it's her turn in exile, but I don't have time to wonder why.

I can't risk her speaking. As far as I know, the door from the kitchen to the rest of the house is open and the noise will go straight up those stairs to Borz. Paralysed, I go round and round the problem in my head, and in the end all I can do is step into the room with my finger to my lips.

'I've come for Zarifa. Let me take her.'

I whisper it as quietly as I can, and we look at each other, and there's no love there, none at all. If she felt threatened by me before she hasn't relaxed now the threat has gone. She doesn't say anything, just keeps her eyes on mine, and I think we understand each other. I think. She's tough, but that look has changed. If I was guessing I'd say she still hates me but not as much as she hates Borz.

I don't like to turn my back on her but I have no choice. From the kitchen I start across the hall, careful with every step, there's just enough light from the kitchen to see by, and then I'm by Zarifa's door and here I don't hesitate, I go right in, take a step inside and whisper her name.

Her breathing is loud, almost snoring. The room stinks of unchanged air and sweat and the things Borz does in here.

'Zarifa.'

She's not waking. I close the door behind me and feel on the wall for the light switch.

The room is tiny, and Borz is asleep on the single bed. I don't see Zarifa at first, she's lying on the floor in the gap between the bed and the far wall, and she doesn't move. Borz does. Thick with sleep, eyes screwed up, he turns his head to me. I need a knife, a chisel, but all I have is this stupid gun and if I fire it the brothers will be in here in an instant and I'll get us all killed. I should just switch the light off and go, run past Hafa into the night, but what kind of human being would I be then? I've made mistakes but I've never been a coward.

I step back and point the gun at Borz, whose eyes are now awake, completely awake, and drilling right into the heart of me. Right now, just woken up, staring at a gun and the wife he's planning to kill in the morning he shows nothing, total calm, like a lizard, like a stone.

I have no idea how I'm going to do this.

'Zarifa. Get up.'

She's awake, I doubt she's slept, and she's pulled herself into the corner, her arms round her knees.

'We're going.'

I look at her quickly, show her she can trust me, keep my gun on Borz's heart.

'Now. We're going.'

As I look back to Borz his hand swipes up and knocks the end of the gun away and then he's up and as hard as I push at him I stand no chance, his hand's on my throat and the other is ripping my gun away from me. He lifts me up off the ground by my neck and no breath will go in, I'm going to die here now, of course he will be the one, in this room, full of his stink, his own pit of hell. I won't look at him. I won't give him the pleasure.

Two minutes go by. Abraham has no watch and he's in no state to count but it's been at least two minutes, maybe five now. In his hands and around his neck the gun weighs heavy. Such a simple thing to work, and so difficult to use.

He steps inside the passage, listens, hears nothing. One of the two doors ahead of him is open; he steps through it and listens again, and now there's noise, indistinct and far off, that he strains to catch.

Slowly, gun first, he heads towards the light, and finds himself in a kitchen – fitted, jarringly banal, it's like walking back into his flat in London – and standing the other side of the white-topped table a woman in a dressing gown with a kitchen knife in her hand, the blade up and uncertainly in front of her. She's walking towards the door into the house but as she sees Abraham she stops, fear in her face, and at the same moment there's a thud from outside and a sort of cry. Abraham and the woman exchange looks and it's clear from the confusion in her face that whatever's happening she's not part of it. Abraham drops the barrel of the gun, then makes for the door himself.

He's barely taken a step when Borz is there. Naked, giant, demonic, taking up almost the whole frame, a machine gun in one hand and Sofia by the neck in the other, her eyes half screwed shut in pain. By instinct, Abraham raises the gun but as if reflecting the action Borz calmly brings his gun across himself so that the barrel sticks into the soft flesh under Sofia's chin. His eyes cut through Abraham; now they terrify him.

Borz shakes his head like a weary parent bringing play to an end.

'No more.' His words are like rocks.

Abraham can take no more. It feels like the end. From fatigue alone he keeps the gun on Borz, who circles round the other side of the table, pulling Sofia after him. He seems to be making for a phone on the counter. The other woman, the wife if that's what she is, has let the knife drop to her side and is standing by the cooker looking dazed and out of place, barely even a witness. She glances at Abraham, up at Borz's face, then down at the ground.

'Now. Finish. Over.'

Through her pain Sofia looks at Abraham and he knows what the look means. Kill him. Don't worry about me. Put a stop to this man.

But he can't. Doesn't even trust himself to shoot the right person, with a gun like this, in this tiny space, and so he lowers the barrel and accepts the death he's been imagining: tomorrow, in the full sun, dressed in orange, beside and in the same instant as his daughter.

Borz looks over his shoulder, pushes Sofia so that she stumbles into the table, and reaches for the phone behind him. As he places it to his ear the other wife brings her hand up, Abraham barely sees it, and the knife sinks into Borz's side, up towards his heart; blood spurts from the wound down her arm and onto the table. Rage and shock twisting the thick pig skin of his face, the knife still stuck in him up to the handle, Borz swipes at the wife, his chest and belly suddenly rigid. The back of his hand cracks her cheek and she falls. Borz lifts the gun and brings his arm across but now he's on his own, in the clear, just him and the gun, and Abraham, without thinking, fires. The first bullets puncture his chest like blots of red ink, and Abraham keeps his hand on the trigger until the torso is more blood than flesh and Borz's face stops protesting and then stops altogether.

Silence and gun smoke fill the room. Borz is propped against the cooker, eyes dead, mouth open, still supported by his massive frame. Sofia is the first to move.

'Go!' she says, to Abraham, who's staring at Borz, ears ringing, eyes in shock. 'Dad! Now!'

Through his stupor Abraham can hear shouting and knocking somewhere outside, a commotion of voices. Sofia moves round the table, disappears through the door into the hall and reappears just a second later dragging a young girl behind her. A shot cracks the silence and the door frame splinters as she comes through it.

'Go!'

Abraham turns and starts to run. Behind him he hears his daughter.

'Come with us.'

'You killed him,' says the wife. 'Why should I run?'

More shots. The three of them run across the yard, scramble into the darkness.

6

I'm in black, they can't see me, not out here. As soon as I'm past the light coming from the house I'm safe, but Zarifa is wearing white and my father's conspicuous enough. Bullets begin to tear past us, wailing above the brothers' shouts. I've heard them when they're just working each other up into a frenzy but this is different, they're furious, and scared, because they were meant to be keeping Borz safe.

I'm faster than the others, and I stop to let them catch up, make sure they're okay, watch to see who is behind us. Zarifa has no shoes but she's light and she moves okay across the broken ground. I can make out one brother standing in the back doorway, flashes of fire coming from his gun, it's difficult to tell but I'm guessing he can't see any of us now. He's not coming after us, he's just standing there. My poor father is stumbling so much, it seems wrong to see him struggle with his weakness in the same moment that he has finally been proved strong. What he needs is rest, and peace, and here in the night I vow to give it to him.

But not yet. We have so far to go.

The 4x4 is maybe four hundred metres from the house and we're closing on it when I hear a car's engine off to our right and in a moment the light from its headlamps shows past the last house in the row. Then it appears, beams cutting through the night, skidding in the dust and fishtailing towards the 4x4. I think I see a brother leaning out of the window, sitting on the sill like they do, gun in hand.

We'll never make it. By the time we get to the car and open the doors and get the engine started, even if Dad wasn't in this state, they'll have torn us all in two.

'Stop!'

I hold out an arm and pull them both round.

'Follow me.'

I hope to God I can find it again. I'm sure I saw it as we crossed this ground to the house, but there's so little light, and what there is isn't where I need it. For a moment I think I've missed it and my heart sinks because any moment we're going to be picked up by the headlights and then we're gone. The ground is so broken it could be anywhere. But then in the darkness I see a patch that's darker and I can feel fresh adrenaline pumping through me, I didn't know I had any left.

'Here. Down there.'

Zarifa goes first, I help her down. My father takes a moment because he's still in pain, I can see it in every movement, but I have to hurry him, get in, hurry, we've got to go. I jump down and push them both towards the deep darkness.

Soon none of us can see a thing. Not each other, not a hand

in front of our face. The tunnel is maybe four feet high so even I have to crouch.

'Move down. Quickly.'

Together we claw our way a few feet further inside and then I *shh* them and we all stop. When I look back the entrance is a grey disc and it grows brighter and darker as the car sweeps its lights across the ground. It's so rough up there they may not see it, I pray they don't. I can tell that in the darkness we're all praying for the same thing. As if from a mile away I hear shouts, muted by the earth, and a door slamming, and two shots, one right after another, like they think they've seen someone. Then more shouting, and the engine revs and I can feel the vibrations through the ground as the car races away.

For maybe a full two minutes we sit and listen and breathe. When I whisper, it's so quiet I can barely hear it myself.

'We need the car. But they may have left someone there.'

Above us I can hear airstrikes somewhere across the city, not so far away, the walls of earth shake. Suddenly I'm exhausted, and I just want to stay here in the dark until it's safe to go out. Wait until the khilafa is built and the men who built it gone. Wait forever.

'Where does this go?'

I tell him I don't know. It runs parallel to Borz's street, and most of these tunnels are round the perimeter of the city where they're easy to dig, like a ring road round Raqqa. But I have no idea where this one comes out, and we need to get right across town.

'Do you know what time it is?'

'The clock in the car said two when we arrived.'

The sun comes up at seven. It could be five miles round the outside, it could be more. But if we try to go through town we'll be dead. Even if we weren't on the run we'd be dead, a woman with no veil and a gun on her back, and a Yazidi girl, and an Egyptian who's limping and in pain. I could brave it, make out the others are my prisoners, march them at gunpoint, but by now the brothers may have raised the alarm. But then I wouldn't want to be the one to tell an officer that Borz was dead before I'd found and killed the people who killed him. And no one uses the tunnels at night.

'Come on.'

I squeeze past the others so that I can lead from the front. I take the gun from my father, then I feel for my shoes in the dark, pull them off and reach out to Zarifa.

'It's okay,' I tell her, and together we manage to put them on her feet.

'This is going to take a long time,' I tell them both in Arabic. 'And we don't have long.'

Where the ceiling dips, Abraham has to crawl on all fours, sometimes for minutes at a time. More than once the earth roof brushes against his back and the pain leaves him sprawled in the dirt, but he has the will to pick himself up. Now he has something to escape to.

The tunnel is roughly built, propped up every yard or so with timber, but the floor is rocky and soon his knees hurt as much as the rest of him. His neck aches. So much has happened that only now does he realize that he hasn't drunk any water for the best part of a day; his mouth is cracked and dry with thirst and sand. With every step – every inch forward – he wonders whether it wouldn't be easier to be on the surface, where at least he could breathe. The air down here is thick and empty at the same time; he has to pant to suck the oxygen from it.

After twenty minutes the tunnel surfaces, and they wait by the entrance, listening for activity above. Then, like some burrowing creature, Sofia raises her head slowly above the parapet, crouches down to let a car pass, then repeats the process and eventually pulls herself up. The first time this happens they have to cross a road; they sprint to the other side, Sofia first, Abraham at the back, this young girl they've brought with them in between, and for a while they run about in the darkness, still crouching, desperately trying to find the entrance to the next stretch.

For hours, many hours, this goes on. Sofia lets them rest, but not for long, and she doesn't seem to need it. Abraham hates this city like he never knew he could hate anything, but he's strangely proud of the way his daughter navigates it. She doesn't flag. She's clear and courageous. Going back to Borz's for the girl was an insane thing to do, like her coming here in the first place. Down here, in the heat and the intense dryness and the total dark, where the images that come to his mind are of himself taking the cable across his back as he hangs in space, of the shock, almost puzzlement on Borz's face as the bullets sink easily into his chest, he concentrates on an idea of her future and for the first time in a long time knows it can be bright. It's the only thing sustaining him.

The sky is turning from black to the darkest blue when they emerge at the exit to yet another tunnel. There's just enough light for Abraham to see that his hands and the sleeves of his jacket are black with dirt. The streets are quiet. Quietest before the dawn.

Sofia throws the gun out, pulls herself up after it, and tells them to wait for her, she'll be back in a moment. Abraham hates any separation now. He wants to protect her, absurd though that is – she's protecting him – and if something bad happens he wants it to happen to them both. With an almost physical certainty he feels that all life is now bound up in her.

By an old instinct he puts his hand on the shoulder of the girl to reassure her, but she shrinks from him, and he apologizes. He can see her face now, the outline and essence of it, and it seems to tell him what he knows already, that she has more reason to be terrified than him.

'It'll be okay,' he says, in Arabic first and then in English, to himself.

7

I'm sure this is it. There's a building on the corner that's collapsed on itself and I remember the shape of it, like a tooth with decay, the four corners still standing and everything else sagged into the middle. From that crossroads it's two or three minutes to Badra's but we have to be really quick now because dawn is on its way and any moment the first call to prayer is going to start and the whole city will come alive again.

Out here my legs barely work, they're cramped with crouching and crawling, and my energy is almost gone. My feet are badly cut, each step is agony, and my mouth is so dry I can't move my tongue. If we're not in the right place I won't be able to go on, I don't think I can.

That first stretch is so long, it feels like a hundred miles, and with each step I'm praying that no brothers drive past or take this moment to look down from a window. There's enough light to see by now which means we can be seen, we might as well have a giant spotlight trained on us. And the call to prayer must be minutes away.

Twice cars pass, and twice I have to decide whether to just keep on walking or try to find some dark spot out of sight. Both times I keep on walking, and my heart pounds so hard I swear I can feel the fabric of my niqab shaking. I'm praying we look like a family, husband, wife, child. They drive straight by, and my heart rests a little, not much.

After what seems like hours we're there. My first home in the khilafa.

She'll be awake now, she always is. I press the buzzer and tell my father what to say. After maybe a minute, just when I'm thinking she's somewhere else, something must have happened, there's her voice as hard as ever.

'Yes?'

'I have a message from Umm Karam.'

'Why can't she call?'

'There are documents.'

He does well. The door clicks and we're in. Even the smoothness of the tiles under my feet is a relief.

The lights aren't working and neither is the lift. It takes us so long to get to the fifth floor, one flight at a time, that I'm sure by the time she comes to open the door Badra must already smell a rat. After two flights the first call to prayer starts, and outside the day has really begun.

My first idea had been to talk to her on my own but the other two are in such a state, they need water and rest and I don't want her just shutting us out. The sight of them may be the best appeal we can make.

I knock, firmly, trying to make it sound like a man's knock.

She's unveiled, dark against the light in the hall of the apartment, and her strict blue eyes stare right at me like she was expecting me the whole time.

'You.'

'I need help.'

'They came for you.'

When, I want to ask. Did they come before or after we killed Borz? But instead I say, 'Then they won't come back.'

She just looks at me, and as usual I have no idea what she's thinking, none at all. All night I've been wondering what I tell her, and now that the moment is here I can't think of any lie that she won't instantly see through.

'They want to kill us this morning.'

'Who is this?'

She juts her chin at Zarifa.

'She's Yazidi. Borz's.'

'You took her?'

'No one should live that life.'

328

'You still think there are rules, don't you?'

I'm not here for one of her discussions. I'm here for water, and money, and help from another human being.

'You said it. The khilafa is not for us. Not for her, not for me.'

She shakes her head, and her mouth makes something like a smile.

'No one leaves. That is the only rule.'

'I thought there was only sharia.'

'You don't listen. You never listened. There will be sharia. One day. Now all we have is force.'

God forgive me, how I hate her logic and her coldness. She knows what I've been through. I don't want to hurt anyone else, I never want to hurt anyone again, but I will shoot her if she doesn't get out of my way.

'I just need some water and some food. That's all.'

'Then you better hurry.'

I feel like I've swallowed a cold stone. I don't even have to ask what she means, she volunteers it.

'I called them the moment you buzzed.'

The door's open three inches and she's kept her body behind it the whole time, but now she steps back and in her hand I see a pistol coming up at me. I kick at the door, lean into it with all my weight, shout for the others to get back – she's surprised and her first shot goes past me somewhere, does no harm. Now I barge the door because my only hope is to keep her close, don't let her take aim, and as she fires again she staggers backwards under the weight. I feel that one, it flies past me and I flinch from it but I keep pushing, and the door gives, and she falls backwards and with my balance gone I fall onto her, veil pulled off centre, on the floor we roll and grope in the dark through the black fabric for each other's arms, trying in the mess to stop a shot and trying to get one away. Waiting for His will to choose one or the other.

I can't see a thing but I sense someone by me and Badra shouts, a muffled shout and when I finally shift my veil I see Zarifa kneeling down, she's got Badra's head wrapped in the folds of her abaya and with one hand she's pulling the material tight against her neck. I keep fighting but the fight is going from Badra, the hand that clutches me loses its power and I pull away, keeping my hand on her gun hand.

'Zarifa. No.'

Either she doesn't hear me or she can't stop. I can't see her eyes but I know she wants it, and I can't let her, she's too young.

With some wild last burst Badra brings her fist blindly up into my jaw. It sends me over and I shoot, and for a second, two seconds, I think I've hit Zarifa and that God has chosen the most awful punishment for me. No. Not this time. Zarifa still kneels, still tightens her grip on Badra, and I shout at her again because I can see that Badra's back is no longer arched and her chin is slumping onto her chest.

Have mercy on her, Lord. Have mercy on me.

'Zarifa. Zarifa.'

I take her hands and unlock each in turn. She looks at me and I tell her we have to go.

I tell my father to grab the gun and he stands there not hearing me.

'We have to go. Now!'

I pull Zarifa up and start down the stairs, taking them two or three at a time, my bare feet are slipping on the blood I left on the way up but I don't feel the pain now, every nerve in my body is pushing, pushing. God, I hope I'm right. Behind me I can hear the others and I will them to keep up.

At the first floor I tell Zarifa to give me my shoes back. She looks at me like I'm crazy and I have to shout before she understands.

'In there.' I point at the lift.

I run downstairs, out of the door, down the few steps to the street, where the trail I've left becomes smudged and indistinct. It should be good enough. I put on the shoes, my fingers shaking as I unlace them, and as I race back inside I hear a car, many cars, driving at speed.

On the first landing they're still trying to prise the doors open. Together my father and I wedge our fingers into the crack and pull, him on one side and me on the other, and by leaning our weight into it they start to open, enough for me to stick my head in and look, but it's pitch black, I can't see anything.

I take one of the shoes off again, pass it through the opening and let go, and almost straight away I hear the thud of it hitting something solid. The lift is right there, it must be.

'A little more.'

The opening is now a foot and a half. I squeeze through, the gun slung across my back, and even after everything it's not easy, just to drop into space, it's so hard to find a grip but there's a sort of lip on each of the doors and I hold on to that while letting myself down, and finally I'm hanging from the floor by both hands and there's nothing for it but to pray and breathe and just let go.

The lift is right there. Maybe four or five feet down.

'Zarifa. Now.'

She appears between the doors and my father hands her down to me and as I guide her I can tell she's quivering. The call to prayer is finishing and the engines are close.

'It's going to be okay.'

He slips through next, and stands with one foot either side of the opening where there must be a little ledge. Now they're here for us. Two or three cars, maybe more, they sound like they're in convoy, getting nearer.

'Close it.'

'I know.'

I can see him against the blueish light, can sense how hard it is for him to find a final scrap of strength. The door is old and the mechanism hasn't been serviced for years, it's all dry and the parts scrape against each other with a terrible screeching sound. From outside I can hear wheels crunching to a stop, car doors slamming, and that same crazed shouting that followed us into the night at Borz's.

'Dad. There's no time.'

I'm whispering-shouting now, they're so close. I hear the door open downstairs, hear their boots on the tiles. So many of them. The gap is down to three inches, it's still too much, but I have to tell him to stop, he has to leave it.

He gives it one last heave that closes it another inch and then hangs back into space, one hand on each lip of the door, and past him and through the gap I see glimpses of the fighters as they tear up the stairs. I don't breathe. It takes so long it feels like there are hundreds of them but it's probably only ten or twelve, and in a pack they're gone. Now their footsteps are up above us – they echo round the lift shaft – growing higher and fainter.

'Drop down,' I say, but my father gives the doors one last almighty go until they're almost shut. Not completely but as good as, just a thin blue line of light shows between them.

8

All Abraham can do is listen to the sounds above and hope that the men who have come for them are the kind who act rather than think. Down the lift shaft come sounds of shouting and doors being kicked open and slammed shut. Much shouting, and much frustration. Borz wanted them kept alive, but Abraham knows that this time they'll die the moment they're found.

Executing the spy and his daughter is one thing. Parading the sorry trio who killed your most feared commander is another.

Boots on the stairs, hammering on a door far above, the door being kicked in, everything accompanied by a constant yowling of shouts and instructions. Christ, what a horrible sound, like dogs in a frenzy. A group of four or five come all the way down the stairs and pass the lift doors at a run, boots clattering. Everyone seems to be making noise, and above it no one seems to be in charge. A group comes down a floor, then another, until the men are so close that Abraham can make out individual voices and imagine them in each room of the apartment on the floor above. In amongst them a woman's voice pleads and a child cries, and he prays that he hasn't brought fresh misery on the head of another innocent.

Beside him, Sofia is holding Zarifa and comforting her, rocking gently forward and back.

Now the men are on the first floor, and Abraham can see looming through the crack the figure of a fighter in his fatigues, enough of him to know that he's carrying a gun at his side and wearing a black scarf on his head. Now they don't even knock, they kick down the door to the apartment and storm the place, yowling harder than before; but it seems to be empty and in less than a minute he hears one of them saying they're not here, let's go.

This is the moment. When they leave the last apartment the lift doors will be right in their line of sight and if one of them is quick, and thinking, this is the time for him to work it out. Abraham holds up a hand and all three of them stop breathing while the heavy footsteps start down the stairs. He keeps it raised until what he thinks is the last pair of boots has appeared and gone.

One more door kicked in on the ground floor, more shouting, inside then outside, and conversation that he can't catch. He lets a breath out slowly, closes his eyes, wills them to leave.

Boots coming up the stairs now. They've figured it out. Like a child playing hide and seek Abraham keeps his eyes shut in the hope that when they force those doors open and look down the shaft they won't see him there.

But the boots go past at a run. Sofia shrugs, her arm still round Zarifa. Upstairs they hear more shouting, and after five minutes, maybe ten, the fighters come back, talking the whole way down and issuing commands, if you could call them that.

'Get a fucking move on.'

'Stop that fucking noise.'

The crack in the lift doors turns briefly black as a dozen women in their niqabs are hurried down the stairs. The women from the makkar, leading their children. They're carrying bags, it looks like, and more than one of them is crying.

Finally, engines start up outside, one, two, three, and the place is quiet. All he can hear is the crying of a child, maybe two, on the floors above.

They're not clever enough to be waiting, he's sure of it, and he knows Sofia is thinking the same, but they wait anyway, for what feels like a century but is probably half an hour. The building creaks like a ship in the wind. He puts his hand on her shoulder and whispers.

'Now?'

She nods.

Together the three of them climb warily to the top floor, checking to see from the windows on the stairwell whether anyone has been left behind to stand guard. Outside, there's no one, and when they reach the makkar everything is quiet. Badra's body lies by the threshold, crumpled and awkward, her head lolling back heavily on her neck, which has stretched to its full extent, long and white. Her blood has splashed the wall but none shows on her black niqab. Sofia stands over her for a moment, looks into her open eyes, and shakes her head before leading the way inside.

Her gun is up, and she moves in quick arcs from room to room, checking for fighters. After each she holds up a thumb for Abraham to see. From the hall, a corridor heads left and she swings into each of the doorways like a professional, like she's done it a thousand times, and all Abraham can think of is the bullet that's waiting for her inside. But there's no one there. She lets her gun drop, and in that moment he sees the exhaustion she's been storing up flood her young body and, as if stumbling on her niqab, she takes two clumsy steps and collapses.

9

Water feels like a sacrament. God-given. My father sits me up, splashes me with it to bring me round and lets me drink a little, not too much, from the glass he raises to my lips.

'You okay?'

I nod but I don't mean it.

He finds food in the kitchen and prepares it with Zarifa. She's still terrified, poor thing. We sit at the table where I sat on that first night, it feels like years ago, and watch the sun rise across the rooftops. From the minarets all over the skyline the call to prayer sounds again.

'I have to pray.'

'We need it.'

The bathroom is already a mess again. I wash my tattered feet, make myself clean and go to my old room, which is strewn with the things those poor women didn't have time to pack as they were forced from the building. I'm guessing that the makkar couldn't continue with its leader dead. I hope it's that. I hope they haven't taken them all to be questioned, that they think someone else is mixed up in this.

I pray for them. I pray for us, and for Badra. For her faith, which was strong, and for her understanding, which was blind right up until the end. For those two brothers, except that word doesn't feel right any more. Those two fighters. Two men. When I close my eyes I feel like I'm in a room with the three people I've killed, that we're all sitting in a circle, and I want them to say something, to forgive me, or rage at me, but they're mute, and they just look past me into space.

Finally I pray for Zarifa, and for Abraham, and the millions caught in this war. And then for myself, that I might finally understand. What do you want, Lord? What would you have me do?

I don't hear Him. He doesn't speak to me. It is unlawful for a believer to kill another believer. He may cast me out, the most glorified, the most high. But I will not cast Him out.

Empty, hollowed, I finish praying, find antiseptic and cloth, and boil water. Then I have my father sit with his back to me and the light from the city and I clean his wounds. Some have begun to heal over tiny pieces of fabric and as I carefully pick them out he jerks and does his best not to scream. You have to be quiet, I tell him. There are spies everywhere.

In the end they all sleep, because Sofia is right; there's nowhere left to run. In Badra's room they find an alarm clock and set it to ring in four hours. When they wake, they search the apartment and find fresh niqabs, shoes for Zarifa and a too-large shirt for Abraham in a suitcase of a husband's clothes. In Badra's room Sofia is ruthless: she pulls out all the drawers, drags the mattress off the bed, goes through every pocket of every piece of clothing. Abraham suspects that there's something beyond mere thoroughness to it, and at one point, when he catches her eye, he thinks he sees a strange kind of guilt there, as if by showing Badra no mercy after death she's convincing herself that there was no need to have shown her any in life. It doesn't sit well with her.

'Who was she?'

'I have no idea.'

'You knew her.'

'She made out she was my friend.'

Sofia was taking books from the shelves, thumbing through the pages.

'But she was a hard woman.'

Taped to the back of the cheap plywood wardrobe they find a plastic envelope, and in it a paltry collection of documents: Badra's passport; statements from a bank in Germany, the most recent dated six months earlier; letters from her mother, begging her to return to Munich; and cash, which Sofia counts out onto the floor. Four hundred euros and three hundred and sixty dollars.

'Some commitment.'

'What do you mean?'

'If she was so committed to the khilafa why keep all this? To get out. When it didn't work for her.'

She shakes her head and counts the money again, then holds it in her hand and looks at it as if it holds the answer to something.

'Is it enough?' asks Abraham.

'To what?'

'To get us out.'

'It helps.'

She explains the rules. No woman can go anywhere in the city without her mahram. That's clear and paramount. No woman under the age of forty-five can leave the city at all, except in the case of a genuine medical emergency, and then she still needs to be with a male relative. And for foreigners, men and women, it's more or less impossible to leave because it's assumed that if you're foreign, you're ISIS, which is mainly true. So having papers wouldn't see them out – but not having papers makes it worse. With good Syrian documents, a decent story and a few hundred dollars, maybe that would be enough, but looking like they do and having no papers? They'd need thousands.

'What about force?'

'You're serious?'

Abraham shrugs.

'When you came in how many fighters were there? At the checkpoint.'

'Four.'

'There's always at least four. Sometimes more that you can't see. There are three of us. We have two guns. Only one machine gun. And none of us has fired one before today. Then, if we make it, chances are they're ready for us at the next checkpoint.'

For a few minutes they sit and consider their assets: some money, a phone, two guns, and a car, the key pulled from Badra's pocket. It ought to be better than nothing and yet it feels like nothing at all. Finally, Abraham breaks the silence.

'What if we stay?'

'Sorry?'

'What if we stay, get papers, do it properly?'

Sofia shakes her head.

'They'll find us.'

'It's a big city.'

'It's full of spies. I told you. There's no way. Every hour is bad.'

'Why?'

'You have to ask why?'

'Stupid questions can be useful.'

She shakes her head. 'Because, because. Because they'll come back here and find us. Because word will get round and everyone will be looking. Because even if we did find some-where to stay we have no way of going out and getting food.'

'How efficient are they?'

'What do you mean?'

'I mean, can we assume that every checkpoint already knows to look out for a man of my age and two girls of yours?'

'Yes. Of course.'

10

There's much talk of when to leave, before or after dark. At night they're less likely to be recognized, but who would be sharp enough to distinguish these two veiled women and this bearded man from a hundred other identical groups that walked the city? Now I see a use for the veil, says Abraham, expecting a sharp look from Sofia, but instead he receives a smile. In the end they decide on dusk: everyone was more obtrusive at night, because locals simply slipped off the streets.

Sofia goes down first, and in the five minutes she's gone Abraham again feels that sense of peril that seems to be growing sharper the closer they come to making it out – a possibility he daren't think about and can't help but imagine. Sofia and Zarifa with him on the dusty old bus north from Akçakale.

The stairwell is clear, the street seems clear, and so at six thirty, with the sun nearly gone and the mosques emptying from the last prayers of the day, the three of them walk swiftly down to the street and round the corner to Badra's car in its spot, wary of every face they pass. Abraham is sure his eyes are too bloodshot and nervous for anyone who's half-awake not to notice them, and wishes he had a veil for himself, but they reach the car easily enough, and it starts, thank heaven, and he sets off to the hospital with as much confidence as he can feign.

Sofia goes in slightly before Abraham, pushing Zarifa ahead of her at the barrel of the machine gun. She's tried to explain how this is going to work ten times, but Zarifa hasn't understood, and she mutters and half sobs as she walks.

God, Sofia was convincing in this role. The way she walks, all power and certainty, occasionally nudging Zarifa with the gun – if he didn't have that final faith in her he'd swear she was still a member of the brigade and about to turn the tables on them. He follows in her slipstream at about twenty paces, past the battered and makeshift ambulances and the waiting mahrams, down the ramp, in through the main entrance of the building, along that ugly corridor with the sandbags in the windows, and the fighters milling about with more time than everyone else, and the dimly lit wards on either side. Sofia checks one closed door, doesn't like it, tries another and without turning to look at Abraham goes inside after Zarifa. No one challenges her. Who would? She belongs.

One thought keeps cutting in: if they're waiting for us this could be the shortest of all escape attempts.

The long main corridor is U-shaped, and the room where they store the gowns and scrubs is at its furthest end. So many people to pass. Fighters, nurses, doctors, patients. Walk steadily, ignore the pain, you're just a normal person.

Don't look anyone in the eye. Be like Sofia, quick and sure.

It feels like a mile uphill but he makes it, and in the storeroom finds a clean set of scrubs that he puts on over his jacket. The gun is there. He ties on a surgical mask and for a moment is paralysed by the choice it presents. Mask up or down? Up, and someone with sharp eyes might wonder why, if he wasn't operating. Down and he might be recognized. In the end he settles for down. Now the difficult part. Now to steal an ambulance.

Walking back towards the entrance he keeps his pace even and his eyes on the furthest point, resisting the strong urge to check every face, and as he turns the first corner, heart pumping at the base of his throat, fingers swollen at his sides from the surging blood, he sees Huq absently rounding the second, head down in someone's chart that he almost certainly can't understand. Twenty yards away, no more.

Abraham pulls up his mask and keeps his eyes on the floor. The rooms he passes are busy and there's nowhere to go. So he carries on, watching the floor, wishing he had his own chart to look at; he should have found himself a chart. His hand slips through the hole in the gown and after some fumbling finds the gun in his jacket pocket.

With only feet between them, Abraham senses that Huq has looked up, and at the moment he hears his voice start to protest he steps close in to him so that his mouth is by his ear and the gun is in his side. Huq's breath still stinks of meat and decay, but there's something else in there, a tinge of immediate fear, and Abraham knows that his only hope is to count on the considerable coward in him.

'So help me I will put a bullet up through your heart if you make a single fucking sound,' he says, in English, hardly believing the words as they flow from his mouth, grinding the barrel between two ribs.

I'm not sure about this plan. I've heard better but I can't come up with anything else. The one advantage, the one thing that might help, is that it plays on the fighters' fears. Of their commanders, and of women. We'll see.

I manage to calm Zarifa down, but it takes a couple of minutes, poor girl. Heaven knows what she thinks is going on. Just sit, I tell her, we'll stay here for a few minutes and then we're going to be leaving. I just need you to be quiet. Everything will be okay.

It's a crazy plan.

I think we're in housekeeping. Ragged mops, buckets, filthy cloths, empty bottles of cleaning fluid. The floor is stained and the air smells of damp and mould more than anything else. I'm glad I didn't get ill in the khilafa. Zarifa sits on the floor and I stand by her with my hands on the gun, for appearance's sake.

When I was in the makkar I thought time passed slowly, but this is something else. Each minute by the clock on Badra's phone feels like ten – at each voice I hear outside my finger tenses on the trigger. I reckon it should take him five minutes, no more. Get in, get dressed up, get out.

Something's happened, no question, and soon I'm going to have to go and look. At twelve minutes, I stand by the door and I hear noise out in the corridor, shouting, the kind fighters do when they're not getting what they want. Somebody's in a real state, like the world's about to end. Get me a doctor. Get me a fucking doctor. If my friend doesn't get a doctor in the next thirty seconds I'm going to start shooting people. It's getting closer – I can hear him opening doors, screaming into rooms, and I know that if he doesn't find what he wants he's going to be in here any minute, and there's nowhere to hide. Zarifa has gone stiff again and I put my hand on her shoulder to reassure her. When the door opens I have my gun and my story ready.

'In here,' says Abraham, and pushes Huq into the storeroom where the gowns and the scrubs are kept. 'Over there. Sit on the floor.'

For pride's sake Huq attempts a scowl, but he sits compliantly enough, cross-legged by shelves of old linen, and now Abraham wonders what on earth he's going to do with him. He can't shoot him – even in Raqqa, gunfire in a hospital would bring people running – and anyway he couldn't shoot him. Compared to some of these people, Huq was more or less a saint. Leave him alive, though, and he would sound the alarm immediately, and sure as Abraham was that he could concoct some story that would have kept the poor idiot terrified for long enough to secure a decent head start, only one course of action seemed safe. He was going to have to tie him up.

God. How to do that without help? He began to regret the plan. Sofia should have come with him.

It's only Huq. Think, be careful, don't rush. From a box by the door he takes two masks and throws one to Huq. The gun is out on display now.

'In your mouth. Like this. Then tie it behind your head.'

'I knew you were a spy,' said Huq, not loud – not loud enough to risk a bullet.

'I'm not a spy.'

'All those trips upstairs. Is Saad in on this?'

Abraham takes a deep breath and shakes his head.

'Enough. Tie that thing. Tighter. Okay. Let me tell you why I came here. I came to try and rescue my daughter from the insane killing party you people are having. That's all. Saad gave me work because I wouldn't only treat the killers. You do the same and there's still hope for you. You could be a good doctor. You could make a difference.'

That wasn't true, and it wasn't half of what Abraham wanted to say. But humiliate Huq and Huq would eventually take it out on somebody else.

'Okay. This one round your ankles. In a figure of eight. Jesus, tighter. Okay. I'm going to put the gun down now but if you move an inch I'm going to pick it up again and I'm going to shoot you. Okay? And if you live I'm guessing you won't be high up the surgical priority list.'

Abraham rests the gun on the nearest shelf, checks that Huq isn't about to try anything, and takes a white sheet from a pile. He bites at the edge, works his teeth against the threads, opens up a split and tears the fabric from end to end. It's worn and thin but good enough. In a minute he has two long strips and as he finishes he takes the gun and squats down by Huq.

'Nearly done. Same deal. Don't move.'

He puts the gun behind him, within reach, maybe two yards from Huq.

'Your hands. Like this.'

As he holds them out Huq shifts his weight and throws himself forward with unlikely speed, grips Abraham by the throat and topples him onto his back, stretching with his free hand for the gun. Through the gag he's making a roaring noise as if he's finally become the warrior he's always wanted to be, and his eyes are a crazed mixture of wild and afraid. Abraham is shocked, and his back is on fire, and he can't breathe. He pushes helplessly against the weight, with all the strength he can find, but nothing gives. The little power he has is going. Huq's fingers touch the gun, nudge it an inch further away, and as he adjusts his position to lunge for it again Abraham brings his knee up between the two of them and straightens it, pitching the other man awkwardly onto his side. Abraham kicks at him again; Huq grabs him by the ankle and pulls, recovering his momentum and launching himself forward.

Huq has the gun. Rolling on his side he twists and brings it round to point at Abraham, who finds just enough spring in his legs to push up and then fall. He falls on Huq and his hand closes on his wrist and for a moment the two men are locked together, bodies and wills rigid in struggle, the gun like a third player pointing first this way then that. A feeble amateur fight to the death, neither of them skilled, even competent. But Abraham has his legs, and now he brings his knee up hard into Huq's groin, and again, and Huq's body tightens and then relaxes, and his hand opens.

In one movement Abraham takes the gun, clumsily by the barrel, and without thought swipes it across Huq's cheek, which seems to bend under the force and whips his head away so fast and so utterly that his neck might be broken. He raises his hand again, but Huq is gone. Not dead – his pulse is there – but out, and for a while.

Abraham kneels by him, panting from the effort and the heat, sweat across his screaming back. When his breath returns he finds the two strips of sheet and ties Huq's hands as tight as he can, and his feet again, and finally he takes a mask and reinforces the gag. He drags him across the storeroom and, as an afterthought, passes a length of sheet around his ankles and ties it to the upright of one of the shelves.

What a waste, Abraham thinks as he fixes his scrubs and his mask and closes the door behind him. What a pointless life. What a worse than pointless life.

11

This brother is immense. Bigger than Borz, if anything, he fills the doorway of the storeroom, great dark head like an ox, a huge V of a chest, two chains of bullets crossed over it, gun pointing at the floor in his hand. The sight of me stops him, standing with my gun, he doesn't know what it means. Thank heaven he can't see how dry my mouth is or how fast my heart is beating.

'Who the fuck are you?'

'Al-Khansaa Brigade, brother. What's wrong?'

'I need a fucking doctor. Find me a fucking doctor.'

'I have a prisoner.'

'Fuck your prisoner. He's been shot in the neck.'

'I can't leave her.'

Every sinew in him is about to snap. He looks away, jaw clamped, head shaking, and when he turns back he lays each word down like blows.

'You don't have a prisoner any more. Move.'

He raises his gun and with the barrel motions me out of the way. I hold up a hand to him.

'Wait. I'm coming. I'm coming.'

'Why do you care about another dead cunt? Move out of the way.'

'Your friend is dying.'

'So stop holding me the fuck up.'

345

'I'll lock the door. It's okay. It's okay.'

By the look of him he's a thought away from unloading his gun into me as well. Hand up, I tell him we'll find a doctor, it'll be okay, and I steer him from the room, making a show of locking the door behind me.

'What happened, brother?'

'Sniper cunt.'

He's striding away, possessed by his mission. With a sweep of his arm he sends me on ahead of him.

'Run. Fuck sake. Find one. He's in an ambulance out front.'

As I start to run I see a doctor at the far end of the corridor and I will him to turn back, but the fighter has seen him too.

'You. You! Come here.'

My father looks at the fighter, looks behind him, and with a sigh I can actually see walks to us.

'Run you fuck. Run!'

Abraham manages a sort of jog. He hasn't the strength to run and with each step he can feel the wounds on his back peeping open. His eyes are on Sofia, who still has her gun. That's good. If she'd been caught they'd have taken it, or worse. This was something else. Some new reversal they didn't have time for.

A beast of a man. Massive body and short legs, like a Minotaur, raging and tossing his head and giving off heat. How easy it would be to shoot him through that great wall of a chest. Abraham begins to understand why he and his kind killed so many. It was easy. It didn't require effort, courage, thought. Anyone could do it, even pharmacists.

'Fucking run!'

The fighter stomps off towards the entrance, and Abraham does his best to catch up. As he draws level with Sofia he exchanges a look with her through her veil. We have no choice. Let's go.

Outside, the fighter walks to the back of an old government ambulance that's been driven almost into the hospital and is now blocking the entrance. Its back doors are open and inside are two men, one an ISIS medic who Abraham recognizes as a regular driver. Both his hands are bright red with blood and pressed to the neck of a fighter lying on his back on the floor of the ambulance, one leg twitching intermittently.

'Where the fuck have you been? He's going, brother, he's fucking going,' says the driver, who seems to have no idea what to do.

'Do something,' says the fighter, and Abraham climbs in beside the patient. The blood has stopped spurting, which probably means the heart is giving up, and his face is turning grey from lack of oxygen. Saad had told him about this. Probably a haematoma is constricting his airway and no breath is getting through to the lungs. Stick a tube into his trachea and maybe he can be saved, but it's a five per cent chance.

'Let's get him on a stretcher. You two. Let me see the wound.'

'Hurry,' says the fighter. Now he has nothing to do he's less certain of himself.

Abraham applies pressure to the wound while the driver positions the stretcher, and as soon as he touches the man he knows that he won't live.

'You two carry him. I'll stay like this. And you, sister, move this thing. It can't stay here.'

With his eyes he tells her take it, take the opportunity. There won't be a better.

'She can't drive this.'

'It's a few yards.'

'She's a sister.'

'So?'

'It's not ordained.'

'I don't care what's ordained, I'm not having someone die

because the next ambulance can't get to the hospital. Give her the key.'

The driver is shaking his head.

'Every moment you delay is killing him,' says Abraham, and the fighter growls in agreement.

'It's in the ignition. Bring it to me after.'

'Get it out of the way. Over there.'

Abraham gives Sofia a look that he hopes says everything he needs it to say and the three men carry their dying load inside.

Half of that was brilliant. Really, I didn't think my father had it in him. But he knows I can barely drive. One lesson. That's all.

Then I remember. I'm one of the brigade, I can do what I want.

I pick one of the older mahrams because I figure he'll give me less trouble and hate myself for that instinct. An old man with thick grey hair and a black beard and sad eyes that are somewhere else, like he's waiting for news of something, which he probably is. I ask him if he can drive and he looks at me for a moment as if to say, Really? I'm standing here while my wife or my daughter is inside dying and you're going to point your gun at me and get me to do the thing you were asked to do? I wish I could explain. But even if I could explain it would make no difference. Who am I, that I deserve to escape from this city? There are thousands, tens of thousands more deserving than me.

He does what I say. Of course he does.

*

I wait with the ambulance. I thank the old man, not that that means anything, and I wait. I'd cut off my hand to know what's going on inside. How my father's going to get himself out of there, and whether Zarifa is safe. If they don't make it I still have to leave. Not for my sake. Nothing is for my sake any more.

It's eight o'clock, by Badra's phone. He's been in there for fourteen minutes. That's too long, way too long – they must have found him, and right now they'll be questioning him, and he's had enough, poor man, he'll give me up and quite right, he must. And there's Zarifa. If someone else finds her I dread to think what could happen to her now, and I realize something I hadn't before, that by trying to save her I've made her life ten times more dangerous.

So I take the key from the ignition and I go back in. And as I'm going down the ramp, going as fast as I can but trying not to stand out, I see my father coming through the doors pulling Zarifa by the hand, head down and eyes straight ahead.

'Go. Just go,' he says, and passes me without checking his speed. When I can't see anyone coming after him, I catch up.

'He's been dead for ten minutes. Idiot's had me operating on a corpse.'

'Where's the driver?'

'I sent him for blood and drugs. We don't have long.'

Zarifa and I go in the back, as agreed. Nurse and patient, as per the story. There's no gurney in here, just a thin mattress on the floor and it's already covered with old blood and new blood, the fighter's blood, which is good. I tell Zarifa she has to lie on it and she shakes her head and says no, no, but as we drive off I unveil and I hold her, and I look her in the eyes and tell her again it's okay, everything's going to be okay. There's not much more I can do.

But slowly I think she's coming to trust me. There's a roll of blue paper in here and I tear off a length and spread it over the top half of the mattress. I'm staggering about as we jolt and jump on the rough streets. We're going too fast, I think, we shouldn't be doing anything to attract attention, but it's okay, it's an emergency, we have the right markings, I've seen a thousand ambulances tearing through the city like this. As long as he doesn't get lost. We went over the route ten times but it's dark and it's not easy. If it was earlier and the sun was going down you could just keep it ahead of you and eventually you'd be fine. For the sake of our story we're heading west, towards Al Tabqah, and when we're clear of the city we'll circle back up to the north. Zarifa lies down, and I arrange things as best I can so it looks like some of the blood is her blood. No one will look too closely. That's the last thing they'll want to see.

12

They must know by now. Word will be out. Even if no one's realized these are the same people who killed Borz, they'll be after the ambulance. As clearly as the broken roads in his headlights, Abraham can see the driver phoning a commander, and the commander phoning the checkpoint commander, and the checkpoint commander narrowing his eyes against the dark, tightening his hold on his gun. A stolen ambulance. Was he stupid, to have taken that opportunity? Should he have found a way of sneaking out?

Have faith in yourself, and in fate. What will be will be.

Left here, onto a wide and empty street. Two cars ahead of them, a handful passing the other way. Abraham pushes on, waiting every moment to pick out the cars angled across the road and the barbed wire and the fighters doing that slow strut they loved so much. Every time he checks his mirror he expects to see headlights and sirens, and imagines bursting through the checkpoint pursued by the full might of an angry ISIS. Better to die like this tonight than tomorrow on his knees.

But there are no sirens, and when the checkpoint comes the fighter who waves them down shows no signs of urgency or tension, just sets his feet squarely on the road and calmly raises a hand, squinting at the headlights. By the arc lamp shining down from a post Abraham can see two more men in fatigues leaning back against a 4x4 parked by the side of the road. All are hugging guns to their chests. The city has almost run out here; there seems to be nothing but wasteland on each side, and concrete blocks have been lined up along the verge to stop anyone pulling round in a wide arc. Abraham slows as evenly as he can, everything nice and smooth, his heart going like bells.

'Evening, brother,' he says as he winds down his window and puts his arm with the black band on it on the sill. The sentry looks tired; a round man for a fighter, fleshy, his cheeks droop and the lids sit heavily on his eyes. Ten o'clock now, probably a new shift at midnight.

'Where are you going?'

'Al Tabqah.'

'Road's closed this time of night, brother.'

'No one called you?'

'No one called me.'

Abraham *tsks*, shakes his head.

'I knew they wouldn't. Idiots.'

'What's going on, brother?'

'I have a patient in the back. An important patient. And she's losing blood.'

'So take her to the hospital.'

Abraham shakes his head again, a different emphasis this time: I would like nothing more than to be doing that, my friend.

'They don't have the blood. A rare type. They have it in Al Tabqah.'

'You serious, brother?'

'She'll die in two hours if she doesn't get it.'

'Who is she?'

'I can't say.'

'You can't say?'

'Really, brother. It's worth both our lives.'

He didn't like that. Don't tell me what my life is worth.

'Open the back.'

'She shouldn't be disturbed.'

'Open the back.'

Abraham shrugs, steps down from the cab, and the brother follows him round to the back of the ambulance.

The bastard knows, of course he does. He can see the blood pulsing in my throat, the exhaustion in my eyes, the pupils dilating from the fear.

'When I say.'

The fighter sets himself, gun ready and trained on the doors, and now he nods at Abraham to open them. Inside in the blue light cast by an electric lamp are two black forms, one lying down, the other kneeling by the first.

'What's wrong with her?'

'Wounds to the abdomen.'

'Fuck does that mean?'

'She's been assaulted.'

'What's all the blood?'

Abraham keeps his eyes wide and on the fighter's: you don't want to ask any more questions, believe me.

'Who's that?' The fighter gestures with the gun.

'A nurse.'

'Why d'you need a nurse?'

Hand cupped to his mouth confidentially, Abraham steps towards the fighter.

'The girl's dying. And she's important.'

'This is bullshit.'

Just their luck, to get a thinker. Abraham feels panic leap in him as he sees the first leg of their flimsy story begin to buckle.

'Brother. If I don't get her to Al Tabqah in the hour she'll be dead. And I don't want that on my head. Or yours.'

'Get her out.'

'I can't move her, brother.'

'Get her the fuck out. You. Down here.'

Sofia is frozen, but almost to his surprise Abraham is still trying.

'Brother, do you know Abu Selim?'

That checks him. Just a little, but a distinct pause in his reply.

'You think I'm an idiot?'

Abraham leans in again, almost whispering.

'This is his daughter.'

He pulls back to watch the reaction. Now the sentry is thinking.

'Serious?'

'Fatima. She's twelve years old. She dies, it's bad for everyone.'

A conundrum. A thinker he may be, but the fighter doesn't seem equal to figuring it out.

'I need to call it in.'

Oh Jesus.

'To who, brother?'

'This is Abu Selim's daughter, I'm going to call it in.'

'I wouldn't do that, brother. This isn't a normal situation. He won't thank you for it.'

'Fuck does that mean?'

Abraham stands back, hands on his hips, and shakes his head.

'Don't make me spell it out.'

'Spell it the fuck out.'

The fighter turns to Abraham and now the gun is up and on him. Abraham pauses, partly to collect himself, partly for effect.

'Who do you think assaulted her?'

'How do I know who assaulted her? The fuck do I care?'

Abraham just keeps his eyes on the fighter's, lets him work it out for himself.

'This is not a public situation, brother.'

The man's thoughts turn slowly. Abraham can almost see them, caught in a simple calculation; will it be worse for me if I let them through or if I don't? The look he finally gives Abraham may even have some sympathy in it. Rather you than me, brother.

'Fucking go. And watch the road around Madan. There were Kurds down there two days ago.'

Abraham nods – doesn't thank him, because why should he be grateful? – and under the incurious gaze of the other two sentries gets back into the cab and drives away.

13

From the back I hear most of the conversation, with my finger on the trigger under my abaya and the gun ready to fire. If they want to kill me they can shoot me, and I'll kill as many as I can first. But the first checkpoint was easy.

I sit on a bench by the door next to Zarifa and through the dirty square windows watch the night slipping away behind us. I see planes high in the sky and orange bursts of flame in the city and wonder at the cruelty of killing a hundred innocents to wipe out maybe one fighter. The old me wasn't wrong about that. The old me wasn't wrong about many things.

It's lonely here in the back. I can't imagine what it's like for my father, staring into the darkness and praying, praying hard that the road is clear.

Apart from the airstrikes there's not so much fighting at night and none where we're going – this whole area was won months ago. Half an hour west, a tiny road like a track goes north and then curves round to meet the main road between Raqqa and Akçakale. The journey is fifty miles at most, and it should be clear. We don't see anything, don't hear anything, and I'm beginning to think that we should pull over, rest for a while, work out exactly how we're going to get across the border once the night is over, when the ambulance starts to slow down and I pray silently to the most glorified that my father's had the same idea.

I hate not being able to see. We come to a stop, and my chest tightens, and in the near darkness I pull my veil back across and do the same for Zarifa. I feel her stiffen beside me, and I put my arm around her. We sit and listen, both blind, only one of us able to understand.

'What is this, brother?'

A voice I don't know, not friendly. A checkpoint voice. And then my father's, higher and tighter than it should be, even through the metal between us I can hear the fear in it.

'Picking up a patient from Tell Abyad.'

'This time of night?'

The story has changed now. We worked on this. We must be ten miles from Tell Abyad now and there's no earthly reason to be bringing patients here. It has no hospital.

'We got a call an hour ago. That's all I know.'

'No way I wouldn't know about a thing like that, brother. Not a fucking word about an ambulance.'

Stick to the story. I will my father on. This can work.

'Some fighter's being brought across the border. Maybe it's sensitive.'

'So they wouldn't tell a piece of shit like me, that what you're saying?'

'It's just they told me not to talk to anyone about it.'

'You're talking to me about it.'

Please God. I close my eyes and pray. I know this kind of brother, the kind that likes to tease before he pulls the trigger. I can smell cigarette smoke seeping in like a bad omen.

I hold the handgun steady under my abaya. I wish I knew how many are out there.

'All I know is, I have to get to Tell Abyad and pick up a patient.'

'In this ambulance.'

'In this, yes.'

'You're picking up a patient. In this nice ambulance.'

He knows. I know he knows. It's in his voice. All the checkpoints have now been told. The only reason my father's still alive is this idiot's love of his own voice.

'Really. I have to go. I was told to be there by twelve.'

Poor man. He has no idea. As quietly as I can I shush Zarifa and inch towards the door. There's movement outside, I can see it, one brother at least.

'What's in the back, my friend? Medicines? Surgeons? How you planning on saving that brother?'

He hesitates. He shouldn't but of course he does. These people are experts in making you live at a pitch of fear.

'Nurses.'

'Nurses? Are they pretty? Could they cure a man of his loneliness, brother? Because it's lonely out here, believe me. Man could fuck his own daughter out here, brother.'

Now there's silence outside. My hand is sweating on the gun.

But we're finished. If I shoot whoever's beyond these doors my father's dead in the same instant. I thought when we came through the last checkpoint that He was guiding us out of here, I felt sure I could feel the soft warm touch of His hand on my back, but now I know we weren't meant to leave this place. Our destiny is here. I have brought us all to this point.

Then the shot comes and the metal round the lock tears open. They don't need to do it but they want to frighten us and Zarifa is shaking, I'm tied in to her now, I feel her terror like my own. One of the doors is thrown open and the light comes on in the back and shows a brother standing there with a machine gun pointing at us.

'Hands on your head. You, now.'

I leave my gun in my pocket and raise my hands. Zarifa does the same.

'Kick that to me. Easy.'

I slide the machine gun towards him. He takes it, slings it over his shoulder, steps back so we can get down.

'There.'

This one isn't a talker. With his gun he points the way, and we walk to the front of the ambulance. By its headlights I see a brother grinning and my father kneeling on the road with his hands on his head. He looks up at me with eyes that say I'm sorry and God I wish I could do something – and I want mine to show him that none of this is his fault, but the veil is between us. The checkpoint is just a 4x4 slung diagonally across the road. This new brother tells us to make a row, and as I kneel next to my father I'm trying to work out the odds. There are only two of them, I'm sure, but their guns are out and more powerful and I can't move my hands. It's so cold out here. Then he tells me to unveil.

'Forget it.' I shake my head. Even by his own rules it's wrong.

He nods, and the second brother brings his gun up, I can sense it behind me, and brings it down hard on the back of my neck. I collapse onto my face. It's like being hit by a car.

'Get up.'

My cheek is on the tarmac. Pain splits my back. I can smell dust and oil and I'm looking at the brother's boots.

'Up, you cunt.'

I play dead. Not quite dead.

'Get the fuck up.'

I see no reason to help him.

'All right. You want it there, that's fine.'

He kneels by me, turns me over and pulls my veil off, and I see his face properly, the desire in it, the yellow poison – then his hand is up my abaya and between my legs. I think he's expecting me to struggle but I don't, I let him do what he wants to do. He grins over me and when his hand opens the top button of my trousers I close mine round the grip of the gun, take it from my pocket and fire twice through the black cloth at what must be his heart. Like Borz when he was finished, he reels off me.

Spinning on my back, tangled clumsily in my abaya, I try to

get the gun out into the air and in that single scrap of time I can see the second brother's eyes freeze in a fear that has come on him so quickly. His gun lines up with mine, and my father sweeps it out of the way as both guns fire, mine a single dead crack and the other a burst of light. Zarifa screams. The fighter's shoulder snaps back, and he brings his gun back round and again we fire in the same instant, and this time his whole body jolts backwards, and so does my father's.

14

Abraham doesn't feel it as pain but as a burning, a fire consuming the life from him, hot and cold at once; and the single thought in his head isn't that he's going to die but that he's never loved his daughter so much. As life fades, his love seems to grow to fill the world.

Her face is over his, her hand on his cheek.

'Dad. Don't. God God God. Let me see.'

The wound is almost in the same place as the boy's, the boy Saad saved that day. But higher, a crucial inch or two, the liver may have been hit and he won't last long without that.

'God, Dad, Dad. Stay with me. We're so close. I can drive.'

Abraham shakes his head. When she was born she cried and cried, every night for weeks, a restless soul always, as if she arrived with some foreknowledge of the troubles that lay ahead. So sensitive to pain, and so hopeful about banishing it. He, he had accomplished so little. Her mother's daughter, she might still do so much.

'Zarifa, help me. His legs, take his legs.'

'No.' He smiles, and she'll think he's being brave, but he means it. 'Leave me. You have to go.'

Sofia, Ester, Abraham. The three of them are together, he

knows it as surely as he knows he's going to die. One again, as they were when he and Ester lay either side of her in bed and watched her sleep. That instant of time is no different from this. There's no line now. No direction, just love. She's talking to him and he sees her words, they drop like water.

'I can't leave you.'

'You haven't. You're here.'

Now she cries, and his hand goes to her face, and all its beauty is restored, her eyes are light and liquid, the light is the old light, it shines on him forever.

15

I don't hear her at first because my ears are full of sound, gunfire and the wind and his voice, the words repeating like a chant, like holy words, they wrap themselves round my soul. The night, Zarifa, the dead men, my dead father, the desert that can't quite swallow us up, none of it exists. Just his voice and the tears that hold me. I'm helpless with them, rigid, they build and build like a flood trying to escape through a crack.

Why did I leave him? Why did he come here?

She's rocking my shoulder and saying my name. Sofia. My real name. I don't know how she knows, but of course she's heard him say it.

'Come, Sofia. Now.'

I wake into the darkness and I don't think I can find the strength to go on. Three men dead in the blue light of the headlights, dawn coming, two teenage girls and some guns. It's not enough. There's an army ahead of us and an army behind and all I want to do is lie here until the sun scorches me into the road. But Zarifa's veil is off and there's hope in her eyes, and we may not be only two. I must remember.

'We can. Come.'

She tugs at my sleeve, then stands and pulls off her abaya and lays it carefully on my father's body. I look at her, nod, take my hand from his face so she can cover him for the last time. Then I take off mine and shiver in the dawn air.

'Sofia.'

'Zarifa.'

Together, by some instinct, we know what to do, and we do it quickly. We drag the fighters to the 4x4 and somehow wedge them into the boot. They weigh two tons each. Then I drive the ambulance forward and we lift my father into the back.

I don't want to leave anything on the road so I drive the 4x4 a little way into the scrub first before I come back for the ambulance and drive it away from the sun, which is beginning to lighten the sky. We lurch and stumble over the rough earth but after half a mile the ground dips down and I leave the ambulance in the hollow where it can't be seen before running back for the 4x4. By the time we're done, a pale light has washed over the whole land and we're alone in an empty world of vast dead plains.

I have to leave him here but I can't leave him here. I know it doesn't matter and I know it's stupid and I know above everything else that it has to be done. Zarifa and I lift him from the ambulance and find a level spot and set him down. I feed a corner of my abaya into the fuel tank of the ambulance and leave it there for a minute for the fuel to soak in. Then I spread it over his body and with a final word to him and to my mother, and a final prayer to both our Gods, I light a match and touch it to the corner of the cloth.

*

After that we walk, a mile or more west of the road with the sun on our right, over the rocks and the stubby grass, across broken fences and crumbled walls, past the dead shells of buildings like animal skeletons in the heat, heading north to the border with the guns bouncing on our backs. I have no clue what we'll do when we get there. Step through a hole in the fence, like I did last time, when I was a hundred years younger and everything I thought was so difficult was so easy.

We have water left, two small bottles, and some food, but I don't want to eat and by the time the sun is fully up and on our backs I can feel my strength slipping and I know Zarifa is struggling too. Even the slightest hill is so hard, it's like we're carrying huge loads. The heat is like its own weight. I drape my sweatshirt around my neck to stop my skin from burning and it's wet with sweat in minutes. For hours we walk without talking. Sometimes I reach over and touch her arm and make sure she's okay and I wonder to myself how many journeys like this she has made before, less alone than she is now.

We will do something together or we will do something apart, but we will do something. The women are the future of her people and mine.

Ten miles, I thought. It begins to seem like twenty. After four hours the plain looks exactly the same as it did after three, nothing seems to change and for a time I think maybe I've died, or gone crazy, and I'll be stuck forever walking in this wilderness. But then at noon we come to the flat top of a long, low rise and there, a final hour's walk away, is Tell Abyad, and the border, and Turkey beyond, and by the fence just west of the town like a black pool a huge crowd of people and cars, and flowing into them a queue that stretches back for miles along the road from the west and seems to shimmer and shuffle in the heat.

They're coming from Kobani. From Kobani and from everywhere around, pushed out by the advancing brothers – by Daesh. There are thousands of them. Zarifa and I sit and share the last inch of warm water from the last bottle and I wonder how I'm going to get both of us through. I can see tanks on the Turkish side, patrol vehicles, soldiers everywhere. There won't be any holes. And we don't have any papers.

Ten thousand. As we get closer, I think ten thousand at least.

There are so many, it's like a new town. We ditch our guns and walk down to join them. No one notices. We're two more drops in a sea of hungry and tired people. They think I'm the same as them. But every face I rest on makes me want to walk back to Raqqa in shame.

Fighters stand in groups a way off and watch like jackals. I don't know why they're here. I don't know why they don't stop us all. I don't know why they do anything any more.

We settle at the back of the queue, where people are still arriving. A woman smiles at me and I'm amazed she finds the strength. She's big, she rocks from side to side as she walks and her breath is short. Her headscarf is colourful with blue and purple flowers and it's stained with sweat around the edge. On her hip she has one child, a girl, maybe four years old, who looks at me with tired eyes that don't give anything away. Who is this person, she's thinking. In what new way will she make things worse? Wearing a bright orange dress that's so pretty, so wrong here, her sister holds her mother's hand and squints ahead at the backs of the men in front. Together we all smell, of the journey, of fatigue, of fear.

I left my home by choice, but until I came here I don't think I knew what home meant. Home is what every person here has lost. The children stab me, deeply, each one. Every girl, every boy, looking around them into the heat with no expectation of anything good, and something missing from them, there's no shine, no spring, their spirits have been boxed away. But the mothers are worse. In the pain of the past they carry that tiny jewel of hope. They need to make things all right, and probably they won't be all right. I can feel the soreness in their feet, the weight of their possessions, so little and so heavy, the greater weight of the responsibilities they can't meet.

How Badra was wrong. This is where we must start.

Why didn't I see these people before? When I drove through the city with her, how did my eyes see one thing and my brain register another? We're by this one man, he has three bony cows and five children, and his back seems broken by the effort of carrying them all – there's no wife in sight, he's lost her somewhere, somehow – and he's giving sips of water to his children and all the while glancing at his cows because he knows that unless he finds some for them they'll die. A week ago I would have told him there was no progress without pain, that his sacrifice would lead to a golden future once the revolution was secure. And now? Now I can barely look at the lines in his face, the fear and the exhaustion there. It's like my eyes had become filmed with some madness that turned white to black and finally they've cleared – like I've been living in a dark room for years and have come blinded into the light.

I want to tell them all that I'm sorry. If I could feed them, bring them water, house them, return their lives to them, I would. I pray for the opportunity to redeem myself and more clearly than He has ever told me anything He tells me to start right now.

That first day I do the little I can. I carry things for people whose strength is going. I try to occupy a child so his mother can comfort his crying sister. I walk the length of this new town, past family, after family, after family – so many – and I huddle with everyone else in the crazed crush at the border itself as we desperately stretch for some shred of news. They're letting people through, but it takes time, each refugee has to be processed, no vehicles are allowed, livestock is doubtful. I find a Turkish soldier and tell him people need water, he has to do something, and he just shrugs.

When I've taken the news to the back of the queue – it isn't the back now, hundreds more have come, are still coming, and it isn't a queue, either, it's a shifting press of people – I go to talk to the fighters.

There are five of them a few hundred yards off, standing

with their guns, shifting on their feet, bored, fed, hungry. The usual look. Apart from the world. Black. Waiting for the moment they can feed on us again.

It's a lonely walk with the sun burning down. They watch me come like big cats considering prey that isn't worth the kill, and on my back I can feel the anxious eyes of the Syrians. Don't make this worse for us.

You can always tell the leader. I don't know how. Maybe because the others look to him and he only looks at me. When I'm six feet away I stop and I hold his black eyes which seem to boil with that blackness.

'These people need water.'

I don't know what they were expecting but it wasn't this. Some of them seem to think it's a joke but I ignore them.

'They'll die without it.'

The leader is the smallest of them, he isn't much taller than me and his gun almost reaches the ground like a crutch.

'There's water in their homes,' he says. One of the others laughs.

'You drove them from their homes.'

He doesn't reply to that. His face doesn't move, doesn't look like it's ever moved.

'You could bring water from the town,' I tell him. 'Allah would reward you, the most high, the most glorified.'

He takes his time. He knows all the tricks.

'Who's this "they", sister? What are you?'

Until this moment I hadn't even stopped to think how crazy it was to come up here. They could have pictures of my face. The truth is, Raqqa, my father, our journey, it all seems so far away and already I seem to have become part of something else.

'I'm not from Kobani.'

'You don't sound like you're from Syria, sister.'

One of the fighters brings his gun round onto his chest and the others begin to stiffen, wake up.

'I was brought up in Sudan. Not that it's any of your business.'

'Why not, sister? You come up here and tell me mine.'

'God's people are all His business.'

'Not when they're dirty kafirs, sister. Not then. How is it my business these godless cunts didn't bring enough water?'

I start to relax. He thinks this is about him.

'Alms shall be for the poor and destitute, and for the traveller in need.'

I hope the Lord's words will shame him. He's silent for a long time and then he calmly takes his gun from his shoulder and points it at me.

'We will put chains round the necks of the unbelievers. And they will be rewarded according to their deeds.'

The muzzle of the gun is an arm's length from me. I look at it, and I look at him, and I wonder why I came to talk to these people who take light and make it black, who could turn the water of God's love into a burning desert. I think I wanted them to see. But they will never see, and I walk away.

As the sun sets on the third day Zarifa and I are finally processed, funnelled into a tent where four Turkish army officers who look as exhausted as we do sit at tables. They try to separate us but I explain that Zarifa doesn't speak Arabic or Turkish and, when I insist, they let us sit together. There's a new calmness about her now. I don't know where it comes from.

Where are our papers? They were taken from us. Where have we come from? Raqqa, I tell them. We escaped from Raqqa and now we're here and we need asylum. She is Yazidi. Her family is dead.

We need your papers. Otherwise you could be Daesh. Without papers you could be anybody, and you will stay in Syria.

My mouth is so dry I can hardly speak, and when they bring me water I can't find the words. Instead I find the piece of paper my father gave me before we left the hospital and I give it to them. He smiled as he pressed it into my hand. How did he find the strength to smile?

'Call him. Please. He will understand.'

When he comes at last, I think he must be the wrong man. I'm expecting someone clean and purposeful, slick, I suppose, not this shambling type in a dusty suit who reminds me of a supply teacher.

'You are Sofia.' He says it in English, and stoops to hold out his hand to me. It's the middle of the night and Zarifa and I have been put out of the way in a little tent that's thrashing in the wind like a sail in a storm. There's a guard for us, but this man waves him away.

'I am Vural.'

He offers his hand to Zarifa, who nods and stays silent, as wary of this new figure in her life as I should be. But his face is open and his eyes are human, and he sits cross-legged on the ground in front of us like our equal.

'Your father?'

I can't say the words. They harden in my throat.

'Did he find you?'

I nod.

'And they kill him?'

I force my eyes up to his and wonder if I'm the worst thing he's ever seen.

'They didn't kill him.'

I think he understands enough not to make it easy for me, not to say the right thing. He looks at Zarifa and starts nodding slowly, like he's understanding for the first time.

'No good man can live there.'

He smooths his moustache with his fingers and asks me what I want.

'We have no papers. My friend should be with her people.'

His head tilts from side to side, like he's deciding something that could go either way. The wind blows in the sides of the tent and with a snap sucks them back out. It's like my god is waiting for me.

'And you? I should arrest you. Give you to the British.'

'I'm not ready.'

'Not ready?'

He's smiling now, smiling and frowning, like it isn't for me to judge. But I'm not being arrogant, it isn't that.

'I need to repair what I've done.'

An atom of good against an atom of evil – that's what God will weigh, the most high, when He is ready to show me my labours. Not yet. Please not yet. For now the scales hang round my neck, twisting me down, a great rock on one side and nothing but air on the other. This man holds the fate of my soul.

'Please.'

'What will you do? If I let you go.'

I've thought about it. It's been in my head for longer than I realized. Ever since I started teaching the class maybe, slowly coming up to the surface all that time. I look at Zarifa.

'First, take her to her people. I have to know she's safe.'

'I can do that for you.'

'No. I'm responsible for her.'

'And then?'

'I work with other sisters for a true Islam. Somewhere, I don't know.'

He looks at me with an eyebrow raised.

'I try to level the scales.'

One hand goes to my belly and I stroke Zarifa's arm and pray that God will help me protect her and His children everywhere, the living and the unborn.